Grown Women

Grown Women

A NOVEL

Sarai Johnson

HARPER

An Imprint of HarperCollins*Publishers*

GROWN WOMEN. Copyright © 2024 by Sarai Johnson. All rights reserved. Printed in the United States of America. No part of this book may be used or reproduced in any manner whatsoever without written permission except in the case of brief quotations embodied in critical articles and reviews. For information, address HarperCollins Publishers, 195 Broadway, New York, NY 10007.

HarperCollins books may be purchased for educational, business, or sales promotional use. For information, please email the Special Markets Department at SPsales@harpercollins.com.

FIRST EDITION

Library of Congress Cataloging-in-Publication Data has been applied for.

ISBN 978-0-06-329443-1

24 25 26 27 28 LBC 5 4 3 2 1

For Margaux Mae and all the daughters before her.

PART I

The Snakes

Charlotte

TENNESSEE

1974–1977

CHARLOTTE REPOSITIONED HERSELF in her hospital bed to get a better look at the crying baby. Though she could sympathize with the feeling of outrage that came from being torn violently from a position of warmth and comfort, she did nothing to comfort the child. Instead, she watched it wail desperately until a nurse forced the warm lump of wiggling flesh into Charlotte's arms.

"It will get easier," the nurse said, but Charlotte knew that it wouldn't.

Charlotte hadn't bothered to think of a name for the baby, as she had not planned on keeping it. But now that she was holding the fat little thing, she decided to name her Corinna, after her father's favorite song. It had always made her sad, like looking at this baby.

Months earlier, Charlotte had fled her mother's home in Atlanta and sought refuge in a small town outside of Nashville. She liked the name, Chilly Springs, when she saw it on the green-and-white interstate sign. So she pulled up to a motel with weekly rates in her muddy white Mercedes Benz and unloaded her single Gucci suitcase. The man behind the desk spit chewing tobacco into what looked like a rusted urn. His pale gray eyes stood in striking contrast with his skin, tanned and coarse.

"Honey," he said in a gravelly voice. "I think you got the wrong spot."

"Are there rooms available?"

"Yup."

"I'm in the right spot, then."

She dropped her handbag on the low counter, removed her driving gloves, and put them in her purse. She briefly flashed the small handgun as she rummaged through her bag to locate a twenty, and when she passed it to him, he handed her a key.

She went to her room and fell asleep on top of the burgundy polyester bedspread. It wasn't until she woke up hours later that she realized the room smelled like body odor, saliva, and—somehow—bleach. A wave of nausea crashed over her. She rolled off the bed and crawled on her hands and knees across the grainy low-pile carpeting to the toilet, where she released the contents of her stomach: only a little more than a strawberry milkshake from miles down the road. She put her cheek to the cool tile floor for comfort.

Not even twenty-four hours had passed since she'd last seen her mother, but Charlotte wished she could go home, to the freshly laundered and delicately lavender-scented thousand-thread-count sheets on her four-poster bed. But she could not go home as she was. Though she knew about *Roe v. Wade*, Charlotte was afraid to get rid of the baby any other way than to give birth to it. She thought she would wait out her pregnancy in Tennessee and return home without a baby. (She hadn't given much thought to what would happen to the baby, but any outcome had to be better than what Charlotte could offer.) She and her mother would go back to their normal lives. As everyone expected, Charlotte would go to Spelman, though she really wanted to go to Howard. She would do whatever her mother wanted her to do; things would work out, she thought.

In the meantime, though, she needed a job. Without any practical experience, Charlotte took the first one she could find, which happened to be waitressing at Whiskers, a catfish restaurant. The grease and fish smells made her stomach churn in the late stages of her pregnancy. A few times per shift, she excused herself to the dumpsters out back, where the smell was worse, but a breeze might carry through the arid air. She would lean against the cement wall, and, sometimes, when she was feeling weak, she'd place a hand on her swollen belly. More often than not, a tiny hand or foot would push back, and she would startle as if a rattlesnake had leaped out of the tall switchgrass hissing with its fangs bared. She never got used to it.

Charlotte had never worked a day in her life. Her hands were soft, and she didn't have the upper-arm strength to carry plates the way the other waitresses did. In the past, she would have considered rigorous pageant preparation "hard labor." She hadn't understood the pain or exhaustion of being on your feet all day. But she did know how to plaster a smile across her face when she didn't feel like it.

When her water broke, she was carrying two heaping plates of fried catfish and hush puppies to a pair of men in hunting gear. She set down the plates at their table and asked if they needed anything else, then walked calmly through the swinging kitchen doors and asked Irene, her only friend at the restaurant, to cover for her. She drove herself to the hospital, where she labored, alone, for sixteen hours. She had not intended to leave with the baby, but she did.

The nurse gave Charlotte a large supply of mesh underwear and painkillers, and she was back at work within days, though she was still in a considerable amount of pain. She took the baby with her in a wicker bassinet, which she set on the rarely used prep station in the back, far enough from the fryers. Fortunately, Corinna wasn't a crier. She laid in her bassinet for hours at a time, sleeping or staring at the ceiling or grasping for the dream catcher some-one tied to the handle of the basket when Charlotte wasn't look-ing. And none of the other servers or kitchen staff was allowed to complain, because Charlotte was the most popular waitress in the restaurant. It wasn't because she was the friendliest or the fastest, or remembered the regulars' orders. No, the owners, a pair of big, corn-fed white-boy brothers from Mississippi, knew she was good for business because she was beautiful.

She was the prettiest woman many of the patrons would ever see. Her skin was pale gold, with an ethereal glow. Her eyes were light brown with flecks of yellow in the irises. Her thick black hair tumbled down her back in loose, shiny waves. If you had never seen her dark-skinned baby, you would have thought she was an exotic European or North African and not a light-skinned Negro. And Charlotte knew it.

She did her best to exploit it, too. Most importantly, she ad-opted their manner of speech and flashed her wide, blinding white, orthodontic wet dream of a smile to every man, woman, and child who entered the restaurant.

When Corinna started playing at getting out of her basket, Irene helped Charlotte get a job as a receptionist in a real estate office. The pay was worse, but the work was easier, the sort girls like her did if they wanted to keep busy between typing school and marriage. Her new boss, Nate, was a handsome Black man who fa-vored brown suits. Charlotte thought he might have a little crush on her, because he never apprehended her for how horribly she did her job. But he was married, and never lingered at her desk, and she never caught him looking at her.

As Charlotte couldn't afford childcare, she brought Corinna to the office. Sometimes, in the middle of the day, when Corinna grew tired of coloring and rummaging through drawers looking for candy, she would stand quietly nearby and stare at her mother. Charlotte, who was sometimes typing and sometimes gazing blankly into the distance, could feel the girl's eyes on her, trying to get her attention. Charlotte knew she should acknowledge her daughter, but Corinna's reptilian eyes, lopsided smile, and peanut butter complexion made her think of Wayne. And almost always, Charlotte felt sick. She knew it wasn't how she was supposed to feel. But she couldn't help it.

One evening, when Corinna was maybe two or three, she sat in the shallow water of her bath playing with a yellow rubber duck. Corinna held up the toy so that she and the duck were looking Charlotte right in the face. She held her mother's gaze for a long moment before squeezing the duck with her tiny hand so that it squeaked.

"I love you," said the little girl. Charlotte didn't know what to make of it, as she couldn't remember uttering the phrase to anyone, ever. Perhaps to her father? But he'd been dead for over a decade. So where would Corinna have learned it? From the television Charlotte let her watch, or from hanging around with adults all day at the office? Whatever the case, the words made Charlotte's already tumorous shame grow. She carried the shame in her belly, where it squirmed like a pit of snakes.

1978

Charlotte sat at the makeshift kitchen table—a card table with broken legs supported by orange crates—reading a weeks-old copy of the *New York Times* that someone left behind at the office, smoking, and drinking a cup of instant coffee spiked with cheap bourbon. It was early on a Friday evening, and she was feeling unusually hopeful. Corinna sat at the other end of the table, filling in a picture of a giraffe with the wrong colors; she was using purple for the spots and green for the rest. Charlotte watched her daughter for a moment and almost smiled to herself. Instead, she went back to reading about the uptick in maternal filicide in Japan. Charlotte wondered why more women didn't kill their children. The thought crossed her mind at least a few times a week. That's why it was important that she have time for herself. Just as much for her daughter's good as her own, Charlotte reasoned.

At eight thirty p.m. on the dot, Charlotte tucked Corinna into the bed they shared. It was only a full-size mattress tucked into the corner, but Charlotte took good care of the sheets and made it up every morning. She sat next to her daughter on top of the covers, and they watched the end of *Donny & Marie*. Usually, Corinna was asleep by the end of the show, but her eyes were still wide open when the credits rolled. Still, Charlotte turned off the TV and went to the closet to pull out the only going-out dress she'd managed to bring with her from her old life: a long yellow floral silk Treacy Lowe wrap dress with a deep-V halter neckline. It had been a really nice dress when it was new, but now it was coming loose at the seams. She slipped it on and did not bother with her hair or makeup. Before she left, Charlotte considered giving her daughter a gentle kiss on the forehead but didn't.

She chain-smoked with the windows down on her drive into downtown Nashville. There were nicer places she might have gone, places where she might have landed a man with money. But she'd had money, and it hadn't done her much good. She was looking for somebody to take care of her, give her some relief. As she walked into Mama's, her favorite bar, she took a moment to survey her surroundings, the unfinished wood floor covered in peanut shells. She wasn't looking for the most handsome man in the room, or the one with the most money. She was looking for a few free cocktails to help her forget about being a mother. She selected a very tall, very fat man with a snow-white beard; a silver braid down the middle of his leather-clad back; and a small, single gold hoop earring, and let him buy her a few gin and tonics while he nursed a Heineken. He was a good talker, and good-looking in a peculiar sort of way. He could have easily played a heroic pirate in a movie. But he wasn't quite right.

She scanned the crowd and found an older guy standing alone in the far corner drinking what looked like a Bloody Mary. His white hair was receding, and she knew intuitively that he had large tufts of hair growing out of his ears. He might also have been married. She knew the type. She was planning to cut a path through the crowd, but before she could make a move, the scrum split like the Red Sea and offered her her Moses. He was tall with wavy, dark hair to his shoulders, and he was square-dancing in a pair of rugged brown and yellow cowboy boots, light-wash jeans, and a T-shirt with the sleeves cut off and a large sweat stain that spread symmetrically across his back like wings. He was holding a bottle of Natural Light in each hand, taking a sip every third beat, and smiling the biggest, warmest smile that Charlotte had ever seen. She set down her drink, walked right up to him, and asked him to teach her how to square dance. He gulped down the last of his beer, handed the bottles off to an unsuspecting stranger, and used his right arm to take her around the waist while he clasped her right hand with his deeply calloused left one.

"I'm David," he said, with a smile that seemed brighter now that he was looking at her. His teeth were perfectly square and bright white, but just crooked enough that Charlotte could tell he had gotten lucky with good genes, not good orthodontia. His eyes were dark blue, almost navy. "You're real pretty. I think I'm gon' have to marry you."

Charlotte felt herself blush, something she never did. Her body felt light, and the knots in her stomach loosened a little. Her mother had warned her about white men and their smooth-talking with brown women, but maybe he didn't realize that she wasn't white. After all, his skin was tanned several shades darker than her own.

"Oh, don't go blushin' on me like you ain't know you're beautiful."

They swayed slowly to a rhythm that did not match the music while the crowd do-si-doed around them.

"You look like somebody painted you," he said. "Like you belong on some rich fella's wall. That's how pretty you are. You ain't tell me your name, darlin'."

"Charlotte," she replied softly, almost shyly.

"Shah-lot," he said, disregarding the *r* in the middle of her name, and she thought it sounded a lot better that way. "That's a beautiful name," he said. "I never met a *Shah-lot*." He placed her hand on his thick, bulging shoulder and put his own hand on the side of her face, and kissed her. "I think I'm going to have to marry you," he repeated, his forehead pressed against hers.

Flustered, Charlotte stammered, "I've got a kid," to which he smiled and shrugged. It was important to mention her child upfront. Any man she dated would have to be okay with a kid, but also not eager to have more.

They danced until the bar emptied out. David went home with her that night, and slept fully clothed on the floor by the mattress. He spent much of the next day playing with Corinna. So she decided she would marry him.

A month later, she wore a white pantsuit from the Salvation Army to the courthouse, and he wore the same outfit he'd worn the night they met.

Afterward, David moved her and Corinna into a small but comfortable blue clapboard house with two bedrooms and one bathroom. It also had a laundry room with a washer and dryer, a small luxury. He bought brand-new furniture and installed an air conditioner in the window of the front room. He went to work on construction sites every day and came back smelling like liquor and a locker room, but he paid the bills on time. Sometimes, he took her out to halfway decent restaurants in Nashville and flirted with the waitresses, or they went out square-dancing, and he danced exactly like he had the first time she saw him, a beer in each hand, smiling.

EARLY 1980S

A few years into their marriage, Charlotte came home early one day and found that David was gone. He'd left a short note.

Charlotte,
I got to get back to Louisiana to take care a some business.

David

A man with as many whims and secrets as David was bound to do something like that eventually.

Corinna was devastated; her dramatic sadness annoyed Charlotte. She felt Corinna didn't have the right to be so upset; David was more Charlotte's husband than he was Corinna's father. Anyway, she figured he would come back, but she wouldn't make it easy for him when he did.

Nate, her boss, had recently divorced, and Charlotte quickly won his attention. She liked him because he always smelled fresh out of the shower. He bought her flowers and jewelry and paid for babysitters. He was predictable. But he was not a good dancer. How was she supposed to enjoy life with a man who not only couldn't dance but didn't even *like* to dance? He preferred long, slow dinners with expensive wines and tiny desserts.

In addition to being boring, Nate barely acknowledged Corinna, which left Charlotte with the sole responsibility of caring for the girl, and she found that burden far too great.

Two months later, David came back with all his belongings packed into the bed of his truck and tears in his eyes. He was carrying a bouquet of peonies, her favorite.

Nate took the news well. Charlotte suspected he was relieved, actually. Everyone attempted to go back to the way things were, but Charlotte couldn't really forgive David. He'd run around on her and had drunk too much from the start, but he'd done one very important thing right: he'd promised he would stay and be her husband, and he'd broken that promise. Though she could have left him, there was nothing she wanted less than to be alone again. Or be with a man who didn't like to dance.

But there was turmoil. Several times, she threw heaps of his clothes out on the front lawn and set them on fire. More than once, she chased him out of the house, wielding the ball-peen hammer she kept under the sink. They fought over things as small as the mushrooms in the sauce for the frozen Salisbury steak and as big as the mortgage. Most of their fights occurred after nights out at the bar, especially after Charlotte started accepting offers of cocaine in the bathroom and quickly developed a nasty habit.

Shortly after a promotion to office manager, she was arrested and jailed so many times for disorderly conduct, public intoxication, and driving under the influence that she got herself fired. So she started doing hair in the kitchen. There weren't many places for Black folks to get their hair done in Chilly Springs, so the competition wasn't fierce. With the population looking like it was, business would never boom, but it would be better than nothing. Charlotte could do a decent roller set, and she practiced on Corinna's hair for the more complicated styles.

Corinna would sit patiently between Charlotte's knees while her mother attempted to re-create hairstyles from an outdated copy of *Ebony*, eventually developing a passable finger wave. Corinna briefly rocked an impressive, feathered blowout that was absurd on a second grader, and she thought her mother did the best side ponytail she'd ever seen (especially when she was also sporting a feathered bang), and her edges suffered when Charlotte practiced her cornrows.

Not long after Corinna's ninth birthday, Charlotte tried to do a relaxer for the first time, and the child's hair went both very limp and very straight, slipping through Charlotte's hands like overcooked noodles. She panicked. When she slammed the faucet off, Corinna's little crocodilian eyes popped open. Charlotte hastily attempted to rinse out the rest of the chemicals, but it was no use. Corinna's head was nearly bald in some patches, and in others, her hair was as long and as strong as ever. Charlotte hadn't known what to do but cut it very short, almost down to the scalp.

Afterward, Corinna smiled wide into the cheap pink pearlescent hand mirror like her mother had blessed her with the most beautiful hairdo the world had ever seen. "Oh, Mama," she said as she smoothed imaginary hair around her shoulders. "It's perfect."

"Stop playing, girl," Charlotte said and snatched the mirror away.

"I'm not playin', Mama." Corinna looked up at her mother. "I really do like it cuz you did it."

Charlotte managed to plant a kiss on her daughter's prickly head before retreating to the bedroom with a fifth of whiskey.

1985

Charlotte was peeing when she realized it was her thirtieth birthday. She lingered on the toilet, sighed noisily, and lit a cigarette. This was not where she thought she would be at thirty. As a child, she hadn't even known people could live like she was living now. Even the people who worked in her mother's house probably didn't smoke on the toilet or resent their children the way that she did. Charlotte could have been like her mother and smoked on a much nicer toilet in a much nicer bathroom, but she'd made different choices.

For Evelyn's thirtieth birthday, Charlotte's father had thrown a lavish literature-themed party on the back lawn of their large, Victorian-style home. Charlotte was rather young but had been allowed to stay up until past ten o'clock to watch people arrive, elaborately dressed as literary characters: several guests wore full suits of armor, one woman's gown bore a painted crimson letter, another woman sported a flapper dress, a man carried a magnifying glass and wore a deerstalker hat. Charlotte's parents had dressed as Lord and Lady Macbeth. Evelyn wore a deep blue, floor-length velvet gown with gigantic bell sleeves and golden embroidery snaking along the hem and placed a gold crown at a rakish angle in a pile of her loose, ash-blond curls and smeared red blood paste up to her elbows. Despite the unsettling texture of the paste, Charlotte held her mother's hand until she was forced to go to bed. Even now, in the tiny bathroom with the peeling paint and chipped porcelain sink, Charlotte could still feel the crackling wax on her palms.

Now, Charlotte wished she'd spent that evening with her father. She couldn't even remember his costume in detail. Her memories of him were generally scarce. James Jackson was one of two Black surgeons in Atlanta during her childhood, so he was in high demand. When he was home, he showered his wife and daughter with gifts and attention. Evelyn was kinder when he was around, and the house felt brighter.

There was a timid knock on the thin plywood door. Charlotte's cigarette was almost burned down to her fingers. The ash dissolved on the floor. She realized she'd been crying.

"Mama?" Corinna pleaded from the other side of the door when she didn't answer. "You all right?"

"I'm fine," Charlotte said and hastily wiped her cheeks, but only managed to cry harder. The backs of her hands were streaked black with the prior night's mascara, and her eyes stung badly from the running makeup. When she finally looked up, Corinna was standing in the open doorway.

"Mama? What's wrong?" Corinna reached for her mother, but Charlotte recoiled and scrambled to pull up her pants.

"Leave me be," she said and hit her hip hard on the sink when she fled the bathroom.

1990S

After an exceptionally good detox in county jail in the early nineties, Charlotte woke up gasping for air as if she'd been drowning and whatever had been holding her down had turned her loose.

During Charlotte's lost 1980s, Corinna had become a teenager. She hadn't grown much in height, but her chest was heavier, and her hips wider. Her hair had grown back from the relaxer incident, but it was never as thick as Charlotte thought she remembered it being. Corinna kept it boyishly short, cropped close at the sides and straightened within an inch of its life, like she was trying to emulate Lisa Bonet from *The Cosby Show*. But the amount of hair grease she used to make it appear slick made it stringy, and Charlotte suspected the oil may have also been responsible for her ruddy, blemished skin. But it wouldn't have really mattered how Corinna wore her hair, Charlotte thought, her daughter was simply not pretty. Her eyes were too small, her nose was too wide, and her lips were oddly thin and pale pink against medium-brown skin with ashy undertones. Her eyelashes were short like a dog's, and her posture was bad. The prettiest thing about her was her teeth, which were a bit crowded in her mouth, but gleaming white and chiclet shaped. Charlotte envied her daughter's average looks. Corinna had probably never looked up from doing something, perhaps a math test or whatever she did at school, to meet the gaze of a man or boy (or girl, for that matter) who would then sort of pretend to have been looking just past her.

Charlotte laid eyes on Corinna only a few times a week. She had no idea what the girl did outside of school; she only assumed she attended as she had no evidence to the contrary. When they were in the same room, they had little to say to each other. They usually discussed the weather—almost always dry and hot, except in the winter when it was occasionally less dry and less hot. Sometimes they sucked their teeth in frustration while watching game shows on the thirteen-inch antennaed television. But years had passed since they'd had anything resembling a real conversation. When Charlotte had been Corinna's age, her own mother never missed an opportunity to volley sharp critiques at her. "Is that what you're wearing?" "Those shoes? With that dress?" "You should grow out your nails. Your hands look like a man's." Charlotte didn't understand much about her childhood, but she did know that she would never speak to any child that way.

Charlotte had considered having a second child with David. She thought she would get it right the second time, or closer, at least. But she had two abortions when she was with him, and she told herself many stories about why, including that a new child wouldn't be fair to Corinna. Charlotte did not resent Corinna as much as she had when the girl actually needed her. Corinna, who had clung to her mother as a child, now treated Charlotte like a roommate.

One afternoon in April, Corinna came slamming into the house soaking wet and hollering about another tornado; one had narrowly missed their house only the month before. She claimed she'd barely escaped getting herself, and the fifteen-year-old Ford David had won in a bet, swept up in it.

"Best get in the tub," David said. He knocked back the last of whatever was in his glass and groaned. "Charlotte, I told you to stop buying that cheap shit."

Corinna was flitting around the house, pulling blankets and pillows off the beds and flailing them into the bathtub, which Charlotte eased into with a fresh glass of "cheap shit." Her bare feet dangled over the tub's edge, losing circulation; she was uncomfortable but didn't bother to rearrange herself.

"How many tur-nay-ders y'all think this house can stand?" David asked, sitting on the toilet seat lid, taking another shot of Jack Daniel's. Corinna sat next to Charlotte with her legs crossed. Corinna looked up from an old, crusty copy of *Woman's World*.

"That wind out there howlin' like a wolf," he continued, and released a convincing howl of his own.

"Where'd you learn to do that, Daddy? There ain't wolves in the bayou, is it?"

"There's wolves everywhere, darlin'. Even in your own home sometimes."

He continued. "I ever tell you about how I lived in Montana with my great-uncle one summer?"

"That's where you learned it?"

"You never told me you lived in Montana," Charlotte said, but was ignored. The snakes in her stomach stirred. Quickly, they slithered around, flicking their tongues across each other's bodies and her internal organs.

David let out another howl. "You try," he said to Corinna.

"Y'all stop that," Charlotte said. But she was ignored again.

Corinna howled. David howled. Corinna howled again.

Charlotte crossed her arms over her chest and closed her eyes. Soon, it was completely quiet inside the bathroom, except for storm sounds and David's sips from a bottle of whiskey.

Charlotte woke up several hours later and found herself curled up in a fetal position. Corinna was also asleep, her head resting at a ninety-degree angle on her mother's hip. Charlotte repositioned Corinna's head it so that she would not wake up with a sore neck, though she knew it was already too late. She climbed out of the bathtub and stepped over David, who was asleep on the ratty bathmat that had once been the color of deviled egg yolk but was now the color of Tennessee Honey whiskey. It was five thirty-five a.m. and the sky was beginning to turn a dusty, blushing pink that reminded Charlotte of an Easter dress she'd had as a little girl, tulip-hemmed, with silk flower petals floating loose in layers of rosy chiffon. That year, uncharacteristically, Evelyn had made matching fresh-flower crowns for the two of them, something Charlotte still could not fathom.

Charlotte stood on the front porch in her bare feet and the flannel pajamas she'd been wearing for several days and lit a cigarette. The air still smelled moist and static, but it was going to be a nice day. She stepped off the porch to assess the damage. Gravel from the driveway had been tossed about the lawn, but the house was mostly intact, except for a large panel of clapboard that had blown off and away, and the weathervane was gone. There was also a long crack in the window above the kitchen sink, she noticed.

She hobbled across the gravel to the side of the house where Corinna's Ford was parked, and cringed when she saw a branch lodged across the front of the car. In addition to the dents on the body of the vehicle, the windshield had been obliterated. The branch surprised her, as there were no big trees in the immediate area. She looked around, trying to imagine what might have caused this, but there wasn't much of anything for miles besides a creek behind the house. Their closest neighbors were several hundred yards away in any direction; theirs was a ramshackle island in a sea of dry grass and red clay dirt.

She turned her attention back to the car. The repair would probably cost more than it was worth. Charlotte decided she would give Corinna her car, a Chrysler LeBaron she'd been driving since she sold her Benz for coke money, until she could buy her a new one. It must have been the mild euphoria of the nicotine hit that made her feel so generous.

*   *   *

That summer, Charlotte started temping, primarily because they needed the money to repair their house, but mostly to prove a point.

At her first gig, working in the front office of the local State Farm Insurance agency, Charlotte met Delia Washington. Charlotte's job was to answer the phones and Delia's was to shuffle the endless heaps of paperwork coming in and out. Like Charlotte, she was a temp and, like Charlotte, appropriately bad at her job, spending most of her day filing her nails or chewing gum and staring off into space. Charlotte liked her immediately.

Delia had the thickest Alabama accent Charlotte had ever heard, but she spoke so slowly that she couldn't help but concentrate on what she was saying. She was very, very short and favored clothes with the loudest possible prints Charlotte could imagine. Her husband, Reggie, worked nights on the line at the Saturn plant, and they had two sons, Johnny and Jimmy. Johnny was a big, tall, strapping kid who played football at the high school so well that college coaches had been looking at him since he was in elementary school. Jimmy was nine, and Charlotte suspected he might be a bit slow, but Delia never said anything about it.

Delia talked about her boys with an enthusiasm that made Charlotte's eyes water with guilt. Johnny wanted to stay close to home for college, Vanderbilt being his top choice. His grades were good enough, even without the football, Delia said. He had himself a "little girlfriend," a white girl who lived in Franklin in a big white house on Highway 31 that looked like the one in *Gone with the Wind.* Charlotte knew that her friend was proud of her son's choice, but she was not entirely sure why.

Charlotte had never seen *Gone with the Wind,* but she knew it was racist because her mother told her that once, in the dressing room of a downtown Atlanta department store. They were shopping for Charlotte's cotillion dress, and she was trying on her eighth frilly white gown in a row.

Evelyn sneered. "We'll have to get you something made. These are stinking of Scarlett O'Hara in *Gone with the Wind,* if you catch my drift. That movie's racist, you know that, right? Happy slaves and all that *mess.*"

When Delia tired of talking about her sons or, more likely, realized she was talking too much about herself, she asked after Corinna. And since Charlotte didn't know the answers to her questions, she invented them. She said Corinna wanted to go to an HBCU, because Charlotte had always wanted to. She didn't tell Delia that she'd been *expected* to attend an HBCU because she was descended from a long line of Black academics, including the former president of Spelman College, because she was ashamed. Not because she'd gotten so far away from where she'd come from. She didn't tell Delia any of that because it was more complicated than that. She hadn't been protected when she'd needed protection. But though she and Delia were good friends, she didn't know if she could ever admit all of that to anyone. It was easier to lie and say that her father and mother were both dead and that she'd been raised by her grandmother, who had also died. It might have been gratuitous to add that Corinna's father was Charlotte's high school boyfriend, who also died tragically in a horrible car accident on I-65 before Charlotte could even tell him she was pregnant, but it was the same story she'd always told Corinna. The only person who knew the truth was David.

Charlotte suspected that Delia did not totally believe the story, which she'd patched together when Corinna was about ten years old and had first asked. But retelling it under the harsh fluorescent lighting in the insurance office break room, Charlotte felt ashamed for lying to the first real friend she'd made since she got fired from the real estate office years earlier. (Irene from the restaurant had stopped talking to Charlotte long before that, after an incident involving a pair of flared-leg jeans and a bottle of Everclear.)

She considered telling Delia the truth, especially once they started spending more time together outside of the office. They'd spend Saturdays riding around in Delia's old hooptie—a twenty-year-old Cadillac—drinking gas station lemonade and rum out of a rusty Thermos, perusing estate sales in the nearby county where retired country music stars and old agriculture money resided. They walked through houses like the one Charlotte had grown up in, with elegant staircases, vaulted ceilings, and Tiffany light fixtures. She pretended to be in awe, for Delia's sake, but internally balked at the unimaginative tastes and habits of rich people. Some were coated with dust; others were slightly newer with better landscaping. Some of the faucets were rusted brass; others gleamed like gold. But the houses Charlotte liked best were the ones that appeared immaculate from the outside but were packed to the rafters with junk: old newspapers, Playbills, bags and bags of cat litter, boxes of cheap cooking gadgets. Though all of the homes Charlotte and Delia saw had likely been cleaned to a degree by embarrassed family members, these were the ones Charlotte liked the best: the obvious sites for real chaos and sadness. That's what she liked most about this part of Tennessee. It wasn't like Nashville or Atlanta, where it was harder to hide. It's why she stayed out there in Chilly Springs. David had wanted to stay where he'd been living when they first got married—in the northern half of middle Tennessee—but Charlotte insisted. She said she needed the quiet.

She and Delia rarely bought anything, except one afternoon, when she spotted a pair of earrings on the dusty windowsill of a vast, derelict Tudor. Someone must have picked them up and changed their mind. The sun glinted on the large ruby-colored stones set as the eyes of gaudy gold-colored serpents. They reminded her of her mother, whose jewelry often featured serpents. She said they represented the balance between good and evil.

Before she knew what she was doing, she was approaching a beautiful redheaded woman carrying a clipboard, preparing for a vigorous haggling, but the woman barely looked at her or the earrings.

"Ten dollars," the woman said in a clipped accent that wasn't local.

"Five," Charlotte answered.

The woman shrugged and pointed at a metal cashbox. Charlotte assumed the woman was a distant cousin of the owner, or a put-upon niece, or perhaps an estranged daughter. Whatever the relationship, the estate was a burden that she was only interested in unloading.

"Where you gon' wear them?" Delia asked in the car on the way home. "You got a gala somewhere I don't know about?"

"Worry about yourself," Charlotte said, laughing.

But as Charlotte turned them over again and again in her hand, she started to become repulsed by them. When she got home, she shoved them in Corinna's direction. Corinna looked at the earrings, at Charlotte, and back at the earrings. "Mama, my ears ain't pierced."

"I know that," Charlotte lied. "For when you do get 'em pierced."

The exchange kept Charlotte up at night, reminding her of interactions she'd had with her own mother. Evelyn forgot or disregarded things about Charlotte, things that felt important to her. She once heard her mother refer to Charlotte's eyes as green, the color of her own eyes.

*   *   *

That fall, Charlotte bought Corinna a car for her seventeenth birthday. It was a used Honda, but the engine turned over reliably, and it was painted the same color all over. She might have spent the money differently, but it made her feel better. Whatever peace she could get was a reprieve from her immense shame. Corinna accepted it with a smile and hug but continued to hold her mother just a little past arm's length.

Charlotte was drinking less and therefore having fewer violent arguments with David. She spent almost everything she earned on the house and that goddamned car note when she really wanted to spend it on alcohol and cocaine. She was trying, and she wanted that to be worth something.

The Monday after Mother's Day that year, Delia came to the real estate office where the temp agency had placed them the month before wearing a gold charm bracelet with her sons' names etched onto gaudy ovals. There were also charms in the shapes of footballs and basketballs, to represent the boys' favorite sports, and roses, Delia's favorite flower. Charlotte forced a smile with difficulty.

The day before, Corinna had come home in the late afternoon, flustered and carrying a bouquet of grocery store flowers for Charlotte and a stack of Styrofoam containers full of food. She'd smelled horribly of fish grease and her forest-green polo shirt said WHISKERS in small print above her right breast. Corinna saw her looking at it.

"We got new uniforms," she said, her mouth full of food, before Charlotte had a chance to ask.

Charlotte ate the catfish and fries without a word. She could not say anything, even if she wanted to, as the wind had been knocked clean out of her. It felt like the universe had reared up like a horse and kicked her square in the chest.

Now, Charlotte took Delia's wrist in her hands and carefully examined the yellow gold charms, biting her lip to hold back tears.

"Johnny saved up his money from painting houses and mowing lawns," Delia said. "I told him not to get me nothing. It's pretty, ain't it?"

It was not pretty. In fact, it may have been one of the ugliest pieces of jewelry Charlotte had ever seen. Still, it was better than *pretty*. It was not only thoughtful, but meaningful. Delia's children knew her in ways that Charlotte's daughter didn't her. And it was nobody's fault but her own.

Charlotte went to the bathroom and cried. She went home early, but not before stopping to pick up a bottle of Jack Daniel's and a liter of Coca-Cola.

WINTER 1992

On Valentine's Day of the following year, Corinna told Charlotte that she was pregnant. Her daughter was eighteen years old, working at Whiskers, and pregnant, just like she had been.

"Your grades are good enough for community college, maybe even a state school, if you work for it," Charlotte told her. "Why would you have a baby right now?" She was digging around in her purse for her yellow faux-snakeskin wallet. "Good thing I went to the bank earlier. If you call now, you might get an appointment for tomorrow."

Corinna looked like she'd been struck, but her voice was steady. "Did anyone ever try to talk you out of having me?"

"Does it matter? Look where it got us." Charlotte placed the money on the table and lit a cigarette. "Who knows who I could have been. I wanted to be a dancer, you know. I could sing pretty good, and was in pageants, too," she said wistfully. "Who knows who I could have been."

"Well, Mama . . ."

"How you gon' afford it? The daddy gon' help? Babies *cost*, you know?"

Charlotte glanced up to blow smoke and saw that her daughter's fists were balled up at her sides. She knew she should apologize and make it right. But no one had ever apologized to Charlotte. She was trying to make this right for her daughter, which was much more than her own mother had done. So, she said nothing.

Corinna snatched the money and fled the house without a word, while Charlotte just listened to the Honda pull away. When she returned home after three a.m., Charlotte was waiting up. She flicked on the porch lights, went to sit on the steps, and beckoned for Corinna to sit next to her. Up close, she could tell her daughter had been doing some real crying and that she wasn't done; a few new tears rolled down her cheeks.

"I'll help you raise it," Charlotte said. "If you really do want to keep it, I'll help you."

Corinna looked at her mother with narrowed eyes. "What?"

"I said, I'll help you if you want to keep it. Whatever you need me to do."

"I do want to keep it."

"All right, then. It's settled." Charlotte stood up, brushed off her light-wash jeans, and turned to go inside.

"Mama?"

"Yeah?"

"Why are you helping me?"

Charlotte shrugged. "It's the right thing to do, ain't it?"

"Is it?"

"Girl. Don't ask me either of those questions ever again."

SPRING 1992

As the reality sunk in, Charlotte resolved to stop drinking altogether. After a few days of debilitating headaches and nausea, she decided to drink less. She allowed herself two drinks per night and forbade herself any before noon. She slipped up from time to time, and still carried a flask in her purse, but she really did cut back.

It was an exceptionally hot spring and summer, and Charlotte was almost perpetually sunburned. One Sunday, David grabbed Charlotte's left arm and a large chunk of the top layer of her skin peeled off in his hand.

"Look at you," he said. "Shedding skin like the snake you is."

Charlotte spat in his face and pulled a knife from a drawer when he lunged at her again.

"Get out," she said.

"Don't come back here till I say you can."

Charlotte went inside and wrapped her arm with gauze and went to the bathroom to cry. She wanted to call Delia, who would have brought over one of those big bottles of cheap wine from the grocery store and some of her homemade chocolate chip–walnut cookies. They would have sat on the porch and laughed about other things. But Delia had been pulling away ever since Charlotte had told her about Corinna's pregnancy. For a week or so, Charlotte called and left messages, but Delia didn't return her calls and didn't even bother to make plausible excuses. Then, she stopped showing up to work. Charlotte asked the agency, and they said Delia had asked to be placed elsewhere. Charlotte's feelings were badly hurt. She allowed herself to mourn for an entire week.

SUMMER 1992

Late in Corinna's pregnancy, Charlotte had trouble sleeping and often woke in the middle of the night to find Corinna stumbling toward the toilet to vomit. One night in July, when Corinna was eight months pregnant, it was a night like many nights before, Charlotte found her heaving. Fighting her instinct to flee, Charlotte moistened a washcloth in the sink and repositioned her daughter so that her head rested in her lap. She gently wiped away Corinna's sweat, tears, and vomit residue. She placed a hand on her daughter's belly, and the fetus pushed back against Charlotte's hand, but she did not startle.

"Mama, I'm scared," Corinna said, her voice raspy from crying.

Charlotte knew she should say something to make her daughter feel better, but she was not well versed in platitudes. She decided to tell the truth. "I know. I'm scared, too," she admitted, and Corinna's eyes flickered open.

"Why are *you* scared?"

"Because it's fucking *scary*," Charlotte said. "Having a *baby*? It's scary, and it hurts."

Corinna stared up at Charlotte with blank eyes.

"What?" Charlotte said.

"You're *supposed* to be reassuring."

"Well, I *am* reassuring you it's a scary thing. You know, people act like it's always this joyous thing, and even if everything is the way it's supposed to be, I can't imagine that it's not still really fucking scary. And that's okay, I think. Normal. That's my two cents, anyway."

Corinna smiled weakly, but it was still a smile, and Charlotte rubbed her daughter's cheek with her thumb. "Will you let me do your hair?"

The next morning, she cut Corinna's hair very short. "I wish I'd done this myself when you were born," she said.

Corinna smirked and Charlotte felt something soften in her. A tear streamed from each eye, but she turned away so Corinna could not see.

Evelyn always said crying was undignified; she hadn't even cried at Charlotte's father's funeral. But that same day, Charlotte had crept into her parents' bedroom to steal one of her father's shirts and heard her mother wailing in the adjoining bathroom. Charlotte pressed her ear to the door and listened. These were angry, hysterical sobs, the kind she hadn't even seen on television. Charlotte never saw her mother cry again, but had deduced that it was okay to cry in private, which is what she'd done ever since.

LATE SUMMER 1992

"I'm gon' name her Camille," Corinna told Charlotte as they drove to the Goodwill one evening to look at cribs. Charlotte had tried to convince Corinna that a crib could wait, if they even needed one at all. Corinna had slept in a drawer or a wicker basket for her first months and a laundry basket after that.

"How do you know it's a girl?"

"I just got a feeling," Corinna said, a hand on her belly.

"Well, can you name her something that doesn't start with a C?"

"No, I don't think so," Corinna said. She was chewing a piece of ginger candy, open-mouthed. "I think it's cute."

"People will think it's on purpose."

"Well, it is."

"What's the letter C to you?"

"It starts your name, and mine. Where'd you get my name from, anyway?"

Charlotte shrugged. "Heard it somewhere and liked it," she lied. "Where'd you get it? What's it? Camille?"

Corinna shrugged. "Heard it somewhere and liked it."

The following week, Corinna and Charlotte were playing spades at the kitchen table when Corinna's contractions started. At the hospital, Charlotte stayed in the delivery room, but began to feel faint when the baby crowned. The baby's hair was thick and curly, which is all Charlotte saw before she went to the bathroom and vomited. Then she went outside and smoked a cigarette and then another. She managed to eat a honey bun from the vending machine and smoked another cigarette. It was an oppressively hot and dry August day, but she paced outside anyway, sweating from each and every pore. Finally, she went to see the baby. The sight of the beautiful, healthy, chocolate-brown baby girl nearly took her knees right out from underneath her.

FALL 1992

Charlotte sighed and lit a menthol cigarette from a new pack. She reapplied lipstick in the rearview mirror and practiced a look of nonchalance. If he were to stop by, David usually met her on the porch, but today she found him in the living room holding the baby. Corinna was seated next to him, tucked underneath his right arm like a throw pillow. Charlotte cleared her throat when no one greeted her.

"Oh, hey there, Granmama," David said, smiling wide.

"I'm gonna go take a shower," Corinna said, excusing herself.

"There's my baby," Charlotte said. She lifted the baby out of David's arms using both hands and held her in the air for a moment as if to inspect her for signs of neglect or abuse. Finding none, she cradled the baby close. "What are you doing letting this strange man hold you?" Charlotte said, pointing a red varnished nail at David. "She usually don't like strangers."

The baby grinned, baring her gummy gums.

"Well, I ain't no stranger, am I?"

David looked grayer than the last time she'd seen him, but that might have only meant the Walgreens was sold out of Just for Men in A-40/Medium-Dark Brown.

"She don't know that. She's just a baby."

"Well, I thought I might as well come on over and introduce myself, being the baby's grandaddy and all."

Charlotte avoided eye contact by dancing around the cramped living room with the baby, who was wearing only a diaper and a pair of pink leather moccasins Charlotte hadn't seen before.

"Well, you seen her," she said, backing away.

David stood. He was a big man, especially in his twenty-pound work boots. "You like them little boots I got her? I got 'em a bit big so she can wear them for a little while."

"Yes. They're just fine, just fine." She hated them, and she would get rid of them as soon as he was gone.

"Well, I know well enough to leave when I've worn out my welcome." He opened his wallet and produced two crisp hundred-dollar bills. "Here," he said. "For the baby."

Charlotte snatched the money as he made his way to the door. She looked down at Camille, who was only about seven weeks old and was more blob than baby. A wave of sour nausea came over her. She'd had this feeling only once before: when she realized she was solely responsible for Corinna's life. She was not solely responsible for Camille, but she was responsible. Responsibility for another human was a big task, one she hadn't done very prudently before. She had to do better this time. She needed help, love, and support. But most importantly, she needed access to another income.

"Wait," she said. "Don't go."

PART II

Blue Magic Women

Camille

WINTER 1997

MOST NIGHTS WHEN Camille was very young, she sat peacefully between her mother's knees to have her hair braided. This was the best time of day. Corinna was gentle, gentler than Camille's grandmother, and Camille loved the smell of the goop her mother smeared on her scalp. The goop was called Blue Magic, and it smelled like nothing Camille had ever smelled: nutty, spicy, chemical. When Corinna was done braiding, she tightly secured her work with a silk scarf.

Then Corinna tilted Camille's head back so that their eyes met. They'd smile at each other, and Corinna would whisper: "Now, keep this on your head while you sleep." Camille always laughed like it was the funniest thing she'd ever heard.

Camille obediently climbed into their full-size bed so that her mother could tuck her in. They kissed each other's cheeks with the same left-right, right-left choreography every night, then Corinna turned off the overhead light and got ready for work, guided only by the flashing lights that spilled in from the living room television.

Camille pretended to sleep but opened her eyes as soon as she sensed her mother's back was turned to watch her get dressed. Even in the same jeans and one of three black T-shirts, Corinna always took great care. Camille watched her mother slick her hair tight to her scalp to produce a little ponytail to which she attached a scrunchie covered in a coarse plasticky material meant to resemble hair. When Corinna wasn't wearing it, she kept the scrunchie on the brass bedpost, and Camille liked to run her fingers through it, letting the oils from her mother's hair get into her hands so she could smell her for a little.

Corinna closed the bedroom door behind her when she left, and then Camille usually slept until around two or three a.m. when her mother would come home, smelling like sweat and spilled liquor, and wake her with kisses and the rustling of plastic bags. Camille loved the sound of Styrofoam containers squeaking open to reveal hot French fries, fried fish, or chicken wings, and thought her mother seemed happiest when they were alone in their creaky bed eating fish 'n' chips and drinking Coke out of glass bottles. After they ate, they went to the bathroom to wash the oil and crumbs from their hands and mouths. Then, Camille sat on the toilet seat lid while her mother washed her T-shirt in the sink with the tiniest amount of Fels Naptha soap that she could manage, humming while she scrubbed. Then Corinna would put the shirt over the shower curtain rod and her pants on the towel rack and go back into the bedroom. Sometimes, Corinna had Camille read one of her small collection of Dr. Seuss books until one of them fell asleep.

When the sun came up, the house was usually quiet. Charlotte would be cooking breakfast with her satin kimono over her pajamas, accidentally dropping cigarette ashes in the eggs.

"There she is!" Charlotte would say, too loudly. "My beautiful girl! How'd you sleep? You hungry?"

"Real good," Camille replied every morning, regardless of how she actually slept. But she was never hungry in the morning, still full of whatever her mother brought home from Copperhead. If Grandaddy happened to be up, which he rarely was, he wanted to hear about her dreams, and she knew to have a few to tell him about, even if she hadn't dreamed at all. Sometimes, he let her have some of his coffee when Charlotte wasn't looking. She didn't like the taste, but she loved when Grandaddy smiled at her, despite his morning breath.

After Charlotte had finished her first cup of coffee, Camille followed her into the living room and sat between her knees to have her scalp rubbed and her hair rebraided. Almost every day, Charlotte invented a new constellation of braids and ponytails. She braided tighter than Corinna and could be aggressive with the sharp end of the rattail comb, but Camille knew not to complain because Charlotte would say: "Oh, you want crooked, loose, raggedy braids, huh?" And Camille definitely did not want crooked, loose, raggedy braids. She wanted the best braids in school, and her grandmother delivered.

But Charlotte's diligence almost always meant Camille missing the bus. So Charlotte drove her to school in her old red convertible, wearing a silk scarf around her hair and dark glasses. She blasted disco music and chain-smoked.

Camille enjoyed school because she was good at it. She didn't consider many kids her friends, and never invited any of them over, but she was never lonely. Still, she always looked forward to seeing her mother's soft-topped jeep outside school at the end of the day.

Sometimes, she and her mother went out for a milkshake at the diner by the park, or to the park itself, which was just a circle of land dotted with enormous bales of hay and bordered by blacktop. Camille practiced her cartwheels in the grass and picked wildflower bouquets for her mother. Occasionally, they went to Goodwill, and her mother let her pick out a book or two but rarely a toy. Camille knew not to argue; her mother always said the same thing.

"You like to read, don't you? You read like a big girl. You gotta practice."

Camille loved it when her mother said she was a "big girl" doing "big girl" things.

No matter what day it was, when they got home, Grandaddy was sitting on the porch with his New Orleans Saints commemorative plastic cup in his left hand and a cigarillo in his right, playing Robin Trower on the battery-operated CD player delicately balanced on the porch railing. This was Camille's other favorite time of day: before Grandaddy got too drunk and before her grandmother and mother got to arguing. Camille liked to sit on the porch with no shoes on and eat Popsicles or watermelon right out of the rind. Sometimes, Grandaddy told stories about the bayou, and other times, they sat quietly together and watched the sun go down.

1999

Corinna often forced Camille to go outside to play with the neighborhood kids, telling her it wasn't normal to sit in the house reading all day. But Camille didn't really like other children, and especially not the neighborhood kids, who were older and often shoeless. So she usually took a book to read by the creek, the part where kids didn't play because it was just a ditch unless it had recently rained. There was a big, smooth ledge on the far side of the creek, where Camille liked to sit and dangle her feet as she read.

One afternoon, she was looking for four-leaf clovers as she headed toward her spot, and was just about to leap into the creek basin and climb to the other side when she noticed someone was in it. A girl about her age was sitting cross-legged, a book open in her lap, watching her. As Camille noticed her, the girl smiled and said hi. And Camille found herself smiling and saying hi back.

"I'm Jenny. I'm six," the girl said.

"I'm Camille. I'm six, too." She paused. It was February, so her half-birthday had just passed. "Well, six and a half. You stay by here?"

"I live down thattaway," the girl pointed. "Where there's water in the creek. But it's quieter down here. You wanna come sit by me?"

Camille shrugged, leaped down into the bone-dry basin, tossed her library copy of *Ramona and Beezus* up onto the stone, and scrambled up the bank. "I like to do my feet like this," Camille said, demonstrating, and the girl followed her lead. "What are you reading?"

"*Sideways Stories*," Jenny said, and flashed the cover of her paperback book.

"That's an orange-level," Camille said. She also read at the orange level. Everyone else in her class read at the pink level or below.

"Yeah. I'm the only one in my class that reads that high."

"Me, too," Camille said.

"I'm in Miss Partridge's class," Jenny said. Miss Partridge was the youngest, nicest, prettiest teacher with the coolest classroom that overlooked the playground. That classroom was also removed from the other three first-grade classes, which explained why Camille had never seen Jenny. "She cries a lot."

"I have Mrs. Johnson," Camille said. She knew her mother had chosen Mrs. Johnson because she was the only Black teacher of first grade, but Camille had wished she had Miss Partridge. But now she was glad she didn't. There was something very unsettling about a crying adult.

"You wanna read together?"

The girls sat side by side, reading quietly until it started getting dark and Jenny said it was time for her to go home. Each day, after school, Camille willingly went outside to meet her new friend. Sometimes they read, sometimes they searched for wild strawberries, and other times they pummeled dandelions with rocks to make yellow "ink" they used to write their names on their rock over and over again. They never argued about rules or fairness like the other kids did.

One afternoon about a month into their friendship, Camille

and Jenny were building a delicate Lincoln Log–style structure with pine needles when she heard someone calling her name. She looked up to see her mother standing on the opposite bank, hands on her hips.

"I been calling you, Camille."

"I'm sorry, Mama," she said and scampered across the creek bed. She used one hand to hold her mother's and the other to wave goodbye to Jenny.

"So you got a little friend?" Corinna asked as they walked back to the house.

"Yeah, she's nice."

"That's great, baby!" Corinna said, a little too exuberantly for Camille's comfort. "You know, when I was your age, I didn't have *any* friends. Nobody lived around here. I only saw other kids at school."

Camille didn't understand what her mother meant. The place was full of kids, as far as she could see. As they approached home, she saw a bunch of them riding bikes on the main road. From her spot at the creek, she'd see high school students get dropped at the mouth of a different main road. There were kids everywhere. She was about to tell her mother this when she noticed that her mother's lips were unnaturally red, and her eyelashes were spidery and long. This was makeup, something her grandmother sometimes wore when she was "feeling fancy." Camille had never known her mother to "feel fancy." She squinted in confusion but said nothing.

She started coming inside from playing in time to sit on the toilet seat lid to watch her mother apply mascara and lipstick. Corinna was spending more time in the kitchen at night, muttering softly into the phone. She was also buying new clothes and growing out her hair.

Then Corinna's schedule changed again. Before, she'd had every Sunday off, and they spent the day at the park or doing whatever activity was free at the library in downtown Nashville. But now

Corinna was gone by the time Camille woke up on Sundays, and didn't get home until late. So Camille spent more of her waking hours with her grandparents, but it was Corinna's presence that she craved. Her mother was her God, her Blue Magic woman.

When her mother was gone, they'd put on loud disco music, and she and her grandmother would dance while Grandaddy kept time tapping his big dry hands on his bony, denim-coated thighs. When it was time to go to bed, she nestled between her grandparents in bed and read to them. Sometimes she fell asleep there, but she preferred to be in bed when her mother arrived home because she smelled nice, like Blue Magic and flowers.

One night, on the fly, she trailed Corinna to the door on her way out, expecting her to get into her Jeep. Instead, she got into a silver car with a man at the wheel. She could barely make out his face, but saw his hair and beard was the bright, deep orange of the twenty-five-cent Austin Cheese Crackers she got in the school cafeteria.

"Who's that?" she asked her grandmother, who wasn't paying attention.

Charlotte stood up to join Camille at the door, but the man was driving away. "I don't know. Close this door 'fore the flies get in."

Every night after that, Camille followed her mother to the door to see if she got in her own car or the Austin Cheese Cracker Man's. Most of the time, it was her own, but every now and again it was his. More alarmingly, sometimes Corinna didn't show up until morning. One night, Camille was next to her sleeping grandparents on the couch when she saw headlights flashing in the dark living room. She leaped from the couch, met her mother at the door, and followed her into their bedroom.

"Whatchu doin' still awake?" Corinna asked.

Camille shrugged. She likely would have fallen asleep on the couch, too, if a few more minutes had passed. But they hadn't. "Who's that man, Mama?"

"What man?"

"That man you was in the car with?"

"Oh, a friend of mine."

Camille had never heard of her mother having any friends. She was supposed to be her mother's only friend. "What's his name?"

"Isaac."

Camille started to see more of him through doorways and windows, coming and going. He did take the time to smile at her when they made eye contact, but it was always a tight-lipped one that gave Camille the impression that it didn't matter whether or not she returned it.

There had always been a tension between her mother and grandmother, but it had stayed in the kitchen in the middle of the night or in hushed tones on the gravel driveway. Slowly, it became more audible, though Camille still didn't see anything. There was shouting and door slamming, but never when she was around. As soon as she stepped into a room, the mood would change so quickly that she thought she'd imagined it. She learned to eavesdrop. She crept from bed at night and flattened herself against the wall of the short hallway to listen to her mother and grandmother at the kitchen table.

"Mama, I'm *trying*," she heard her mother say. "She's all I care about, really. I just want her to have something close to normal."

Charlotte sighed. "By not being around?"

"By working hard. By giving her a *father*."

Camille went back to bed. She didn't like the sound of "father." Camille knew that she had a good life and that she didn't want it to change even if there was one of those elusive fathers waiting for her on the other side.

Soon, Charlotte began to fill the void her mother had left. It wasn't a perfect fit. Her grandmother's body was not soft like Corinna's, but when Camille pressed her face into Charlotte's belly and inhaled, she smelled like home; Corinna always smelled like somewhere else. Charlotte never encouraged Camille to go outside and play with the neighborhood kids, not minding if she stayed close.

A few times a week, women came to the house to get their hair done. After Charlotte applied a relaxer to their hair and washed it, they sat in one of the kitchen chairs to have it straightened with a hot comb heated on the stove, Camille's favorite part. Somehow, Charlotte managed to smoke while she applied Blue Magic to the scalp and hair, the cigarette coming perilously close, but never making contact. The whole thing was like magic. There was a bit of magic to everything Charlotte did, even when she was just sitting and staring into space. Charlotte spent a lot of time out on the porch, but when it was raining, too hot, or too cold, she took the rocking chair by the window with a cigarette and something to drink. Sometimes, she played different music: low and slow, and the singers muttering rather than belting like they did in disco.

"Granmama, whatchu call this type of music?" Camille asked as she climbed into her grandmother's narrow lap. Charlotte tapped her heel in time with the music.

"The blues, baby. You like it?"

"Why they call it the blues?"

"Don't it sound blue to you, baby?" Charlotte winked.

"Yeah, I guess so."

"When people are sad sometimes, they say they're blue, or they got the blues. So they sing the blues."

"If it's sad, why you listen to it, Granmama? Are you sad?"

"I get sad sometimes, yeah."

"What you get sad about?"

"Oh, all kinds of things."

"Like what?"

"Your mama, for one," she said under her breath.

Camille pretended not to have heard. "Huh?"

"Nothing, sugar."

But Camille heard. She reclined farther into Charlotte's angular body to consider what it meant. She wondered, Did she make her mother sad? She didn't want to do that.

When Corinna told her they were moving out of the house, Camille cried, though she could see that she was making her mother sad.

"You'll have your own room," Corinna offered.

Camille didn't want her own room. She loved sharing her space with her mother.

"You'll see Isaac more. You like him, don't you?"

Camille wasn't "studyin'" Isaac, as her grandfather would say. She was aware of him, but she didn't spend much time thinking about him.

"You'll still see Granmama and Grandaddy all the time."

"But why, Mama?"

"For you, baby. Everything I do is for you."

Camille didn't know if she believed this, but she acquiesced because she was the baby, and her mother was the mother.

WINTER 2000

It wasn't that Camille didn't believe Isaac when he said all the computers would crash at midnight on New Year's Eve. She just didn't see how it mattered. Fourth graders at her school used computers to play some dumb-looking game called Oregon Trail. There was a computer in Jenny Rhodes's basement where they played Barbie Magic Hair Styler, and a few at the public library and maybe one at the doctor's office, but she failed to see the horror in any of them crashing.

Isaac was collecting nonperishables on industrial pallets in preparation for Armageddon; he covered them with blue tarps and stored them on the open carport where Camille once practiced pirouettes and no-handed bike riding. But he'd collected so much by October that Camille couldn't so much as sit out there, and the house was similarly cramped and cluttered. Worse, he lectured Corinna about the Bible and the Rapture, sometimes making her and Camille pray for hours in the living room. Once, Isaac woke Camille up in the middle of the night and asked her to confess her sins. When she said that she did not have any sins because she was seven years old, Isaac smiled and put his sweaty hand on her head and spoke in what she recognized from the late-night TV sermons she'd watched with her grandfather as "tongues." His irises moved so rapidly that they seemed to vibrate, and the whites of his eyes were almost always pink, which looked strange in contrast with his bright orange eyelashes. Obviously, something wasn't "right" with Isaac. In general, something wasn't right. And yet, she and her mother proceeded as if nothing were the matter.

On a trip to Food Lion, Camille was in the middle of trying to convince her mother to get Capri Suns instead of Little Hugs for her lunch when her mother snatched the box out of Camille's hand and then used the same arm to pull Camille close to her. Camille assessed the aisles for danger but only saw a big, dark brown woman wearing an unreasonable amount of jangly jewelry. She was wearing lime-green cargo capris and a coordinating patterned top. There was a word her grandmother sometimes used to describe women like that: "Tacky," she said with a frown about anybody on television wearing a color brighter than navy blue.

"Oh, Corinna," the strange woman said. "I just wanted to take a look at her."

"Oh," Corinna said and pulled Camille closer, while Camille pressed her face to her side. When she was younger, she'd bite her mother's fleshy bits whenever she got the chance, convinced that her sweet mama must taste sweet, that some of her mama's sweet would work its way into her bloodstream. She was always disappointed and confused to find that she actually tasted salty and soapy, and finally stopped when her mother laughingly threatened to bite her back. She thought about the Little Hugs and how she would agree to drink them if her mother kept holding her close.

"She's a pretty little thing, ain't she?" the woman said.

"Mm-hmm. She is."

"A pretty little chocolate thing."

Camille did not like when people referred to her skin color this way. She just wanted to be brown like the white kids were beige or tan or whatever. You never heard anybody calling white girls "pretty little sand-colored things" or "pretty little egg-colored things." Sure, chocolate was superior to sand or eggs, but that wasn't the point. She actually wasn't certain of the point.

"Mm-hmm," Corinna answered again.

"Big ole puppy-dog eyes. She's gonna be pretty. Better watch her."

"Oh, I will, Ms. Delia."

Ms. Delia walked away wearing a tight, painful-looking smile. Corinna did not release Camille for a beat, but as soon as she did, she snatched the box of Capri Suns off the shelf and threw it into the cart.

"Oh, it's buy one get one," Corinna said to herself and grabbed another box.

Back in the car, Camille asked her mother: "Who was that tacky lady?"

Corinna laughed. "Oh, just some lady."

"Why'd you try to hide me from her, then?"

Corinna turned around to look at Camille in the back seat. "I wasn't trying to hide you."

"What was you trying to do then?" Camille didn't expect her mother to answer. Only Grandaddy tolerated this many questions.

"If you see that lady again, don't speak to her. Tell her your mama said not to talk to strangers."

"Why?"

"Because I *said* so. You hear me?"

"Yes'm."

Corinna clicked on the radio as they left the Food Lion parking lot. The host was taking calls about kids saying the "darndest things." A woman told a story about her son running after his father and his friends with his toy golf clubs in hand, wailing about not being allowed to play with those "mean old men." Another woman laughed as she recounted her daughter explaining to her with a straight face that "it's all the same when you're laying down." Corinna smiled to herself at some of the stories, none of which Camille found even vaguely funny. Another caller had to explain to his three-year-old daughter that she could not marry her grandfather.

"Well," the host said. "Did you tell her she could marry a man *like* her grandfather?"

"I'd like to marry a man like Grandaddy, I think," Camille said.

"No, you don't."

"Why not?"

Corinna sighed loudly and clicked the radio off. "I love your grandaddy. But there's stuff about him you don't know."

"Like what?"

"I'll tell you when you're older."

"You promise, Mama?"

"Well. We'll see. Maybe he'll tell you himself."

SUMMER 2000

In May, once it was evident that they were in the clear regarding Y2K, Isaac bought a computer and a modem to connect to the internet. He sat at the computer night and day and latched on to various conspiracy theories about John F. Kennedy, the Illuminati, and various aviation incidents. Camille asked her mother if Isaac was crazy like those people on *Ripley's Believe It or Not*.

"He's just passionate, honey." Her mother flashed a stiff grimace that Camille was meant to interpret as a smile, and held it for a beat too long.

Isaac continued to follow her mother around the house, telling her about the New World Order and the occasional alien abduction. By June, he no longer seemed to be going to work.

Luckily, Camille was able to spend most nights with her grandmother and most days with Jenny, exploring fields and graveyards. After the day they'd met by the creek, the girls were elated to learn that they were enrolled in the same ballet class. Once, after class, Jenny asked her mother if Camille could come over, Camille's mother said yes, and they'd been best friends ever since. They even wore matching necklaces from the mall; they'd made lanyards and sold them at school to save up for them. Each necklace had a pink flower-shaped, lacquered pendant with a purple rhinestone in the middle. Above each flower was a smaller, silver pendant; Jenny's read "Best," and Camille's read "Friends."

Camille was warming up to the kids from the neighborhood but still found them childish; they wanted to play games like basketball or tag, or they were skinning their knees on the slip 'n' slide in somebody's front yard. Camille infinitely preferred Jenny.

That summer, the girls spent hours and hours outside, even when it rained or was almost unbearably hot and Jenny's scalp turned pink with sunburn. Jenny's mother kept Capri Suns in the freezer and cut the tops off so the girls could drink the juice and chew on the ice. They tied two long jump ropes to a young tree by the creek, and they took turns jumping double Dutch, even though the ground was so soft that sometimes the mud sucked their shoes right off their feet. But Camille got very good that summer anyway. Eventually, Granmama told her to leave her socks and shoes at home: "Can't be ruining your damn shoes all the time." Soon, Jenny started doing the same, and they spent their days barefoot: running down to the creek, catching tadpoles, and daring each other to eat them.

One afternoon in July, Jenny failed to show up at their regular meeting spot, an old-fashioned gas station at the intersection of Kedron and Old Highway 37. They were both sleepy roads with a few subdivisions sprouting from them like tributaries. You could walk safely along either road's shoulder in broad daylight, assuming the drivers who came along were sober. That's what Charlotte said, anyway. The gas station was about a quarter mile from her grandmother's house and maybe a bit farther from Jenny's, and it sold a few things like cigarettes and canned goods. There was also a lunch counter where Ms. Wallis might make you a sandwich on gooey white bread if she was in a good mood. Camille usually arrived first and waved to Jenny when her skinny figure appeared, sometimes alongside her older brother or on the handlebars of her sister's bike. That day, Camille sat waiting on the curb outside the station for over an hour, the jump rope clutched in her fists.

After a while, Ms. Wallis came out. She was a fat woman, barely taller than Camille, with big pink cheeks. She was almost always smiling, but she looked serious now. Before she had a chance to speak, Charlotte's red LeBaron came tearing down the road.

"Oh, Charlotte, I was just gettin' ready to send her home. It's just awful, ain't it?" Ms. Wallis said when Charlotte leaped out of the car, still wearing her kimono and house shoes.

"Oh, baby," Charlotte squatted down in front of Camille, who hadn't moved, hadn't loosened her grip on the jump rope, hopeful that she and Jenny might still play. "What did you hear?"

"What do you mean, Mama?"

Charlotte sighed. "I don't know how to tell you this, baby, but I got real bad news."

Camille looked at her grandmother, who seemed thin and old in her floral house dress, more like a grandmother than Camille had ever seen her look.

"What happened?"

Jenny Rhodes and her entire family were dead, Charlotte said. Camille didn't know what to say next, so she said nothing at all, only stared at her bare thighs once she climbed into the car. *Dead?* How could Jenny be dead? She was only seven and a half. Had she been sick? That didn't explain why the entire *family* was dead. Had they been in a car accident, maybe?

"Granmama?" she asked as they pulled into the driveway. "How'd they die? Were they sick?"

Charlotte put the car into park. She opened her mouth, closed it, opened it, closed it again. Finally, she said, "Her daddy killed them."

Camille felt dizzy. "Killed them?"

"Yes."

"That means they're in heaven?"

Her grandmother did not seem to know what to say.

"Isaac says don't everybody go to heaven when they die," Camille added.

"Well, I don't know," Charlotte said.

Camille waited for her to say more, but she didn't, so she started to cry. Charlotte reached over to touch her hand. "I wish I could have protected you from this."

At the house, Camille crawled into her grandfather's lap; she knew she was getting too big to do it, and he was fragile, but she did it anyway. She wrapped her arms around his neck and sobbed. David said nothing, only rubbed her back until she fell asleep. She woke up several hours later on the couch, wrapped tightly in an itchy blanket. Her mouth felt hot and painfully dry. She could hear her grandparents and mother talking in low, aggressive voices in the kitchen.

"She'll be fine. It's no different than if she moved away or something," she heard her mother say.

"She's little, not dumb, Corinna," Grandaddy said.

"I agree. No point in lying to her," Charlotte said. "It's too late anyway. I already told her the daddy did it."

Camille heard her mother inhale sharply. "You *what*?!"

"She asked me! What was I supposed to do? Lie to her?"

"Yes! She's seven years old, for the love of fucking God, Mama! You told her her friend was *murdered*. By. Her. *Father!*" This was followed by yelling. A lot of yelling. Camille was not surprised when she heard glass shatter and the front door slam. That was how most conversations ended between her mother and grandmother. She didn't know how there was any glass left in the house.

When Charlotte came to take her to bed, Camille pretended to be asleep so that her grandmother would carry her into the second bedroom. Once there, she lay awake all night.

FALL 2000

When Camille was forced to ride the bus, which wasn't often, the route took them right by Jenny's house. It was an unusually nice new home for the area, set back at least a hundred yards from the road, and built out of brick, also a rarity. Jenny's parents' cars were still parked out front in the long, paved driveway, the only paved driveway Camille had seen. Camille had always assumed life had to be real good in a house like that. Jenny was always happy. She always smiled in spite of her big ole buck teeth. Jenny's mother, who looked like an older, more haggard version of her daughter, was always kind. Camille tried to remember Jenny's father, but all she could pull up was the outline of a man leaving a room or driving away. Camille had envied Jenny with her two parents, two siblings, and a house with enough space for everyone. They even had pets: two cats and a dog. She hoped Jenny's dad hadn't killed them, too.

Jenny's father had smothered his wife with his bare hands. He'd shot Jenny and her two older siblings in their beds as they slept. He'd moved all the bodies into the master bedroom and tucked them into the California King. Then he took a handful of Percocet, washed it down with an entire bottle of Smirnoff, got in bed with his family, and died. At least, that's what Camille patched together from eavesdropping on grown folks' conversations.

On TV, when someone died, moms or dads went to their kid's room and sat on the bed to explain that so-and-so was in a better place. That didn't happen for Camille. Once when she asked her mother if Jenny was in a "better place," Corinna replied, "That's too much for a girl your age to be thinking about" and left it at that. And Charlotte, never short on words, could not seem to carry the conversation beyond "I don't know."

Camille's grandfather, though, explained to her that sometimes men are weak and take it out on their families.

"But why, Grandaddy?" she asked.

"Now, *that* I do not know."

I don't know. I don't know. She heard it over and over. These were adults. Adults were supposed to know things! More than that, these were *her* adults. How could they not know the answers to her most pressing questions?

Ultimately, she was at the mercy of her imagination about Jenny's death. And her imagination took her to many dark places. Had Jenny known she was going to die? Had she been scared? Every time she closed her eyes, she saw her friend's frightened face in the backs of her eyelids.

*   *   *

Camille got in trouble a lot that year, primarily for terrorizing her classmates. Samantha Miller, the redheaded new girl, got the worst of it. She wasn't much different from anyone else. Her clothes were from Walmart like everyone else's; her single mother was working class and undereducated, just like everyone else's. She was unremarkable in appearance; her hair was unkempt, and she smelled like cat urine or tobacco smoke. The same could be said about many of Camille's classmates.

Camille also managed to pull her classmates into the "harassment campaign," as the teachers would eventually refer to it. If Samantha scratched her nose, she was accused of picking her nose. If she moved to scratch her head, the kids said she had lice. When she wore the same shell-toe Adidas with glittery pink stripes that Camille had, she was called a copycat wannabe. When she traded the Adidas for her old canvas Keds, it was because she was poor. When Samantha attempted to retaliate, Camille only had to wield what had come to be known as the "Mrs. Urkel," an increasingly exaggerated and manic rendition of Samantha's laugh, though Samantha hadn't laughed in weeks. When Samantha started missing school, Camille was reprimanded and made to apologize.

Though Samantha was nothing but kind to Camille, Camille continued to tease her. She was less frequent in her ridicule, but she still made fun of Samantha's glittery leggings and her gap teeth. She tried to stop, but she found herself constantly saying mean things. Sometimes, she got mad and did not know why.

Though she was hard on other kids, Camille wanted friends. She *needed* friends, actually. She was tolerated by most of the class, but she knew it was more out of fear than anything else. Now that

Jenny was gone, she had no friends. She decided the easiest thing would be to befriend the least-liked person in the third grade: Samantha Miller. When Camille approached Samantha with an invitation to play with her at recess, Samantha's eyes lit up.

"Really? Me?"

Camille's first instinct was to mimic Samantha, but instead, she smiled. "Yes," she said. "You."

Camille didn't like that she asked a lot of questions, something Jenny had never done.

"Where's your daddy?" Samantha asked once while they sat on the swings, not swinging but twisting the chains together so that they would be spun in circles when they released the tension. "Mine's in the pententerry."

"The what?"

"The pennytentcherry."

"Huh?"

"He went away for being bad."

"Oh, he's in jail."

"Yeah. Where's yours?"

Camille released the tension in her swing and started spinning. She closed her eyes to focus on the whirling sensation, like she was a Sky Dancer toy. When she stopped, Samantha was looking at her.

"I don't know. My mama said he moved away."

"You don't ever see him?"

"No. I don't care, though," Camille answered honestly. There was no man-shaped void in her life, especially after learning what Jenny's dad did to her.

When Samantha came over to play for the first time, she asked Camille why her grandparents were white. "Is your mom adopted?"

"They're not white. My mama's not adopted."

"Are you sure?"

Camille was positive, because she heard her grandmother yell: "I labored for sixteen hours to give birth to you, and this is how you repay me?!" And she was pretty sure her grandmother was not white because she often said things like, "White folks are some of the shittiest drivers." She was not, however, sure whether her grandaddy was white. She'd never really thought about it. Her grandaddy was her grandaddy. But Samantha got her thinking, and so she asked him later that same night.

"Grandaddy?" she asked as she crawled into his lap for their nightly bedtime reading.

"Yes, baby?"

"Are you white?"

"White?"

"Yeah."

"Well, *yes*. I guess we never told you, but," he said, and nuzzled her cheek. "You and me ain't blood-related. We got something better than that."

"Whatchu mean, Grandaddy?"

"Well, I *chose* to be your grandaddy."

"And Mama's daddy?"

"That's right."

"Why you choose us then?"

"Because I love your granmama."

"Oh," she said, leaning against his chest, and opened up *Matilda* to where they left off the night before.

*   *   *

One day during recess, she and Samantha tied jump ropes to the only tree in the playground, which stood alone by the basketball court. Samantha was turning, and Camille was jumping, but the rope kept getting caught in her shoes, sometimes wrapped around her ankles. Camille was out of practice; she hadn't jumped double Dutch since the summer. When it happened for the third time, she felt a pain in her throat and tears welling in her eyes. She touched her "Friends" necklace for comfort but found very little.

"You all right?" Samantha asked and stepped toward Camille, who shoved her in return. The girl tripped and fell backward onto the blacktop. "What'd you do that for?!"

Camille immediately regretted it and was going to apologize, but Mrs. Greenwich saw the whole thing from yards away, and started to lumber across the schoolyard in her clunky white orthopedics.

Shit, Camille thought to herself as Mrs. Greenwich took her by the upper arm, her long, acrylic nails painted in the French style that Charlotte said was tacky. Tacky or not, they pinched.

"*Camille*," Mrs. Greenwich said as she dragged Camille into the school building. "What has gotten into you?"

Camille just sighed.

"Huh? What do you have to say for yourself?"

She didn't have much of anything to say for herself. "I don't know why I done it," she replied, and Mrs. Greenwich's grip got tighter.

"She's mature for her age," Mrs. Greenwich once explained to her mother. "It makes sense why she's so impatient with kids in her class. She's *so* intelligent. But it's just unacceptable behavior, Mrs. Brown."

"Have you ever heard of *positive discipline*?" Camille's dance teacher had asked Corinna on another occasion.

Corinna usually sighed in response to strangers' advice. Camille knew the word for her mother's feelings was *exasperated*. She always looked tired. She was beginning to do the sitting and staring that Camille saw her grandmother do.

Camille wanted to change but didn't know how. She didn't know why she behaved the way she behaved, and she wished someone would explain it to her. But no one did.

One morning, she woke up and found that her "Friends" necklace had broken while she was sleeping. It was nestled between her pillow and the bed. She took it to her mother.

"Mama, it's broken!"

Corinna took the necklace from Camille and tossed it in the trash without looking at it. Camille, so shocked that she stopped crying, dug through the trash and took the pendant back to her room. She wiped her tears as she placed the necklace inside a small wooden box Jenny had given her days before she died. She swore to herself that she would never go to her mother for help again.

FALL 2001

Camille was nine years old on September 11, 2001. But for years and years, she swore up and down that she was in the third grade that year and, therefore, eight. The confusion likely originated with the fact that Mrs. Greenwich, her third-grade teacher, who had retired (possibly influenced by Camille's wild behavior) and become a substitute, was filling in for Mrs. Lee, her fourth-grade teacher.

Camille was late for school that day, as her grandmother had taken her to Sonic for breakfast burritos. She walked into her classroom drinking the last of her cherry limeade and found the room empty, besides Mrs. Greenwich, who sat behind the desk looking significantly paler than usual. The TV hanging from the ceiling on a hydraulic arm usually featured *Zaboomafoo* or *Wishbone* in the late afternoon, especially on Fridays. But on this day, there was a skyscraper with the fin of a plane sticking out of it. The image made little sense to Camille. Why would you put a plane into a building like that? Must have been an accident of some kind, she thought, squinting. The intercom clicked, and Camille was called to the office for dismissal.

On her way into the office, Camille heard her grandmother tell the office manager that her favorite disco channel stopped playing Sylvester to announce that a plane had hit the World Trade Center and that it was a suspected terror attack. When Charlotte heard "terror attack," she'd pulled a hard, illegal U-turn in the street to retrieve her granddaughter, whom she'd dropped off only a few minutes earlier. Camille didn't know what that meant, but it made her feel kind of like she did when Jenny died.

Camille found herself seated on her grandmother's couch between her grandparents and mother watching TV, with the volume turned up uncomfortably high. When the South Tower collapsed, Charlotte sent Camille outside to play. She got her bike from behind her grandfather's unused tool shed and rode to the strip of gravel along the main road. It was midmorning, and normally there would have been old people sitting out on their front porches, waving as she rode by. She didn't ride for very long, because the empty porches spooked her. Was this the end of the world Isaac had been talking about? Had it been happening this entire time?

She returned to her grandmother's house and knelt on the porch by the living room window to get a view of the television. Another tower collapsed. Charlotte burst through the front door and screamed Camille's name.

"I'm right here, Mama," she said.

"Come on inside," Charlotte said, grabbing her by the arm.

"Ow, Mama."

Corinna, who Camille hadn't realized was standing in the doorway, snatched her away from Charlotte. She took her by the shoulders and shook her.

"I'm Mama," she said. "Do you hear me? *I'm* Mama."

Camille, unsure what to do, began to cry.

"Tell me that you understand!" Corinna shouted. Charlotte pulled Camille out of her mother's grasp, and they proceeded to yank her back and forth.

"Stop that!" Grandaddy shouted. When he had everyone's attention, he said: "I think emotions are running a little high." He spoke with a clarity that surprised Camille. "Maybe we oughta pray," he said.

"Pray?" Corinna and Charlotte asked in unison.

"Maybe Camille and I ought to go home," Corinna said.

"No, no. That's a good idea, David," Charlotte said. "Let's pray."

"Do you even know how to pray, Daddy?" Corinna asked.

"Shut up, girl. Can't be that hard. Give me your hand." He beckoned for Camille to sit next to him on the couch, took her hand, and extended his other to Corinna. Corinna slowly lowered herself to a kneeling position on the carpet by his legs and took his hand. Charlotte did the same thing on the other side, and they formed a circle. This seemed right, but also very strange, like "seeing an owl in daylight," as her grandfather would say.

"Okay," he said. "Lower y'alls heads."

Camille's mother and grandmother both lowered their heads and closed their eyes, which Camille hadn't seen anyone do since Jenny's funeral. Lots of people she knew prayed over their food, but not their family. *And* Camille's grandmother never did anything anyone told her to do, so Camille figured that something very serious was about to happen, and so she bowed her head, too.

"Dearly Beloved—"

"I don't think that refers to God, Daddy," Corinna said.

"Shut. *Up*," Charlotte hissed.

"God, Jesus, Whoever," David continued. "Keep us safe. I hope them dying people ain't too scared. Welcome them to heaven or wherever the hell people go when they die."

Camille looked up at her Grandaddy. His eyes were closed, but his wrinkled eyelids trembled. She moved to sit closer to him. A replay of the towers falling was playing on mute on the television.

"Amen," Charlotte and Corinna said in unison. Charlotte eased her way to stand with help from Corinna.

"We ought to go see about Isaac," Corinna said.

Camille did not want to go home. Isaac almost never spoke to her these days unless it was about something creepy, but he was often staring at her or, more accurately, staring in her direction. Sometimes, when her mother was working, she had to have dinner alone with him. He'd heat up TV dinners and insist they sit at the table. When she looked up from moving food around in its plastic tray, Isaac would be looking at her, though looking *through* her might be more accurate. There was an emptiness there, in his eyes. It reminded her of Tequila Cooper, a narcoleptic girl in her class who slept with her eyes open. You could only tell she was asleep because her head drifted toward her desk and her eyes lost their light. Camille hadn't noticed that people had light in their eyes until she met Tequila.

Mrs. Lee kept a pillow underneath Tequila's chair. If you saw her nodding off, you were supposed to place it on the desk before her head hit the table. If you were able to do it in time, you got to choose a piece of candy out of Mrs. Lee's top drawer.

But Isaac wasn't asleep.

"What?" he would say, as if she were the one staring at him.

Camille didn't think she would slip a pillow under Isaac's head, even for a giant Tootsie Roll.

The thought of Isaac, on a day like this, was especially unappealing. "Can I stay here, Mama?"

"Why do you always want to stay here?"

"Corinna, don't go getting all worked up. We just had a lovely moment. Let her stay. You ought to stay, too," David offered gingerly.

"Don't tell me not to get worked up!" Corinna started gathering her things. "Y'all always telling me what to do. I have to go home to my husband."

"Husband?!" Charlotte gasped.

"Yes, my husband."

"You *married* that crazy nigger?!"

"Charlotte! The baby don't need to be hearing all that," said Grandaddy, clasping his hands over Camille's ears.

"You told me to, Mama! She needs a father!" She heard through her grandfather's hands. "She needs *two* responsible parents, better than what I had!"

Charlotte had an expression Camille had never seen on her, like she'd been slapped. Camille was so surprised that she didn't protest when her mother took her by the arm and pulled her out of the house.

*   *   *

The day the towers fell, Camille and Corinna drove to the home they shared with Isaac, who was waiting for them on the front steps of the small, gray house. His hair had grown out into an unkempt Afro. It was flat in the back, and his orange hairline was receding so that he looked like a menacing clown, especially when he displayed his graying, gap-toothed smile. He crouched down and opened his arms for Camille, clearly expecting her to be relieved to see him. But she took a step back, and then her mother grabbed her by the arm and pulled her into the house. Camille was getting really tired of being pulled around, but she didn't dare say anything.

"Do you have homework?"

"No. We ain't have school today."

"Well, write an essay or something," Corinna said, then dragged Camille into the kitchen and shoved her roughly into a chair. "I'll get you some paper."

Corinna dropped an entire package of unopened wide-ruled paper and a couple of unsharpened pencils in front of her. Camille knew her mother was angry with her, but she wasn't sure why. She opened the package, took out a few sheets, and positioned them neatly in front of her. She picked up a pencil and stood to find a pencil sharpener. Corinna was now sitting at the other end of the table, watching Camille carefully, a glass of something brown and smelly in front of her.

"Where are you going?"

"To sharpen my pencil."

"Give it here. Sit back down."

Camille tried to think about what to write. Maybe she would write something nice about her mother so that she would stop being so mad. Her mother returned with the pencil and a sharpener.

"Sharpen it," she said.

Camille stuck the pencil into the sharpener and turned.

"Use paper to catch the shavings, Camille."

Camille knew she was on thin ice when her mother punctuated a sentence with her name like that, but usually she knew why. Today, she did not know what she had done, and this scared her very much. Was it because she called Granmama "Mama" again? That couldn't be it. Was it because she hadn't hugged Isaac? That couldn't be it, could it?

Camille took the top sheet of paper from her pile and put the one curly shaving on it. She continued to sharpen the pencil and listened to her mother pour herself another glass. Camille got ready to write. She hoped she might make her mother laugh by gripping the pencil in her fist.

"Like this, Mama? Like a monkey would?"

Her mother had laughed just two days earlier at the same silly joke. Now, she was stone-faced.

"Act like you got some sense, Camille," Corinna snarled, and Camille sat up straight.

Camille held the pencil correctly and began to print because she wasn't so good at cursive.

My Mama is a very good mama. She makes sure I have food to eat and that I am always where I am supposed to be. She lets me take ballet classes and says I am very talented, even though I am not as good as Jennifer Evans. She is very beautiful. And I love her very much, even though she—

Camille turned the pencil around and started to erase her last three words, but Corinna, who had been watching more closely than she realized, snatched the paper from the table.

"Even though what, Camille?"

Camille's mind went blank; she could barely remember what she planned to write. It might have been about how her mother came home every night at three a.m. smelling like a tub of liquor. It might have been because her mother married Isaac and Camille wasn't invited to the wedding, and hadn't even known about it until weeks after it happened. Maybe it was something lighter, like the fact that Corinna never let Camille have ice cream for dinner. In school, she was learning about sentence connectors, and "even though" happened to be her favorite because you could say a nice thing followed by a less nice thing, and Ms. Lee said it was good that she was such a "complex thinker."

"Even though what, Camille?!" Her mother repeated, louder this time. "Even though I work my fingers to the bone for you?"

"Mama, I was going to erase it."

"My question is, why would you *think* it to begin with."

"Mama," Camille pleaded. She stood to retrieve the paper from her mother. She extended one hand toward the paper her mother was now holding out of her reach like a schoolyard bully. When she stood on her tiptoes, Corinna slapped Camille so hard that she fell to the linoleum floor. Camille had never been hit in her face before. She had only seen someone get hit in the face on television. She thought it was something adults did to each other, not to children. Adults could hit kids almost anywhere else, including the head (she had been hit countless times with brushes on the back of her head because she wasn't holding her head still when she was getting her hair braided), but not the private parts and *definitely* not the face.

Camille was accustomed to whoopins. She hadn't gotten many in her lifetime, but when she did, it was for things like following a basketball into traffic or throwing a tantrum in the grocery store. Her mother might smack her across the legs or bottom with her hand. But those whoopins weren't painful as much as they were embarrassing. She knew there was a difference between a whoopin and getting beat like some of the kids who came to school with black eyes or bruises. But recently, her mother had started making her lay across the bed to be struck with one of Isaac's big thick leather belts.

Her skin stung, and her ears rang. Tears streamed down her face, but she was not yet crying. She looked up at her mother, who looked as surprised as Camille felt. Now, Camille began to cry in earnest.

"Baby, I'm sorry," she said, trying to hold Camille, but Camille wiggled away and fled to her bedroom.

Camille went to bed thinking she would wake up the next morning and her mother would be so sorry that she would take her out for a breakfast burrito. But through the thin walls, she could hear Isaac telling her mother once again, "The Bible says, 'spare the rod, spoil the child.' And that girl is spoiled."

Corinna must have really taken that to heart, because Camille wasn't allowed to do much of anything anymore. All of a sudden, she was only allowed to watch TV for one hour a day, and none of the exciting channels like MTV or BET, and even some cartoons were prohibited. She had to bring her books to her mother for approval. She watched Isaac watch her mother go through her closet and put everything that was too "grown" into a big, black trash bag. When her mother was done, all that was left were a couple of dresses usually reserved for picture day, two pairs of patent leather shoes (both too small), a few T-shirts, and a pair of jeans that rose almost all the way up to her belly button. Her mother even took the purple converse sneakers right off her feet and left her with a pair of white Keds instead.

Her mother was still her mother. But she wasn't her Blue Magic Woman anymore.

*   *   *

When Camille got into trouble again for bullying another new kid, Principal Keys asked her why she did it, leaning forward with a sad look in her eyes. She looked tired, like Camille's mother often looked tired. Ms. Keys was a tall, brown-skinned woman with milky-chocolate eyes. She wore her short hair roller-set close to the scalp, like all the Black women Camille knew with jobs outside the house.

"Is everything okay at home?" asked Ms. Keys.

Camille could not count how many times she had been asked this same dumb question in the past few months. What was she supposed to say? No? Was she supposed to say: "My stepfather is crazy. And he's getting crazier all the time. Was she supposed to tell the truth? "My stepfather tells my mother to beat me. And he stands over her while she does it." Is that what this woman wanted to hear?

"Yeah," Camille said, holding Ms. Keys's gaze.

"What are we going to do about you?"

Camille shrugged.

"Well, you need to apologize to Randy Lynn. And you need to leave her alone. Otherwise, I'll have to suspend you next time."

"Yes, ma'am." Camille definitely did *not* want to get suspended. That would likely mean more time with her mother and Isaac, who were almost always home during the day.

"But I do need to call someone at home, okay? Is someone there?"

"No," Camille lied.

"I'll leave a message then."

Camille gripped the seat of the chair as the woman dialed her home phone number. She could tell Isaac answered the phone because Ms. Keys seemed uncomfortable.

For the rest of the day, Camille thought about nothing but the ass-whooping she was going to get. Her friends sometimes talked about their parents' manner of corporal punishment like it was a joke or something. But Camille knew there was something different about the way she was getting whooped lately.

That night, when she was told to lie across the bed, she refused. She crossed her arms over her bony chest and said: "Call my granmama and tell her to come get me."

Isaac lashed her hard across the backs of her legs, but Corinna stopped him before he could do it again. It hurt, but Camille did her best not to show it.

"I'll take her," she said. "I'll take her."

"If you take her over there, she'll never know discipline. 'A rod and a reprimand impart wisdom, but a child left undisciplined disgraces its mother.'"

Corinna grabbed Camille's arm, hard, shoved a few things in a bag, and drove her over to Charlotte's. Camille ran up the porch stairs into her grandmother's arms while her mother stood at the bottom. She looked down at her crying mother and felt a strong desire to get away from her. But she also felt responsible for what had happened. She'd *made* her mother beat her; she wouldn't have done it if it weren't for her own good. "Everything I do, I do for you." That's what Corinna said all the time, and Camille had always believed her.

"I don't know what to do, Mama," Corinna said through loud, mournful tears. "I'm tryin' and tryin', and I just don't know what to do."

PART III

"Whole Baby, Whole Invalid"

Corinna

1984–1992

CORINNA WAS NINE years old the first time she saw her stepfather hit her mother. He hit her so hard that her front teeth tore through her bottom lip, and three of her ribs cracked when she hit the kitchen counter and then the floor.

This wasn't the first time David had hit Charlotte, but Corinna had never seen it with her own eyes. Still, she knew her parents' relationship was tempestuous; she could hear the arguments through the thin walls, and they were both often bruised or cut up. Charlotte got her own licks in, but she was a small woman, five feet, six inches and 120 pounds soaking wet, up against a broad-shouldered man over six feet tall, 200 pounds at his thinnest and healthiest.

If Corinna asked her mother about the bruises, Charlotte might say "Oh, you know. I can be real clumsy sometimes." But this was untrue. Charlotte was the most graceful woman Chilly Springs had ever seen. Once, on a rare trip to Sears, Charlotte plopped down at a baby grand piano and began to play. An elderly white woman stopped in her tracks and literally clutched her pearls with astonishment.

"My God," the woman said. "I have never heard anyone play 'Für Elise' so beautifully. Where did you study?"

Charlotte responded by standing up from the bench and gripping Corinna's wrist to pull her away without a word.

Most children believe their mothers are beautiful. But Corinna knew that her mother actually was very, very beautiful, objectively speaking. Charlotte's face was symmetrical, her eyes were big, her eyelashes were long and lush, her lips were full and pouty, her nose gently sloped upward. Her fair skin and golden eyes glowed despite her hard living. Though she always wore her thick, dark hair in a ponytail, it was impossible not to notice its volume and glossiness. Corinna liked to run her fingers through it when Charlotte was passed out on the couch. Her mother was loveliest when she was sleeping, her expression neutral rather than aggrieved. Sometimes, she almost looked content. Charlotte saved her pleasant looks for the clerk at the liquor store, who sometimes threw in a little something extra, and smiled only for David. It was a real treat when she smiled. Her eyes brightened; her dimples revealed themselves. Her teeth were so well shaped that they looked like the windup chattering teeth Corinna could buy at the school's "merit store," where the currency was little plastic tokens awarded for good behavior.

Charlotte also had a certain presence about her. She walked like she'd been taught to walk by the preeminent, globally recognized expert. Corinna never tried to emulate her mother's graceful strut. She knew her mother's walk had no place in their sleepy little town. And Corinna wanted to fit in.

Corinna felt so different from her mother. So much about her mother was alien to her. She wondered if her mother might have loved her more if they looked alike, if they had more in common.

One thing she understood was her mother's choice to love David. Some people might not have understood what a woman of Charlotte's charms and beauty saw in a man like David, who was bow-legged and belched in public, but Corinna understood. As violent as he could be, he could also be incredibly kind to her mother. As many times as Corinna heard or saw her parents screaming at each other, she had also seen them sitting on the front porch laughing or dancing in the living room. But things could get real bad, real quick.

On the morning in question, in the time it took to toast a Pop-Tart, Charlotte and David went from laughing over spiked coffee to arguing about who would drive Corinna to school for her first day of fourth grade, as the school bus wasn't running that week for some reason or another. Charlotte insisted that David drive her. David said he needed to get to work. When they got to be toe-to-toe, Corinna should have known it would be bad. Still, she screamed when David hit her mother with a deft left hook. David pushed past Corinna on his way out, shaking the hand he'd hit Charlotte with. Charlotte yelped but quickly quieted. She appeared dazed. Corinna noticed something wasn't quite right with her eyes. It scared her. It reminded her of the girl who'd fallen headfirst off the big slide the year before. That girl had been taken off the playground on a stretcher. She knew her mother needed to go to the hospital now too.

Corinna was wearing brand-new sequin sneakers and marabou hair ties, both of which David had brought home the day before. She wore her hair in two perfect afro-puffs she'd spent forty-five minutes styling. She helped her mother to the car and drove them both, very slowly, to the nearest hospital, a half hour away. Corinna told the nurse that her mother had fallen down the porch steps and that a neighbor had dropped them off. And the nurse held Corinna's gaze for a long moment, as if waiting for her to crack.

"All right, well, good thing you were there to help your mama out. She's lucky to have a daughter like you," said the nurse, who was short, chubby, and dark-skinned like Corinna. The woman held Corinna by the shoulders briefly, and the warmth of the gesture nearly brought her to tears; she couldn't remember ever being touched like that. She turned Corinna around and palmed her a dollar bill. "Now, go get yourself something out of the vending machine while I talk to your mama, ya hear?"

Corinna drove her mother home, tucked her into bed, and kissed her forehead, just like she'd seen on TV. That's how you're supposed to treat someone you love. Perhaps you also hit people you love sometimes? Well, Corinna's mother never hit her and never tucked her in. So, assuming her mother loved her, she wasn't sure how love was supposed to look.

Corinna went to the kitchen and got up on the step stool she used to get a good vantage point over the dishes in the sink. She gave her head a good shake to reroute her train of thought and started thinking about *Family Ties*. She had been trying to figure out if it was okay to be in love with Alex P. Keaton.

Corinna stayed home for three days to take care of her mother and keep watch for David. Though she'd been horrified by what she'd seen, she was also concerned he might never come back. Corinna wasn't sure what frightened her more.

When she finally started school on the fourth day, she didn't wear the marabou hair ties or sequin sneakers, not wanting to attract attention to herself. Her teacher, a heavy white woman with watery gray eyes, pulled her aside to give her one of the free lunch vouchers that had been handed out to half the class on the first day. "I got to report it to the truancy office if you miss ten days, dear," she said. "It won't do any good if your mama's got to take off work to go down to the courthouse. Welfare office might start sniffing around."

Corinna's mama didn't have a job to take off from. She wondered what made this woman assume such a thing. Hardly anybody's mama had a job. There weren't enough jobs to be had. Either way, she knew she didn't want the welfare office involved. If that happened, CPS could get involved. If CPS got involved, she might disappear like Casey Craig, who came to school dirty, until he didn't come to school at all. Nobody knew for sure what happened to him. Maybe he had clean clothes and enough food to eat now. Or maybe he was dirtier and hungrier.

"You never know how that could end up," her teacher said and gently took Corinna by the shoulder, as kindly as the nurse had, and guided her back to her desk.

*   *   *

When she got home that afternoon, David was on the porch reading a newspaper, which struck Corinna as strange because she'd never seen David read anything except the screen during *The Price Is Right*. He dropped it when he saw her coming up the driveway from the bus stop.

"Howdy," he said with a goofy grin as he stood to greet her. He was sweating through his shirt, like always. He was reliable in his own way. The year before, when Corinna had played Frenchy in *Grease*, David arrived an hour and a half early carrying an enormous bouquet of lilies and sat in the very first row in the school auditorium. He had even showered and replaced his old, dirty work boots with newer, slightly cleaner ones; she wasn't sure where he got them from, but he was there. That was the important part.

From the beginning of fourth grade on, Corinna did the best she could with what she had. She quit the drama club and went home as soon as class was over. She rose early in the morning to clean the house and prepare breakfast and was tired by the time she got to school. When her grades dropped, she pretended to be her mother on the phone when teachers called the house and forged her mother's signature. She never asked her parents for anything, but she did steal money out of her mother's purse to buy household essentials, taking her bike up and down the steep Tennessee hills to and from town several times a week to keep the house stocked with frozen meals and cereal. David would come and go, and Charlotte would *always* take him back. And the cycle of fighting and dancing started again.

*   *   *

When Corinna was fifteen, she got her first job at Whiskers, the local catfish restaurant. She was hired to smile at people as they came in and show them to their tables with the appropriate number of menus. She liked that job, finding that people were pretty easy to please and that she was rewarded simply for doing what she was supposed to be doing. The validation could be outright intoxicating. Getting paid was almost like a bonus. She saved half of her money but spent the other half on things for the house. No one ever seemed to notice.

At school, Corinna sometimes ate lunch with Emily Perkins and Glory Rodgers, both of whom wore long denim skirts and did their waist-length hair in strange, intricate updos. They weren't her friends, but they were the only people with nowhere else to sit. Usually, they spoke only to each other in low tones, with their backs hunched toward each other, creating an invisible but impenetrable force field around their whispers. She wanted a friendship like theirs, but she didn't even know where to begin.

She noticed sorts of pairs everywhere she looked. On the bus, she noticed that Diana Davis and Tiffany Dozier always sat next to each other and became irate if anyone tried to disturb this ritual. Sometimes, Corinna saw their heads turned toward each other so close they might have kissed, but then one of the heads would bob rapidly to indicate emphatic listening. Sometimes, they sat in absolute silence, filing their nails or eating sour cream and onion potato chips. Corinna noticed they brought each other small things.

"Here, I brought you a scrunchie like the one you said you wanted."

"They didn't have grape, so I got you cherry."

Corinna found these acts enormously tender. She craved the feeling of knowing someone was thinking about her when she wasn't around, of receiving a gift she hadn't asked for, of being part of a whole.

When Corinna was in the eleventh grade, Charlotte got clean ... or clean*er*, rather. Either way, Charlotte got a job outside the house for the first time in years. Corinna was not sure why. That's when Delia and Johnny Washington entered the picture.

Delia was Charlotte's good friend from work who came over to smoke and drink. Johnny, her son, played football for the local high school. Delia was short and round with a cherubic face, while Johnny was tall and broad-shouldered. They had identical smiles, even if there was nothing to smile about, unlike Corinna and her mother.

Johnny was the most beautiful person she'd ever seen, even from television and the movies, better-looking than Michael Jordan and Sean Connery combined. There was something feminine about his enormous eyes and luxurious eyelashes, but they looked right on his rectangular face. And when he talked, people listened. When he walked, people followed. Corinna had even seen her own mother lean in to listen to him talk.

When Johnny approached Corinna at her locker, she fumbled her books but didn't drop them.

"Hey," he said, and Corinna looked over her shoulder to be sure he was speaking to her. Johnny was digging around in his bookbag for something, produced a Ziploc bag half filled with coupons, and handed it to her with a smile. His teeth were big and white and straight. "My mom said to give this to you."

Corinna hesitated.

"You know. To give to your mom."

"Oh," Corinna croaked. "Thanks."

"Yeah," he said and zipped his bag. "Hey! Jason, wait up," he called.

This started to happen every few days. Sometimes, Corinna had something to give to Johnny, but she never approached him, because he was usually surrounded by a small entourage. The items varied greatly. Once, it was a pair of seemingly unworn pale beige kitten heels. Another time, it was a single sewing needle. Corinna did not know why their mothers couldn't just exchange these things at work, but she never questioned it, because each time she and Johnny swapped items, he lingered a little bit longer.

Most Saturdays, Corinna came home from work in the late afternoon to find her mother and Delia cackling either on the front porch or in the kitchen. Delia often took Corinna's hand and thanked her for passing along whatever she'd given Johnny. Delia was almost always midlaugh when she did this, sometimes tears of laughter still streaming down her round cheeks.

"Thank ya, baby," she'd say. "For giving that little bottle of perfume to your mama." The plastic perfume bottle had been half empty and tied up in a plastic shopping bag. When Charlotte opened the bag, she took a sniff from the spritzer and said to no one: "She's right about that one."

Delia and Charlotte were like Glory and Emily, Diana and Tiffany, Cagney and Lacey, Kate and Allie. Corinna wasn't exactly jealous of her mother's relationship with Delia, but she did wonder what they talked about. More specifically, she wondered what kinds of things Charlotte told Delia. Did Charlotte talk about her life? Her life before Corinna was born?

One Saturday, she came home and found Delia, her mother, and Johnny in the living room, Delia and Charlotte cackling as usual. But Johnny was propped up in the ratty easy chair with his eyes closed, his mouth open enough that Corinna could see that it was packed with gauze.

She must have been staring.

"Oh, don't worry about him, honey," Delia swatted at the air with a laugh. "He just got his wisdom teeth out. Can't leave him home alone, so he don't choke on his own blood or whatever."

Corinna wondered why they both hadn't just stayed home, or why Charlotte hadn't gone to their house. Instead of asking, she took a shower. When she left the bathroom, Johnny was awake. He looked over his shoulder at Corinna, who wore a crusty old shower cap and a threadbare towel that barely covered her butt cheeks. Johnny was obviously not in his right mind because he wiggled his eyebrows and winked, which caused Corinna to briefly forget what she was doing. When she remembered, she was flustered and forgot that in order to open her bedroom door successfully, she needed to push and pull at the same time. She fumbled with the door with a hot neck for what felt like ages. When she finally got it open, she was too embarrassed to show her face for the rest of the night.

She could not escape Johnny after that. He started appearing at the house more often, supposedly because his mother was shuttling him around town because his truck died. Sometimes, they watched TV together while their mothers and David played cards and drank whiskey in the kitchen. But sometimes the noise from the kitchen was so loud they couldn't hear the television, so they sat on the porch and talked.

When Johnny talked and Corinna leaned in to listen, he leaned in even closer. It was an incredible feeling; it made her feel warm and liquid, like her joints were loose and she might slide right off her seat. She didn't even notice that he never asked her about herself.

He told her about his girlfriend, whom Corinna knew existed but had never laid eyes on. Her name was Georgia, and she was white. Her parents weren't thrilled that she was dating a Black boy, but it sounded like they tolerated him because he played football "like nobody's business." They thought he would be famous one day.

"Everyone thinks I'm going to get drafted."

"Like, into the military?"

"No," he laughed. "Into the NFL. The National Football League. Heard of it?"

"Oh. Yeah."

After some time, they started driving around in Delia's green Cadillac, the color of baby shit. They often drove all the way to Nashville, more than fifty miles north.

It didn't take long for Corinna to understand that he didn't want to be seen with her, but she didn't mind; at least, Johnny wanted to be with her at all. And she enjoyed the drive. Depending on the time of day, they would watch the sunset over the maple trees or drive in near absolute darkness as there wasn't much between Chilly Springs and Nashville to illuminate the highway.

Sometimes, she fantasized about what it might be like to really leave Chilly Springs, though she had no actual plans. She figured she would do what everyone else did: graduate from high school and get a job at the car plant. Maybe she could even get a permanent office job like her mother had before her record caught up with her.

Corinna knew Johnny didn't come over entirely of his own volition: Delia often left Charlotte and David's company pissy, maybe even blackout, drunk and needed someone to drive her home. But Johnny could also have just dropped his mother off and come back to get her later. He didn't have to stay. He didn't have to drive around with Corinna. He did not have to tell her that he didn't love Georgia or that he didn't love football like he did when he was a kid or that he actually thought he'd be a good doctor or something.

Corinna felt the most chosen she'd ever felt when he leaned over and kissed her one night as they sat on the hood of the Cadillac parked in Centennial Park by the duck pond. But then he backed away from Corinna, until his back was almost turned to her.

"I shouldn't have done that," he said. "I'm sorry."

Corinna almost felt hurt, but not quite. Instead, she almost pitied him, recognizing something familiar in him: shame. Corinna knew it could be painful, crippling even. So she reached out to comfort him.

"Don't feel bad," she said, touching his back for a moment. When he ever-so-slightly turned toward her again, she rubbed his back, which was muscular in places she had never considered a person might have muscles. He was like a child, how easy it was to comfort him. He pulled his shoulders back and straightened up.

He cleared his throat. "I'm sorry," he said again, his back still mostly turned. "I hope this doesn't change anything. I don't want to lose you as a friend."

"Of course not," she said. Of course, she would do nothing to jeopardize this opportunity to feel wanted, to feel part of something. Even if no one knew about it, she was finally part of a pair.

Finally, he turned toward her, and she wrapped her arm around his waist. Almost begrudgingly, he wrapped an arm around her shoulders and squeezed gently. He released a long sigh, and she looked up at him and saw that a single tear was falling from his left eye. She kissed his cheek. She had never kissed anyone's cheek other than her sleeping parents'. Johnny very slowly turned his head so that their lips touched again. The moment lingered until Corinna halted the kiss.

They drove back to Chilly Springs in silence. For several days, Corinna did not hear from Johnny. He did not come by her locker, and Delia did not come by the house, which wasn't necessarily a bad sign as Charlotte sometimes drank at Delia's. Still, Corinna wondered if she'd done something wrong.

The following Friday, Corinna came home from work around nine to find Delia's Cadillac parked on their gravel driveway. Inside, Charlotte, David, and Delia were playing cards at the kitchen table while Johnny sat nearby drinking lemonade. Two very separate conversations were going on. Delia was recounting the Mr. Softee bit from Eddie Murphy's *Delirious* for the umpteenth time while David and Johnny talked football. David was impressed that Johnny was being scouted by Vanderbilt, his first choice. When Corinna stood in the doorway, Johnny turned to look at her. She was sweaty, tired, and her feet hurt, but she smiled, genuinely happy to see Johnny. She dropped a plastic bag with styrofoam containers full of leftovers from the restaurant on the table. After showering and changing into her fleecy Tweety Bird pajamas, she found Johnny in the living room watching TV. He stood up as soon as he saw her, and walked out the door to his Cadillac. She knew she was meant to follow him.

"It's late," she said, stopping short of getting into the car. She crossed her arms over her chest. "I have to work in the morning."

Johnny, already halfway into the car, sighed.

She wished she could take it back. "W-Why don't we stay here? Sit on the porch?" she said.

"I got something to tell you," he whispered.

Corinna's heart leaped into her throat at the suggestion of secrecy. She was in the car before she knew it. This may have been the moment she had been desperately waiting for. He was going to confess his feelings for her. She was buoyant as they pulled out of the driveway in silence, but it started to dawn on her that if he had anything good to tell her, he would have said it already.

Fifteen minutes passed before she could untie her tongue enough to ask: "Well?"

"Well," he said, not taking his eyes off the road.

Corinna made a fist, digging her thumbnail into the side of her index finger. Fantasies of them as a couple assembled in her mind: holding hands in the hallway, coordinating formalwear for prom, going on double dates to the bowling alley, her wearing a T-shirt with his football number painted on it with a glitter paint pen. As promptly as the images came to her, they blurred and dissipated. Though she knew he couldn't know what she'd been thinking, she was hot with embarrassment. What place could she possibly have in his life?

Johnny sighed noisily as he put the car into park by the duck pond at Centennial Park, then turned in his seat to look at her.

"I like you, you know that?"

Corinna was still hopeful, though she knew a "but" was coming. "I understand," she said. "Your girlfriend . . ."

"Right, well. We can still hang out."

Corinna had watched enough television to know what he was suggesting. But it was better to have some small piece of Johnny than nothing at all.

They sat by the duck pond that night, and from then on, they returned every night they could. As always, Johnny did most of the talking. But when Corinna spoke, it felt like Johnny was listening, an unfamiliar feeling. She told him everything—about her parents, her job, and her difficulty imagining the future. And he always asked the right questions, nodded or shook his head at the right time, followed up on things she'd told him weeks earlier.

It was the most heard she'd ever felt in her chaotic life, and things escalated quickly. Within weeks of their first visit to Centennial Park, they were regularly having sex in the grass by the Parthenon.

One night, Johnny rolled over so that he was lying on his stomach, head propped up on his elbows like Corinna thought she would pose for her senior portrait later that summer. He raised an arm to point at the building, which was bathed in light from the ground. "You know it's a reproduction? Not the real thing." Corinna had never thought about it. She'd gone inside once on a second-grade field trip and had been too horrified by the statues, all of which seemed to be looking right at her, to pay much attention to the tour guide. "Why bother, you know?"

"Lots of people will never be able to see the real thing. I think a reproduction is better than nothing at all."

"Even if it's something as dumb as this?"

"It's not dumb to everyone. Some people might think it's—"

"Like who?" Johnny laughed and started talking about Vanderbilt again. He'd committed by then. They gave him a bunch of gear, he said. She could have a T-shirt if she wanted. She wanted it because it had belonged to him.

*   *   *

While Corinna felt the relationship intensifying with the introduction of sex, little changed about how they interacted when other people were around. They still exchanged their mothers' items at Corinna's locker and chatted about inane things. Otherwise, Johnny never so much as smiled at Corinna in passing. It didn't bother her, though. She'd never entertained any delusions about his loving her. She wasn't deserving of love. If she was, someone would have loved her by now.

Corinna realized she was pregnant around Valentine's Day. She took the test in the single-stall bathroom at Whiskers on her lunch break. She was not surprised. She was not scared. She felt very little at first. But as she stood by the door for the second half of her shift, Corinna started to feel something she wasn't familiar with, like warmth was rising in her chest to her cheeks. It turned out to be a mixture of heartburn and, possibly, happiness.

She kept the news to herself for a few days. When she told her mother, Charlotte immediately tried to give her money for an abortion. Corinna hadn't considered not having this baby. Of *course* she was going to have this baby. She would care for the baby and the baby would give her something back: love.

The same night, she met Johnny in the Food Lion parking lot, where he hoisted his big, solid body out of his mother's Cadillac, looking like something out of a perfume commercial. He'd been out to dinner with his girlfriend's family, so he'd shaved and gotten a haircut, and was wearing clothes she'd never seen before. He looked very handsome, like someone who would want nothing to do with her and her bastard baby. She'd run through the various ways this conversation could go, and debated not even telling him, but she figured he deserved to know.

He got into Corinna's Honda, looking far too big to be in a car so small. "I think I know what this is about," he said.

She stared at him, feeling flustered. "What?"

"You're pregnant, ain't you?" Johnny did not often speak colloquially. He told her he made an effort not to sound "backwoods." But he slipped up in private. When he spoke to his mother, he talked just like her, leaning on his vowels and throwing *r*s where there weren't any. The accent also slipped in when he got worked up over something, like when he complained that his coach called him a "slap-dick punk-bitch baby" for fumbling the ball.

She dropped her gaze to her hands. She figured that shame might come later, when her belly was big, and wasn't sure why she was feeling it now, especially considering that Johnny was just as responsible. She badly wanted out of the conversation, the car, and her body if possible.

"You don't have to do anything," she said after a long silence.

"Well, I'll pay for the uh—" he whispered, "procedure. But I— I—uh—"

"I'm keeping it."

Johnny craned his neck to catch Corinna's gaze. "'Scuse me?"

"I'm keeping it," she said again, more loudly. "And raising it."

"But *why*?" He looked genuinely confused. "Why would you do that? We're seventeen. We've got our whole lives ahead of us."

"No, you have your whole life ahead of *you*."

"What's that s'posed to mean?"

Corinna wished she hadn't told him, wished she could have anticipated how embarrassed she would feel. She shrugged.

"I told you you don't have to do anything. I'll do it on my own."

"Then why did you tell me?"

"You wouldn't want to know?"

"Well," he said, looking at his hands. "Don't tell anyone."

She nodded. She wouldn't do anything to hurt him. This wasn't about him anyway. This was about *her* baby. Her baby. She liked the way it sounded.

"My mama's gonna have a conniption," he said with a sigh.

"You're going to tell her?"

"I tell my mama everything."

"Everything?"

"Just about. Don't you?"

She shook her head.

"Well," he said. "Good luck telling her 'bout this. Just leave my name out of it, will you?"

She nodded. He exited the vehicle with a loud sigh and uncharacteristic, "*Fuck!*"

When Johnny and the Cadillac were gone, Corinna pressed the heels of her hands against her eyes in a futile attempt to keep the tears from coming. In a different universe, maybe she and Johnny might have been something vaguely resembling a family. Johnny's rejection felt like a loss, but only because she allowed herself to believe they'd had anything at all. But now she did have something; she had a baby, her very *own* baby, to grow and love. In light of this revelation, Corinna decided that she would only cry this one time over Johnny. Then she would let it go. Move on. Get over it.

*   *   *

Pregnancy was worse than she thought it would be. On TV, pregnant women were worshipped by their dopey husbands, ate strange food combinations, and collapsed comically into sofas. This wasn't that. Though her condition wasn't completely uncommon or looked down upon, it wasn't exactly celebrated either. Two years earlier, Susie Clemmons left school and married the father of her two children. People said Jessamine Bush planned her pregnancy so that she could give birth over the summer. Both girls had been subjected to unkind gossip, but also had the privilege of wedlock or something adjacent.

As soon as she started showing, Glory and Emily stopped sitting with her at lunch. Johnny stopped coming to her locker. She heard the whispers. She was sick all the time, the headaches were constant, she could barely eat, though the lunch ladies kindly gave her generous portions. Patches of her hair fell out, and the skin above her lip darkened and resembled a mustache. But her mother was kind to her for the first time in recent memory. Corinna couldn't exactly say that her mother had ever been cruel or abusive, but she wasn't like the TV moms who prioritized their homes, children, and husbands. Now, Charlotte cooked, cleaned, and often picked up and dropped off Corinna from late shifts at the restaurant. When she saw that Corinna was using rubber bands to make her jeans fit, she bought enough maternity clothes to get through an entire week without doing laundry. Sometimes, Charlotte alluded to the existence of the baby's father but never asked about his identity, for which Corinna was grateful. After all, they had never been the kind of family to ask questions.

Corinna did not attend graduation, because the thought of wearing the hot polyester cap and gown in the hot gymnasium for several hours was far from appealing. She was relieved that she would no longer be the Pregnant Girl. She went about her life, being sick and working at Whiskers. Delia had stopped coming around as much, so Charlotte and Corinna spent more time together. Charlotte taught her how to play spades, which they played at least once a day. Corinna tried her best not to think about Johnny.

When Corinna was about six months along, the Baby Shit Cadillac pulled into the Whiskers parking lot. Corinna assumed it was Delia and Reggie, who both loved hush puppies and catfish fried hard. They drenched their Festive Feast—meant to serve four—in Louisiana Hot Sauce. They often came by when Reggie got off the line at the plant. Delia was always polite when Corinna showed them to their seats, but Corinna knew that Delia's opinion of her had changed. But it was Johnny who emerged from the driver's side tonight. He craned his neck and squinted, obviously trying to see into the restaurant. Corinna lifted a hand without thinking and waved, and he gestured for her to come outside. She shook her head. She couldn't leave the host stand unattended, which he should have known. Apparently annoyed, Johnny lumbered up to the restaurant. He was wearing overalls with one of the straps off, like the Fresh Prince, which was odd. Johnny usually dressed more like Carlton. He stood in the doorway for a moment, saying nothing, just staring at her blankly.

"Yes?"

"Can you talk?"

One of the big brothers who owned Whiskers loudly greeted Johnny and sent Corinna on her break, which felt like the worst thing that could have happened. Several thoughts crossed her mind. Was he here to ask her to get an abortion again? It was too late for that. Was he going to say he'd found a nice family for the baby? She shuddered at the thought.

They walked to the side of the building hidden from the street where workers usually took their smoke breaks. No one was there. Was he bringing her back here to *murder* her? No, that was crazy. Corinna shook her head to redirect her thoughts.

"Why you dressed like that?" she asked, looking at his red Converse sneakers. She felt stupid for asking. She didn't want to wade back into the detritus of the fantasies she'd had about her relationship with Johnny. But here she was, ankle-deep.

"Costume party."

"Okay. Well," Corinna rubbed her stomach, still looking down. Of course he had parties to attend. "What did you want to talk about?"

"Look," he said. "I'm sorry about what I said at the Food Lion."

She shrugged. He'd only said what she already knew. "It's okay," she almost whispered.

"I've been stressed out with everything. I shouldn't have talked to you like that."

Corinna shrugged again.

"Well, I've been thinking, and my mama says I can't have nothing to do with the baby. It would ruin my reputation," he said, rubbing the back of his neck. "But I know I should help out somehow. Maybe one day things will be different, and I can figure out a way to be part of the baby's life."

Corinna frowned. "Part of the baby's life?"

Johnny shifted his weight. "Well, yeah."

"I mean, I'll take your money, but you don't want her . . ."

"Her?"

"I don't know yet. I just have a feeling."

"Well, my mom says I have to pay child support cuz that's the right thing to do."

"But she also said it would ruin your life, right?"

"Well, right *now*, it would."

Corinna stepped away from Johnny and protectively spread her hands on her belly. Slowly, she started to shake her head. "No," she said. "I don't think so."

Johnny sighed. "Well, you don't have to make up your mind now."

They looked at each other.

Johnny finally broke the silence. "Well, I'll tell my mom what you said. She said she'll take care of it."

"Okay."

"Okay. Well." Johnny started toward his car, and Corinna turned to watch him go. Before he got into the Cadillac, he turned toward

Corinna again. "I'm sorry about what I said the other night. You always were a good friend to me."

SUMMER 1992

Camille was born silent. Corinna held her breath until the infant released an inhuman wail. A young nurse took the slippery baby, wrapped her in a pink blanket, and handed her to Corinna. The baby opened her disproportionately large, ink-pool eyes for a moment, and Corinna immediately began to cry. She pulled herself together before Charlotte reappeared at her bedside, smelling of tobacco smoke, peppermint, and dollar-store perfume, and plucked the child away without an inkling of hesitation.

"Oh, my God. Would you look at this sweet thing? She's perfect." Charlotte swayed with the baby in her arms, whispering to her. "And, oh! Would you just look at those big ole eyes!"

The next day, Charlotte pushed Corinna away from the hospital in a wheelchair, humming a gospel song Corinna recognized but could not name. Charlotte, who didn't go to church or believe in God, *loved* gospel music. And it was Sunday in the Bible Belt, so there was nothing but gospel on the radio. To protect her manicure, Charlotte used the second knuckle of her index finger to punch at the radio buttons while Corinna fumbled with the car seat. Finally, she settled on "Amazing Grace."

"Grace would have been a lovely name for her. She kinda looks like a Grace. Where did you even get that name? Camille? Sounds white," Charlotte said for the umpteenth time as she reached for the cigarettes in the cupholder. Corinna noticed for the first time how filthy the cupholder was, crusted with dark, unknown liquids that could have been anything from Coca-Cola to rum. She touched her mother's hand, and Charlotte withdrew.

"I was just going to put 'em away," Charlotte said. She picked up the gold and white box of Virginia Slims—not her usual brand—tossed them into the glove box, and slammed it shut. Then, she snapped her fingers. "This was on the radio when I brought you home from the hospital," she said, pulling out of the parking spot without checking her mirrors. "Did I ever tell you how my water broke . . ."

Corinna stopped listening. Though she had many questions about the past, she had learned to withhold them. Once, when she was very young, she'd asked her mother about her own mother.

"She's dead," Charlotte answered, and took a long swig of something brown. "And when she was alive, she was otherwise occupied."

Corinna raised the question several different ways over the years, and always got the same response: "She's dead." Charlotte never offered any additional detail and became hostile when Corinna pressed for more information. So she'd dropped it.

"Thank you for bringing us home, Mama," Corinna said once she heard a break in the story. Charlotte smiled in return and reached over to squeeze Corinna's knee.

They were silent for the rest of the drive. Corinna watched the baby sleep, glad to have something to look at besides cornfields, wild turkeys, and raggedy-ass houses. Every once in a while, her daughter opened her tiny, gooey mouth wide, as if to suckle. When the car stopped, Corinna crawled into the back seat and watched the baby's closed eyelids until Charlotte knocked on the window.

"It's going to get awful hot in there real soon," Charlotte said as she opened the driver's-side door and slammed the seat forward to gain access to the coupe's back seat. Corinna turned away from her mother as she leaned forward to take the baby.

Charlotte sucked her teeth, trickles of sweat forming on her forehead and upper lip. "Give her here. Let's go inside. I'm going to have a fucking hot flash."

After a short standoff, Corinna handed the baby over, crawled out from the back seat, adjusted her postpartum diaper—careful not to put too much pressure on her stitches—and waddled after her mother into the house.

"You really ought to know that you're supposed to put the car seat facing back," Charlotte shot over her shoulder.

Corinna tried her best not to feel wounded. She couldn't let her mother hurt her feelings now, not when things were going so well.

1993

Corinna popped a handful of ibuprofen as she walked into the restaurant for her shift, washing them down with warm water from the fountain by the bathrooms. She went to the kitchen to clock in, greeted everyone in English and Spanish, and shoved a chilled slice of bread into her mouth on her way back to the host stand. It would be a slow night. Somewhere, she'd heard that hostesses made tips in cities where people wore coats. She figured she wasn't pretty enough to work in a restaurant like that, anyway. She imagined tall, slim women like her mother wearing sleek black dresses and tasteful jewelry. She drew flowers on old menus and thought about Camille.

On nights like these, when she got cut early, she drove over to Copperhead Tavern, the only real bar in town, to see if she could work a few hours behind the bar. Her mother did not know about this and would not have approved. That night, though, she wasn't needed. Three pretty blond women she didn't recognize were on duty, laughing with the customers, mostly older men just off work from the plant.

The bar manager, Isaac, poured her a glass of white wine. "You look tense," he said.

She and Isaac had gone to high school together. He was two years ahead of her and was on the football team with Johnny. He was what Charlotte called one of those Orange Black People. His skin, the color of raw sugar, was covered with freckles. He even had freckles on his lips. His hair, eyebrows, and beard were all bright orange. He was not attractive in any traditional sense of the word, but he stood out from all the other boys, and girls of all kinds wanted to date him in high school. She was sure he'd never noticed her, but he'd greeted her warmly the first time she'd come to the bar.

"How's it going? You good?" he'd said, like they were old friends, before stepping back from the bar to shake a cocktail.

"You really got to shake it more than that," she said. She ought to know, living with two alcoholics who sometimes cared about the quality of their cocktails.

"Oh, yeah? Show me."

After that, Corinna worked as a fill-in bartender when she could. It was good, mostly easy money. And she was good at it. She knew the regulars and how they liked their drinks. The drinks were easy—beer; Beam and cokes; margaritas; shots; sweet, cheap wine; and the occasional old-fashioned. But she knew how to make other things because she studied the binder behind the bar with detailed instructions for drinks like Sazeracs, tequila sunrises, whiskey sours, Long Island iced teas, and cosmopolitans. Sometimes, she convinced regulars to try something new so she could practice, but they almost always went back to their regular order.

Isaac was always trying to convince her to go full-time, but she demurred, not interested in the conversations she would have to have with her mother. She didn't think Charlotte would like that, she told Isaac eventually.

"It's more money, though," Isaac responded. "The tips aren't consistent, but they can make a big difference."

She hadn't thought of it this way. The waitresses at Whiskers made minimum wage because the tips were so bad, probably because people were saving their money to get drunk at Copperhead.

They were in the kitchen, where Isaac gave Corinna a generous pour of Moscato, a drink she didn't particularly like. She took a big sip and mulled it over. Isaac was pouring bitters from mason jars into dropper bottles through a funnel.

"What are you doing on Friday?" he asked, and Corinna hoped he was finally going to ask her on a date. "You working at Whiskers?"

"Yeah," Corinna said, smiling, still hopeful.

"Why don't you call out and do a shift over here? A real one? See how you feel about it."

He'd suggested this at least half a dozen times, but she said yes this time.

When Corinna arrived home, the house was dark except for the blue flash of the TV in the front window. Charlotte was seated exactly where she'd been when Corinna left, but she was asleep, with her cheek resting on her fist. David sat next to her, also asleep, but with his head tilted back and his legs splayed out in front of him. Chinese food takeout containers were spread out on the coffee table. Corinna spotted two half-eaten egg rolls and some leftover lo mein. She carried the food into the kitchen and ate quickly. When she walked through the living room to get to her bedroom, her parents stirred slightly but did not wake.

Camille was asleep in the crib next to Corinna's bed. Corinna had had to move her dresser into the closet, where there was hardly enough space, and the crib still touched the wall and the edge of Corinna's full-size bed. She had to kneel on the bed in order to retrieve the baby from the crib. David had brought it home and set it up a few days after the baby was born. He said nothing about where he'd gotten it. It didn't matter. It was better than sleeping in someone's arms as she had been for the first few days of her life.

Corinna lifted the baby, who momentarily opened her eyes but did not wake. Corinna sniffed her diaper and was surprised to find that it was dry (she didn't quite trust her parents with Camille at this point). She returned the baby to the crib and got ready for bed in the light from the television and the moon. She whispered good night to her sleeping child before she drifted off to sleep herself.

*   *   *

Two days later, David fell four stories from scaffolding on the old movie theater on Main Street right onto a parked Volkswagen Beetle. The doctors said he should have died. In the hospital, Charlotte and Corinna stood over David's mangled body while Camille slept soundly in her mother's arms.

"He's like a fuckin' cockroach, ain't he?" Charlotte said, folding her arms over her chest with a loud sigh.

Before Corinna could fix her mouth to respond, Charlotte was on the move down the hall, going uncharacteristically fast. Corinna followed slowly, for fear of jostling and waking Camille.

When Corinna finally caught up with her mother, she was sitting on a retaining wall behind the hospital, her hand cupped around the end of a cigarette as she attempted to light it. Corinna sat next to her, using one hand to support her baby's neck and back and the other to light her mother's cigarette. "We've got some of the worst luck," Charlotte said, her cigarette dangling from her lips. "It would have been better if he just died."

"Mama, you don't mean that."

"If he *died*, we could have got life insurance."

"He's got life insurance?"

"Or *something*. Damn. Now, we got a whole baby *and* a whole invalid. That's not cheap, Corinna."

"Babies and invalids don't come in halves," Corinna said, and Charlotte gave her half a smirk for her trouble. "He probably gon' get disability. We'll be all right," she continued.

"'All right' was fine before we had a baby to take care of."

This puzzled Corinna, who'd once been a baby, hadn't she? Had there been similar concern for her well-being? Hard to imagine.

"The medical bills gon' bury us," Charlotte said, a far-off look in her eye.

Corinna didn't know what to say. They'd never had any money, and it was hard to imagine having even less. But it was easier now to make the decision about Copperhead. The night before, she'd come home from her first shift with a hundred dollars in tips.

"I got a new job, Mama."

Charlotte looked at her in surprise. "Where?"

"At Copperhead, over on—"

"I know where it is. You're eighteen, you can't work at a bar."

"Yes, I can."

"You'll be out late. What about the baby?"

"I figure she'll be asleep most of the time. She sleeps well, don't you think?"

"All right," Charlotte said. "We'll do what we gotta do."

*   *   *

For the first few months after his accident, David could barely do so much as wipe his own ass, as Charlotte put it. But she surprised Corinna by nursing David back to health with a great tenderness that Corinna had not known her mother was capable of, and happily tended to him and to baby Camille while Corinna worked. Financially, they were not doing great. The disability payments and an undeserved settlement helped, but it did not completely fill the void where David's salary had once been, especially with the added cost of his medical bills.

Over time, David got back some of his mobility, but he didn't regain the vigor that helped drive the tumultuous chaos that the women had grown accustomed to. There was an entirely new energy in the house. Corinna's parents were totally enthralled with the baby—singing to her, dancing with her, reading to her, playing with her. Once, Corinna walked into the kitchen to find Charlotte reading aloud to David from a book called *Touchpoints—Birth to Three: Your Child's Emotional and Behavioral Development*. Corinna had never even seen her mother hold a book, let alone read one.

David was staring into the middle distance with intense concentration. "Underline that," he told Charlotte, who obeyed. "Then," he said. "Let's go back a chapter. I wanna review something he said about attachment."

Somewhere they read that it was good for babies to watch the news, and Corinna soon found her parents sitting on the couch, the baby propped up between them, watching the television.

"'Rina," David said one evening as she was on her way to work. "Did you know a whole slew a Black churches been burned down in Mississippi in the past year?"

Corinna turned her attention to the TV screen, where a pretty anchor was introducing a guest: "Here to comment on the scourge of hate crimes in the American South, Dr. Evelyn Gwendolyn Jackson."

"What a name," Corinna said, continuing to the front door. "Can't help but be somebody with a name like that."

She felt something change in the room but didn't have time to linger on it.

"Y'all sure it's best for Camille to be listening to sad shit like this?"

Her parents didn't say anything. And she was running late, so she left.

SPRING 1996

The Tennessee Tornadoes drafted Johnny in the spring, making him the biggest story in town since the plant opened in the eighties. Corinna couldn't turn on the local news without seeing something about him. The high school hung a large congratulatory banner over the entrance of the building. The City Council named him the first-ever Chilly Springs Citizen of the Year, even though he'd been living in Nashville since he started Vanderbilt a couple years earlier. There was even a life-size cardboard cutout of Johnny standing by the entrance of the Food Lion.

Walking into the grocery store one night, Corinna overheard two older Black men, who were standing by the cutout with their fists on their hips.

"And they say ain't nothing out here but meth and guns," said one.

"Mm-hmm," said the other. "Got us a hometown hero."

"Thassright."

Corinna wished she could tell Johnny how proud of him she was.

They had rarely spoken since their meeting at Whiskers, but he'd been quietly making child support payments for the past few years. They'd started coming one day a few months after Camille was born, when Corinna got an envelope in the mail with no return address but with a check inside from the account of Delia

D. Washington. They continued to arrive until one month Delia included a note saying it was "too dangerous." Was she worried someone would steal the checks, or figure out the connection? Corinna wasn't sure.

Either way, Corinna went to Delia's house once a month to pick up an envelope full of cash, enough to keep Camille in new clothes and shoes and to pay for field trips. There was also enough that Camille could eat pretty good, but not much more, which was fine with Corinna. She was assistant bar manager now, and ends were meeting for the most part.

Delia, who Corinna once knew to be a kind woman and a very good friend to her mother, had become cold and condescending. She seemed to take pleasure in withholding information about Johnny's life while absorbing details about Corinna's, and implying that Corinna had gotten pregnant on purpose. In reality, Corinna got pregnant because she'd only known what she learned from television and in sex ed (which involved all the girls in the class spitting into a paper cup and tearing petals off wilting flowers).

Otherwise, Corinna hadn't heard a word from Johnny in almost five years, and she didn't expect to. But a little more than a week after the news of his draft broke, he called the house. Corinna was standing in front of the open refrigerator, trying to figure out how to make a meal for four out of leftover baked beans, three slices of grayish lunch meat, half a slice of bologna, and a bottle of mustard.

"Yeah?" she sighed into the phone. From where she stood, Corinna could see through the window above the kitchen sink that Camille was running around the front yard in the frilly, yellow-striped bikini Charlotte bought for her at Walmart. Before, Charlotte had paid for only her own manicures and liquor with the money she'd squirreled away from doing hair, but now she spent it on Camille, whether or not she needed anything. Corinna couldn't make sense of it.

"Corinna, it's Johnny."

Her ears started ringing, and she felt slightly faint, though it was probably because she was hungry. Without answering, she tore off a piece of bologna, which only made her hungrier.

"Hello?"

"Mmmph," she said as she shoved the rest into her mouth.

The slice of bologna would likely be all Corinna ate that day, because she wasn't working that night. In her head, she calculated the tips from the night before, wondering if they'd cover gas and a few groceries to hold them over; they weren't getting a check for at least another week. She could eat for free at Copperhead and even bring some food home if she worked a double. She could pull at least a few doubles, hopefully make some tips and not eat any groceries if she bought them . . .

"Listen," Johnny said. "I'm going to do the right thing. I'm not going to leave y'all with nothing."

"Mm-hm," Corinna said, still running the numbers in her head. Was there something she wasn't thinking of that would throw a wrench in the whole thing? A field trip or something? Camille's preschool seemed to go on one every damn month.

"Come up to Nashville tomorrow, and we can talk about it. I'll give you some cash when you get here, okay?"

"I work at six. I need to come during the day."

Johnny told her to meet him near campus at Pancake Pantry, a place she'd always wanted to go. "Come *alone*," he stressed.

Corinna hung up without another word. She paced the small kitchen and massaged her aching temples. Camille was still running around outside in her little bikini, smiling and giggling with a clod of dirt in her fist. Neither Johnny nor his mother had met the little girl. They'd never even asked for a picture. What a loss for them, Corinna thought. Camille was magic. She'd come into this family and sobered up two far-gone alcoholics. Imagine what she could do for Johnny and his family.

In the morning, Corinna drove to Nashville, a heaviness in her gut that may have just been gas from guzzling 7-Eleven coffee she found a coupon for. She sat in the car for a few minutes before she was able to work up the nerve to go inside. Johnny was sitting at a table that looked child-size in relation to his hulking frame. He was staring into a cup of coffee, twiddling his thumbs, bouncing his left knee. He would have appeared to be a jittery junkie if it weren't for the Ralph Lauren rugby shirt, boat shoes, and white baseball cap.

"Hey," he said. He smiled, but it was not the smile that was plastered all over Chilly Springs, just him peeling back his lips to expose his teeth. Corinna did not peel her lips back in response. A man clapped Johnny on the back before Corinna could take her seat.

"Congratulations, kid," said the man, who, with his chiseled jaw and huge hands, looked like a cartoon of an aging football player.

"Thank you, sir," Johnny said, smiling a different smile and reaching out his hand. "That means a lot."

"You know him?" Corinna asked after the man had gone.

"No."

"Oh, right. You're a celebrity now." Corinna rolled her eyes and put her napkin in her lap. She ordered orange juice and the Caribbean pancakes, and Johnny asked for a three-meat omelet with a side of ham and extra pancakes. Johnny dropped his menu when he was finished ordering and stared at it unblinkingly. Corinna knew this meant he was thinking through what he was going to say next. She'd watched him do the same thing in front of his mother, at school, and among his friends, but never when they were alone.

"What did you want to talk about?" Corinna asked, looking at the manila envelope under Johnny's right elbow. He followed her line of vision and seemed surprised to see it there.

"Oh, right. We'll get to that." He patted the envelope like it was a stranger's dog. "First, things are good? How's your dad doing?"

"Disabled and indigent," Corinna said, which came out sounding like something Charlotte would say. The waitress—visibly uncomfortable with the tone of the conversation—delivered Corinna's juice.

"Doesn't indigent mean—"

"Doesn't matter. We're here to talk about Camille, right? Camille is doing great. She's reading a little bit, doing some addition when she feels like it."

"Does she ask about me?"

"Specifically about *you*? No. What kind of question is that?" Corinna drank her orange juice and gestured to the waitress for another. "I assume you're picking up the check?"

"I *meant*, does she ask about her dad?"

"No. She doesn't. You know what she does ask about? Ballet classes. A lil' studio just opened in town and every time we drive by, she sees this little ballerina on the sign and goes, 'That's going to be me.' You really should come by and tell her we can't afford it."

"Okay, Corinna. I get it."

"*Do* you?"

"Fine. You wanna talk money? Let's talk money." Johnny opened the envelope with an unfamiliar scowl, took out a stack of papers, and started reading in a loud whisper.

Corinna listened carefully as she ate her pancakes. Ultimately, he was going to quadruple his child support payments, create a trust, and pay for her school expenses, under the condition that Camille's parentage never be revealed to the public.

"That means your mama, too," Johnny said. "She got a big mouth."

"How you know she doesn't already know?"

"She would have told somebody by now."

Corinna couldn't argue with that. "What about Camille? Can I tell her?"

"No. Not until I say so."

Corinna wanted to spit her masticated pancakes at Johnny's smug face. But she did not. "I ain't signin' nothin' here. Give it. I'll read over it and get back to you."

They finished eating in silence, and Corinna drove home feeling lighter. When she got far enough away from the city, she rolled down the windows of the Honda and stuck her left arm out of the window, like her mother did when she was in a good mood. She stopped and bought a SuperSonic burger with some of the cash from the bank envelope thick with twenty-dollar bills that Johnny had given her.

When she got home, Camille was sitting on the porch steps combing her doll's hair and shimmying her shoulders to something David was playing on the tape player.

Corinna went to her bedroom and spread the papers out on the bed. She read through them again, highlighted the dollar amounts, and noted that they needed to be 25 percent higher. She'd gone back and forth about whether 25 percent was too much or too little, but knew this might be her only chance to get Camille what she deserved. She sat on the bed, feeling suddenly winded. For some reason, for the first time in her life, she ruminated on the ways in which Charlotte had been a terrible mother. Corinna knew she was already doing better than Charlotte. But "better" wasn't good enough. She bit the end of her ballpoint pen so hard the plastic ruptured. She tried to think of some examples of good mothers. Delia? She loved her children, but she also coddled them. Claire Huxtable? Too much to aspire for. The mom of Kendra Allen from Corinna's fourth-grade class? She brought cupcakes for every holiday, but Kendra had killed the class hamster by hanging it from the jungle gym with a stolen shoelace. Corinna did not know how she would do it, but she would be a Great Mom. She would figure it out. And the money was a start. It would open a lot of doors for Camille that had been locked for Corinna.

She couldn't imagine her own mother having the same concerns about her. Corinna's biological father was dead, so Charlotte couldn't have asked for anything from him. But there must have been something she could have fought for for Corinna. She might have kept her nose clean so she could hold down a job. She might have married someone with more sense and self-control than David. Corinna decided to stop thinking about it. She didn't have the time or resources to be angry. She had to get to work. She read over the paperwork again. Johnny was offering not a small sum of money: an increased amount of child support per month, college tuition, and a generous lump sum deposited into a trust fund. Camille would be fine. But she wouldn't be *set*. Corinna thought about the children

Johnny would have with his wife, who would get so much more—not only college and a trust fund, but private schools, vacations, tutors, computers, cars, nice clothes, big birthday parties, and a father who acknowledged them. Johnny wasn't making much yet. But what if he did one day? Corinna ran the numbers in her head again. A lump sum wouldn't do.

A few days later, she had an appointment to meet Johnny at a lawyer's office in Bellevue. When she arrived fifteen minutes early, she was ushered into an empty office. She chose the chair closest to the door and attempted to channel her mother's poise. She was wearing her best dress: a thrifted Calvin Klein sheath that was at least one size too small, maybe two. It was so tight that she was forced to sit up straight and hold her breath. She crossed her legs at the ankle, like she'd seen her mother do, and folded her hands in her lap.

Corinna knew Johnny had arrived before she saw him, from the way the people at the front desk greeted him. He entered the room wearing a big smile, and gently squeezed Corinna's shoulder. She despised him at that moment.

Right behind Johnny was a woman with an enormous head of blond hair so stiff with hairspray that it didn't move as she strutted into the room. She introduced herself only as Lydia, but Corinna assumed she was a lawyer.

As soon as the pleasantries were over, Johnny clapped his hands. "Let's get these papers signed, huh?"

Lydia produced a stack of papers, presumably identical to the ones Johnny had given Corinna at the Pancake Pantry.

"I'm not signing those," Corinna mumbled. She'd imagined sounding more assertive in her head, perhaps even snatching the papers off the desk and ripping them in half.

"What'd you say?" Johnny said, still smiling.

"I'm not signing those," she repeated, more confidently.

Johnny's face changed like it had in the Food Lion parking lot when she told him she was keeping the baby. "What?"

"It's not enough."

"What do you mean it's not enough?"

Lydia cut in. "I can assure you this is a very generous package—"

"It's not enough," Corinna said for the second time, sweating. She hadn't expected this much resistance. "I want what you're offering, plus five percent of your annual earnings every year deposited in the trust until she's twenty-one."

"Twenty-*one*," he said as if surprised to learn there were numbers higher than twenty.

Corinna nodded.

Again, Lydia intervened. "The standard is—"

"I don't give a damn about the *standard*," Corinna said, surprising herself. "I don't think it's too much, considering what you're asking of her. She's a secret, yeah? Well, she won't be no secret if she don't get her five percent." Corinna's speech slid into its natural vernacular though she'd practiced to avoid doing so.

"Corinna, I—"

"Oh, don't look at me like that. *You* took advantage of me."

"So that's what this is about?"

"It's about Camille!" Corinna said, louder than she meant to. Maybe it was a little bit about the way he'd treated her. And the way her mother treated her. And the way the world treated her. But Corinna would never touch the money. She cleared her throat. "So what if it is?"

"Well," he said. "I need to talk to my mother."

"No, you don't."

"*Yes*," he said. "I *do*."

"No, Johnny. You do not. Have the lady draw up some new papers. Or else I'm leaving, and I ain't signin' shit," she said, sounding so much like her mother she could hardly stand it. "I might even call the papers," she added, bluffing. She never wanted to blow up her daughter's life like that.

Johnny looked like he'd been force-fed a lemon. He was sweating, too.

"Mr. Washington?" Lydia asked.

For the first time, Corinna looked right at Lydia, whose heavy makeup was impeccable, especially considering the temperature in the room. Lydia looked bored, despite the scene she'd just witnessed. She'd probably seen much worse. This was a family law practice, after all. The world's most horrific violence probably happened in the home.

Johnny reached for a Kleenex and wiped his forehead and neck. Corinna wanted a tissue but couldn't risk moving in that dress any more than she had to.

"All right," he said with his head bowed. "Let's get some new papers drawn up. Lydia, how long will that take?"

"Not long, Mr. Washington. We use computers here."

Lydia asked a few questions that Corinna didn't pay much attention to because she felt faint from the heat and the tight dress, then Corinna and Johnny sat quietly while they waited for the new papers. The office must not have belonged to anyone because there were no signs of life—no degrees on the wall or family portraits on the desk. Perhaps this was strategic. She wished she had something to focus on, but she'd brought only her car keys and wallet, which now looked juvenile. Her mother was right; she needed a purse. She wasn't a kid anymore. She was a mother.

She thought of Camille, her pretty little girl, at home with Charlotte, probably dangling her feet from a kitchen chair, eating a cheese and tomato sandwich, and giggling at something her grandfather was saying.

When the papers came back, there were a few concessions, but nothing that outweighed the gains she'd made. After she got in the car, turned on the air, and unzipped her dress, Corinna felt buoyant. She couldn't remember ever feeling so light. She leaned her head back, closed her eyes, and exhaled.

The following Tuesday, Camille started her ballet classes.

PART IV

"Still Your Mother"

Charlotte

FALL 1998

CHARLOTTE'S FAVORITE PLACE for thinking was at the kitchen sink, from which she could look out the window to watch Camille play, see cars full of hooting teenagers pass by, and, most importantly, monitor Corinna coming and going.

One Monday morning, she was smoking her third or fourth cigarette of the day when Corinna pulled up in her brand-new soft-topped Jeep wearing a low-cut black racer-back tank top with COPPERHEAD TAVERN emblazoned across the chest, a cartoon snake slithering along the feet of the letters with its fangs bared. GET BIT, the shirt read across the back. Charlotte frowned. She didn't love that Corinna worked in a bar and, worse, a low-class dive.

Copperhead hadn't been around when Charlotte moved to Chilly Springs. It popped up after the Saturn plant opened and the population boomed. Before that, you had to go all the way to Nashville to go dancing. Now, you could get sloppy drunk, dance, and eat fried Oreos right there in town. Not that it mattered much to Charlotte. Charlotte was becoming concerned as of late with "upward mobility," a phrase her mother, Evelyn, often used in her work. There simply wasn't much mobility to be had where they lived, upward or otherwise. But she was starting to think about Camille's future and wasn't seeing many options.

Camille would need only more as she got older. Would Corinna be able to provide it? Charlotte thought she might try working again herself, now that David was in better shape. But what would she do? She was forty-two, and her only experience in the past decade was temp work. And somebody needed to be home for Camille in the afternoons, make her dinner, and put her to bed. Maybe she could get something part-time, in the mornings.

"Where you been?" she asked when Corinna came into the house. Her daughter frowned. "Hellooo?"

Corinna let the door slam behind her and headed toward her bedroom. Charlotte followed. "You know, you may pay some lil' bills around here, but it's still my house, and I'm still your mother. If I ask you a question about where you been—"

Corinna attempted to slam her bedroom door, but she had to push several times until it closed completely.

Charlotte was too surprised to react. They argued often, but Corinna's refusal to engage this morning felt more hostile than a shouting match. Charlotte cracked her knuckles and went to find her cigarette, which she found still burning in the kitchen sink.

David called for her, finally awake. He tried these days to get up to see Camille off to school, but usually went right back to bed if he did. She helped him to the couch, then picked up the remote and turned it to the local news. Johnny Washington was on TV again, a clip from the week before of him heading to the locker room at halftime. His helmet was off and he was dripping with sweat; he spoke breathlessly about the second-quarter touchdown pass. Then he asked for the microphone and announced his engagement to his high school sweetheart, Georgia. He looked directly into the camera and said, "I can't wait to spend forever with you, baby."

The clip had been on the news every day for the past week, along with a snapshot of his new fiancée flashing her engagement ring that Charlotte estimated to be around five carats, about the same size of the ring her mother had given her on her sixteenth birthday. She wished she hadn't left that behind in Atlanta. She could have sold it and bought the house they lived in.

Charlotte sighed.

"Whatever happened with you and his mama?" David asked.

"I don't know. I guess she got real full of herself, too," Charlotte said. "Ready for your coffee?"

David nodded. "Fix me some eggs, too?"

On her way back into the kitchen, Charlotte saw an envelope crumpled on the floor and recognized the pale pink of her mother's stationery. Evelyn had been using the same damned stationery for thirty years. She ordered it custom from New York; a "suite" of the stationery cost the same as Charlotte and David's light bill. Each Monday, Charlotte watched for the mailman, ran out to the mailbox, retrieved her mother's weekly letter, and put it in a shoebox in the closet. Somehow, she'd always been sober enough to do this one thing consistently. But this one must have come early. Heat rose in her esophagus. She'd never missed a letter in more than twenty years, amassing a half-dozen shoeboxes' worth of them, though she assumed a few must have gotten lost in the mail. But she'd never had an issue with them. If Corinna was around when the postman came, she'd dump the entirety of the day's mail into the trash.

"Nothing but junk," she'd say, and collect the pink envelope later.

She even rehearsed how she would respond if Corinna or Camille ever asked: "Must be running for office or something. You know how these politicians can be. Remember how Clinton sent that little postcard?"

Charlotte never opened the letters, though she did sometimes read the return address, which changed fairly regularly. This return address was in Washington, DC. It had recently been somewhere in California, and in Mexico before that. Many years had passed since there had been one in Atlanta. But none of that was important. What was important was the name printed in the upper-left-hand corner of the envelope in gilded block letters: DR. EVELYN GWENDOLYN JACKSON. Jackson: her first husband's name, the name under which she'd earned her PhD.

The name had been on TV a few times in the past few years, a talking head during national news segments, commenting on various race-related events: Rodney King's beating, Bill Clinton's apology to the victims of the syphilis experiments, Tiger Woods's status as a cultural phenomenon, and so on. She'd once seen some fellow named Henry Louis Gates describe her mother as having "walked so Cornel West and I could run" on CNN. Charlotte didn't know who Cornel West was, exactly, but she knew it was high praise. Watching her mother on TV wasn't as emotionally fraught as she might have thought. Her mother wasn't her mother on the screen, she was Dr. Evelyn Gwendolyn Jackson, and Charlotte had never really known Dr. Jackson.

David knew about Evelyn and played along by never mentioning her.

Charlotte picked up the envelope and carried it with her to the kitchen, where she prepared David's breakfast of salty eggs, black coffee, and a handful of medication. She served it to him on the little wooden TV table Corinna had brought home for him shortly after the accident, and sat next to him while he ate. *The Price Is Right* was on, but Charlotte wasn't paying attention. She was thinking about the letter she'd put away with the rest but realized there were more pressing issues at hand. Corinna must have spent the night with someone; if Corinna was seeing someone, she might try to move out and take Camille with her. Charlotte couldn't have that. She loved that little girl—sticky hands, sharp teeth they'd finally got her to stop biting people with, and all.

"You think she's seeing somebody?" she asked David.

"Hmm?" he responded, his mouth full of eggs.

"Corinna?"

"Yeah. You ain't seen him in the Mustang?"

"Mustang?"

"Charlotte. Come on now."

"Why didn't you say something?"

"Why would I?"

Charlotte sucked her teeth.

"Sometimes, I wonder what you be thinking 'bout in that pretty lil' head. You always standing by the winda. I figured you seen him."

*   *   *

Sure enough, several days later, Charlotte was by the kitchen sink when a Mustang pulled into the driveway. A very tall, very thin man with a shock of curly orange hair emerged, dressed like a Mormon in black pants and a white shirt without a tie. She tapped out her cigarette and went to the front of the house, opening the inner door and leaving the screen door between them.

"Who the fuck are you?" she said before he was even all the way up the porch steps. She'd assumed he was a white man, but upon further observation, she saw that he was what Evelyn had called an Orange Black Person. His hair, eyebrows, and patches of facial hair were all bright orange. His skin was pale but spattered with dark brown freckles that bloomed from the middle of his face, tightly spaced on the bridge of his nose and sparser toward his hairline, cheeks, jaw, and even his pale pink lips. She wondered if his tongue was freckled, too. He was too skinny for her taste, but he was not unattractive. He was too far away to judge his teeth, but, based on the way he carried himself, she assumed his parents could afford orthodontics.

"Oh, hi, Mrs. Jackson," he said. He touched his own chest and bowed slightly. "I'm Isaac."

"Who?"

"Isaac. I'm, uh, I'm here to pick up Corinna," he said, his cheeks turning red. "And Camille, too," he added.

"They're not here."

"Yes, ma'am, I know. I came early because I was hoping to introduce myself."

Charlotte considered this for a moment. It was four o'clock on a Saturday, and her only plans were to sit on the porch and drink and smoke. David was napping and wouldn't be up for a while.

"Well, it's Mrs. Hart, actually," she said, giving him her legal name, though she wasn't entirely sure why, other than to throw him off. She'd been going by Jackson since Camille was born because it was easier.

"Sorry, ma'am."

"You drink beer?"

"Yes, ma'am."

She left him outside and went to the refrigerator for a six-pack of Natural Light. They sat on the porch, and Charlotte asked him rapid-fire questions about himself and his personal life for the next forty-five minutes.

"You from here?"

"Yes."

"What your parents do?"

"Ma is a kindergarten teacher; Pop is an electrician."

"Where do they live?"

"Right off Kedron, past the new subdivision."

"Where do you live?"

"Just down the road from my parents, ma'am."

"What's your full government name? I know people at the police department," she said, which was true. They were very familiar with her there.

"Isaac Kenneth Brown."

All of his answers were just fine, but there was something off about him. He spoke too quickly, and he took only one swig of beer and let the bottle grow lukewarm at his feet. Something about him reminded her of someone, but she couldn't quite put her finger on it. Also, it was terribly strange of him to just show up like that. She couldn't imagine Corinna had advised him to do that.

When Corinna and Camille drove up, Charlotte was panicked to see her granddaughter, who had just turned six, sitting in the front seat with no seat belt. Charlotte stood up quickly, prepared to confront Corinna, but Camille came skipping up the driveway in her pink ballet tights and black leotard and leaped into her arms, and she forgot that she had anything to say at all.

This was the first time Charlotte noticed that Camille was not just beautiful to her, but objectively beautiful. She was actually the most beautiful child she had ever seen, with oversize almond-shaped eyes; long, lush eyelashes; and deep, raw-cocoa-colored skin. It startled her and not in the best possible way.

Camille wrapped her arms around Charlotte's neck and planted a firm kiss on her grandmother's lips. It was unclear where she'd learned to do that. Corinna thought it was cute, but Charlotte found it strange and far too *familiar* of a habit for a young girl.

Charlotte carried her inside, plopped her at the kitchen table, and served her a slice of manager's special chocolate pie and a tall glass of Hi-C, apologizing that the grocery store had been sold out of the Orange Lavaburst flavor.

Camille smiled and exposed the gaping hole where her two front teeth should have been.

"Dat's okay, Granmama. They have the red flavor at school," she said and used both hands to lift the glass to her lips. Charlotte rested her face on her fist to watch Camille. She barely noticed when Corinna came clattering into the house.

"Mama! You're going to ruin her dinner."

"Huh?" Charlotte said, not taking her eyes off Camille, who was chewing so slowly that it seemed she was not chewing at all. Charlotte wiped a smear of chocolate from the corner of the child's mouth.

"Mama, I told you—"

"Oh. I was planning on taking Camille over to the fairgrounds." This was not true. She vaguely remembered Corinna saying something about the movies. But Charlotte just had one of those *feelings*.

"Mama, I told you—"

"Why don't we just ask her what she wants? Camille, baby, what do you want?"

Camille stopped chewing altogether and dropped her eyes to the table.

"Do you want to go to the movies with Mama and Isaac, or do you want to stay here?"

"Or do you want to stay with Grandma and finish your pie and go to the fair? There's a Ferris wheel. Didn't I tell you we could go on a Ferris wheel one day?"

"We can see *Stuart Little*, Camille."

"Oh, honey. You can see that any day. The fair is gone day after tomorrow."

"Then go tomorrow, Mama," Corinna said.

"I'm busy tomorrow," Charlotte lied.

Camille's eyes ping-ponged back and forth between her mother and grandmother. "I'll stay with Mama," she said, her mouth still full of gooey chocolate. The women stopped talking and looked at her.

"You mean you'll *go* with Mama."

"Yes, I'll go with Mama to the fair."

Corinna dropped down to her knees so quickly, Charlotte felt her body instinctively pull itself in Corinna's direction to stop her from hitting the ground. Then she realized that Corinna was only getting ready to plead with Camille.

"Camille, honey. *I'm* Mama."

"I want to go to the fair," Camille said meekly. She choked down the pie in her mouth and took a sip of her sweet drink.

"Okay, you can go to the fair with *Gran*mama. *Mama* is going to the movies with Isaac, okay?"

"Okay."

"Give kisses?"

Camille kissed her mother, and Charlotte and Corinna locked eyes for a moment.

"You're up to something," Corinna said calmly. "And I don't like it." She snatched her keys from the counter where she'd tossed them, and slammed the door behind her so hard that the only picture hanging in the kitchen rattled and shifted on its hook. Charlotte stood quickly to straighten the picture, a drawing by Camille of their family that she'd framed.

"What's all that racket?" David called from the bedroom.

Charlotte ignored him and turned her attention to Camille, who was staring at her half-eaten pie. "Finish your pie, sweetheart, and we'll go, okay?"

"I lost my appetite, I think."

Corinna

FALL 1998

Corinna needed to introduce Isaac to the realities of having a six-year-old. He'd met Camille but had never spent meaningful time with her, and didn't know how poorly she could behave in public. He hadn't seen her chew up and spit out a fistful of Swedish fish into the cup holder of his car like she'd done to Corinna's. This was important because Corinna was moving on to the second part of her journey toward becoming a Great Mother: providing a reliable second parent. Corinna figured her own life had been better—she wasn't sure how exactly—because of David. If anything, her life had simply been better because it wasn't just her and Charlotte.

Isaac had maneuvered their schedules so that they would both be off on a Saturday night—almost impossible for the two assistant bar managers, but he'd made it work. And then her mother had ruined it. And in the midst of her ruining it, Camille called Charlotte *mama*, not once but twice.

Instead of going to the new movie theater in town, which had originally been their plan, Corinna suggested they go to Bluebird Café, over an hour away, so that she would have a little more time away from her family. When they arrived, a live band was playing. She and Isaac briefly attempted conversation by shouting over the table at each other, but promptly gave up and sat in what might have been an awkward silence if it weren't for the music.

Corinna turned in her seat when the band started to play "Jolene." The beautiful blond woman behind the microphone didn't have the strongest voice, but the crowd stomped and hooted and sang along. When the song was over, the singer threw her thick hair behind her shoulders and announced that they were taking a quick break.

Corinna turned around, and was surprised by Isaac's deeply inquisitive expression. The food arrived, but Issac's expression didn't change.

"Whatcha thinkin' about?" Corinna asked.

"Nothing. I was just thinking about Camille."

Corinna attempted a joke. "'Jolene' made you think about Camille?"

"Who's her father?"

"Hmm?"

"Camille? Who's her dad?"

"Oh," she said, pulling her lips away from her teeth in a piss-poor attempt at a smile. "That's not important, is it?" She put her fork down and reached across the table to touch his hand, which was wrapped around a glass of dark, opaque beer. His hands, like his face, were freckled. He released the glass and allowed her to hold his hand, which was moist and cool.

"Well, no. But it *matters.*"

Corinna took a moment to consider the distinction, but couldn't figure it out. "Well," she said. "It doesn't really matter to me. It will probably never matter to her or to Johnny—" *Oh, shit.* She'd said too much.

"Johnny who?" he asked, his expression changing as he made the connection.

"Just somebody from school."

"Only Johnny I know is Johnny Washington."

Yes, *Johnny Washington*, the most famous graduate of their high school, the all-American football player who was now the starting quarterback for the Tennessee Tornadoes. If you were to walk into Chilly Springs High School at that very moment, you would have been greeted by a twenty-foot-tall mural of Johnny holding a football in between two big brown hands and smiling at you like he knew you and cared about you and wanted you to be well.

"Well . . ." Corinna averted her eyes.

Isaac opened his mouth but said nothing. She knew what he was thinking. *How? Why?* Johnny *fucking* Washington and Corinna Jackson? He closed his mouth and opened it again. Still, no words came out.

"I'm surprised you wouldn't have guessed," she said and smiled nervously. "Y'all played together and all. She looks just like him."

Isaac finished his beer in one big gulp and slammed the glass down. "Does he *know*?"

"Yes, he knows."

"And he isn't supporting you?"

"He pays child support, and there's a trust," she said, knowing she was violating the contract she'd signed. "She'll be able to go to college, do whatever she wants."

Isaac nodded. "What about you? And your parents?"

"What about us?"

"He don't take care of y'all?"

"We're fine. We'll be fine as long as Camille's fine," she said. And it felt so obvious. Maybe this wasn't the father for Camille. "You know, I'm suddenly not feeling very well," she lied. "Can you take me home, please?"

He drove almost all the way back in complete silence.

"You know," he said as they got close. "I don't judge you or anything for having Camille out of wedlock. I think choosing to have a child is always beautiful."

Corinna hated the word *wedlock*. It sounded permanent and condemning, not like something you'd want to have a child in.

Before she got out of the car, she asked him not to tell anyone. "It's a condition of the arrangement," she explained.

"You can trust me," he said, but she didn't believe him.

She wished she could start the entire evening over again. She walked into the house, where Camille was reading something out loud, and saw her daughter with new eyes. She saw her for the first time as Johnny Washington's daughter.

"'Don't be silly,' said Frog. 'What you see is the clear warm light of April,'" she read, terribly literate for a girl her age. Corinna had been average in every possible way, but Johnny had been exceptional, and Camille would be exceptional, too. "We will skip through the meadows . . ." She sounded confident and clear, like a parent reading to their child at night with all the inflections of an older, wiser storyteller, but she suddenly clapped the book shut.

"Hi, Mama."

Corinna snapped out of her trance, and crouched down to greet her daughter, who wrapped her arms around her neck and planted a kiss on her lips. Corinna picked her up and carried her to their bedroom. When she closed the door behind them, Corinna realized tears were welling in her eyes.

"What's wrong, Mama?"

"Nothing, baby. Nothing. I just missed you today."

A few days later, Corinna and Isaac were working the same shift when he pulled her into the kitchen, which had just closed.

"I've been trying to call you," he said, looking slightly panicked.

That was odd, Corinna thought. She didn't know about any calls.

"I hope nothing has changed between us. I didn't mean to pry—"

Corinna was warmed by this show of affection. She grabbed him and kissed him so forcefully that their teeth clinked together painfully. They went home together that night, and she woke up next to him in the morning. She didn't love him yet, but hoped it was possible she would.

LATE WINTER 1999

The name sounded familiar, but it was the envelope that stood out to her because it was beautiful, the color of a summer sunset. The return address was printed in golden letters. And Charlotte's name was printed by hand.

After a few weeks of cooking on it, Corinna realized that she'd seen Evelyn Gwendolyn Jackson on television occasionally. But it didn't explain why she'd written a personal note to Charlotte. Was she running for office or something?

She put the mail on the kitchen table with the intention of bringing it up with her mother, but it disappeared. She must have dropped it somewhere, she figured. Corinna thought about it from time to time but never quite found the nerve to ask her mother about it.

But she thought about it more that winter, mostly because Isaac asked a lot of questions about her family, ones that anyone might ask their significant other. Are your mother's parents alive? What about your father's parents? Who *is* your father? Corinna didn't know. She'd been told all those people were dead, and she'd accepted it. After the sixth grade, when Corinna asked what her biological father's name was for a class project and her mother threw three heavy glasses into the wall, she stopped asking any questions. Corinna manufactured a family tree on her own instead, naming her father Jeremiah because that seemed like a good name for a nice man.

But she knew that name, Evelyn Gwendolyn Jackson, was significant. It wasn't just that it was printed in gold that tipped her off or simply the fact that she recognized it. It was something more than that.

"Mama?" Corinna asked her mother one morning in early February as they sat across from each other at the kitchen table. It was so cold inside that Corinna could see her own breath. Camille was at school, so David had turned off the heat for the day to save money, even though Corinna told him that they could afford it.

"Hmm?" Her mother took a large sip of coffee and turned the page of *Woman's World* without looking up.

"We don't have *any* living family?"

"What?"

"I was just thinking. You said your mama and daddy are dead, but they didn't have brothers and sisters? You don't have any cousins or anything like that?"

"Not that I know of."

"And what about my daddy? What about his parents? All those people can't be dead."

"You've got a dad, don't you?"

"Yeah, but—"

"But what?"

"It's my blood, Mama. It's Camille's blood."

Charlotte looked up and sighed loudly, releasing a cloud of vapor. "What's your point?"

"They ask about that kind of stuff at the doctor."

"That's not why you're asking, is it?" Charlotte asked, looking back down at her magazine.

Corinna changed tack. "I was just thinking that Camille might have another set of grandparents out there somewhere, and they might like to know her."

Charlotte took another sip of coffee. "Can we talk about this another time?"

"But Mama—" she pushed. "You don't even talk about him. It's like he don't even exist."

"Corinna, I can't," she whispered.

Corinna had never known her mother to whisper. That's when she knew for sure that something wasn't right.

*   *   *

In the waiting room of Gail's Ballet School, Camille leaped in front of her mother with her arms outstretched. "Hi, Mama!" she said and wrapped her arms around Corinna's neck in a tight hug, then gleefully waved goodbye to the teacher on their way out.

When they pulled up to the house, where David and Charlotte were sitting on the front porch, they greeted Camille like a celebrity. David hummed the theme to Miss America, and Camille knew this was her cue to strut toward the porch smiling, with one hand on her hip and the other waving with the palm slightly cupped. Usually, Corinna was genuinely delighted by how well Camille could perform at the drop of a dime. But on this particular day, she didn't have the stomach for it.

Corinna went inside, opened the refrigerator, and pulled out the four-liter jug of wine she'd been saving for nothing in particular. As she was pouring, she heard her mother finish the song: "Fairest of the fair, she is . . . Miss America. There she is, Miss America 1999!" Corinna looked out of the window and caught a glimpse of Camille, now gracefully ascending the porch stairs blowing kisses and holding a phantom bouquet. Corinna gulped her wine. The phone rang, an aggravating sound.

"Hullo," she said.

"Corinna, is that you?"

It was Delia. Delia summoned Corinna a few times a year to remind her of the terms of their arrangement and ask for updates on what she was doing with her monthly payments, at least 75 percent of which had to directly benefit Camille or be put into savings. The remaining 25 percent could be used for "indirect costs," which Corinna learned was actually a business term for things like transportation and administrative fees. Initially, Corinna had provided official reports, which she prepared using a typewriter at Isaac's parents' house with the help of his mother, but Delia eventually asked her to just come by the house every now and again instead.

Corinna was indifferent about most people, but she hated Delia. She wore too much jewelry, which rattled together when she moved around. Delia was constantly chewing gum and filing her nails. The sounds that Delia's body made reminded Corinna of the way rattlesnakes sound before they strike.

The Washingtons lived in the same house they always had. At its core, it was just a larger version of Corinna's house, with a white clapboard exterior instead of a blue one. But since Johnny signed with the NFL, more than a few improvements had been made. A large brick addition had been made to the western side of the house. There was also a new sunroom out back that Corinna had never been inside of, but you could see it from the road. The small porch had been extended and now spanned the length of the house, and shrubs and flowers had been planted strategically, obviously by a professional. But what Corinna envied the most was the paved driveway. Camille could learn to ride her bike safely with a paved driveway.

When Corinna arrived, less than an hour after their phone call, Delia was standing in the doorway behind the glass outer door with her fists on her wide hips. Delia had always worn her hair short and roller-set close to her scalp. Charlotte used to do Delia's hair the same way but had done a much better job with it than whoever did it now.

Corinna knew she would not be asked into the house, so she took a seat in one of the pure white rocking chairs that were lined up on the porch like at a Cracker Barrel.

"How's the girl doing?" Delia asked as she settled into a nearby chair.

"May I have a glass of water, Ms. Delia?"

Delia huffed. "I wish you would have said something afore I set down." She eased her large body back out of her seat. "Good thing you ask, though, because I forgot your money indoors."

As Corinna waited, she took in the grass, which was lush and green. She wondered what a person had to do to get grass that green. She knew the grass outside her own house would never be that green. Delia returned with a plastic cup of water and an envelope, which she handed over before she sat down again.

"And the girl?"

Corinna hated that neither Johnny nor his mother would say Camille's name, treating it like a swear word. Delia, a God-fearing woman, would never, ever swear. "Camille is doing real good. She's very smart, reads real well."

"Oh, that don't surprise me one bit," Delia said and smiled. "Johnny was reading real well before he even started school."

"Well, you could come see her anytime."

"Oh, honey. Bless your heart. You know I can't do that."

Though she had just drank an entire glass of water, Corinna's mouth went dry. Every time Delia and Johnny declined offers to meet Camille, she was newly offended on her daughter's behalf. But she quickly shook the feeling.

"Yeah, I'm sure y'all are busy with the wedding and everything."

Johnny was going to marry that white girl from Franklin that he'd been dating since the ninth grade—Georgia or Virginia or something.

"I was thinking y'all might want a picture of her or something?"

"Come on now, 'Rinna," Delia said, using the nickname David had used when she was younger. "You know we care about that baby. We just can't go getting attached." She leaned away. "You open up that envelope, and you see she's gon' be better off when she comes of age than any of his legitimate children."

Legitimate? She felt tears coming. "Anything else?"

"Well, I was thinking about something," Delia said with a hiccup.

"Yes'm?"

"You got a plan for when she starts asking about her daddy?"

"No, ma'am." Corinna avoided eye contact.

"Well, I was thinking that girl going to grow up in the middle of a pack of lies. No reason we got to add another one."

"Why you say that?"

"Say what?"

"About the lies."

"Oh, honey. You ain't dumb. You know something ain't right with your mama."

Corinna sat up straight, and Delia continued.

"She says she don't got *no* family? Everybody got somebody somewhere. I really don't like to be talking like this. It's gossip, and gossip is the devil's work. But I don't see no point in adding one more lie. When she starts asking, you bring her right here to me, ya hear? I'll explain about protecting Johnny's future."

Corinna fought to keep from rolling her eyes; she knew that she would never bring Camille there. She would take their money, but as long as they treated her like a shameful secret, her daughter was hers. Corinna, Charlotte, and David had been the only ones who wanted her. And that's who was going to raise her. And that's who would control the narrative around how she came to be and why she didn't know her father.

She didn't even know why she wanted them to know Camille to begin with. What was the true value in knowing where you come from, anyway? Corinna had no idea, and she was doing just fine.

But Corinna was angry. Her neck grew hot and itchy. "My mama ain't a liar."

"You sure 'bout that?"

Corinna was not, and Delia seemed to sense her uncertainty; she leaned back and crossed her arms over her chest to signal that she knew she was right.

On the way home, Corinna drove down Main Street. When it came time for her to make a right on Gibraltar to go home or a left up the hill to the town center, Corinna took a left without thinking about it. She parked in front of the library, which was just a couple of double-wide trailers stacked up on cement blocks. She went inside, and asked a librarian to help her get online. Corinna had never used a computer before. From TV, she knew that in other parts of the country, even in other parts of the state, people were using beige machines to do things like send messages to each other and learn things that were previously only in encyclopedias or the phone book. On the news, she'd seen children in Nashville using bright, candy-colored computers to play games that taught them how to type and read. She wasn't sure, but she didn't think Camille had ever used a computer either.

"Sure," said the librarian, who was ghostly pale with big, thick, red hair. "Are you looking for anything in *pahtikahlah*?" She didn't recognize the accent, though it struck her as high class.

"Yes," Corinna replied. "I'm looking for somebody." She was self-conscious of the way she spoke in this woman's presence.

"Okay. Do you have this person's name?"

This woman talked proper like Charlotte sometimes did, and it surprised her to hear someone else speak that way.

"Yes."

Corinna and the librarian sat at a computer. She thought she might also ask about Y2K, something Isaac had been going on about. The librarian pulled up something called Netscape on the screen and instructed her to type the name. Corinna tapped at the computer keys, one by one, to form the name Evelyn Gwendolyn Jackson.

The librarian typed quotation marks around the name. "This helps the search," she said, before pressing Return.

Overwhelmed with the number of results, Corinna asked the librarian to help her print the first three articles:

"Evelyn Jackson, PhD, Opens Bookstore and Café Near Monterey."

"Scholar Evelyn Jackson Names Bookstore for Daughter."

And "Acclaimed Scholar Accepts Prestigious Professorship at Howard University."

The first article opened with a quotation from Dr. Jackson: "I named it for my daughter, Charlotte."

Over the next few days, Corinna went back to the library while Camille was in ballet class. Sometimes she read articles on the internet; other times, she asked the librarian to order Evelyn's books. Corinna was somewhat surprised to learn the books were not like the books in the grocery store, but thick, dense, impersonal texts with titles like *The Black Bourgeoisie and the White Imagination* and *Twentieth-Century Academia and Blackness* and *The Crooked Looking Glass: Reflections on the Talented Tenth and the Black Leisure Class*. All of the books published after 1980 were dedicated to Charlotte.

Corinna hadn't noticed it when she'd seen the woman on TV, but Dr. Jackson looked exactly as one would imagine Charlotte's mother would look, very fair-skinned with graying dark blond hair and green eyes. She almost looked like a white woman. Most importantly, Evelyn Gwendolyn Jackson was sure as shit *not dead.*

If Charlotte lied about this, Corinna could hardly begin to imagine what else her mother might have lied about. Corinna didn't feel angry that she'd been lied to, not exactly. She considered confronting her mother, but she didn't want to create tension where there was none. She and Charlotte were doing okay. They played spades and sat on the porch just to chat. Sometimes, her mother even hugged her when she left for work in the evenings. Corinna had no memory of her mother ever hugging her as a child. Why would she imperil this? For what? A ghost?

In spite of herself, Corinna found herself arguing more and more with Charlotte. After several extraordinarily, inappropriately explosive fights over expired deli meat, gas money, the light bill, whether David's CD collection should be organized alphabetically or by genre, who drank the last of the "good" Johnnie Walker, the temperature of Camille's baths, Kool-Aid vs. Flavor Aid, and the existence of hell and whether or not Corinna would go to it, Charlotte told Corinna she could leave.

Corinna saw that this was her best opportunity to punish her mother. On move-out day, she pried a crying Camille out of Charlotte's arms. With tears in her eyes, Charlotte followed Isaac's borrowed pickup truck down the street in her bare feet, both of her hands pressed to her chest. Corinna had never seen her mother cry, not even during knockout drag-out fights with David.

"We're not going far, baby. We're just going five miles down the road," Corinna told a still-weeping Camille. She feared the child might try to climb out of the window and run back to the blue house. However, Camille was asleep by the time they arrived at Isaac's house. Corinna carried her inside to the brand-new twin-size bed and crawled in after her. She slept in Camille's bed for weeks, partly because Camille cried and peed the bed if she didn't, and partly because she feared what the distance from her daughter might mean.

LATE SUMMER 1999

Each day, Camille was less like a baby and more like a complete and complex person. Corinna could no longer anticipate her attitudes and moods. She realized that she'd assumed Camille would be like her as a child: docile, anxious, and yearning for affection and affirmation.

But Camille taught herself backflips and cartwheels. She played with bugs and frogs, climbed trees, and never expressed fear. Where other children seemed to require playmates to enjoy themselves at the park, Camille seemed the same whether or not there were other kids around.

She also loved to read, something Corinna had never found much pleasure in doing, and it was yet another way she felt she was losing touch with her child. The year they moved in with Isaac, Camille won an award for reading the most books in her grade. The prize was a subscription to *Highlights* magazine and set of buttons that read I ♥ BOOKS and I'D RATHER BE READING that she wore proudly on her bookbag.

That year, Corinna caught her reading a romance novel. "What's that?"

"What?" Camille asked.

"This book." Corinna took it from Camille, who reached after it with both hands. The cover was mostly blank, except for the title, which was printed in swirling, metallic letters. *Love and Lust in Las Vegas.* "Where did you get this?"

Camille stared at her blankly.

"Where did you get this?!"

Camille continued to stare. In certain light, Camille's eyes appeared so dark that you could not see her pupils. The effect was both chilling and lovely.

"Camille *Jackson.*"

Camille crossed her arms over her chest, mad. It was when Camille was angry that Corinna saw herself most in her daughter's face. Corinna popped Camille across her butt with the book and sent her outside. She considered reading the book herself but wound up throwing it into the trash.

A few days later, Corinna caught her with *Valley of the Dolls,* which Corinna knew was inappropriate because whenever the movie came on television, Charlotte changed the channel.

"I thought it was about dolls. It was actually about old white women." Camille shrugged. "Can I go play?"

Not long after that, Camille's teacher Mrs. Clayton requested Corinna's presence for a meeting.

"She's clearly a very intelligent, curious child," said Mrs. Clayton, an elfish-looking woman with brown hair cut into an unflattering pageboy. "She's reading above grade level."

Actually, Camille was reading far above grade level. Corinna sensed a *but* coming.

"She's a wonderful student. But she . . . lives in her own little world."

"She daydreams?"

"Yes, and she tells these funny little fibs sometimes."

"Fibs? Like *lies*?"

Mrs. Clayton sighed. "I don't mean to offend you. But, sometimes, she tells these *fantastical* stories. I think she gets them from those books she reads—"

Corinna felt defensive. Her first thought was to ask for an example, but she didn't want to give the teacher an opportunity to prove her point. "My child doesn't lie."

"Ms.—"

"My child doesn't lie," Corinna volleyed on her way out.

She slammed the door of the classroom in an attempt to convey outrage, though she was unsurprised. After Jenny died, Camille had started lying, and the lies were becoming more and more outlandish. She'd overheard Camille tell a neighborhood kid that she was the product of an "immaculate conception, like Jesus." She was also telling people that Jenny moved to Cambodia because her father was in the CIA. More alarmingly, she'd also seen her bite a kid and then tell them she was a vampire.

She drove directly to her mother's house and recounted the meeting to Charlotte, who was standing by the kitchen sink with a cigarette while Camille practiced cartwheels in the front yard. After the move, Charlotte had been cold with Corinna. She still watched Camille, but Charlotte never asked Corinna to stay or waved from the front porch as she drove away.

"And what did *you* say?" Charlotte asked.

"What do you mean?"

"You let her talk about Camille like that?"

"Like what?"

"'Rinna, come on," Charlotte said, and sighed. "That's *racist*, what she said. She wouldn't say those things about a little white girl."

Corinna wanted to ask her mother how she knew, but she cleared her throat and sat up straight.

"You know. They write books on raising children. But they assume we got all this time and money and good husbands and all that kind of shit," Charlotte said, waving her scrawny arms around to insinuate all these assumptions.

"How would you know, Mama?" Corinna asked, knowing the answer.

"Because I read them, Corinna." Charlotte knocked back the rest of her drink with a slight wince.

"You read them after Camille was born. Why not when I was born?"

The two women stared at each other in silence. Color rose in Charlotte's pale cheeks.

"If you have something to say, just say it," Charlotte said.

"Look, Grandaddy," Camille called from out front, where she might have been turning cartwheels or backflips or any number of tricks she'd taught herself.

"I'm lookin'," David called back.

"Ta-da!"

"Oh, would you look at that? My little Olympian."

The light was just right that Corinna saw her mother as she had been as a young woman. At forty-six, she wasn't old, but the skin under and around her eyes was loose and had permanently darkened. The angles of her cheekbones and shoulders were becoming harsh as she grew increasingly gaunt. But she was still beautiful for a woman in her apparent misery. Corinna wished someone would paint a portrait of her mother at this exact moment. A photograph wouldn't do her mother's beauty justice, and at the rate she was going, Charlotte would be unrecognizable in a few years.

Corinna gently backed away from the confrontational question. "I didn't mean it like that, Mama. I was just wondering."

"I didn't exactly have the time, you know? I was alone."

There was another pause. "The teacher asked if there is something going on at home," Corinna said finally.

"Well," Charlotte said. "*Is* there something going on at home?"

Corinna relented. "I don't know. Maybe. Teacher said I should sit down with her. Pour me some, Mama?"

Charlotte sat down at the kitchen table and poured another glass of Jameson. She crossed her legs and draped an arm over the back of her chair. They sat in silence for a moment while Corinna took small sips of her drink. And then Charlotte started talking.

"Maybe y'all should get married, let her know y'all's situation is permanent."

Corinna was surprised at the suggestion, both the idea and that it was coming from Charlotte. Corinna and Isaac didn't laugh together like her parents, but they also didn't fight like her parents. That had to count for something.

"He's a good guy," Charlotte said. "Right?" she added when Corinna hesitated.

"I just don't *love* him, Mama."

"Love's not everything, I'll tell you that right now," Charlotte said, shaking her head.

Corinna knew her mother was at least a little bit correct. And that was going to have to be enough.

LATE SUMMER/EARLY FALL 2001

Isaac wasn't particularly warm with Camille, but nor was he icy. If she asked him for something, he never hesitated to give it to her. He never yelled, even when she deserved to be yelled at. He left parenting up to Corinna, though he had plenty to say about how she parented.

Why had she thought he would be able to provide anything other than that? Because he drank in moderation? Because he didn't have a drug problem? She'd been mistaken. But she could move on. They had an okay life together. There was no fighting. There was no extra money, but they had enough. She owed her daughter a stable partner. She couldn't provide everything Camille needed. Corinna was not sufficient on her own. Sure, Charlotte and David were happy to step in and provide love, but what about everything else? Corinna wasn't even sure what "everything else" meant, but she wanted Camille to have it. She and Isaac liked each other. They didn't fight. He didn't hit her. He earned a steady paycheck. That *felt* good enough.

She suggested they get married.

"All right!" he said. And it was the last enthusiastic thing he ever said.

She didn't tell her mother that she was getting married because she didn't see the point. Though it had originally been Charlotte's idea, she knew Charlotte wasn't capable of celebrating what was meant to be a happy moment unless, perhaps, it was Camille's happy moment. She was no longer sure how her mother would interpret the wedding. Marriage had been Charlotte's idea, and yet she resented Isaac for separating them. She decided Charlotte's validation wouldn't mean much one way or another.

They did a ten-minute civil ceremony at the courthouse, then drove twenty minutes to Applebee's to celebrate. Other than her decision to have and keep Camille, it was the most important one she'd made in her life. And she was satisfied with it.

However, after a few months of marriage, something was up. Isaac had always been a little strange. He got excited about everything from making bitters to quoting Bible verses. And he'd been excited about her. But things started to change not long after they got married. He became sullen, spending long stretches of time lying on the couch watching *M*A*S*H*. They rarely had the same shifts at Copperhead, but she noticed he was making mistakes at work: he forgot to tilt the glass when he pulled a pint, he stirred margaritas, he told a customer there was pinot noir when there was only pinot grigio.

"Is everything all right?" she asked him several times. "You seem off."

"Yeah, yeah," he'd answer. "I'm fine."

But he wasn't fine. He started missing shifts because he couldn't get out of bed if Corinna wasn't around to mobilize him. She covered for him as long as she could. But it was only a matter of time before their boss noticed. He didn't even tell him to his face that he was fired; he told Corinna. She brought home Burger King and told him that he'd lost his job.

He barely shrugged. "A man reaps what he sows."

At first, Corinna tried to help him get a new job, but it became clear that he was in no condition to work. He wasn't quoting just scripture anymore. He'd become convinced that the earth was flat—which was somehow related to the New World Order and their insistence upon deceiving good hardworking Americans. He became frenetic and fast-talking, rambling loudly about Johnny Washington "shucking and jiving for white folks."

"That man don't even take care of his kids. I do more for his damn kids than he does," he said once within Camille's earshot. Corinna froze, but Camille didn't react; she continued sorting the beads in her jewelry-making kit. This, too, concerned her: how easily Camille ignored him.

She considered taking him to the doctor, but they didn't have insurance. She thought about going back to the library and doing research of her own but was frightened of what she might find. She went to his parents, and they told her to pray.

The consequences of losing Isaac's income came faster than the unemployment check could arrive. She picked up doubles, then asked for and was granted a raise. But it wasn't enough. She could have moved back in with her parents, but she couldn't take Isaac to their house. And she couldn't leave him. She felt like she was running across quicksand, but she wasn't fast enough.

The first time Corinna hit Camille—really *hit* her—she couldn't even remember what Camille had done. She had no recollection of picking up the belt, but she did remember standing over her daughter with her arm raised. She dropped the belt and sobbed. Camille promised she would do better, which was the first time she'd acknowledged her bad behavior. Maybe they were finally on the right track.

But Camille did not keep her promise. Isaac was no longer bathing. Corinna wasn't sleeping or eating enough, and in her rare moments of quiet and stillness, she could feel the quicksand pulling on her. Her throat constricted. Her vision blurred. Her hands went numb.

Eventually, Corinna had a profound, sparkling moment of clarity as Camille stood with her arms crossed over her chest, refusing to get beat. Again. Corinna wasn't proud of it, but she'd hit Camille several times over the course of several months, even leaving bruises. There wasn't enough time to reflect upon her parenting. But suddenly, it occurred to her: she was not being a Great Mom. This was not the best place for Camille to be.

She was doing the right thing, she told herself over and over again as she drove away from her mother's house, without Camille and without plans to retrieve her.

Corinna's body ached for days. She took ibuprofen. She drank whiskey. She tried a couple of Percocet provided by a coworker. Nothing helped.

Charlotte

FALL 2001

A banging sound woke Charlotte from a deep sleep. When she stood, her right leg was completely numb, and she almost fell to the carpet. She dragged her foot behind her and hobbled to the door. Before she had a chance to say anything, her granddaughter was in her arms. Corinna stood behind her, her hair askew and clothes rumpled. She wasn't wearing any shoes, and her feet were ashy and dirty. She looked like she'd been in a fight.

"What the hell happened to you, Corinna?"

"Oh, Mama. I'm tryin' and tryin', and I just don't know what to do," Corinna said. And then she half ran, half stumbled, to her car and drove away.

Well, *shit*, Charlotte thought to herself as she carried Camille to the bathroom. She had dreamed of this moment. But she hadn't seen it coming.

She set the girl down on the lid of the toilet seat and ran the water as hot as it would go. When the tub was full, Charlotte poured in cucumber-melon scented bubble bath, and gestured for Camille to stand and lift her arms. As Charlotte undressed her, she saw that Camille had bruises on her arms and scars and scabs on her back and across the backs of her legs.

"Oh, my," Charlotte said and tried to steady her trembling lower lip.

She'd never seen Corinna hit Camille in a way that would leave such marks. But Camille had been acting up. And she was getting older. Maybe she required and could handle a little more discipline. Maybe there was something Charlotte did not understand. Maybe Corinna just needed a break.

That don't give her the right to be beating my baby like this, Charlotte thought. Where would Corinna even have learned such a thing? Charlotte had never ever laid a hand on Corinna. Not *ever*.

"What happened tonight?" Charlotte asked.

"I said I wasn't going to get beat." Camille was now sitting in the bathtub with her knees pulled to her chest. Steam forced her edges and baby hair up and away from two crooked braids.

"That ain't the beginning of the story, is it?"

"No," Camille answered.

"No, what?"

"No, ma'am. It ain't the beginning of the story."

"Then start at the beginning." Charlotte undid Camille's braids and pulled her thick, curling hair into a high ponytail.

"Well," Camille said and pressed her lips together. "I guess it starts with Samantha Miller. She's that redheaded girl who was in my class last year. She's weird." Camille took her hands from around her knees, spread her fingers wide, and held them around her head to indicate how big the girl's hair was. "And," she said. "And."

"And what?"

"Well, Jenny died."

Charlotte squeezed a washcloth, sending soapy water cascading down Camille's bruised shoulder, as she waited for Camille to say more. "That made me extra mad . . . and bad. And that's when I really started getting in trouble, and Mama started beating me."

Charlotte felt something catch in her throat. How had she not noticed things had gotten so bad? Jenny had been dead for over a year.

"She says she don't know what to do with me. I think she means about bullying Samantha. But Samantha and me are friends now. But she still bothers me sometimes cuz she's always so *happy*," Camille said with disgust.

"And what's wrong with that, baby? What's wrong with being happy?"

"You ain't that happy. Mama ain't that happy. Why does she get to be so *happy*? Her daddy's in prison, and she's *still* so happy. It just makes me so *mad* sometimes," Camille said.

"I *am* happy. You make me happy," Charlotte said, stroking the back of Camille's head. Tears rolled down the girl's face, but she made no sound. Children were not supposed to cry like that.

"Oh, honey," Charlotte said, using her thumb to wipe tears from Camille's cheek. "Don't cry. You're going to make me cry." But it was too late. They were both crying. Charlotte lifted her grand-daughter out of the bathtub, wrapped her in a towel, and carried her to the bedroom, where Camille quickly fell asleep. But Charlotte couldn't. She was thinking of her mother. Charlotte knew she'd messed up a lot along the way. But at least, she told herself, she wasn't like Evelyn.

To the wider world, Evelyn was a public intellectual, well known for her work as a scholar, writer, and teacher. Everything about her was immaculate and intelligent, but her knowledge of Black folks and books was especially so. She also liked art. She'd been gifted a beautiful Aaron Douglas original by the artist himself; she hung it in the front hall and lectured everyone who entered the house on the legacy of the Fisk University Art Department.

"That's where I earned my master's," she would say. "Not the Art Department, of course. The English Department."

But though Evelyn may have been the type of woman to give keynote speeches, she was also the type of woman to chase her daughter around the house because her concentration had been broken by "obscenely loud" piano practice. Charlotte was practically invisible to her mother until she was twelve or thirteen, at which point Evelyn became invested in Charlotte's "development into womanhood." She paid close attention to Charlotte's grades, clothes, hair, makeup, and general presentation.

When Charlotte started competing in pageants at her mother's urging, Evelyn made Charlotte practice her walking late into the night. She'd sit in the formal living room, her papers splayed out on the glass coffee table, while Charlotte walked the nearby corridors on her tiptoes with a book on her head. Mostly, Evelyn seemed to be working, but every now and again, Charlotte saw her mother watching her over the tops of her half-moon reading glasses. Sometimes, Evelyn added books to the stack or adjusted Charlotte's posture brusquely. But Evelyn rarely attended the pageants themselves. Instead, she hired people to help Charlotte prepare at the venues. When Charlotte brought home a third-place trophy, Evelyn slapped her and threw the trophy in the trash.

"I expect nothing but the best from you," she told Charlotte, who cradled her own cheek. "And don't be such a damn baby about it."

Evelyn slapped, pinched, and yelled at Charlotte all the time. Those were not the worst things she did to Charlotte. But Charlotte had done none of those things to Corinna, and had assumed it meant Corinna wouldn't do those things either. She realized now that she'd simply enacted a different sort of violence on her daughter. That violence had transmogrified into bruises on her granddaughter's back.

*   *   *

Charlotte startled awake near dawn with the uncanny feeling that her mother was nearby. She looked around the bedroom. David was lying flat on his back with his hands clasped at his torso like he was in a casket, and Camille was smack dab in the middle of the bed, swaddled tight in the comforter. Charlotte smelled something fresh and flowery, which was odd. Charlotte preferred fruity scents. She sniffed Camille's neck and smelled the cucumber melon bubble bath from the night before, but there was another distinct scent in the air. It was lavender, Charlotte realized. Her childhood home in Atlanta was lightly scented with lavender, particularly the sheets and towels. Evelyn sometimes used her pinky to dab lavender oil on her personal correspondence. Charlotte looked at the closet, where she kept the shoeboxes of letters. She slipped out of bed, picked up one of the newer letters, and sniffed it. It smelled like paper. She sniffed at the box. Nothing. She reached for an older box, and still nothing. She inhaled deeply, and the smell seemed to have dissipated.

Charlotte checked the return address on the most recent letter. It was sent from Washington, DC, where a plane had crashed into the Pentagon a few months earlier. Charlotte knew Evelyn was fine, because her letters kept coming like clockwork. But for some reason, Charlotte tore open this envelope and looked for a phone number. And then another envelope. And then another. When she finally found a phone number, she went straight to the beige phone in the kitchen and dialed. The phone rang and rang and rang. She started to hear her mother's voice through the tinny sound. *Chahr-lotte. Charlooootte.* And very suddenly, she snapped out of it. She hung up and poured herself something to drink. She sat at the kitchen table she knew ought to be replaced. She crossed her legs and folded her arms.

She sat there, clutching at her own throat, until Camille came to sit in her lap, dressed in one of David's old work shirts. He must have put it on her because she'd fallen asleep naked.

"I'm sorry," she told Camille. "I'm sorry."

Camille wrinkled up her little brow. "Why are you sorry, Mama?"

"Oh, I just am. Do you forgive me?"

"Of course I do, Mama."

Charlotte clutched Camille tighter. "I love you. Your grandaddy loves you. Your mama loves you. She just don't know how to be a good mama all the time. That's my fault."

"Granmama, you're squeezin' me too tight."

"I'm sorry, baby."

"Granmama, why you cryin'?"

"Because I love you so, so much."

"Can I have a Toaster Strudel?"

"You can have two."

Corinna

WINTER 2001

The unemployment checks eventually arrived, and Corinna's finances improved. But she didn't retrieve Camille from her mother's house. Even when she was able to stop working doubles, and had enough to eat, she didn't go get Camille. She was concerned with Camille *feeling* safe, and she knew that wasn't with Isaac. Corinna didn't think Isaac was dangerous. He did sometimes fly into rages, not unlike David once had. But, unlike David, he never directed his anger at his wife. She did realize that this could change, as she understood so little of what was happening in his head. Either way, it was better not to have Camille there.

When she thought about it, she got angry that her parents hadn't considered her feelings—especially feelings of safety—as much as she considered Camille's. But she always pulled herself together, shook her head, and moved on. There was nothing she could do about the past, she reminded herself. No point in being sad about it. And how embarrassing to be jealous of a child.

She knew she needed to give her mother money at some point, but she couldn't face her just yet. It wasn't shame that kept her away, more that she didn't have a plan. It wouldn't be good enough to just do the best she could for Camille. Now that her head was above water, they could do better than survive, but not without a plan. Now that she had time to think, she thought of Dr. Evelyn Gwendolyn Jackson, the living ghost. She returned to the library to research her grandmother. The woman clearly had money; her house had been featured in an interior design magazine. And in the article, she mentioned that this house was her "West Coast base," which meant she must have *other* homes.

Corinna went to the dollar store and bought a small notebook. On the first page, she wrote in capital letters: "BETTER THAN GOOD ENOUGH."

She thought about it for weeks. She made notes, she did calculations, she researched schools and guardianship. She talked to Delia, who surprisingly didn't have much to say about the revelation of Charlotte's origins.

"Yeah, I knew she wasn't like us," Delia sighed. "Life broke her down pretty good, but it was a different kind of broke down, ya know what I mean?"

Corinna did know what she meant. Charlotte's brand of sadness didn't come from discrimination or hardship like most Black folks in their part of the world. Still, she didn't know what had happened to her mother.

She also considered that since Charlotte had lied about her own mother, she had likely lied about Corinna's father. If he was dead, he hadn't died how Charlotte said he did. She didn't know the truth about him, but she could deduce that it wasn't good. Corinna found it difficult to manage all of her feelings at once. She decided to focus on what might be most advantageous.

She took the cash from Delia and cash from the month before and put it into an envelope, so full of bills that she couldn't seal it. She carried the open envelope around with her for several days until she got up the nerve to drive to her mother's house while Camille was at school.

Corinna had been so distracted for the past few days that she'd forgotten about her black eye until she was in the driveway. Isaac had hit her with a half-hearted swipe when she tried to wake him up from a nap to eat lunch. When he realized what he'd done, he'd cried for an hour.

"I'm really losing it," he'd said. "I'm really losing it."

She tried to hide her eye with her hair, but knew her mother would notice. It was too late to leave, as her mother was in the doorway, looking at her.

Charlotte

WINTER 2001

Corinna didn't call or visit Charlotte for a while. It was the first time since she was born that Charlotte did not hear from her at least once a day. When Camille was at school and David was asleep or watching *The Price Is Right*, Charlotte took her usual post by the window above the kitchen sink. Usually, when she looked out, she wasn't looking for anything in particular. During the day, in the middle of the week, there wasn't much to see out there but patchy grass, uneven gravel, and the hoopties parked in it.

A month and two days passed before Corinna finally came. When she saw her daughter emerge from the Jeep, Charlotte's feet walked her to the front of the house. She opened the inner door and watched Corinna through the glass. She wore her Copperhead tank top and a pair of cutoff jean shorts that hung loosely from her hips. She was far too thin, almost sickly. But her hair was styled into a side-swooped bob that complemented her face shape. She was wearing lip gloss. She carried a handbag that looked like it might be made of genuine leather. From a distance, she looked good, almost glamorous. However, as she approached, Charlotte saw that the hair was only partially hiding a black eye.

"What the fuck happened to you," Charlotte said when Corinna reached the top of the steps.

Corinna turned around and started to descend the steps.

"Wait, wait," Charlotte said and pushed clumsily through the door to the porch. "Wait. I'm sorry. I'm sorry," she said. Corinna stood very still with her back to her mother. "Come inside, please."

Silence.

"Please, honey."

Corinna turned around and let her mother usher her into the house.

"You look like you need a drink."

They sat at the kitchen table, which Corinna had offered to replace months earlier, and Charlotte declined.

"Mama?" Corinna said after she knocked back some Jack.

"Yes, baby?" Charlotte said, surprising herself by leaning forward, eager to hear what Corinna had to say. She straightened up and threw her shoulders back.

"I don't think I can protect her like I'm supposed to."

"From what?"

"From me, mostly," Corinna said, eyes downcast.

Charlotte's stomach sank. "Why don't you leave him? You know you can come back here."

"It's really not about him. Anyway, I can't. He's sick, Mama. Would you leave Daddy?"

"That's different."

"Different how?" Corinna looked up at her mother without lifting her head. The effect was aggressive.

"We never laid a hand on you!" Charlotte whisper-shouted.

Corinna lifted her head and squinted softly. "Well," she said, sounding exasperated, "maybe you should have."

"What the hell is that supposed to mean?"

"I mean that I just never learned what I was actually supposed to do with a child."

Charlotte's cheeks went white-hot. "You're just going to keep punishing me and punishing me, aren't you?"

"You know what? I'm not here to talk about me. I'm here to talk about my daughter," Corinna said. She picked up her purse and produced a thick envelope stuffed with money; bills were literally spilling out. "This is Camille's money," she said. "Some of it, anyway. I'll bring the rest soon."

"What do you mean?"

"I need to give it to you."

"Corinna, if you got something to say, just say it."

"Camille's life is better than mine, but better ain't good enough, Mama."

Charlotte swallowed and cleared her throat. "I know that."

"Well, I don't want her to end up like us, okay? I don't know anything else, but she has so much life ahead of her. She could be a real dancer, take real classes at least. She can do anything she wants if we let her."

Charlotte looked down at the envelope and found herself unable to speak. When she finally found her words, she said, "That's a lot of money."

"And there is more. So much more. She can have the best education, the best everything. I wanted to wait until she was a little bit older, but—"

"You ain't making sense."

"I know that your mother is still alive," Corinna said.

Charlotte clutched her throat. "I don't know what you're talking about," she lied, her cheeks somehow growing even hotter. The heat was spreading throughout her body. She thought bursting into flames might be a small mercy.

"I done some research about the name on that letter. She's a professor. In Washington, DC. She named her bookstore after you."

Charlotte felt like someone had snatched her chair right out from under her, and the only thing keeping her upright was her own strength, pathetic as it was. She was shaking from the effort of keeping her composure.

"Mama, it's okay that you didn't tell the truth. I'm sure you had a good reason. We just gotta do something different." Corinna reached across the table to take her mother's hand. "We gotta try, at least. All I need you to do is reach out to her, and I'll take it from there."

Though Evelyn had not been a wonderful mother, she had always been a fantastic teacher. Charlotte suspected that the years had changed Evelyn like they'd changed her. Even if they hadn't, maybe Evelyn could love Camille like she hadn't loved Charlotte. After all, Charlotte loved Camille like she knew she should have loved Corinna. If nothing else, Evelyn could teach the child about something other than problematic men and brown liquor.

"I haven't seen or talked to her in almost thirty years."

"I know that she writes you. Don't you write her back?"

"No. I don't." Charlotte shrugged and avoided her daughter's attempt at eye contact.

"But why not?"

"That's none of your business."

Corinna recoiled. "Well, could you do it for Camille?"

Charlotte knew that she couldn't say no to doing anything for Camille's good. And the more she thought about it, the more she thought it might be best.

"Okay," she finally agreed, and Corinna's shoulders dropped so heavily with relief that Charlotte thought her arms might dislocate and fall right to the floor. "I'll give her a call."

"Thank you." Corinna smiled a little. "Either way," she said, "I think Camille oughta stay with you. Is that okay?"

"Of course," Charlotte said.

When she was alone again, she poured herself a drink and looked at the money. She didn't count it, just *looked* at it. There were easily a few thousand dollars just lying there on the table, and she still had a great number of questions. She'd never heard of surplus child support. She thought the whole point of child support was that it was *just enough*, but then again, what did she know about child support? Why hadn't Corinna just written her a check?

Hours later, when Camille came crashing into the house, Charlotte was still in the kitchen, staring at the phone mounted on the wall, thinking about what she would say to her mother. Camille pulled herself onto Charlotte's lap. She was heavy, but Charlotte looped an arm around the girl's waist and planted a kiss on the side of her face.

"What are you thinking about, Mama?"

"You."

"You're thinking about me? Why?"

"There's plenty about you to think about, you know. Lots of things to think about when it comes to you."

PART V

Ghosts

Camille

SPRING 2003

CAMILLE CAME HOME from school one afternoon and found a pristine woman sitting at the kitchen table. She froze and looked around. There was no sign of her grandparents. Grandaddy should have been on the couch or porch. Granmama should have been smoking at the kitchen sink. They should be greeting her loudly and enthusiastically, just like they'd done every day for the past two years that she'd lived there. She looked over her shoulder and saw that her grandmother's LeBaron was parked outside. Was this a ghost? She squinted, not sure what signs she was looking for. Perhaps blurry at the edges? Hovering a bit off her seat? A bit translucent, perhaps?

At first glance, Camille thought she was a white woman, but the longer she looked at her, the more her features came into focus: full lips, freckles across her button nose, and kinks in her curly hair. Camille relaxed. Maybe she was just there for a hair appointment.

But where was Granmama? She wouldn't leave a stranger alone in the house like that.

The woman sat with her arms crossed over her chest, and her legs crossed at the ankles, she appeared graceful rather than aggressive. Camille knew she was in trouble if she came home to find either her mother or grandmother sitting like that. But she didn't feel worried. There was something familiar about this woman, though she was positive she had never seen her before.

"Hello," the woman said, with what sounded to Camille like a vaguely British accent. The woman removed a large pair of sunglasses from atop her head and set them down on the table, before she thought better of it and reached into her large handbag and produced a small leather box that she put them in.

"Staring is rude, Camille," said the woman, beckoning her. "Come, come."

Camille was unnerved to find that this woman knew her name. She thought she might be there to get her hair done, but the woman's hair seemed very much "done." The hair was entirely icy gray, cut short on the sides and curly on top, like a lady lawyer she'd seen in *Ebony* the week before.

"Sorry," she said. "Ain't mean to be rude."

In the magazine, the haircut had seemed terribly *modern*.

"Come here and let me have a look at you."

Camille did as she was told. Up close, Camille saw that the woman's eyes were the color of ripe honeydew melon. She'd read about Black people with green eyes but had never seen one of them.

"You're going to be pretty," the woman said as she took Camille by the upper arms and turned her left and right to examine her. "You've got lovely cheekbones," she said with a frown, like she was looking at a pair of shoes at JCPenney's. "How old are you?"

"Ten."

"What's that? Fifth grade?"

"Yes, ma'am."

"And how are you in school?"

"All As."

"Ah. That's very good. Very good. Let me ask you something else. Does the name Evelyn mean anything to you?"

"Ev-eh-lin," Camille repeated. "No."

"That's good. That's good."

"Are you Ev-eh-lin?"

"Yes, I am. That's sharp deduction, little girl."

"Why are you in my granmama's house?"

"Listen here. You're not going to believe this," said Evelyn. She pulled out a package of sugar-free mints and popped two into her mouth without offering one to Camille. "I'm your great-grandmother."

Camille laughed. "That's funny. You're too young."

Evelyn also laughed. "That is funny, isn't it?" She was digging through her purse again. "Honestly, money keeps you young."

"Money?"

"I'm just kidding."

"Oh. Okay. Well, where's Granmama?"

"Oh, I sent her and that man out for some proper food."

"You mean Grandaddy?"

"Well, he's not *my* grandaddy," said the woman. "They've been gone a while. Should be back soon."

"Grandaddy don't really go nowhere," Camille said.

"Pardon?"

"Grandaddy doesn't really go anywhere, sos I was just wondering why he went with Granmama."

"You're a fast one," Evelyn said. "Tough getting anything past you. I wanted to meet you alone."

"Granmama says I'm not really supposed to talk to strangers."

"It's a little late for that, no?" Evelyn had finally stopped digging around in her purse. "Besides, I'm not really a stranger. I'm your great-grandmother. I've just never met you. That's different," she said, seeming ready to talk about something very serious. She gestured to the chair across from her. "Sit down, little girl. We need to talk."

Camille sat down and looked at the woman across from her. She would have guessed she was maybe a little older than Charlotte but not old enough to be Charlotte's mother by any stretch of the imagination. Also, the idea of Charlotte having a mother, someone to tell her what to do, was preposterous.

"But if you my great-grandmother, where you been all this time? How come I've never met you?"

"We can talk about that at another time. Right now, I just want to let you know that I'm here because your mother and grandmother asked me to come."

Camille crossed her arms over her chest, feeling defensive. "Why'd they do that?"

"Because they need some help."

"Help? With me?"

Evelyn paused, closed her eyes for a moment, and said slowly, "Well, *yes*. I heard your mother is having some trouble. Is that right?"

Camille shrugged. "It's more my stepdaddy than anybody."

"Well, she had your grandmother call me and ask for my help."

Camille thought she was doing well. She and Charlotte were waking before dawn to make the forty-five-minute drive to downtown Nashville where Camille was attending a new magnet school on the Eastside. She was taking real ballet classes on the West End, taught by skinny white women and short white men. She didn't have to take the bus past Jenny's house anymore, and she didn't have to wake up in the middle of the night to pray. She hadn't been in trouble for anything in months. Aside from learning that her family was poor, she thought things were good. She had been feeling at ease, even. But now, she knew things were about to change again, and it made her stomach churn.

"Are you here to take me away?" she asked.

"Well, no. Not if you don't want me to. I'm here to start a conversation about what's best for you. And I want you to be involved in the dialogue, okay?"

Camille nodded timidly.

"So, if you decide at the end of this conversation that you want to stay here, you stay here. End of story."

Evelyn

SPRING 2002

Evelyn lived on the corner of 15th and S Street in Northwest Washington, DC. The house, which once belonged to Harlem Renaissance–era poet and playwright Georgia Douglass Johnson, was a new acquisition. An offer to be a full professor at Howard brought her out of partial retirement from her cliffside home in Half Moon Bay, California, where she'd been running a bakery and bookstore specializing in African diasporic literature.

Though her DC neighborhood was not yet fashionable—she'd heard a politician describe the 14th Street Corridor as being "good for nothing but hookers and heroin"—Evelyn hadn't cared. Georgia, whom Evelyn always referred to by her first name, had been a great connector of people; she threw parties in that house. Langston Hughes, Anne Spencer, Zora Neale Hurston, and—of special interest to Evelyn—Gwendolyn Bennett had all set foot in it. The house may have been DC's outpost for the Harlem Renaissance movement. Evelyn could practically see the poets and writers she admired walking around on the aging hardwood floors. She *needed* to own that house, but it was in disrepair. So she did a quick and very expensive renovation to it and the smaller carriage house out back.

But something was off, she realized not long after moving in. Several times, she came home late at night to find every light on, even though she would never have done such a thing. Once, she went to the cabinet for a pan, she found the pots, and the pans were where the pots should have been. She thought her house-keeper was an idiot and fired her. But one night, she set herself up at the dining room table to edit, neatly arranging her tools: a high stack of pages, red felt-tip pen, and a fresh bottle of Wite-Out. She went to fetch herself a glass of wine, and when she returned, her pages had been turned as if someone had been carefully reading through them. She looked cautiously over both shoulders before she shrugged and got started.

She was working on a manuscript about the sacrifices made by women in the Harlem Renaissance. She was having a particularly hard time writing about Gwendolyn Bennett, who died in obscurity after decades serving the movement. But late one night in March, she'd been making notes on her draft with a red pen. After a quick trip to the bathroom, she returned to find a sheet of paper turned over to the blank side. In bloodred writing, there was a message: "Did she know any different? Would the world have allowed anything else?" Evelyn searched the house for signs of an intruder, checking the doors and windows, but all of them were locked. Eventually, she decided that she must be overtired, must have written the words herself and forgotten. She went to bed.

In the morning, the words were still there, and it was clear that the handwriting was not hers. It swirled and looped in a way that Evelyn's block lettering did not. She folded up the page and carried it with her like a gris-gris for weeks. She pulled it out in her office between classes to stare at it and ponder what it meant. She focused on the first of the two questions: "Did she know any different?" *Did* Gwendolyn even realize she had other options? The assumption was that she was ambitious, that she wanted to be remembered like Hughes and Locke and the rest. But many of the women she'd studied from the movement had really been canonized only after they were dead. So Gwendolyn probably did not really have anyone to model her success after. Evelyn swore out loud when she realized her mistake. But was it true? Was this new hypothesis arguable? Obviously, women figured shit out for themselves all the time, but it must have been much harder when you did not see people who looked like you doing what you wanted to do. Evelyn knew a thing or two about that.

Maybe that's why she'd been such a horrible working mother; she'd never seen it modeled for her. No, she admitted. That felt wrong. There was no excuse for the way she'd behaved, not even academia. And as much as she believed in it, academia could not solve her specific emotional troubles.

And so, she couldn't write or edit for days. On a Thursday evening in early spring, she was sitting on her back deck, drinking a glass of sparkling rosé, and thinking about how to save her book. There was only a week left of classes, and this time of year always seemed to be rough on the undergraduate spirit. Three students had come to her office just that afternoon and promptly burst into tears. Evelyn was exhausted, not so much from teaching but from *caring* so damn much.

She realized she was hungry and decided to go out. She splashed water on her face, tucked a thick folder of student papers under her arm, and headed to the little Afghan joint around the corner on U Street, where happy hour ran late. The guy at the door very politely asked to see her ID. She laughed. He laughed. She took a seat at the nearly empty bar. It was an unusually warm day, and everyone else would be on the roof deck.

"The usual, Ms. Jackson?"

"Yessir," she told Josh, the bartender. This was her favorite bar, but was also one of the only bars she'd ever entered in DC because she lived her life only as far north and south as R and W Streets, if she could help it. Occasionally, she took a car over to Georgetown or GW or American, but she never ventured far within the city if she didn't have to. She had never even visited the Smithsonian museums downtown. She didn't want to be in DC. She hadn't wanted to come out of retirement, but a full professorship was too good to be true. At Emory, she'd been an assistant professor. Then, she was an associate at Spelman and again at Stanford, where she stayed for almost a decade, publishing consistently and appearing on national television, but the promotion she expected never came. Granted, she didn't ask for it, but she felt she was too old to beg for what she knew she deserved. So she retired and opened

Charlotte's in an attempt to find a new sense of accomplishment. Around that time, she published what critics deemed to be her best work, a mainstream nonfiction book about women in the civil rights movement. The book got Howard's attention, and they offered her an endowed professorship. She barely even had to teach. She decided she had to take it. Running the bookstore had been fine work, but academia was her first love.

At the bar, Evelyn organized herself to grade, pulling out the papers and putting them in alphabetical order. She produced the rubric she designed especially for the assignment and opened the slim velvet box that contained her beloved rose-gold Caran D'Ache pen, a gift from a customer in Half Moon Bay. She desperately missed her home in California, where it was quiet and cool.

"The mantu, as well?" The bartender turned around from the cash register.

"Of course." She smiled. "I'm a creature of habit, Josh."

She sat and graded until the noise from upstairs became too much. It sounded like there might be belly dancing or something. There was still plenty of work to be done, but she went home to soak in the bathtub with a nice chablis.

*   *   *

Evelyn had never wanted to be a mother or a wife. But she'd done what she thought she was supposed to do. Respectable, upper-middle-class Negro girls were supposed to go to either Spelman or Howard and get engaged before graduation. Her father, Gordon, was the president of Spelman, so naturally she went there.

When she was three months from graduation, and single with no prospects in sight, her mother panicked. Pearl took it upon herself to search high and low for a suitable mate—which meant politely and subtly inquiring with the other Black elite in town. Evelyn was never quite sure where her mother had found James, as he was not quite in their circle.

Evelyn had been skeptical. She'd never heard of James Jackson. And she wasn't fond of the last name. It was *common*, as Pearl

would say. Evelyn liked her own last name: Baudin. But it was un-
heard of for a woman to keep her name back then.

According to her mother, James was a "catch." He came from a
good family. He was dark-skinned but not *too* dark-skinned, handsome, and, importantly, he was a Morehouse man with plans to
attend Meharry in the fall. He proposed less than a month after
they met, and they were married in July on a stifling hot day in a
beautiful church with bad ventilation (the windows didn't open,
if Evelyn remembered correctly) and no air-conditioning. Evelyn
tried to convince her mother that they should wait until fall when
it would be cooler, but Pearl and Gordon had gotten married in
that church in July 1920, and so, the wedding went on. One of
Evelyn's bridesmaids fainted on the way down the aisle, and the
groomsmen's suits were covered in sweat stains. Somehow, Pearl
sat in the front row of the church looking pristine in a powder-blue
suit and an enormous matching church hat replete with ostrich
feathers and Swarovski crystals.

Fortunately for Evelyn, she fell in love with James. He was very
kind and thoughtful, and she thought he was handsome, too, with
caramel-colored skin and beetle-black eyes. His smile was bright
and wide, but also humble and good-natured. Evelyn thought he
might have been a movie star if he weren't so smart and so Black.
His father was a prominent surgeon in Atlanta, and his mother,
who had died when he was young, was heir to a small fortune with
indeterminate origins.

They moved to Nashville at the end of the summer, and Evelyn
did her best to be a good wife. She picked James up from class late
at night and cooked all of his meals with a smile. He loved food
that took a long time, like black-eyed peas and collard greens, and
so she stood by the stove reading Baldwin, Larsen, *Nigger Heaven*,
whatever Black or Black-adjacent books she could get her mother
to send her. She smoked a lot. She started to think about working,
an idea her mother dismissed with a laugh.

"We did not come this far," Pearl said, and Evelyn felt the chill-
iness in her bones through the phone, "for you to work like some

common negress. It's not like you have to worry about money. If you're bored, have a baby."

Evelyn felt her body grow colder at the thought, but she would have never said this out loud. Instead, she said she was too busy taking care of James, which seemed to placate her mother.

After his first year at Meharry, James encouraged her to go back to school as well. She enrolled at Fisk to earn a master's in English, which Pearl begrudgingly accepted.

She and James studied together at night, though Evelyn often stayed up even later to prepare the next day's meals. As sleep-deprived as she was, she loved the rhythm and respectability of it. When it was time for James to start a residency, she took her first teaching position at Fisk, teaching five composition courses in her first semester as a professorial lecturer. Pearl was not pleased, but found it respectable. Evelyn's course load was heavy, but she was tireless. She spent hours and hours preparing lessons when it would have been acceptable to simply stand in front of the class and lecture about commas and bibliographies. And she knew every single one of her students—where they were from, their majors, hobbies, and aspirations.

Meanwhile, their families pressured them for children, but James said he wanted to finish his residency first. Evelyn knew she was supposed to want children but could not imagine herself like the women she saw everywhere on the street, in movies, on TV, in magazine ads. She was not *like* those women. But she got pregnant before the end of residency anyway, and everyone was elated. Evelyn did not know her mother could be so happy. Pearl behaved like getting pregnant was Evelyn's greatest accomplishment to date, which bothered her. Getting pregnant was easy. But she was most annoyed by how happy it made James. He was always touching her belly and gushing about how "sweet" she looked in her big, shapeless, horrible dresses and the tops with Peter Pan collars. She would hate Peter Pan collars for the rest of her life.

She stopped teaching, not because anyone said she should, but because she knew that she was supposed to. She stayed home, retyped her syllabus a few dozen times, and obsessed over elaborate meals. She was heavily pregnant when summer came. The summers in Nashville were hot, but this one was exceptionally so, without a single breeze. When labor came, it felt sudden. She wasn't ready. She needed at least another decade to prepare.

They named the baby Charlotte, after James's dead mother. After a few months, Charlotte's bluish, newborn eyes turned their signature golden-brown, and Evelyn admired the eyes like they belonged to her lover. And yet she struggled to feel any affection for the baby. She did everything she was supposed to do, but without enthusiasm. When the baby was a few months old, they moved to a house nearby and hired a woman to help Evelyn with the baby and the housekeeping. She wished the woman would never leave. She hated being alone with the baby; the responsibility of holding a human's life in her hands was too great.

Evelyn went back to work in the spring, which surprised everyone. Though she was often agitated by lack of sleep, she was relieved to return to the classroom.

Her parents came for Easter that year, bringing along James's father, Arthur, in Pearl's brand-new baby-pink Imperial Crown Chrysler. And they had a good visit. They took turns posing with the baby by the car. They ate honey-baked ham, deviled eggs, macaroni and cheese, and green beans prepared by the housekeeper, which Evelyn passed off as her own.

Pearl couldn't find anything wrong at the house, though she tried. Evelyn caught her running a fingertip along the bookshelves and going through the baby's things. But either everything was as it should be, or Pearl was having some mercy on Evelyn because it was Easter. When they were leaving on Sunday evening so the men could get to work the next morning, Pearl, who usually favored superficial air kisses, wrapped Evelyn in a warm embrace.

Early the following day, Evelyn and James got a phone call. Pearl, Gordon, and Arthur had been in an accident. Their bodies were laid out in the Black section of the morgue, which was dirtier, darker, and smaller than the rest of the facility. Gordon's and Arthur's bodies had been so brutalized in the crash that Evelyn was not allowed to see them. But Pearl's body was as pristine in death as in life. She could have been sleeping if it weren't for a trickle of blood from the corner of her mouth, which Evelyn used her handkerchief to wipe away.

Almost fifty years later, Evelyn still kept that handkerchief on her bedside table, in a velvet jewelry bag. The night that Charlotte called, Evelyn took it out of its pouch and stared at it. She started to work the equation of her life before she stopped herself. It was pointless, and the solution would always be the same; she was alone, and she'd made it that way. She carefully folded the handkerchief and returned it to its pouch, then slipped into satin pajamas for bed. She took a few Valium and fell into a deep, dreamless sleep.

Evelyn was unproductive and distracted for the next few days, as were her students. It was difficult to get them to do the reading at the end of the semester when they were also working on their final projects, and usually, she would have lectured them about wasting her time and their own time. Instead, she rambled on about *Beloved*.

"*Beloved* is about ghosts. Ghosts are more than simply spirits of the dead, aren't they? Ghosts aren't just dead people who don't know they're dead or who are angry that they're dead. They are the remnants of the energies of the dead, right? Beloved, who may or may not be a ghost in the traditional, most shallow sense of the word, is Sethe's ghost. As in, Beloved haunts Sethe. But you notice how Beloved isn't just Sethe's ghost, is she? She's Denver's ghost, too. She's Paul D's ghost, isn't she? A ghost haunts the whole damn house, you see?" she said while clicking her Caran D'Ache. "A ghost haunts the whole damn house," she repeated. "And like houses, people can be haunted."

A homely girl raised her hand. Evelyn nodded, and the girl started speaking, but Evelyn barely listened as the student said something about "generational trauma."

Evelyn nodded slowly to give the impression she had been listening. "That's exactly right."

There was more strange activity in the house. Evelyn found notes all over her manuscript in swirling red letters, almost always questions that Evelyn thought she ought to have the answers to: *Are you arguing that frustration is an admirable concept? Is it natural for a young writer to feel anxiety at the dawn of their career? What if she didn't have anyone to model herself after?*

Perhaps Georgia Douglas Johnson or Gwendolyn Bennett, or both of them, were haunting her. But she could not decide if the ghost or ghosts were antagonizing her or offering constructive criticism. Regardless, she had a feeling that something significant was about to happen.

She was sitting at her dining room table trying to decide whether or not she should give up on the entire manuscript when the phone rang, startling her. She knocked over her wine with her elbow, swearing as she tried to locate the phone. She cursed herself for getting a cordless. She was out of breath when she finally answered. It was Charlotte.

"Can you talk?" she asked.

"Of course!" Evelyn said in an odd, high-pitched squeal she did not recognize. Her heart thudded in her chest.

"Well, we have ourselves a bit of a situation," Charlotte spoke with a drawl that reminded Evelyn of Pearl, who had been proud of her aristocratic accent. "*We* being Corinna and me."

"Oh, how's that?"

"I don't really know how to start. Well . . ." Charlotte paused, and when she started again, she sounded choked up. "It's not really about—It's more about—"

Evelyn opened her mouth to say something but thought better of it.

"I'm saying all this really to say that I—I mean *we*—might like to have you in our lives."

Evelyn's mind should have been racing, but it was completely and utterly blank.

"Hello?" Charlotte said after another long pause.

"Yes, yes. I'm here," Evelyn said. "I'm sorry. I just don't know what to say."

"Well, would you *like* to be in our lives?"

"Oh, yes! Of course, Charlotte. That's all I've ever wanted."

Evelyn realized Charlotte had not read her letters. She'd been writing to a ghost. Or perhaps Evelyn was the ghost, haunting Charlotte.

Charlotte

SPRING 2002

While Charlotte worked up the nerve to call her mother, she and Corinna had a honeymoon period. They played a lot of spades and drank a lot of whiskey. Charlotte thought things might be fine as they were, but Corinna still wanted to send Camille away. Her idea was that the girl would live with Evelyn during the year and attend an incredible school in DC alongside the children of diplomats and scholars. She could go to a real ballet school. She wouldn't have to commute almost two hours every day.

"And just imagine the things Evelyn can give her that we can't," Corinna whispered over the table one night when David and Camille were watching *The Price Is Right*.

"Like *what*?" Charlotte asked, knowing the answer damn well.

"Her own room, her own *experiences*, a *role* model."

The idea made Charlotte sick. More importantly, she didn't want Camille to leave. Camille made her the best thing she'd ever been: a grandmother. Who was she without her? Some raggedy old bat with a criminal record, that's who. And Charlotte had had no intention of laying eyes on her mother ever again. The idea of Camille with that woman—

"Fuck!" she shouted and slammed the table with her fist.

Corinna leaned away from the table and asked gently: "Mama, what's your problem with her? What happened?"

Charlotte swiped at a tear rolling down her cheek. She went to pour herself another glass of whiskey but found that her hand was shaking too badly. Corinna did it for her. She thought maybe her daughter would reconsider this plan if she knew. But she couldn't find the words.

She managed to bring the glass of whiskey to her lips. "Does it matter?"

"Of course it matters, Mama."

"She didn't remarry, did she?"

"I don't think so . . . Doesn't seem like it."

That was somewhat of a relief. Charlotte didn't want a man in the house whom she didn't know. But she still wasn't convinced. "You know, you could leave that man, we could all move to Nashville, and she could go to school up there," she offered. "Without all that driving. You could probably get a better job up there, too."

"Ain't no money for that, Mama. You know that."

"What about all that money from her father?"

"I'm not supposed to use it like that. And if we spend it on that, there's no money for anything else."

"We could make up the difference. There's lots of heads to do up there."

"Mama."

"We own this house. It's paid for. We could sell it."

"Even if somebody bought this shithole, the money won't last long up there, Mama. And you'd be spending money that you're not spending now. And there is *no more* money to spend."

Charlotte lit a cigarette. "We could rent it out."

"Who's gon' rent this raggedy-ass house you been smoking in for the last thirty years, Mama?"

"We could fix it up."

"With what *fucking* money, Mama?"

Charlotte sighed. She knew Corinna was losing patience, but that didn't mean she would give up.

"Unless you tell me this woman did something horrible, I think it's what's best."

"She did something horrible."

"What, then? Was it any worse than what you did to me?"

That was a good question. Did Charlotte deserve to lose Camille as a penalty for what she'd done to Corinna, or rather had not done? She caught herself calculating what had happened to her and weighing it against what had happened to Corinna, and knew it would get her nowhere. She'd been fumbling her own feelings for a long time; she was hardly proficient in basic emotion, but she knew comparison was not productive. Still, Charlotte did not like being accused that way. "And haven't I paid for it enough? Raising *your* daughter for you?"

Corinna crossed her arms. A cold smirk crossed her lips. "You getting to raise that girl is a gift to you, Mama. And you know it."

"Well, you're welcome to take her anytime."

"Oh, please. You can't *live* without her."

"And what about you? You *can*?"

"I don't *want* to live without her. But there are more important things than what I want."

Corinna was right. "We don't even know if she would take her."

"Well, call her. See what she says."

"She's a selfish woman; I bet she says no."

"If she says no, we can stop having this conversation. It's getting old."

*   *   *

When Camille fell asleep at the kitchen table—her face landing gently on a grilled cheese sandwich—at five p.m., after another long day at school, Charlotte decided it was time to call.

She loathed the idea of asking for help, especially this sort of nebulous help, from anyone, but especially from Evelyn. She picked up the phone and slammed it back down several times. A sour feeling stirred in her gut. She didn't want anything from Evelyn. And yet she felt Evelyn owed her something, if not everything.

Charlotte held the phone in her trembling fist, thinking of how she got here. She hadn't chosen a life of poverty over one of luxury and privilege for no reason.

She had a wound. Maybe "injury" was more accurate. Perhaps her injury was like David's; he had few visible scars, but his body bore evidence of trauma in his tortured expression and shuffling gait. She hoped bringing Evelyn back into her life wouldn't be like falling four stories off the side of a building for a second time.

Her mother would never be able to hurt her as badly now, though she had more to lose than she had as a young girl. But what could her mother take from her? Her mother wasn't stupid. She would not make the same mistakes a second time. Or she would at least try not to. And there had been no one else to look out for Charlotte. Camille was cared for by more adults than most.

She punched at the numbers with her second knuckle to avoid chipping her new manicure.

"This is Evelyn."

Her mother's voice hadn't changed. Charlotte wasn't sure what she'd been expecting, but she hadn't prepared for the raspy lilt to be the same.

"Hello?"

Her mind went dark. She'd once been quite good at turning her mind off. She'd done it when her mother was being exceptionally truculent or when Wayne came to her door. She could appear present, even have a complete conversation, but be entirely unavailable. She reentered the conversation near the end in time to hear herself say:

"Well, would you *like* to be in our lives?"

"Oh, yes! Of course, Charlotte. That's all I've ever wanted."

Then it was over. She was safe.

The last she saw of Evelyn was her mother as a wild woman. She'd been drunk, sweaty, her dressing gown half off, but somehow, she was steady on her stilettos. Her mother had been terrifying, and Charlotte had not and never would be as afraid of anyone as she had been that day.

She told Corinna what she'd done, and her daughter smiled. "Thank you, Mama." It was the first time in a long time that Corinna had thanked her for anything.

"But—" Charlotte said.

"But what?"

"She's too young. She's just a little girl."

"That's the whole point. She'll go before it's too set in."

"Too set *in*? We ain't no stain. We love her. That's what's important right now."

Corinna crossed her arms. "When, then?"

Charlotte thought of herself at twelve years old. Her father had been dead a few years, and her mother just out of a long depression following it. Evelyn had taken her to get her ears pierced with twenty-four-karat gold studs. When the piercings were healed, her mother replaced the earrings with a pair of dainty diamond studs, given to her while Charlotte sat at her mother's vanity. It was white and gold with blinding, Hollywood-style lights that illuminated the various crystal and crystalline bottles and jars full of perfumes, powders, and creams. Evelyn hummed while she brushed Charlotte's hair away from her ears and pulled it into a low knot. Some kind of jazz was playing softly on the record player.

"Aren't you pretty," Evelyn whispered as she slipped a couple of bobby pins into Charlotte's bun. "Getting to be a real lady. You've got your menstrual. And you've got your ears pierced."

Charlotte smiled at her reflection.

"It's time to start your *education*," Evelyn said as she opened a drawer and produced a brand-new box of *Estée* perfume. "It's time to start preparing for cotillion, for coming out. You're not a little girl anymore." She opened the box to produce the plain, beautiful bottle. "You have to focus on the future now. All you have is your future, really."

She took Charlotte's left wrist and sprayed it generously. Charlotte knew, from watching her mother, to press her wrists together and then to press the moistened wrist to her neck.

"Good girl," Evelyn said and squeezed Charlotte's shoulders. "Do you understand what I'm telling you, Charlotte?"

Charlotte nodded because she thought she understood. But she actually didn't understand at all. Her mother was trying to tell her that becoming a woman would be a painful, challenging experience, and the world could eat her up. Charlotte understood this now and wished she'd prepared better. She wished she'd prepared to defend herself against her own mother, who would become the toughest force she would ever know. But hindsight is twenty-twenty, she thought.

Charlotte could admit that Evelyn had equipped her for a certain world. Whether or not Charlotte was meant for that world was another question altogether. Still, she figured Evelyn was probably best suited to facilitate Camille's entry into that world.

"When she's twelve," Charlotte told Corinna. "She can go."

"Twelve? Why twelve?"

"That's when a girl starts her education, the one that matters."

"Education?"

"For being a woman."

Corinna rolled her eyes and sighed. "Okay, Mama."

Evelyn

EARLY SPRING 2003

Evelyn hadn't been back to Nashville since her parents died. She and James had returned to Atlanta several weeks after the accident with Charlotte and moved into her parents' house, where all of their things were exactly as they'd left them. The housekeeper must not have come because there were still coffee cups on the table in the breakfast nook and clothes in the hampers. Even after she and James had put almost all of her parents' things into the guest bedroom and swapped out much of the furniture, it felt like any minute she could turn a corner to see her mother standing there in her pumps and pearls. James swore the house was haunted. He joked that he could still hear Pearl drumming her nails on the dining room table and Gordon muttering, "Yes, Pearl. Yes, Pearl." She'd stayed in that house for the next twenty years, and the feeling that she was living in her parents' home never wore off.

Evelyn had refused to go anywhere near Nashville after the accident, though it happened over a hundred miles south in Catoosa County near Chattanooga, at the Georgia border. But she'd always associated the trauma of her parents' death with Nashville. She knew she was too sentimental about it but found that she couldn't help it. She was invited to speak at Tennessee State and Fisk several times, but always had a conflict—sometimes fabricated, sometimes real.

She thought she might recognize the city in 2003, but she didn't. The airport didn't look the same, and the area around it had been practically rural the last time she was there; now, a slew of fast-food restaurants lined the road to the east and west.

On her way to Chilly Springs, she drove by the house she'd shared with James and parked across the street. The house was in bad disrepair and smaller than she remembered. They hadn't lived there long, but she'd been happy there, kind of. James had been happy there. Her mother never criticized her in that house.

The neighborhood had once been reserved for Nashville's Black upper-middle class. Black people still lived there, but it wasn't a "good" neighborhood anymore. It reminded her a bit of her neighborhood in DC. Certainly, in a few years, both neighborhoods would be invaded by gentrifiers. As she drove away, she noticed a rusted-out pink Chrysler parked on a nearby lawn.

When she got to Charlotte's house, she found that it was small and mildly dilapidated but painted a pleasant robin's-egg blue. The porch railing was splintered, but two white rocking chairs sat on either side of a small matching table. A child's bike leaned against the side of the house, and a larger bike lay in the middle of the lawn. The closest neighbors were separated by a few hundred yards of patchy, yellowing grass in each direction.

Evelyn lowered her head for a rare prayer, and when she lifted it, a woman was standing on the porch, barefoot, wearing stiff, light-wash jeans and what looked like a little boy's boxy white undershirt. Her brow was furrowed, and she was smoking an unfiltered cigarette. She knew this was Charlotte because of her golden eyes, pitch-black hair, and posture. But otherwise, she was unrecognizable.

After she emerged from the car, she was unsure of how to proceed. Charlotte's eyes were the same eyes that Evelyn knew, surrounded by luxurious lashes but also dark circles; her stare, however, was so cold and so without recognition that Evelyn opened her mouth to say, "It's me." But Charlotte cut her off.

"Hi, Evelyn," she said dryly. "Come in."

Evelyn cautiously climbed the porch steps, uncertain of their stability. She was glad she'd worn flats, as there were many knots in the wood that a stiletto heel might have gotten stuck in.

A tall, very thin man with striking dark blue eyes leaned on a cane in the middle of the small living room, looking like he had been interrupted on his way to do something. Like Charlotte, he had a certain hardness about him, but his face changed quickly into a warm smile, revealing a mouthful of chiclet-shaped teeth, and she saw that he had been handsome once.

"This is my husband, David. David, this is Evelyn."

David reached out to shake Evelyn's hand. He had an incredibly firm handshake and a thick Louisiana accent, and he greeted her politely.

"I'll leave y'all to it," he said on his way out.

Alone again, the women stood in the living room awkwardly. Unsure of what to do with her hands, Evelyn clasped them behind her like a waiter at a decent restaurant, and noticed things around the room. Everything in the room seemed curiously and uncomfortably low: the couch appeared to have been knocked off its feet, the carpeting pile reminded her of a cheap dish towel, and the ceiling couldn't have been more than seven and a half feet high. The only art on the walls were a couple of children's drawings in plastic frames, and they all barely covered places where the wall had been patched. She wanted to tell Charlotte that you're supposed to sand the plaster down before you paint over it, but she knew that would be a stupid thing to say.

Evelyn decided to focus on the photos of the pretty little girl with beetle-black eyes. Without thinking, she picked up one of the framed photos from a wood side table that was the nicest piece of furniture in the room. The girl's front teeth were missing, and she wore two plastic chokers and a cheap-looking gold-colored necklace with an oversize heart-shaped locket. Her collared shirt was rumpled, and her braids were a little crooked.

"She has your father's eyes," she said, sounding much more composed than she felt.

Charlotte snatched the photo away, and Evelyn knew she'd said the wrong thing. There was no way that her daughter remembered James's face, let alone his eyes. He'd been dead for forty years, and Charlotte had left Atlanta with hardly anything, let alone a photo. Evelyn thought of apologizing, but Charlotte's face softened. "Does she?" she asked. She rubbed the glass with her thumb as if it were the girl's cheek.

"She does."

"This is from first grade, I think. Maybe second. She lost her teeth late."

"Can we sit?" Evelyn asked. She was starting to feel a bit weak at the knees.

They sat at the table in the kitchen, which was covered in green, white, and brick red tile that called to mind a quilt pattern. Evelyn watched as Charlotte lit a cigarette and poured two glasses of whiskey. Evelyn never drank whiskey and had quit smoking two decades earlier but took the whiskey when it was offered, and Charlotte lit her cigarette with one hand from across the table.

"Well," Charlotte said as if she might say more, but didn't. She took a long drag from her cigarette. With a cough, she said, "What's in the past is in the past, right?"

Evelyn threw the whiskey back and dropped the glass to the table more forcefully than she intended. "I'm sorry," she said. "I thought you would come back. I prayed that you would come back."

Charlotte stared at the floor. "Without my baby, right?"

Evelyn was not sure how to respond. Of course she expected Charlotte to come back without the baby. How would that have *looked*? Her daughter shook her head. "It don't matter," she said, and Evelyn bit her tongue. Charlotte's natural speech pattern had always been pedestrian, and she didn't have a good grasp of grammar as a concept. Her accent was like molasses. Evelyn spent a lot of time screaming about her ending her gerunds without the *g* and dropping *r*s. She sometimes thought Charlotte was doing it just to piss her off, because onstage in front of pageant judges, her accent went from the fields to the house.

"This is about Camille," Charlotte said, a far-off look in her eyes.

"Right." Evelyn's mind was uncharacteristically blank.

"You'll meet her?" Charlotte offered.

"Of course!" Evelyn said, a little too eagerly. It was becoming clear to her that the power dynamic had shifted. Evelyn had the money, but Charlotte had the child.

"I don't think I oughta be here when you do."

Again, Evelyn waited for her brain to catch up.

"I'll take that little Mercedes as collateral," Charlotte said. "I need to go to the store anyhow."

Evelyn nodded, not sure what else to do. "Can I give you some money?"

At first, Charlotte seemed reluctant to accept the cash that Evelyn pulled out of her wallet, but eventually presented her palm to accept it.

Evelyn was left with no instructions about what to do when Camille arrived, but wound up with plenty of time to think about it. She wanted to take a look around the house but found herself rooted to her seat. She rifled through her purse, looking for something to do with her hands. She took everything out and put it all back in, then pulled the bag into her lap and clutched it to her chest. She scanned the kitchen: it wasn't unclean, but the linoleum was peeling, the laminate on the counter was graying, there were cooking and tobacco stains in the paint and water spots on the ceiling. She had never seen anything quite like it, not with her own eyes. She was ashamed of her disgust.

It felt like hours had passed before she heard the front door creak open and slam. Before she saw the rest of the little girl, she saw James's eyes: big, dark, and almond-shaped. Then the rest of her came into focus. She was skinny. She had Pearl's lips, maybe? Her top lip was bigger than her bottom. When her face was relaxed, you could see her teeth through the crack in her lips. She had not yet grown into her features, but it was clear that she was going to be a beauty, if not the traditional variety. Dark skin like hers had never been in vogue, and Evelyn was not confident it would be, especially not in the middle of nowhere Tennessee. She could tell the girl was intelligent and curious. Beautiful and smart. Good Lord. Her heart rate rose as the realization congealed. Corinna and Charlotte were right to seek help.

Later that evening, as she prepared to leave, Evelyn thanked Charlotte. "She's an amazing little girl. But you knew that."

They were standing on the porch in near-absolute darkness. The porch light flickered but offered very little illumination.

When Charlotte said nothing, Evelyn continued in spite of herself: "I'd be honored to be involved. Whatever you need. I'm happy to have her come and stay with me. Any time. In the summer, during the school year, whenever." She realized she was rambling, but she failed to stop until Charlotte finally cut her off.

"She ought to stay a few more years with me before she goes anywhere with you. Be a little girl a little bit longer."

That stung a bit, but Evelyn acknowledged it wasn't anything she didn't deserve. "Oh," she said, struggling to hide her disappointment and hurt. "Well."

"She's only ten."

Evelyn felt her hands shaking. She took her handbag in both hands to keep from dropping it on the splintered porch floor.

At first, she'd had some hesitation about becoming responsible, at her age, for another living being. But from the moment she laid eyes on the little girl, she'd known she would take her, and hoped it would be sooner rather than later. She was prepared to bring her home that night, just as she was, and figure the rest out later. She wished she hadn't fed her that stupid line about staying if she wanted to stay. Of course, she would want to stay. Evelyn was a stranger. But she didn't want to remain one.

Finally, she nodded.

"You'll get to know her, of course," Charlotte said.

"Of course." Evelyn closed her eyes as she nodded again.

"I'm thinking the summer she turns twelve. Her birthday's in August. She can start the seventh grade with you."

Evelyn's eyes were still closed. She couldn't bear to look at Charlotte and think of her at age twelve. "Yes, of course," she said, before descending the stairs with a sigh. She was seventy-one-goddamn-years-old. She could be dead in two years, though her doctor said she had the heart and lungs of a forty-year-old. She'd taken great care of herself, though she'd never really known why until that moment on the dilapidated porch somewhere south of Nashville. Still, Charlotte's choice to bring Evelyn all the way there, introduce her to the girl, and then pull her away felt cruel. If Charlotte was punishing her, Evelyn had no choice but to be punished.

Why twelve? Evelyn thought as she drove a half hour to the closest decent hotel her travel agent could find within fifty miles of Charlotte's house. When Evelyn was twelve, Pearl likely had a chat with her about "becoming a woman." She'd probably started her cycle around that time. Had Evelyn had a similar conversation with Charlotte? She couldn't remember. When Charlotte was twelve, Evelyn was barely conscious. She was getting out of bed and going about her business, but she did it while floating in a lithium cloud.

Evelyn fell asleep thinking about the coming two years. Two years was nothing, she decided. She would stay close, but not suspiciously so.

PART VI

Becoming

Camille

SPRING/SUMMER 2004

MOST OF CAMILLE'S visits with her mother happened at Charlotte's, when Corinna would come over to play spades and drink or to get her hair done. Sometimes, she drank too much and slept on the couch. Corinna seemed nicer now that they lived separately; she was always asking Camille for hugs that lasted just a little too long. They were almost never alone together.

Camille did not like to sit with her feelings about her mother for too long. If she did, she felt wounded, though she was unsure of the exact location or cause of the injury. Had her mother abandoned her? Or chosen Isaac over her? Did her mother even want to be her mother? Each time she wondered about it, she felt dizzy, lightheaded, confused—kind of how she had felt when Jenny died, but quadrupled. If she examined her mother's love too closely, she might lose the most basic, essential love the world had to offer, so she shook it off as quickly as she could. Though she was able to release herself from the thoughts, she couldn't release herself from the tiny injuries that occurred each time her mind went there. And she didn't understand these smaller injuries any better than the larger ones. She only knew that she was bleeding.

Camille wondered if her mother was in love with Isaac, and if that kind of love might outweigh the one her mother had for her. What was love, anyway? She knew her grandparents loved each other, and they loved her. But their love looked nothing like whatever was happening at Isaac's house, where Corinna seemed to ignore Isaac except for feeding him and making him drink water. He was like a low-maintenance pet, a turtle or a hermit crab or something. So Camille didn't pay much attention to him either.

One Wednesday morning, Camille woke up to see that the sun was out. She and Charlotte were usually long gone by the time the sun came up. Something was wrong. Her thoughts raced: her grandparents were dead in the next room, the world had ended, she was the last human alive. Camille tentatively got out of bed to find Charlotte sitting at the rickety table with her chin in her hand, looking even more tired than usual.

She was relieved. "Oh, good, I thought you were dead."

"What?" Charlotte said. "You're becoming a worrier, you know that? You ain't got nothing to worry about. I've got you."

Camille wrapped her arms around Charlotte's neck, wanting to believe her.

"Go get dressed so we can go get your mama."

"Why?"

"Isaac shot himself," Charlotte said as she prepared to rise from her seat at the table.

"Is he okay?"

Charlotte released a noisy sigh. Camille braced herself for impact.

"No, he's dead," Charlotte said without making eye contact.

This didn't hurt so bad. She felt a bit sick, assuming there was more, but Charlotte only urged her to go get dressed.

"He did it in front of her," Charlotte said in the car on their way to the hospital, almost an hour's drive. She couldn't believe how nonchalant her grandmother was, sipping loudly on a Big Gulp and munching on a chicken biscuit they'd picked up at 7-Eleven.

Camille realized she'd been digging her thumbnail in the side of her index finger. The weight of Isaac's death had not yet landed. But this new information rang loudly in her ears. She wished she was at school. She was in the middle of a complex art project she wanted to finish: a surrealist diorama of the gas station death scene from *The Great Gatsby*.

"But don't say anything to her," Charlotte told her, crumbs of greasy biscuit falling from her lips and fingers. "Just speak when spoken to, okay?"

Charlotte parked, and Camille stayed in the car. She sat on her hands and stared straight ahead, attempting to keep her mind blank. When that didn't work, she opened a sun-bleached copy of *Us Weekly* and stared at a spread of Penélope Cruz and Tom Cruise on vacation. This was better. Camille had never heard of Saint Tropez and she had never been on vacation; she kept busy thinking about what one might do while on holiday in the French Riviera.

When Charlotte finally returned with Corinna, Camille hardly recognized her mother. Her hair was pulled back tight, but stray hairs stood up straight near her temples, like she was a little girl. She was wearing a T-shirt and basketball shorts Camille had never seen before. Charlotte guided Corinna toward the car, like she sometimes did with David when his medication made him forget where he was. Camille pulled down the sun visor for her mother before she crawled into the back seat. She couldn't help but stare at Corinna, who looked like she'd just been slapped across the face with something nasty.

"Go and run your mama a bath," Charlotte told Camille as soon as they parked in front of the house, and Camille bolted up the porch stairs. "Not too hot!" Charlotte shouted after her.

David was sitting on the couch watching *The Price Is Right*.

"Morning, Grandaddy," she said as she rushed past him.

"Morning, baby," he answered with a smile but did not look away from the television.

She turned on the taps, then sat on the closed toilet seat lid to wait. She ran her fingers under the water to check the temperature. By the time her mother and grandmother were at the bathroom door, the tub was full. She stood in the doorway and watched her grandmother undress her mother and help her step into the tub. With painful lethargy, Corinna lowered herself into the water. As she submerged her body, the water turned an alarming reddish-brown, and Charlotte slammed the bathroom door in Camille's face.

Camille did not understand what she'd seen. Was her mother bleeding? She stood for a moment and stared at the hollow, pressed-wood door with its peeling, chipped varnish. A single tear formed and rolled onto her cheek. Annoyed with herself, she wiped at it with the sleeve of her oversize sweatshirt, then retreated to the living room where David sat, unmoved by the calamity.

"You not going to school?"

"Nuh-uh. 'Cause of what Isaac did, Granmama said."

"Oh, yeah," he said casually. "Your mama's going to want you close by."

"That's what Granmama said, but Mama ain't looked at me once."

"Trust me, she want you right here," he said. All of the thin, flat pillows on the couch had been stacked up around David to support his back. He reached behind himself, pulled out the fluffiest one, and handed it to Camille. "You look tired," he said. She knew not to protest, and took it and rested her head on the other end of the couch. She pressed her feet against her grandfather's leg, feeling the comfort of the thick denim on the bottoms of her feet. David repositioned the waffle-knit blanket in his lap so that her feet were covered. He patted them and said: "Take yourself a nap. You'll feel better when you wake up."

As if all she'd needed was permission, she immediately fell into a deep sleep. When she woke up, her mouth was hot and tingling, and her feet were no longer touching denim. Instead, Charlotte was sitting where David had been, and Camille was surprised to find that she had socks on her feet.

"Where Grandaddy go?" Camille sat up, and Charlotte immediately pulled her into an uncomfortably tight embrace, making Camille's spine release a loud, crunchy pop.

"I love you," Charlotte said with a maudlin frown. "You know that?"

"Yes," Camille answered, annoyed at being touched so soon after waking up.

The sun was bright and shining outside, but reality slowly reconstructed itself in her mind. Her heart felt like it was beating just a little too hard against her rib cage. She felt kind of like she had when Jenny Rhodes died. But for some reason, this blow was dulled. Maybe because she was older. Maybe because she knew death better now. Maybe because her heart had been broken a few times since then, always by her mother, of all people. Maybe because she had never loved Isaac. Maybe because this was happening more to her mother than to her. But she knew that anything that happened to her mother was also happening to her.

"How ya feeling?"

She shrugged. "Fine?" She was feeling something but was unsure of what it was.

"You gotta be kind to your mama, ya hear?"

Camille scratched at her scalp. "Why you say that, Mama?"

Charlotte slapped Camille's hand away from her head. "You pat," she said. "Or else the relaxer'll burn you." She took Camille's wrist and patted her palm against her head. "Like this."

"Okay, okay!" She pulled away from Charlotte, who drew her back in, and Camille acquiesced with a sigh.

"Is Mama going to live here now?"

"Of course," Charlotte answered.

"Oh."

"And call me Granmama when she's around. She's always been sensitive about that. Like I said, you gotta be kind to your mama."

"Even if she ain't kind to me?" Camille laid her head down on Charlotte's lap and looked up to see a thick dark hair spiraling out of her chin. She briefly considered if there'd ever been a more beautiful chin hair on a woman.

"Especially if she's not kind to you. Your mama don't got to be kind to you, no way. That's your mama, not your little friend."

"That don't seem fair, Granmama."

"Life ain't fair."

Camille didn't go to school for the rest of the week. When she returned, she told everyone that her mother had been in the hospital, which wasn't exactly a lie. Camille said she'd had appendicitis, a common ailment in books and on television that seemed serious but not fatal, and that allowed broken families to get back together.

She was far from the only student with a nontraditional family; other students lived with their grandparents or didn't know their fathers. But a stepfather who shot himself was too much.

Anyway, telling people that Corinna was sick was hardly a lie. Corinna *was* sick. She didn't eat, and the rare times she slept, she groaned like she was in pain or woke up screaming. Camille started sleeping on the couch, but as summertime approached, it got hotter and hotter in the living room. She slept fitfully, if she slept at all. The itchy brocade upholstery did not help. She dragged herself groggily and angrily through the end of the school year. She started sleeping when she came home from ballet and woke up when her mother went to bed, then did homework into the early hours of the morning. If she had time, she would rest for an hour or two until it was time to get ready for school. She and Charlotte would leave the house when it was still dark to get to downtown Nashville in time for Camille's math tutoring sessions. When the school year ended, Camille was relieved.

In June, Camille started her summer dance intensive in Nashville. Classes were five days a week, nine to three, with only a thirty-minute break. When she was done, she was exhausted both physically and emotionally. She didn't know any of the girls, but they all seemed to know one another. She always left the building in a hurry, with her bleeding feet shoved into old canvas sneakers, as she could barely stand to hear the girls giggle among themselves for one more moment.

When she was waiting for Charlotte to pick her up after class, Camille wondered if she even wanted to be there, instead of in a summer session at her regular studio, where she was the best dancer. Her home studio director, Miss Liz, had suggested the intensive, and the next thing she knew, she was doing it. She was athletic. She was picked first in gym class, and had been drafted on to the Wilma Rudolph Track Team in elementary school. She was fast and coordinated, which meant she was good at performing choreography. And ballet required precision and grace in a way that she could deliver. But she wasn't even sure how she'd become a dance student. Her mother said that as a little girl, she'd pointed at the sign of the newly opened dance studio on Main Street and said, "I wanna do that!" And her mother made it happen. Camille had no memory of it, but she did remember wanting to become a truck driver after seeing a trucker reading a paperback book while he drove, but her mother hadn't encouraged that idea. She knew why: privileged girls do ballet.

Camille did not desire privilege, but only because she didn't fully understand it. For the most part, the people around her were like her. At her magnet school, most of the kids were working-class or barely middle-class. At her home studio, the girls were well-off enough to take dance lessons, but they weren't wealthy. The ballet intensive was her first introduction to true wealth. These girls wore diamond earrings and Ugg boots (even in the summer). Because it was summer, there was no strict dress code: they could wear whatever color or style of leotard they wanted. Camille only had two plain black leotards and two pairs of tights, plus one pair of leg warmers made out of the sleeves of an old sweater. Though the other girls usually wore black, many of them had a leotard for each day, distinguished by lovely little details like cap sleeves, beadwork, lace, or an open back. She particularly admired one with mesh half-sleeves embroidered with red roses that belonged to a translucent-pale girl named Marie Anne. She'd seen it at the dance supply store that spring; she flipped the tag and fought back a gasp: eighty-nine dollars. Camille's new leotard was on sale for fifteen dollars, and Charlotte still asked for a discount. She began to wonder what it might be like to have so many options.

She hadn't made many friends since Jenny died, so she spent her free time that summer at the library, where Charlotte dropped her off a few afternoons a week. She returned her books at the counter and headed for adult fiction. The librarians had guided her to the young adult section several times, but romance, fantasy, and epistolary novels written in internet-speak did not appeal to her, though she occasionally swung by to check if there was a new *Gossip Girl*. Adult fiction was more likely to be glamorous, or at least focused on adults making their own decisions. After she made her book selection, she used the computers to look at leotards on the internet, knowing she wouldn't be ordering any of them.

As soon as she discovered that she could request a free catalog from Bloch, she ordered one from every dance supplier she could find. The catalogs seemed to arrive in the mailbox all at once. She didn't get much time to herself at home, but she used every opportunity to sit on her bed and cut out pictures of torsos clad in spandex, microfiber, or the occasional velvet or satin to paste into her journal. She covered dozens of pages with headless bodies. Eventually, it wasn't just leotards, but costumes. And then she started to order catalogs not only from stores she was familiar with, like JCPenney and Sears, but also from stores without locations anywhere near Chilly Springs—Urban Outfitters, J.Crew, and Bloomingdale's. She read the catalogs' catchy headlines, like "Meet Our English Leather Collection" or "Summer's Brightest Colors Trimmed to Match Your Mood." She also read the descriptions of individual items. Sometimes the captions were straightforward: "Leather-lined" or "Polyester/Rayon." Other times, they set the mood—"This striped poplin cotton skirt is perfectly suited for a coastal summer brunch"—or let the clothing convey its own mood: "The tulle, with a touch of sheerness, is embroidered with intricate lace, velvet trefoil, and satin roses."

When she was done, she assembled images into outfits, creating intricate collages that were less about outfits and more about jamming as many pleasing images as she could into a tight space. She wasn't haphazard; she considered color palettes and composition. She liked most of the things she saw because they were new, clean, and unattainable, though she did tend to prefer the hyper-feminine glitter and sequins. But she also favored the bohemian style being made popular by the Olsen twins and other skinny white women— long, flared jeans and embroidered dresses with bell sleeves. She especially loved images of bodies of water, dedicating several pages to pictures of white sand beaches, cliffs overlooking the sea, and models sitting on boat docks. The closest she'd come to water like that was playing by the creek in her backyard and driving over the Cumberland River and other rivers in Middle Tennessee. She'd heard of Percy Priest Lake, which her grandfather swore was haunted, but she'd never been there.

Her mother and grandmother saw the catalogs come into the house, and even though no one questioned her, she was secretive about her projects. She hid the catalogs and her journal under the bed she shared with her mother, who was too oblivious to notice the errant glue on the kitchen table and scraps of paper on the bedroom floor.

She would have given her left leg for one of the expensive magazines at Walmart—*Vogue, Elle, Harper's Bazaar*—but had to settle for the ones her grandmother kept around the house for the occasional client—*People, Woman's World, Essence,* and *Ebony.* They were all right, but Charlotte tended to keep them around until they fell apart. Charlotte might have given her a few if she'd asked, but instead she stole them or took them out of the trash without being sure why. If she had thought about it, she would have known she was afraid of seeming ungrateful, materialistic, or "uppity." She was constructing worlds with no resemblance whatsoever to the one in which she lived. She craved beauty; and this way, she could create her own.

She scribbled furiously about her small, dull life, on top of and alongside her art. She wrote about the arguments between her mother and grandmother. She wrote about conversations she had with her grandfather. She wrote fictional entries about herself as a character, if she had friends. For an entire week, she wrote about Jenny as if she were still alive. Writing made her feel better in the moment, but reading over the pages made her feel like when Jenny died: angry, empty, and confused. So she mostly looked at the beautiful things.

One Sunday morning, she sat at the kitchen table with her family. Charlotte had just served the eggs.

"Camille," Corinna said, "don't eat them eggs with them cigarette ashes in it."

Camille froze, a forkful of eggs in her hand.

"Excuse me?" Charlotte said, hands on her hips, turning from the sink where she'd just dropped the pan.

"There's no ashes in here, Mama," Camille said, but her mother snatched her fork and her plate and dumped the eggs in the trash.

"I'm tired of you feeding my baby them damn cigarette ashes."

"Ain't no damn cigarette ashes in my food, Corinna."

Rarely, there was a piece of ash in some of Charlotte's food, but it was easy to push aside or pick out. Camille hadn't even had a chance to see if today's eggs had any.

"Then what you call this?" Corinna pointed into the garbage can.

"I'm not looking in no garbage can when you know damn well there ain't no goddamn ash in there."

"Ain't no ash in here," David said, moving around his eggs on his plate.

"Nobody asked you."

"Well, ash or not," Charlotte said. "What's the girl going to eat now?"

"Maybe you should have thought about that before you smoked a damn cigarette while you was cooking."

"She can have mine," David said, standing up on his cane to go sit on the porch. "I done lost my appetite, y'all acting like this."

Camille stood up to follow him.

"Sit down!" Corinna shouted. "Eat your breakfast."

"She probably lost her appetite listening to you actin' a damn fool," Charlotte said.

"I'm the fool?"

"I'll tell you what, Corinna. I'm 'bout this damn close"—Charlotte held up her thumb and index finger an infinitesimal distance from each other—"To throwing you the hell out of my goddamn house."

Camille looked down into the eggs intended for her grandfather; they were steaming hot and might have even been delicious with some seasoning and ketchup. She reached for the salt and pepper, not even thinking about the argument around her. Usually, when the women fought, she and David would sit and eat in silence, sometimes exchanging knowing glances or eye rolls. But he'd left her this time, and she didn't blame him.

"You wouldn't, Mama. You feel too guilty. You know this is just as much your fault as it is mine. And you know what else? I'd take Camille with me. Then what are you going to hold over my goddamn head?"

Charlotte laughed, and though Camille was not looking at her grandmother, she could easily imagine her condescending grin. She wanted to be elsewhere, somewhere beautiful, but she would have settled for one of the blank backgrounds of the JCPenney catalog.

"You crazy," Charlotte said.

"Watch me. It's not going to be today, but—"

Camille looked up to see what made her mother fall silent. Charlotte was holding the pan with its lacy egg remnants over her head, prepared to swing. Her eyes were watery, and her lips trembled.

"I'll kill you 'fore you take that girl anywhere," Charlotte said.

The kitchen was oppressively hot, but Camille shivered.

"You'd rather a stranger take her, Mama?"

"It was *your* goddamn idea," Charlotte screamed at what had to have been the top of her lungs.

The front door opened, and Charlotte lowered her arm.

"What's going on in here?" David asked.

"Nothing," Charlotte and Corinna said in unison.

"Sure don't look like nothing. Charlotte, what you doing with that pan?"

"Nothing," Charlotte replied, throwing it back into the sink with a loud clang. The pan hissed when it hit the cold water pooling at the bottom of the slow-draining sink. "Come on, Camille. Let's get you some breakfast."

They went to Sonic, but Charlotte didn't order anything for herself. Camille wasn't hungry anymore either but ate her burrito and hash browns anyway.

"Mama?" Camille asked with a mouth full of salty, greasy potato.

"Hmm?" Charlotte said.

"What did Mama mean when she said, 'you would let a stranger take her'?"

"Well," Charlotte said, her voice shaking a bit, "remember how your great-grandmother came to visit us?"

Of course Camille remembered. Evelyn had visited a few times since their first meeting, always impeccably dressed in something dark or plaid and carrying a bag that made her look like a soap opera villain. Evelyn was very beautiful, not only because of her looks but because of the way she presented herself, every move seeming flawlessly choreographed, kind of like Charlotte. You could definitely see Evelyn in Charlotte and vice versa. But Evelyn was never flustered or frustrated. And she paid for everything. She opened check presenters without wincing, which impressed the hell out of Camille. But she'd assumed Evelyn was a passing presence, kind of like the out-of-town cousins in that one *Baby-Sitters Club*.

"But she said that if I don't want to—"

"Camille, do you want to keep living like this?"

"Like what?"

"Wouldn't it just be nice to have everything you need? No arguing, no fussing, no screaming, no driving an hour each way to school? You could have your own bed, your own room."

Camille frowned.

"Evelyn can give you a good life."

"But I have a good life."

"A *better* life."

Camille's head started to ache, and acid rose in her esophagus. She thought she might vomit on her new white Keds and the floor, which would have annoyed Charlotte very much. But truthfully, Camille did want a different life, even if she wasn't sure what kind of life she wanted. As much as she loved her grandmother, she didn't want to grow up to be like her. Charlotte didn't seem to have many—if any—pleasures outside of their family. Camille wanted something that was her own.

"Oh, sweetheart. It's just that you deserve better than this. It'd be one thing if there was no other option, but there is another option," Charlotte said, but Camille was hardly listening.

"So I don't have a choice?" Camille interrupted.

Charlotte was quiet for a moment, then said, "It's not about choice."

"But it is! You're *choosing* to send me away."

"I don't feel like *I* have a choice."

Charlotte aged before Camille's eyes. The lines around her eyes and mouth seemed etched so deep they might have gone into her bones, and the bags under her eyes were almost cartoonishly dark and heavy. "But *why*, Mama?!"

Charlotte sat up straight. "It's my job to do right by you, Camille."

Camille shrank back into her seat. The urge to cling to her grandmother was strong. But she trusted Charlotte, more than she'd ever trusted Corinna. Charlotte wasn't perfect; she yelled sometimes, often didn't know the right thing to say, and had even picked her up late from ballet a time or two. But she knew Charlotte loved her, that she was not a burden to her.

Charlotte continued, "You think this is *easy* for me? Well, I got news for you." She put the car into reverse and rolled out of the space without checking her mirrors. "And I'll tell you what else. Don't you question me about this again. I made up my mind, and I'm the one making decisions 'round here. You hear me?"

Camille shrank farther into her seat.

"We're leaving on July twenty-first. You have an audition at the ballet school up there on the twenty-third. You got into a great school, one of the best in the country, very expensive. You can have everything you dreamed of. Everything."

"What about—" Camille was going to say, What about my birthday?

"I don't want to hear it," Charlotte cut her off. "Not another word about it. It's done."

Camille stayed away from her family as best she could through the early afternoon, sitting in her bedroom, cutting up catalogs. Her stomach and lower back were stiff with what she thought was anxiety. In the late afternoon, she went to the bathroom and found blood in her underwear.

"Mama!" she shouted, knowing both her grandmother and mother could hear but only her grandmother would come.

Charlotte slammed through the tumbledown door, holding a skillet full of potatoes in one hand. "What's wrong?!"

Camille pointed at the crotch of her panties.

Charlotte dropped her shoulders with an eye roll. "Girl," she said. "You scared me. We talked about this. It's just your period."

That didn't make Camille feel any better. She had been feeling strange for days, but she thought it was from all the yoga before ballet or not sleeping so good. Charlotte went back to the kitchen to drop off the potatoes and returned with a softer look.

"Let me run you a bath. Give me those drawers, and I'll show you how to soak them so they're not ruined." Camille stepped out of the plain white cotton underwear while Charlotte ran water in the sink. Bottomless and shivering, Camille watched Charlotte drizzle dish soap on the stained underwear and dunk them into the sink.

"This is going to be more important when you start buying nice underwear that don't come in packs," she said before wrapping Camille in a tight hug. "Periods are a real pain in the ass," she whispered into Camille's afro puff. "One of many burdens of womanhood. But you'll be all right."

Charlotte ran a bath while Camille sat on a towel on the lid of the toilet seat. Her grandmother knelt by the bathtub and explained, yet again, what having a period meant.

"You can get pregnant now," she said for what had to be the hundredth time that year. "You know how a lady gets pregnant, right?"

Camille wrapped her arms around her aching middle and nodded.

"Hmm?"

"Yes'm," Camille said, though she actually wasn't particularly clear on the matter. She knew the terminology and some of the mechanics, but she still had big questions about how all of those things worked together to create a baby. But it wasn't like Camille was going to have sex any time soon. She had heard of girls her age and younger doing it, but she was quite sure she would not be one of them. She did not find anything attractive about the boys she knew, and the feeling was seemingly mutual.

"All right. Come on now. Get in."

Camille put one foot in and almost immediately yanked it out again. The water was almost unbearably hot. "Ouch, Mama!"

"I know it's hot. Just take your time. One foot and then the other."

Camille did as she was told. She put one foot in and waited for it to acclimate. It was painful, but the rest of her body experienced relief. She groaned as she lowered herself into the tub and a little cloud of blood dissipated into the water. It made her think of the day Isaac died. She felt a chill run down her spine, even in the scalding hot water. Camille kind of wished her grandmother would leave. But Charlotte knelt down by the bathtub and kept talking.

"You're going to want hot things to help you feel better when you get cramps. Like a hot water bottle. Or you can get a washcloth and wet it, then put it in a plastic bag and heat it in the microwave. Back in my day, we had to boil the water. You're going to want to put it right here—" Charlotte gestured to her lower belly. "Or on your lower back. I was about your age when I started. I read in *Woman's World* that it's genetic. When you start."

"When did Mama start?"

Charlotte was quiet for a moment. "She must have been about your age. There's pads under the sink," she continued. "I don't like tampons. I think your mother does, but I don't know where she keeps 'em."

Camille knew her mother's tampons were in the bottom drawer of their dresser, but she decided she would use pads because that was what Charlotte did.

Charlotte used the side of the bathtub to hoist herself up. "Well, I'll leave you to it." She opened the medicine cabinet and placed a bottle of ibuprofen on the slim bathroom sink. "I think ibuprofen is best for cramps and headaches and things. I should be done with these things soon enough, God willing."

Camille did not know what she was talking about.

"Mama, can you stay?"

"I was in the middle of something when you screamed bloody murder," Charlotte said without turning around. "I'll wash your hair when you get out, how 'bout that? Then ice cream?"

Later, Charlotte washed Camille's hair in the sink. Then Camille sat between her legs on a pillow while Charlotte tightly braided her hair against her scalp. Once she was done with the right side, Camille leaned a cheek against her grandmother's prickly, bony knee and fell asleep.

In the morning, she woke up on the couch, forgetting for a moment about the events of the day before. It was almost just like waking up on any other day. She first recalled the argument in the kitchen, then remembered everything that happened after, as an ache developed behind her eye sockets.

"Hey, baby," Grandaddy said. He leaned against the doorway leading from the minuscule hallway that held the two bedrooms. She rose and helped him to the couch. He groaned as he lowered himself.

"Thank you, honey," he said with a sigh.

Camille had been a baby when Grandaddy had his accident and had never known him to be able-bodied. It was difficult to imagine; even when he told stories in which he was young and running wild around the bayou, she sometimes pictured him with his cane. He never talked about the accident or his injuries, and Camille had never been particularly curious either. On this particular morning, though, she wondered why she'd never asked.

She collapsed next to him, tucked her feet underneath his bony leg, and leaned her head against the wall. He turned on the television to *The Price Is Right*. She was pretty sure his life revolved around *The Price Is Right* and *Jeopardy*. He also tolerated *Who Wants to Be a Millionaire?*, but it was far from his favorite.

"Grandaddy?"

"Mm-hmm."

"What happened to you?"

"Whatchu mean?" His face folded into confusion and then opened up slowly. "You mean . . . Oh. Um. I told you, I fell."

"But how?"

He cleared his throat, and his lower lip trembled briefly before he said: "Well, I went to work drunk and fell four stories off a building."

Camille smirked. "That's not funny."

He looked into her eyes, making her slightly nervous. "I'm serious."

She stared at her grandfather. The man she knew would never do something like that. She felt sick and slightly dizzy.

"Sometimes, you get second chances. And you can take 'em, or you can waste 'em. I could have gone right ahead being the fool I was, but I decided to be your grandad."

Camille felt tears coming and didn't know why. On television, an announcer was describing a tropical vacation as a prize. Camille scratched at the upholstery on the couch and studied the pattern rather than look at her grandfather, who was still watching her. The couch was ugly. If she had any good friends at her new school, she wouldn't have wanted them to come over and see that ghastly thing.

"I wasn't a good husband, and I wasn't a good dad," he said. That couldn't be right, Camille thought. She couldn't speak to her grandad as a husband, but she couldn't imagine a better dad.

"You're lying," she said through tears.

"I ain't lyin', baby."

She wished he'd lied to her. Her world was changing too fast.

"But like I says, we got choices in this life."

"I don't got no choices."

"Well, you will one day. That's why everything's changing. So you can have choices. You'll look back one day, and you'll see," David said as Camille left the room.

She went to the bathroom and slammed the door. This was the only place in the house she could go to be alone. She sat and stared at her hands as it became startlingly clear that the grandfather she knew and the man who went to work drunk were not the same person. They shared the same body, but she wouldn't recognize David as an able-bodied man who drank too much. She only knew the man who needed a cane and loved her. She trusted her grandfather, and she loved him, so she could forgive who he'd been.

She thought of her mother. She thought of the mother who came home at three a.m. with fried food, the mother who encouraged her to read, the mother who whipped her with Isaac's belt, and the mother who moaned in her sleep. And she'd loved some of those women deeply. Maybe, one day, she could forgive the rest.

*   *   *

Camille had never needed a suitcase before. Charlotte had pulled one down out of her closet. It was Gucci, but it was in horrible shape:

scratched and discolored. Camille wondered how it had gotten so beat up as Charlotte had never taken a trip that she knew of.

"Fabric can decay from lack of use," Charlotte explained. "Evelyn will probably get you something new when you get up there. This'll do to get you there."

"Should I bring it back?"

Charlotte stared at the bag with a peculiar look in her eye. "No, please don't," she said and left the room.

Camille decided not to be worried about her grandmother's behavior. She had enough on her mind.

Camille didn't pack much. She didn't have much. Most of her things were either books or ballet-related. She would be wearing a uniform to her new school, so she packed her weekend clothes—a pair of leggings, a pair of jeans, and three T-shirts. Her grandmother had taken her to Books-A-Million in Nashville and told her she could get three things to read in the car; she chose two magazines and a novel, which she packed along with her ballet supplies, her journal, a few pens she'd stolen from Barnes & Noble, and the scarf she wore over her hair at night.

The day they were leaving, she kissed her mother and grandfather goodbye and hauled the decrepit suitcase to the car.

"Are Mama and Grandaddy going to be okay?" Camille asked as Charlotte drove away. "Why don't they come with us?"

"It'd be harder to bring them than leave them."

"What about Mama?"

"What about her?"

"She gon' be okay? I mean, in general?"

"She's a grown woman."

"What does that even mean?"

"What?"

"Grown woman?"

Charlotte paused, and Camille expected her to tell her to hush. "You know, baby," she said instead. "That's a good question."

Camille waited for her grandmother to say more, but she didn't.

An hour or so later, as they hurtled east on I-40, Camille took intermittent bites from a pint of melting cookies 'n' cream and mindlessly flipped pages of an *Elle Girl* with Lindsay Lohan on the cover. *Elle Girl* and *Teen Vogue* were her favorite magazines to read at Walmart; she wished she could have brought them home for her collages, but they were too precious and too rare to cut up.

Elle Girl featured three-hundred-dollar distressed, rainbow-stitched jeans, street-style snapshots of fashionable adult women, and high-end finishing schools for the offspring of multimillionaires. Even the regular column Runway: The Real Way showed a fifteen-year-old wearing Betsey Johnson crinolines, which is what she loved about it. The aspiration. Everyone in the magazine seemed to have *so* much more than they needed. Camille felt like she had exactly what she needed and nothing more. But she didn't want to be a *Cosmo* girl. She did not want to "Look Hot This Summer." She wanted to read about teenage girls on yachts. She wanted to know the details of Kate Moss's drug problem. She wanted to know how movie stars got so thin. If she couldn't have those things, she should at least know about them. She left the magazine open in her lap but she could not focus on it.

She wished she could say something, anything, to her grand-mother about the way she was feeling. But she knew Charlotte would not or perhaps could not say anything to reassure her.

"Why's there no music on?" Camille asked after a period of silence.

"Well, I was hoping we could talk."

"About what?"

"Whatever you want."

"I don't feel like talking."

Camille turned on the radio and turned up the volume just loud enough to reinforce that she did not feel like talking. She had questions, for sure. But she didn't know how to ask them. A song was on that she'd never heard before. Because they were far from home, Charlotte's usual disco channel had become alt-rock.

She reclined her seat and pretended to sleep but was actually staring at the side of her grandmother's face and neck. She'd never seen anyone as striking as her grandmother. She didn't want to be away from that beauty. Somehow, she did fall asleep.

When Charlotte shook her awake, it was dark outside.

"Look," Charlotte said. She was pointing at something in the distance. It was the Washington Monument. It was nothing more than a gargantuan, gray tower, not what Camille would have chosen to be her monument. She would probably never have a monument. But still. The twisting feeling in her gut was gone, but only for the time it took her to remember what was happening.

"Okay," Charlotte continued, lifting one hand from the steering wheel and raising two fingers. "I'll tell you two things. First, your great-grandmother is *not* who she used to be. She is a much kinder woman than when I was growing up. She will be different with you than she was with me, same way I'm different with you than I was with your mother. She loves you, but she probably won't show you the way I show you. She wants the best for you. She likes nice things, beautiful things, so she will probably show you love with nice, beautiful things." Her grandmother sounded like she was trying to convince herself.

Camille sighed loudly to indicate that she wasn't in the mood for a lecture, but Charlotte continued.

They were in the city now, and Camille expected to see something like an episode of *Seinfeld* or *Law & Order*, but the buildings were low, and the streets were clean. They drove by an arch so large that it began on one side of the street and ended on the other. It was painted red, green, and gold, and embellished with gilded dragons and Chinese characters. This was Chinatown, she presumed, something she'd read about in social studies. There weren't a lot of people on the street—it was almost midnight on a Monday—but Camille felt suddenly panicked. Her heart raced. A shirtless man carrying a squeegee approached the car at a stoplight.

"You're going to love DC," Charlotte said, not seeming to notice the man until he tapped on the front window and she waved him away. "There is so much to do here. You shouldn't ever get bored. Almost all the museums are free to visit. You like museums. You like the Frist."

Camille's underarms were growing moist. She turned all of the vents toward her and cranked up the air.

"Oh, man. Haven't been here since I was a kid. What's the matter with you? You having a hot flash or something?" Charlotte laughed and turned the air back down. "You got turned-up-high-air-conditioning gas money?"

Camille wrapped her arms over her stomach and sighed loudly. She wished Charlotte would ask her what she was thinking, even though she had no idea what she would say if she did. Would Evelyn love her? Would Evelyn even like her? Where would she get her *Teen Vogue*? Was there a Sonic in DC? What would her new school be like? What about this audition? How had it even been set up? Why was she moving? The thoughts spiraled and weaved and scampered around in her brain.

She must have sat staring straight ahead for quite some time, because before she knew it, Charlotte was lightly jostling her bare thigh. Camille came to, unsure if she'd been unconscious or not.

"Get out and help me park," Charlotte said as she rolled her window down with great effort.

Camille stood on the sidewalk while Charlotte tried and failed to parallel park. She looked around at the street, which did not seem like it belonged in a "city," but what did she know? The houses were all connected, kind of like the townhome complexes in South Nashville. But these houses were different from one another—some were bare redbrick, and others were painted. Some had shutters, and others did not. Some looked abandoned. Others had elaborate landscaping and outdoor furniture.

The door of a well-maintained house on the corner opened, and Evelyn emerged wearing a red-and-yellow-floral-patterned kaftan and holding a martini glass. Evelyn took a sip of her drink and lifted her hand in greeting, looking like she'd walked out of a movie from the sixties. Camille pulled self-consciously at the hem of the shorts she'd made from a pair of jeans that she'd grown too tall for. Charlotte was calling her name, but she wasn't paying attention; she was too busy looking at Evelyn and her house.

Charlotte was eventually able to get the car in the spot. When she got out, she grabbed Camille hard by the arm. "You didn't hear me calling your name?"

"Sorry."

Charlotte sucked her teeth.

"Are you leaving me here tonight?"

"No, of course not. I'll leave in the morning." Charlotte smiled weakly and pulled Camille's suitcase out of the trunk. Camille took it and lugged it up the front steps of the house. Everything she could see from the main entryway was blinding white; brick; or dark, polished wood. The color came from the large houseplants; brightly patterned accent pillows; and large, abstract works of art.

Camille dropped the suitcase and turned to Evelyn, who was chewing on the mouthpiece of a corncob pipe. She extended the hand with the corncob pipe in it and put it around Camille's waist.

"Come, darling," she said. "Let me show you your room."

When Camille turned around to see if Charlotte was following, the hall was empty. Tears welled in her eyes, and a great pain rose in her throat. She climbed the stairs in a numb, bitter haze.

Somehow, she arrived at the door of a large room with a queen-size bed with a nightstand on either side. It was big enough to hold three or four rooms the size of her bedroom in Chilly Springs. Even with two dressers and a built-in bookshelf, there was enough room for the promised desk with a lamp and drawers. Evelyn walked into the room, but Camille could not seem to lift her feet to enter. Evelyn opened a door inside the room and waved her in. A bathroom of her own! Camille lifted her leaden feet to join her great-grandmother. The bathroom was just as sparkling white as the rest of the house. She ran fingers along the edge of the claw-foot bathtub and the enamel handle of the shower door. Across from the toilet was another door, which Evelyn opened to reveal the cavernous closet with a full-length mirror and a shelf for shoes like the one from *13 Going on 30*.

Camille could hear her heart thudding in her chest. She pointed at herself. "For me?"

"Yes, dear." Evelyn was holding up a big, fluffy robe that had been hanging in the closet on a satin-padded hanger. Camille's name was embroidered in curly, looping script above the breast pocket. "Who else?"

Camille had been practicing how to smile without showing all of her teeth. But she couldn't help herself now, so she covered her mouth with her hand.

Evelyn gently took her by the wrist and removed her hand. "Don't hide your face, dear. You're much too pretty."

Pretty? Me? Camille thought as she looked at herself in the large mirror with the beaming white Hollywood-style lights. She'd never spent much time looking at herself. During ballet, she avoided looking at her face. Even while turning, she always focused on something just off-center from her face to keep her balance. No one had ever called her pretty before, not even her mother or grandmother. The subject had never come up. Black girls couldn't be pretty, after all. Not if they were her complexion. She'd always known this to be fact. But Evelyn would not lie to her. She was like Charlotte in that way.

Evelyn took Camille's hand and guided her back downstairs, where Charlotte was now standing in the foyer.

"Well, it's not as big as the house in Atlanta, but it will do," Charlotte said, rubbing Camille's back. Camille felt Charlotte was really talking to herself. "More windows. More light."

"Have you eaten?" Evelyn asked.

They sat together at a large, heavy table that looked like a slice of an enormous tree. Camille danced her fingers across the growth rings while playing with her lukewarm pad Thai. It was really late, but Camille was not tired or hungry. Her heart was still thrumming in her ears. Evelyn and Charlotte said very little, barely even looked at each other, while they ate. Camille examined their faces, which were so much alike that it was almost unsettling. Charlotte's skin was maybe a shade or two darker, but other than that, they might have been sisters. They looked almost the same age and their faces naturally relaxed into deep frowns. Even the way they held their water glasses was identical. The only real differences were their heights and the color of their eyes. Corinna looked nothing like Charlotte, Camille realized now. She wasn't sure if she looked like her mother or not.

"Darling girl, are you not hungry?"

Camille noticed that her head was nearly resting on her outstretched arm. She sat up straight, embarrassed.

Charlotte placed a hand on Camille's back. "You okay, baby?" she whispered.

Camille nodded, twisted her fork in the plate of noodles, and focused on staying upright.

When she and Charlotte were finally in the big, white fluffy bed, Camille asked why she and Evelyn hadn't spoken for so long.

Charlotte used the back of her hand to stroke Camille's cheek. "Well," she said with a sigh, "she hurt me real bad when I was younger."

"Like she *hurt* you hurt you? Like she hit you or something?"

"Well, yes. That, too. But she also hurt me worse than that."

"But—" Camille started. What could hurt worse than getting whooped real good with a leather belt? Well, she didn't have to think about it very long to come up with a few things.

"It's nothing for you to be worried about. She won't hurt you like that."

"How do you know?"

"I think you'll have to trust me. You trust me, baby?"

"Yes'm."

"Then go to sleep, honey. I'll rub your back." Camille turned to face away from Charlotte, who lifted her pajama shirt and rubbed her big, long hands across Charlotte's bony back. She fell asleep almost immediately.

In the morning, Camille was alone in bed. She briefly panicked, until Charlotte came out of the bathroom, rubbing lotion into her hands.

"You're going to have your very own bathroom. Ain't that something?" Charlotte sighed loudly. "Probably somebody to clean it for you, too. This some high-quality lotion. Why you look like that?"

Camille was squinting at her grandmother, trying to imagine her as someone who had lived like this. In some ways it made sense. Charlotte had beautiful teeth. She didn't walk; she strutted. She'd mention casually that polyester was just as hot as silk, in her personal opinion. She looked at Jennifer Lopez's engagement ring on the cover of *People* and correctly guessed that it was more than eight carats. But Charlotte also swore a lot, mostly used vernacular English, wore men's jeans from Goodwill, and occasionally spit dip.

"Like what?"

"You look like you've seen a ghost."

"I thought you left."

"Without saying goodbye? Never." Charlotte looked blankly out of the window, still rubbing her hands together though the lotion must have been long absorbed. "Bet this place is haunted, though. I think I saw something last night. You like ghosts, don't you? Like in those spooky little books you be reading. *Goosebumps*?"

Camille hadn't read anything from the *Goosebumps* series in years.

"You'll tell me if there are any ghosts. Won't you?"

"Yes'm." *Goosebumps*.

"I love you," Charlotte said and sat down on the bed. She leaned forward and put her forehead to Camille's. "You know that?"

"Yes, Mama."

"You gonna start calling Evelyn Mama, too?"

Camille shrugged. Mama was a term of affection and admiration, and respect. She already had admiration and respect for Evelyn, but she didn't know about affection. "Can I ask you something?"

"Mm-hmm."

"Who decided to send me away? You or Mama?"

"Oh, honey," Charlotte said and touched Camille's ear. "You're not being sent away. You're—"

"That's not what I asked, Mama."

Charlotte's face softened. "We all made this decision together, baby. But when you get angry or sad or whatever, you get mad at me, okay?"

Camille nodded because she didn't know what else to do. Then Charlotte took her hand.

"Shall we?"

They went downstairs, where Evelyn had laid out a bagel spread.

"Look, Camille. No eggs," Charlotte said, but her voice was fading because she was walking down the hallway away from the kitchen. "Camille hates eggs. Don't you, baby?"

Camille forced herself to look into Evelyn's eyes. Her eyes were mint-colored but not like an actual mint leaf, more the color ascribed to mint-flavored food, like mint chocolate chip ice cream. Camille hadn't thought anything in nature was that color.

"No, ma'am. I don't like eggs. I'll eat them, though," Camille said, careful to speak proper in Evelyn's presence.

Evelyn smiled. It was Charlotte's smile, but Evelyn's looked like each tooth had been carefully polished by hand. "Well, we won't have them if you don't like them."

Somewhere in the house, piano music started playing, probably from a radio. Evelyn moved in slow motion to touch her own cheek. "That's Nocturne."

"Number Nineteen."

"You know classical?"

"Yes, ma'am."

"Oh, of course, you do. You dance ballet." Evelyn sounded like she was about to cry.

Uncomfortable, Camille left the room in search of Charlotte. She followed the music toward the back of the house, where she found what magazine folks liked to call the sunroom. There,

Charlotte was playing a baby grand piano, the kind that appeared in the pages of *Architectural Digest* and *Better Homes & Gardens*. Camille had no idea Charlotte could play the piano. As soon as she completed the piece, Charlotte turned around and smiled at Camille.

"Still got it," she said.

"I didn't know you played the piano."

"She could have been a concert pianist," Evelyn said. Camille was startled to find the small woman right behind her.

"Oh, well," Charlotte said, rising from the piano bench and extending a hand to Camille. "Let's eat. Hm? I should probably get on the road here soon."

Again, they ate in silence. At one point, Charlotte and Evelyn lifted their water glasses simultaneously while they chewed in sync, then took sips that looked coordinated.

After breakfast, Camille watched her grandmother shove the few things she'd brought with her into the leather handbag she'd bought at Goodwill for two dollars. It was a nice spacious bag, and Charlotte loved to tell people how little she paid for it.

Charlotte took Camille's chin in her hand. "You'll be good, won't you?"

"Yes'm."

She kissed Camille's forehead and cheeks and waved goodbye to Evelyn. Camille watched her drive away, down S Street, in her LeBaron. Camille sat on the concrete steps leading to the front door, rubbing her palms against her knees in an attempt to keep from crying. Evelyn sat down next to her and touched the small of her back. Camille used all of her might to keep the tears in, but they still came.

"Oh, darling," she said. "I know. I know."

When Evelyn said, "I know," Camille didn't stop crying, but the wrenching inside her waned.

Camille sat up, and Evelyn touched her chin. "Darling girl," she said. "Do you like macarons?"

"I don't know what that is."

"Oh, I bet you'll love them. I got a big box of them just for you. We can watch a film or something. Your grandmother says you like *Breakfast at Tiffany's*. Is that right?"

"Yes'm," Camille said. She sniffed and wiped at her eyes with the heels of her hands. She'd seen the movie once on TV and then Charlotte had let her borrow it from Blockbuster. She liked the clothes, the apartment, and the idea of fleeing a rural life for a glamorous city. "Oh, that's fantastic. I bought it for you."

Camille allowed herself a small smile. And Evelyn smiled back, looking so much like Charlotte.

"Come now. Help me up. I'm old."

Twenty minutes later, Camille was curled up on a couch under the softest blanket she had ever touched. She was in "the den," which was just a second, less impeccably decorated living room, on a large, brown suede sectional big and deep enough for a family. Camille knew some people who lived in newer houses with upstairs living rooms they called bonus rooms or great rooms. But she didn't know anybody who referred to those rooms as "dens," except perhaps in books. This room was vast with a dusty treadmill and a desktop computer with an enormous screen.

Macarons turned out to be delicate, delectable sandwich cookies. And she liked them very much. She could not imagine disliking them. The box was big and rested on the brown ottoman. She counted the macarons. There were fifty of them.

Evelyn had carried the oversize box on two arms, pulled the pink ribbon, and unveiled them with pride.

"I got five of each flavor they had," she said. She pointed at each column as she spoke. "Vanilla bean, chocolate, pistachio, lemon, raspberry, mango, espresso, and um—" she said and shook her head. "Some other shit. I don't know. Let me know what you like. Charlotte said you like fruity things and not really chocolate and vanilla? Is that right?"

"Yes'm," Camille replied.

"You don't have to do that plantation mess here, you know?"

"The what?"

"The yes'm and no'm. I know you have manners. Just say yes or no. That's fine."

Camille nodded, and Evelyn took the blanket from the back of the couch and opened it expectantly. Camille slipped off her moccasins and lay down like she knew she was supposed to do. While Evelyn tucked her in, Camille smelled something expensive and clean.

"Okay, my dear," Evelyn said, blessing Camille with fresh, minty breath as she tenderly touched her cheek. "I'll be just downstairs if you need me."

She had thought Evelyn would watch with her and hadn't even really considered that watching a movie was something someone could do alone. But this was nice. Every so often, she sat up and plucked a macaron from the box, then washed it down with sparkling water. She felt like Holly Golightly. Better yet, she felt like who Holly Golightly wanted to be.

AUGUST 2004

In July, Camille had gone to the DC School of Ballet to audition for placement in the upper division. The day before her birthday, she learned that she'd been accepted into Level Five, much, much better than she expected after looking at the different levels on the desktop computer. She was not certain her small-town Tennessee ballet education was good enough for the lowest level in the upper division, even with the weeks and weeks of intensives in Nashville.

That night, Evelyn surprised her.

"I was going to give it to you tomorrow, but I think you've earned it," Evelyn said, holding an enormous box at Camille's bedroom door. Inside was a smooth leather, caramel-colored bookbag with Camille's full name stamped above the back pocket in gold ink. "I hope you like it. I was going to have it monogrammed but

I learned you don't have a middle name. I didn't think two initials would look quite right."

"I love it," Camille squealed. She'd never seen a bookbag made of leather, not even in her little teen magazines. This was like something from the catalogs she'd seen on the internet. Except this was better because it had her name on it in gold letters.

"There's more," Evelyn said and moved aside some tissue to reveal another leather bag in the same shade, also stamped with Camille's name. "This one's for your ballet things." Camille thought she might cry. Nobody could look down on her at her new school with her perfectly timeless and well-made things.

So Camille woke up on her twelfth birthday feeling light, the lightest she'd ever felt. Her new bed was heavenly, made from something called memory foam, and she didn't have to share it with her mother. And her new home was fully and properly air-conditioned, so she slept well between a big, fluffy comforter and smooth, cotton sheets. At Charlotte's house, she'd had one pillow; here, she had four.

There was a knock on the bedroom door.

"Yes?"

Evelyn, wearing a long, white robe over a matching silk tank and billowy pants, threw the door open. She was smiling, which Camille had come to learn was mildly unusual. It was strange that Evelyn didn't smile more, as her teeth were so perfectly straight and white that Camille was not actually sure if they were real. In her hand, Evelyn held a goblet of champagne with a splash of orange juice. Evelyn often drank mimosas on Sunday mornings. Somewhere in the house, James Brown was playing on a stereo.

"Happy birthday!" Evelyn exclaimed, with an out-of-character hand gesture vaguely resembling a jazz hand. A bit of mimosa sloshed out of the glass. "Oh," she said. "Remind me to tell Miriam to clean that up."

"Thank you," Camille said as she rolled out of bed in the new blue-and-white-piped pajamas Evelyn had bought for her the week before. She slid her feet into a pair of cashmere slippers that Evelyn taught her to keep by her bed, since bare feet were "unpolished." As it turned out, wearing slippers was also more comfortable than going barefoot.

"I have a surprise for you," Evelyn said, gesturing for Camille to get up and follow her. "Come downstairs."

Camille followed Evelyn to the first floor, where she gestured to the coffee table, on which a pink hat box seemed to be desperately panting. Camille yelped so loudly that she surprised herself. Inside the box was a tiny, tiny gray dog with a pink bow tied around its neck.

"She's a teacup French Bulldog," Evelyn said. "And she's your responsibility."

Camille stared at the animal. She'd never seen a dog that small. It seemed like a bad idea for a dog to be that small, especially if it was going to be *her* responsibility. She lifted the dog out of the box and held her close.

"Don't give her a stupid human name, please."

"Thank you, Mama Evy," Camille said. This was her new name for Evelyn, whom she'd called Grandmother for her first week with her. One day, while they were shopping for shoes, Camille called to get Evelyn's attention from across the store. On her way over, Evelyn held up a finger.

"Now, darling girl. What do you *want* to call me?"

Camille shrugged. "What do you want me to call you?"

"Certainly not 'grandmother.' Sounds old and musty, don't you think?"

Camille shrugged again. "I call Granmama 'Mama Charlotte' sometimes. I can call you 'Mama Evelyn'?"

Evelyn nodded with approval. But Camille soon shortened the name to Mama Evy.

Camille held the dog under one arm and used the other to hug Evelyn around the shoulder. After a rapid growth spurt in the past few weeks, Evelyn's head only rose to Camille's jawbone. Evelyn was not much of a hugger, but Camille was used to giving hugs. She hugged Charlotte and David every time she saw them. If she left and came back from somewhere, that was reason enough for a hug. If she'd taken a short nap with the door closed, she instinctively extended hugs when she emerged. Evelyn didn't say that she didn't like hugging, but she didn't seem to know what to do when Camille reached for one. It wasn't that Evelyn never showed physical affection; she did but in much smaller ways. Sometimes, when they were out, Evelyn held Camille's hand. Sometimes, she touched the small of Camille's back in passing. Every now and again, Evelyn placed her hands on Camille's shoulders while she read or wrote at her desk or at the dining room table.

Camille held the dog close to her chest while she ate unsweetened yogurt and farmers market granola. They lingered at the table in the breakfast nook and read the newspaper. Camille read the Style section while Evelyn read the local news, as they had done every morning for the past month. The music had long changed from James Brown to Curtis Mayfield. Much to Camille's surprise, Charlotte and Evelyn had similar taste in music, except Evelyn never danced or sang along, though she did sometimes sway to Al Green when she went through what she called "her pages." However, unlike Charlotte, Evelyn favored playing classical music when she cooked, which didn't happen often.

"I think I'll name her Sozzani," Camille said when she was done reading.

"That's a fantastic name," Evelyn said. "Like the fashion editor?"

"You don't think it's a 'stupid human name'?"

Evelyn smiled, then winked at Camille over the reading glasses positioned precariously on the tip of her nose. "Oh, you'll have to learn when to ignore me. I don't always mean what I say."

Camille found this difficult to believe. Everything in Evelyn's life was precise and curated, from clothes to fruit. Camille had witnessed her go through an entire heap of apples at the farmers market, squeezing and smelling each piece carefully while the merchant looked on, only to buy nothing. Evelyn was most obsessive about fabrics. She could spend hours at Saks, touching, trying on, even smelling clothes, and leave empty-handed.

"Now," Evelyn said, folding her newspaper. "What shall we do today?" She reached out a pillowy soft hand, which Camille slipped her hand into. "Do you have everything you need for school? Have you thought any more about what I said about your hair?"

Evelyn had suggested Camille cut the relaxer out of her hair, starting in about how relaxer was bad for the Black community, how there was a "natural hair movement" approaching, and she could be ahead of the trend. Camille had intuited that Evelyn liked to give lectures, so she sat quietly and listened.

Mercifully, the phone rang this time, and Evelyn went to answer it, then brought the cordless phone back to the kitchen. "It's Charlotte."

"Hi, Mama!" Camille carried the dog onto the back deck and watched it stumble around the small, bright green, Astroturf'd yard like a drunk. "Guess what Mama Evy got me for my birthday?" She waited only a beat to exclaim: "A *dog*! I always wanted a dog!"

"Well, I just called to say happy birthday. So, happy birthday!" She continued, "Boy, I can't believe you're twelve. I can hardly believe it. Just yesterday, you were a little bitty baby."

Charlotte went on to tell Camille about the things that the women who came to get their hair done told her, mostly unfounded and salacious gossip. Apparently, there was a brothel and a moonshine mill in the backwoods run by the sheriff of Chilly Springs. And there was a ghost terrorizing people in the new movie theater. Camille missed how Charlotte confided in her about things that were none of her business, while Evelyn only *told* her things.

When Charlotte was done gossiping, she passed the phone to David, who was very invested in the NFL preseason. "Johnny

Washington is going to have an excellent season. I just know it," he said.

Finally, Corinna got on the line. "I just wanted to say happy birthday, honey," she said in a small, raspy voice, her first real sentence to Camille in months.

Camille ended the call and gathered the puppy from the shade of the high fence, then went inside. "I talked to Granmama about it," she lied, without knowing why. "And I think I'd like to cut my hair like you said."

"Oh, that's great news."

Evelyn would "suggest" many more things to Camille. There would be braces, teeth whitening, waxing, acrylic nails, Howard University, and much more. Camille would do practically anything and everything her great-grandmother encouraged her to do, at least for a few more years.

They drove all the way to Prince George's County, where Evelyn's stylist, Jeanette, worked in an immaculate, well-lit studio attached to the large, white colonial-style home where she lived with her husband and two young sons. Camille realized they had driven over an hour without an appointment but with the expectation that Jeanette would be available.

"Remember, I told you about my great-granddaughter coming to live with me?" Evelyn said to Jeanette at the door of her studio. Jeanette was easily one of the most beautiful women Camille had ever seen. Camille didn't like when people called her "chocolate," but she couldn't think of a better way to describe Jeanette's buttery, flawless skin, the color of the Domori dark chocolate bars Evelyn kept in large quantities in the back of the corner cabinet. "It's her birthday, and she badly wants . . ." Evelyn stage-whispered behind her dainty hand, "the Big Chop."

Jeanette smirked at Camille, gave her a quick once-over. "Is that right, mama?"

"Yes, ma'am," she answered, a bit taken aback by being addressed with a title of utmost respect.

"Oh, you got a cute little accent."

Jeanette was tall, almost Amazonian, in high-heeled, wooden-soled clogs. Her curly hair was wrapped up on top of her head in a colorful scarf, with little corkscrews springing up high.

Camille had spent her life wanting straight, silky hair like all the girls around her, like the girls on television and movies, on the covers of magazines. She'd seen some curly-headed Black women in *Ebony* and *Essence,* but they were all light-skinned, and their curls were big and loose. She had no idea what her hair might look like without a relaxer or hot comb, but she knew it wouldn't be like that. But Jeannie's hair was not like the light-skinned curly-headed women's—she had tight, tight, tight, kinky corkscrew curls. Her hair was nappy, even. And she was beautiful. Camille floated into the shampoo chair.

When all was said and done, Camille's hair was not nearly as long, as thick, or as shiny as Jeanette's. What she thought would be curls turned out more like uneven, crimped waves. Jeannette took Camille by the shoulders and placed her cheek next to hers, and they looked at each other in the mirror.

"It takes time for your hair to remember how it's supposed to be. You ever seen your natural hair, mama?"

"No."

"Ain't that a shame? How old are you?"

"Twelve."

"Hmph. Twelve years not knowing your own hair." Jeanette shook her head slowly, like it was the greatest shame she'd ever come across. "Like not knowing your own name, huh?"

Before they left, Jeanette gave Camille several bottles of her special leave-in conditioner. "It's gonna grow real fast now that you have that horrid relaxer out. And it will grow long and *strong,* honey"—Jeanette flexed both biceps—"I promise you that."

On the drive back into the city, Camille stared into the side-view mirror, trying to recognize herself. She felt Evelyn looking at her every few minutes, but she pretended not to.

As they passed RFK Stadium, Evelyn reached for her hand. "You're the main character now."

"What?"

"This is your story."

"What is?"

Evelyn was smiling unusually wide, which made Camille uncomfortable. "*This is.*"

Camille frowned, folded her arms, and nestled farther into the leather seat.

PART VII

Teeth

Camille

SUMMER 2007

"SO, I WAS reading *Sula*, and it was crazy," Camille explained on the phone to Su Jin, who was struggling with the summer reading. No one seemed to notice, but Camille suspected that her friend had a learning disability of some kind, though it seemed unfathomable that a disability of Su Jin's severity (she was nearly illiterate, in Camille's uninformed estimation) could go undiagnosed in a wealthy private school setting. Instead, the teachers and students seemed to think she was merely "ditsy." She was extremely self-conscious about it. So Camille explained things to her. She couldn't really help with math or science, anything based on memorization or rules, but she could help with language-based work. If Camille explained in enough detail, Su Jin could usually do the analysis and interpretation herself. Camille did this because Su Jin had done her an enormous favor: she chose her to be her friend.

Camille had gone to the Fairfax-Washington seventh-grade

orientation without Mama Evy for fear of looking like a baby, but when she entered the bright white cafeteria and saw all the other kids with their parents, she felt her stomach drop to her knees. She headed to the back of the room and tried to go unnoticed. Shortly after a short blond woman at the front started talking, a door that Camille hadn't noticed behind her flew open, and a flustered girl emerged from a crouched position into a seat next to her. The girl was digging through a satchel, eventually producing a pair of pink cat-eye glasses. She put them on and looked at Camille.

"Hi," she whispered.

"Hi."

"Are you new?"

Camille nodded, wondering what gave it away.

"Me, too! Want to go to the mall after this?"

Camille nodded.

"Cool."

Camille used Su Jin's cell phone to tell Evelyn about her plans. She had trouble keeping up as they walked toward the cluster of upscale stores near the Friendship Heights Metro, Su Jin in a pair of shoes Camille had only seen in magazines: pink patent-leather Dr. Martens.

She'd been explaining things to Su Jin ever since, for the better part of the past three years. Camille had had no problem with *The Great Gatsby*, *Slaughterhouse Five*, or *Call of the Wild*, all of which she'd understood but didn't really *get*. She did, however, get *Sula*. She identified with the title character, who was raised by women and went away to reinvent herself. But she resisted explaining this to Su Jin. She didn't know how to talk about Sula without talking about herself, and she didn't want to try.

"I have to go," Camille said as her mother entered the room and started to pour bright yellow wine from a jug into one of David's commemorative Saints cups.

Camille and Corinna hadn't been speaking very often that summer. Camille didn't know what to say to her mother. She found herself standing with her arms folded behind her back, a display of not knowing what to do with herself that she'd only read about in books.

Corinna looked at her over the top of the white, purple, and gold-colored plastic as she drank. Camille averted her eyes and clomped out of the kitchen.

She thought of *Sula* and the son who returns from war and tries to crawl back into his mother's womb. If she reentered her mother's womb, she could be born again. But she had actually been born again. In this new life, she had straight teeth, access to the internet, air-conditioning, private education, and her own bed. But she'd brought her wounds with her. Her wounds were no longer open, but they'd left her with scar tissue and calluses. Her literal skin, though, was smooth and unmarked, because she'd been taught how to care for it from a very early age. Her mother and grandmother had slathered her with Vaseline every morning and cocoa butter every night and reminded her to wash her face every morning and night. She wished she'd been taught something similar for the rest of herself.

LATE SUMMER 2007

Corinna left—again—that summer. Camille failed to be surprised. She couldn't muster a single emotion on the matter, actually.

Every day at six p.m. sharp, Charlotte took a seat on the front porch with a drink and her cigarettes. If it was too hot outside, she smoked at the kitchen sink until it cooled down. This was not a new schedule for Charlotte. However, she used to lean back in her rocking chair, gazing off into the distance. After Corinna left, Charlotte looked out at the road and sometimes stretched her long neck to watch cars go by.

"What happened with them letters, Mama?" Camille asked Charlotte one afternoon on the porch, referring to the pink papers scattered all over the floor of her grandmother's bedroom. She was sitting between Charlotte's legs, getting her scalp greased. A chunk of ash from Charlotte's cigarette fell onto Camille's knee. She didn't brush it away.

Charlotte didn't say anything for a while, just kept parting Camille's hair and rubbing Blue Magic into the exposed scalp. Camille didn't use Blue Magic anymore, but getting her scalp greased by her grandmother was more important to her than the quality of the product.

"Um," Charlotte said. Though Camille could not see her face, she could hear the expression in her tone: furrowed brows and pinched lips. "You ever wonder about your father?"

Camille thought about it for a moment and attempted to anticipate where her grandmother was going. She assumed whatever happened had something to do with her mother's biological father.

"Yeah," she said. "I guess," though it wasn't entirely true. There were several years following Jenny's death when Camille had been frightened of the idea of a father. In DC, she was asked more frequently about him than she had been in Tennessee— more specifically, what her father did for a living. So she was forced to think about the nameless, faceless entity more often than before, but there wasn't much to think about; he didn't exist. At first, she thought about saying her father was in Belgium on business, but she decided it wasn't worth lying about. She told everyone that she didn't have a father. As far as she was concerned, it was true. And in DC, the dads were even more absent than they'd been in Tennessee. There was no man-shaped hole in her life.

"How do you think you'd feel if you found out he wasn't such a good guy?"

Camille shrugged. "Is that what happened? Her father isn't a good guy?"

"That's right."

"That's why she left, then?"

"Well, no."

"Why did she leave, then?"

Camille felt her grandmother exhale on her exposed scalp. "Sometimes, the best thing you can do for people you love is leave 'em."

She'd heard her grandfather say the same thing, but she couldn't remember the context. Charlotte was done oiling Camille's scalp. She slipped her hands into the mess of curls and massaged her head gently.

"What'd he do?" Camille asked.

"Maybe your mama will tell you," Charlotte said softly.

The conversation was over. But somehow, Camille knew all she needed to know. Though she wasn't sure what it was, she understood that *something* had shifted in her understanding of her mother. The shift wasn't seismic, but it was significant enough to change her behavior.

After that, she spent more time outside, just staring at the grass and tearing petals off wildflowers. She lay on the quilt that had been on her mother's bed and watched the clouds or read a book. She thought of Jenny. Where was she? She'd like to talk about *Sula* with her.

A few times, Charlotte dragged her into the house to eat, but usually let her be. Most evenings, she dangled her feet off the porch and read to her grandparents. After that, she returned phone calls that Charlotte messily kept track of on a notepad, almost all of them from Su Jin. Usually, they could go on for hours about absolute nonsense, but Camille didn't want to talk much after her mother left. Instead, she just listened to her friend complain about her own mother or stepfather. She swore when it was appropriate and laughed when she was supposed to. By the time they hung up, it was usually pretty late, but Camille was never tired. Sometimes, she listened to her MP3 player and danced around the kitchen with Sozzani. Sometimes, she took a shot of whatever was lying around and went to bed. Sometimes, she went out into the near pitch-black night to look at the stars. And other times, she just went to bed and lay awake for hours thinking about her mother. The bedroom where she slept was almost exactly the same as it had been when she was a little girl and her mother was bringing home fried Oreos and catfish at three a.m.: the carpet was still nubby and brown, the walls were still a sickly yellow, there was still cheap dollar-store art on the walls, and the window still didn't open. When she closed her eyes tight, she could still see her mother in her Copperhead shirt and tight jeans, smell the catfish and spilled liquor, and feel her mother nuzzling her cheek with her own.

Corinna

EARLY SUMMER 2007

Corinna had quit her job at Copperhead after Isaac died, saying she needed some time to pull herself together. For a long time, she felt like she was drowning. If she had the wherewithal to figure it out, she would have known it was the feeling of failure that pulled her down the hardest. Marriage gave her legitimacy. More than that, she'd done something better than her mother had. Isaac obviously wasn't perfect, but there was no fighting, no police, no cheating, and he never hit Corinna on purpose. Once, he'd accidentally hit her in the eye with his elbow, given her a black eye, and then cried for two days, he felt so bad. That had to count for something.

But three years later, she still wasn't anywhere near pulled together, though she was *more* together than she had been. She'd located most of her pieces, but she couldn't get them to fit.

She pretended to look for a job. She let her mother drive her all over the tricounty area to pick up and drop off applications, but she never followed up and never answered the phone in case it might be a potential employer. She didn't feel bad about it. She didn't really even need a job now that Camille was taken care of. She had some money saved and didn't have much to worry about beyond food and liquor since she lived with her parents.

She had a hard time imagining herself going back to pouring

drinks and making small talk after what happened with Isaac. He was the only reason she'd become a bartender. That had been his gift to her. It wasn't an easy job. She had to be a chemist, a conversationalist, a therapist, and a bouncer all at once. But there were so many opportunities to do a good job. Every night, there were hundreds of drinks to pour and serve just right, a few dozen people to make laugh. Most of all, she missed the look on someone's face when they took a sip of a well-done cocktail, the impressed frown, and nod. The folks at Copperhead said there would always be a job for her there. But she couldn't go back to touching the same surfaces Isaac had touched and walking the same floors he'd walked. Yes, hundreds and hundreds of people had touched those surfaces and walked those floors since he died. But Corinna still felt sick when she drove by Copperhead.

She couldn't imagine herself doing anything else, though. She'd never really done anything besides bartending, except for her time at Whiskers. She could have gotten some low-skill job, like a cashier at a fast-food restaurant or a clerk in some retail store. But she'd been assistant bar manager. And she'd been a wife. And a mother. And now she was nobody. There was something she kind of liked about being nobody. For the first time in her life, no one needed her.

Camille came to visit several times a year. And each time, Corinna felt Camille getting further and further away from her. It felt like a good thing that they had less and less in common. Camille was becoming a girl Corinna couldn't have imagined, who knew things that Corinna couldn't have imagined.

Corinna was hurting. But she'd done what she thought she needed to do. And it was working out pretty much as she'd hoped. She might not be a Great Mom, but her daughter was doing great, and that was almost the same thing, right?

The summer of 2007, Corinna was thinking about getting her shit together. She would get a job, locate somebody interested in her, or whatever people with their shit together do.

Camille would be fifteen by the end of the summer. Corinna

hadn't seen her since Easter. The cartilage of the girl's upper ear had been pierced since then. The piercing looked fresh, a little swollen. Corinna wondered if Camille's thick curls ever got snagged in the little gold hoop. Did it hurt when this happened? Did it hurt when she got it done? Why had she gotten it done? Did she have permission from Evelyn?

Evelyn was paying for almost everything, which had never been part of the agreement. Still, Corinna didn't protest because it meant almost all of the money from child support was going into her daughter's savings. Evelyn said she didn't believe in private school and that she wouldn't pay for that. But she did pay for all kinds of expensive clothes, shoes, makeup, and skincare. Many of the brands Corinna recognized from dropping into Macy's to check the clearance rack, but others she had never heard of: La Mer, Celine, Miu Miu, and Yves Saint Laurent. Others were so foreign to her in spelling or language that she couldn't commit them to memory.

Evelyn also paid for Camille's braces. Corinna had planned to ask Johnny to pay for Camille's orthodontia when she got a little older, but Evelyn said the girl was already late to the game.

"Oh, darling," she told Corinna over the phone. "You cannot wait any longer. You don't want her in her senior portraits and things with *braces*. Trust me, dear."

Evelyn often referred to Camille as her "darling girl," but when she used "dear," it was almost always infuriatingly condescending. But Corinna demurred more often than not. When it came to the braces, Charlotte said that they couldn't go making decisions about an adolescent girl's face without giving her all the information and letting her decide. It just wasn't right. Corinna did not understand her mother's resistance. Why on earth would Camille *not* want perfect teeth? *Everyone* wants perfect teeth. Never in her life had she heard someone say someone's teeth were too straight or too white. Steve Harvey's teeth did have an overwhelming quality, but that was better than having bad teeth. She really didn't understand Charlotte sometimes.

Camille had always been a pretty girl. But, postbraces, she was stunning. It gave her an aristocratic quality. She looked like a supermodel. Corinna was almost jealous. Her own teeth were not terribly crooked, but they did not have the clinical, mathematical geometry of Camille's new teeth. But different teeth wouldn't have made much of a difference for Corinna. It was too late for her.

In the months following the removal of her braces, Camille had developed a habit for bubble gum; she packed a freezer-size Ziploc bag full of a bubblegum called Babol in her bright pink luggage. She spent much of the summer stretching out for hours on the porch, blowing bubbles, or petting her dog—sometimes all three at once. Camille's dog, who was small enough that she could hold it with one hand, was protective of her, nipping at the air if sudden movements were made in her general vicinity. She fed the dog from her plate and let it kiss her on the lips.

At night, Camille read aloud to David, like she had when she was little. He closed his eyes and reclined his head on the back of the couch. Sometimes, he seemed to have fallen asleep, but when Camille paused, he would come to life with a sharp inhale.

"You don't want to read no more, honey?"

"I just thought you fell asleep."

"Nah, I'm awake."

Corinna witnessed the exact same exchange over and over while Camille read dutifully from *Of Mice and Men* or *Invisible Man*. Other nights, Camille took calls from her friends on the landline, the last of her peers without a cell phone. Sometimes she gossiped with them, and sometimes she talked about their summer vacations or whom she hoped she would get for English. Other nights, she sat on the bed she shared with Corinna, listening to her MP3 player and writing in her black leather-bound journal while the dog lay supine near her feet.

If she wasn't doing any of those things, she was sitting in the living room armchair, telling David and Charlotte stories about her friends, school, and DC. She had so many interests, so many likes, so many dislikes, and so many hobbies. Corinna dissected

Camille's language for evidence that something was even vaguely awry in her new life, but could never find it. She was happy, and doing well, and Corinna felt she'd done something right.

As much as she grieved her relationship with her daughter, Corinna felt victorious that Camille didn't have to worry about food, clothes, the cleanliness of her home, or anything like that. Camille had a good life. No point in regretting the fact that she couldn't provide this life for Camille. But she *had* provided this life for Camille. When Corinna thought about it, which was all the time, she went round and round but landed in exactly the same spot.

She missed Isaac. Maybe not the way a woman ought to miss her dead husband, but she did. She missed who he had been when they'd first started seeing each other. Sometimes she felt guilty for not loving that version of him more. Maybe she would have gotten help for him if she had loved him more, and it was her fault what had happened. She thought she could take care of him. In fact, she thought she had no other choice, as her mother took care of her husband, who was actually a much shittier husband than Isaac. So if Charlotte could love and care for David, Corinna thought she could—and should—at least *care* for Isaac.

She didn't remember much about the events leading up to the moment he shot himself, which doctors said was normal. What bothered her most wasn't the missing memories; the memories she had were the problem. She could very clearly see in her mind's eye the exact second that Isaac's face was obliterated. And it had obliterated, completely disintegrated. She wasn't sure who called the police. She didn't remember going to the hospital.

The next real memory she had was of her mother running her a bath while she waited naked on the lid of the toilet seat. Then Charlotte had bathed her like a baby, gently rubbing her with an old, rough washcloth, and rinsing the suds off with cupped hands of water. Charlotte had washed and braided Corinna's hair and tucked her into bed, where she stayed for several days. Corinna had never felt more loved by her mother. Maybe she'd been marinating in that feeling for the past three years.

No one ever talked to her about what happened to Isaac. Apparently, there hadn't even been a funeral because his parents were so ashamed. They had him cremated and gave half of the ashes to Corinna, who kept them in the nondescript box they'd come in. Originally, she put the box in her lowest dresser drawer, but then she saw it was next to her tampons, so she moved it to her top drawer. Corinna wondered how her mother and daughter felt about Isaac's death, wondered if either of them cried or had nightmares because of it. She doubted it; this was her burden to bear. This was her punishment. For what, exactly? For trying to become independent? For thinking she was deserving of love and security? For being a horrible mother?

Had she been, though? Camille probably thought so. Corinna knew Camille was hurt by the choices she'd made. But Camille didn't know how much more she could have been hurt if Corinna hadn't made those choices. Maybe one day she would tell Camille why she'd done what she'd done. She couldn't tell her now because she didn't know how. She hoped that Camille could forgive her, hoped that someday she would wake up and look around at all of her nice things, her nice life, and she would forgive.

LATE SUMMER 2007

Corinna was beginning to understand that something, or a series of somethings, had happened to Charlotte to make her the way she was. One doesn't leave a wealthy home to live in backwoods Tennessee just for the hell of it. Whatever had happened to Charlotte, it was Evelyn's fault, she knew; in matters of mothers and daughters, it is always the mother's fault.

It was difficult to imagine that Evelyn could do anything wrong, though. She was so smart, so put-together. She could be a real bitch, but Corinna kind of appreciated that about her. She was businesslike in all discussions about Camille, behaving like a

Hollywood agent advocating for her top client: *Camille needs this, Camille needs that, Camille deserves better than this, Camille is too lovely not to have this, I believe in Camille's future so much that I will pay for this, that, and the third.* Corinna felt safe knowing Camille was being cared for by a woman who never hesitated to speak with the manager, whose nails were always manicured, who read the ingredients of everything she ate, who ordered sparkling water in enormous quantities from abroad instead of drinking from the tap. But she could see how it could get aggravating, the perfectionism. But it didn't explain not speaking to your mother for thirty years.

Evelyn hardly talked about herself, so Corinna doubted she'd be willing to shed any light on the question. But she knew Evelyn felt guilty about Charlotte. Any idiot could see that. What Corinna couldn't figure out was whether she wanted to know what happened to her mother. Would it bring her any peace? Any satisfaction?

"What you thinking about so damn hard?"

Corinna looked up to see David sitting across from her at the table, one hand on his cane and the other balled in a fist on the tabletop. He was chewing loudly on an exceptionally large wad of gum (probably nicotine, as he'd never fully shaken the habit). She hadn't even realized he'd entered the room.

"Hm?" she said.

"I said," he repeated, "what you thinking about so damn hard?"

"Oh, I was just thinking about Mama."

"What about your mama?"

Corinna pulled her tongue across the roof of her mouth to make a clicking sound. "I was just thinking. That all right witchu?"

"Well, I was just wondering if I could help. You been sitting there all damn day just staring off into space."

"Well, I don't need no help thinking."

"You sure?"

Well, actually, Corinna wasn't sure. She sighed. Charlotte and Camille were out, probably driving around to all three thrift stores in town, looking for absolutely nothing.

David's tone changed. "You've been thinking a lot lately. Ain't you, baby? You finally in a place you can really think about some shit."

His earnestness made Corinna emotional. Her throat started to ache, and she covered her mouth with her hand. She noticed the table for the first time in a long time. The grout was completely gone in some places, and pieces of tile were chipping away. She quashed the tears and straightened her spine.

"I can tell you this," David said. He spat out his gum and tossed it into the nearby trash can. "If you want to know why your mama is the way she is, you gotta find out for yourself. She's not going to tell you shit."

Corinna nodded. "I know that."

"So you just going to sit here like this for the rest of your damn life?"

They stared at each other.

"What you saying, Daddy?"

"I'm saying there's some shit you can't know and some shit you can."

"Daddy, what the *hell* are you talking about?"

"I got to spell it out for you, girl? You want to know what the hell happened to your mama, don't you?"

Again, they stared at each other.

"Well, do you?"

Corinna nodded.

"It's been right 'front of your eyes, baby."

"Daddy," she said dryly. "What are you talking about?"

He leaned forward and whispered. "The letters, Corinna. The *damn* letters."

Corinna froze. *Oh, shit,* she thought. She stood up so fast the chair behind her fell backward. It'd been there the whole time, just looking her in the face. The closet door in her parents' bedroom had been broken years earlier in a bad fight, removed, and never replaced. So the contents of the closet had since been visible, but Corinna avoided the bedroom as much as she could. As a girl, she had only entered to make sure neither of her parents choked to death on their vomit. Until his injury, the room smelled like body odor, vomit, cigarette smoke, and occasionally perfume that did not belong to Charlotte. It was an ungodly scent that made Corinna's stomach churn. Now, the room smelled sterile, like a hospital. She couldn't decide which scent she preferred.

In the early nineties, when she started making her own money and her parents were starting to act like halfway decent people, she'd bought them a black lacquer bedroom set for Christmas. She'd gotten it from a furniture warehouse off Nolensville Pike up in Nashville, and got a good deal on the set because there were nicks in the lacquer and a scratch on the mirror on top of the dresser. The furniture was too big and heavy for the small room, and allowed only a narrow pathway between the end of the bed and the large dresser to the right.

Pictures of Camille were taped all over the mirror. There were a few photos of Corinna with her, but none of Corinna alone or as a child, almost as if she hadn't existed until Camille was born. Corinna shook off the thought before it could cripple her. She used a stool that Camille had needed to reach the bathroom sink as a little girl to bring herself eye level with the closet shelf, which was overloaded with blankets and shoeboxes. Corinna took the most accessible box and opened it while still standing on the stool. It was packed tight with pink envelopes, just like the one she'd found in the mailbox years earlier. Corinna opened an envelope with great care, slowly slipping the card out of the envelope. She expected a normal sheet of paper, like computer paper or one of those blank notecards you could buy in packs of ten at Walmart. Instead, she found a rectangle of cardstock that was both delicate and sturdy. Corinna had never touched anything quite like it.

At the top of the letter was printed: *From the Desk of Evelyn Gwendolyn Jackson, PhD.* Corinna's hand shook as she read.

Charlotte,
Thank you for sharing Camille with me. She has your father's eyes. She makes me believe it is possible to make my failure lighter and lighter, until it is lost to time and history and generations and generations. I hope to live to see it. I'm sorry I never told you how beautifully you played the piano.

Sincerely,
Evelyn

The stomps that opened David's favorite gospel song startled Corinna so bad that she jumped and dropped the notecard. Her heart thudded with the tempo, and she took a few deep breaths. David had brought this CD home from Goodwill, where he'd bought it for one dollar and forty-nine cents. He did not like the entire CD. He really liked only the fourth track, especially when the lead singer sang in a throaty voice:

God's chemical laboratory of redemption took my black soul
and dipped it in red blood, and I came out white as snow.

He played the song over and over and over while Corinna rooted through the letters wildly. She stopped opening letters with care, tearing the ends and tops off envelopes without abandon. Some of the envelopes contained cards, and others contained small, neatly folded sheets of paper. It seemed that Evelyn always knew what she wanted to write before she wrote it and how to fit it into the space that she had. Perhaps she wrote drafts? It was difficult to imagine Evelyn laboring over anything, let alone a letter. While the presentation of the letters fit the Evelyn she knew, the content surprised her more and more as she went on. Charlotte must have organized them according to receipt or the postmark (which was often missing). Some letters were long and confessional in nature, while many others simply read:

> *Dear Charlotte,*
> *I'm sorry.*
>
> > > > *Evelyn*

As Corinna did not know what she was looking for, she just kept going, feeling wild with it. She took down shoeboxes until she reached the last one, in which the envelopes were so faded they were almost white, retaining only the deep pink along the edges. There was one visibly thicker envelope; she knew she had found what she was looking for. David's song started over for what had to have been the twentieth time that afternoon:

"I knoooow I been chaaaaanged," the chorus sang.

Inside the envelope were several neatly folded pieces of paper covered in a different script. This writing seemed unhinged.

> *Charlotte,*
> *What you have to understand is that I never wanted to be a mother. I thought it was what you were supposed to do. I did a great deal that people didn't expect of me. I went to school, I worked. I thought I had to do this one thing. I did not know how many choices I had. . . .*

Corinna grew annoyed with all of the excuses Evelyn made and tossed the first sheet of paper aside. The next page started:

> *and that's why I let Wayne die. I could have done a great deal of things to save his life—or at least prolong his life. But I didn't. I chose you. I choose you. Come back to me, and we can be a family. I can be your mother. I want to be your mother. I'm sorry I didn't want it sooner. But I miss you, darling girl. At first, I wanted you to come home because of how it looked. I see the error in that now.*

I want you to come home because I love you. I can't bear the idea of your struggling to make a life. We can figure out what to do with the baby. It's not too late to give it up. People do it all the time. You won't want to raise that baby, knowing where it came from. You'll feel nothing but anger and resentment. It's not too late for both of you to have a good life. We can fix this. Let me help you fix this.

Both darkness and strange, glittering light crept into Corinna's vision. She put out a hand to steady herself, found the shiny surface of the lacquered dresser, and placed her palms on the shining surface. She closed her eyes so that she would not have to look at herself in the mirror. She heard a loud ringing and a falling sensation. She hadn't felt like this since she watched Isaac prop his head on the barrel of a shotgun and pull the trigger with his toe. She shook her head as if she might be able to shake her mind back into its proper position.

When Corinna heard her mother clear her throat, Corinna's body jolted. She turned to find Charlotte leaning casually against the doorjamb.

"You look like you seen a ghost," Charlotte said.

Hadn't she? Seen a ghost, on the sheets of pink paper? The ghost was this man, Wayne? No, that wasn't right. There was an acidic, unpleasant taste in Corinna's mouth. She didn't have anything to say.

"Well," Charlotte said, her eyes scanning the floor. "Did you get the answers you were looking for?"

Camille appeared behind her grandmother, wearing gym shorts rolled over several times at the waistband and a T-shirt small enough for an elementary school student without a bra underneath. The shirt read: JONES FAMILY REUNION, '79. She was sucking on the tip of a Rocket Pop.

"What's going on?" she asked, and blue juice dripped on her white T-shirt and the carpet.

Corinna looked at her daughter and then her mother.

"Well?" Charlotte said.

The gospel music clicked off, and Corinna felt steadier on her feet, but the room suddenly seemed impossibly small.

"What's all that on the floor?" Camille asked. "Looks like the stationery Mama Evy uses."

"Nothing to concern yourself with."

"It—" Corinna started but, instead, held up the letter she'd just read. "Mama, this is why?"

"Why what?"

"Why you can't move on?" Corinna's voice cracked.

"Can you leave us for a minute, Camille? Close the door."

Camille did as she was told but as slowly as she could manage. When the door was shut, Charlotte sat down on the bed and patted the space next to her, but Corinna didn't sit. She was too dizzy to move across the room.

"Why ain't you tell me? You could have said something."

"When would have been a good time?"

"When I asked you what she did to you."

Charlotte took a deep breath and exhaled slowly. "Wouldn't you rather not know?"

Corinna felt the room steadying as understanding came to her. She sat down next to her mother.

"Which part? That you were raped or that I'm the product of that rape?"

"Both parts, I guess."

Corinna saw her mother's hand trembling, so she took it. "This explains a lot, Mama."

"About what?"

"About you. Why you were the way you were." Corinna really meant the present tense, *are*, but she decided not to say that out of respect.

Charlotte looked at her hopefully. "You forgive me, because of this?"

Corinna sighed. In various ways, she had already forgiven her mother because it was too painful not to. But if she completely forgave her mother, what happened to her own pain? Did her mother get off scot-free? She would have to run the numbers on that.

"Well, you're not angry that I lied?" Charlotte continued.

"I already knew you lied, Mama. I was never angry about that."

"It doesn't bother you?" Charlotte whispered. "Where you come from?"

Corinna was *very* bothered. But she couldn't admit that to her mother at this particular moment. She would deal with those feelings later, or not at all. "I mean, I don't love it. But I think I already knew somehow."

Charlotte narrowed her eyes. "What you mean by that?"

"I mean, I knew it couldn't have been good. You never said a word about him. Even I acknowledge that Camille got a daddy—" Corinna paused and changed course. "Silence speaks louder than words. That's how it go, right?"

"Well, what happens now?"

"Forgive Evelyn? Move on. It would be good for Camille."

"Who said I don't forgive her?"

"Mama—"

Charlotte looked up from the hand Corinna was holding. "I've tried." She gritted her teeth. "I've *tried*, goddammit. I *can't*."

"Maybe you just don't know how, Mama."

She wasn't sure if her mother was willing to figure out how, or if she was capable of this kind of forgiveness. But she did know she wasn't qualified to determine that about her mother, because she hadn't figured it out about herself.

They sat in silence, Corinna rubbing the back of her mother's silky-smooth hand with her thumb. She looked up from the floor and at her mother. Charlotte seemed different somehow. Her skin was still leathery and lined with age and hard living. There were still bags under her eyes. But she looked different. Relieved, maybe.

"I do know one thing. You can't sit in this house like this no more, Corinna."

"Huh?"

"It's been three *years*." Charlotte's groan was deep and laborious. "I'm worried about you. I know what sadness can do to a person."

"You're kicking me out?"

"I didn't say that. I said you gotta get out of this house."

Corinna watched Charlotte get off the bed onto her hands and knees, army-crawling under the bed until half her body was hidden. She rustled around for a bit before a bulk carton of Natural American Spirits emerged, not even her brand.

Charlotte emerged and put the box on the bed, then pulled herself up. She reached into the pocket of the men's shirt she was wearing, produced a Slim, and lit it. The box had been sealed shut with clear packing tape. Charlotte slit it open with her acrylic fingernail and opened the lid just enough so that Corinna could see there weren't cigarettes in there, but money.

"Looks like more than it actually is," Charlotte muttered, the cigarette dangling precariously from her lips. "It ain't gon' fix nothing, but it'll get you someplace. You've never even left the state, have you?"

"Mama—"

"I'm not going to argue with you about it. You gotta start over, and you sure as hell ain't doing it here."

"But Camille—"

"You ain't doing her no favors haunting this house like this."

"She'll think I'm leaving her again."

"She'll forgive you," Charlotte said.

"How do you know?"

Charlotte slapped her thighs in exasperation, making a satisfying thwack against the stiff denim. She managed not to burn them with the cigarette. "Do I look like a damn fortune teller to you? Do I look like Oprah *Winfrey* to you? I don't *know*."

Corinna rolled her eyes.

"Well, do I?"

Charlotte waited for an answer, and they stared at each other until they both cracked a smile.

"What you doing ain't working. Anybody with eyes can see that. Shit. Don't even need eyes."

Charlotte wrapped her arms around her daughter and squeezed. It took Corinna several seconds to register what was happening. She'd waited for this moment her entire life. She almost forgot to hug Charlotte back, she was so busy trying to savor the moment. Her mother's cigarette was perilously close to her own hair, and her mother smelled like tobacco, cheap floral soap, and just a little bit of liquor. But Corinna had never been more at ease. She squeezed her mother's narrow body so tight that air popped from between the discs of Charlotte's spine.

"You've done me a big favor," Charlotte said softly into Corinna's ear. "Let me do this for you."

Corinna wasn't sure what favor she'd done, or what Charlotte thought she was giving her in return. But she knew her mother was right. What she was doing wasn't working.

PART VIII

Skin and Bones

Camille

A week after her mother left, the floor of her grandparents' bedroom was still covered in pink debris. Several nights in a row, Camille found Charlotte sitting in the middle of the mess, but eventually, her grandmother started sorting through the papers, placing some of the letters back into shoeboxes and throwing others into a black trash bag.

When Camille offered to help, Charlotte's lip twitched with hesitation, but she sat down anyway. She knew Evelyn wrote to Charlotte every Thursday morning. Sometimes, Camille walked the envelopes to the mailbox on the way to school. But she never concerned herself with the content.

Now, she understood that something had gone horribly wrong between Charlotte and Evelyn. Quickly, she understood that she was only throwing away the rectangular pieces of cardstock that had very few words on them. Every single one of them read in Evelyn's block handwriting:

Dear Charlotte,
I'm sorry.

Evelyn

Camille was sad, but it didn't seem like her own to feel.

*   *   *

On the first of August, Charlotte drove Camille to the airport to go back to DC, and Camille requested they drive by Jenny Rhodes's old house. It was smaller and closer to the road than she remembered.

"Somebody finally bought it last year for pennies on the dollar," Charlotte said. "I still think about them sometimes."

"Yeah, me, too," Camille said.

There were no cars out front, but a fence had been erected out back, apparently extending all the way to the creek, where she and Jenny once jumped double Dutch. She wondered why the new owners would fence off the creek. If she could have seen the water, she would always want a view of it. Maybe Jenny's ghost was still wandering along the bank. She wondered what had become of Isaac's ghost. Sure was a lot of ghosts around.

"Granmama?"

"Yeah?"

"I was just thinking about Mama. You know that thing she does with her head?" Camille did her best imitation of Evelyn's erratic head shake.

Charlotte smirked. "Oh, yeah. What they call that? A tic?"

"I guess. I mean. I wonder if it's like she's trying to rearrange her brain."

"Rearrange her brain?" Charlotte smiled graciously. "Girl, you too much sometimes. What makes you think of that?"

"I wish I could rearrange my brain sometimes."

Charlotte paused for a moment. "You mean, change the way your thoughts work? Your memories, stuff like that?"

"Yeah. I think that's what I mean."

"I feel that way too sometimes."

Camille watched the side of her grandmother's face, wondering what her grandmother wished she could change.

On the plane, before it took off, Camille slid open the window shade to look at the vast emptiness around the airport. Sozzani was wheezing and whining in her pet carrier. Camille tried talking to the dog to soothe her, but it only made her more agitated. She unzipped the carrier and dropped in a few low-fat treats. It quieted the dog only for the short time it took her to ingest them. Sometimes, Camille felt overwhelmed by the responsibility of caring for Sozzani by herself. When her mother and grandmother were just a little bit older than her, they'd had to care for human children. The thought alone stressed her out. She decided it could never be her.

She pulled out a copy of *Teen Vogue* and pretended to read, but actually catalogued the ways her life would be better for the remainder of the summer. Evelyn didn't ask millions of questions; she let Camille out of her sight for hours at a time; and Evelyn almost never stared at her.

Camille's knees were sore when it was finally time to deplane; when she massaged her legs, she thought of her grandfather. She wondered if David had ever been on a plane. What about her mother? She figured probably not.

She grabbed a couple of magazines before she exited the terminal, then stepped into the moist heat with a frown. Immediately, she spotted Evelyn, absolutely pristine in a white linen tunic with the collar popped, white espadrilles, and white-framed sunglasses. From a distance, Evelyn looked like a young woman. You couldn't see the particular way the skin sagged on her knees or the way the veins in her hand skimmed so close to the surface of her skin. Nor could you hear her manufactured mid-Atlantic accent, or the way she said "Mondee," "Tuesdee," and "on tomorrow." She was on the phone, but when she saw Camille, she abruptly ended the call and threw the phone through the open driver's-side window.

"There you are! I was beginning to get worried. We really should get you a cell phone."

She grabbed Camille hard by the shoulders, slamming their cheeks together, and blew air kisses at her ears.

"Oh, I missed you!" she said when they were in the car. She sat for a moment, smiling her perfect, big-toothed smile, and looked at Camille. "Oh, you really are a pretty girl, prettier all the time," she said, and Camille couldn't help but smile, too.

"Look in the glove box," Evelyn said. "I got you something."

David was always saying, "I got you something," and it was always candy. Camille had no idea how he managed to get all that candy when he was almost housebound. Camille was no longer particularly interested in candy—Evelyn said it was bad for her skin and teeth, and Mrs. Schumann at the School of Ballet said it was empty calories—but the effort always pleased her.

But this was different. Camille did not feel like she did when David said he had something for her. She reluctantly opened the glove box and was not surprised to find another hardcover Toni Morrison book: *Tar Baby*. Evelyn would expect her to read it and be ready to have high-level intellectual conversations about it within the next few weeks. It wasn't that Camille disliked books, or Toni Morrison. She loved books, and rather enjoyed Toni Morrison, but it didn't feel like a gift, not the way she understood them, anyway. Evelyn bought the book more for her own benefit and pleasure than Camille's. She reminded herself of all the things Evelyn had bought and done for her over the years—maybe more than anyone else. But somehow, the math didn't come out in Evelyn's favor.

Camille forced a smile. "Thanks, Mama Evy."

"You're welcome," she said cheerfully.

Camille expected Evelyn to ask about her visit to Tennessee, as they had spoken only a few times that summer. Instead, Evelyn put on NPR. And Camille was kind of glad to pretend the events of the past month were too inconsequential to discuss. The story on the radio was something to do with climate change or global warming, which made Camille feel sleepy. She rested her elbow on the ledge in the door and rested her head on her fist.

"We have to stop by the store," Evelyn said as they hit the highway. Camille soon fell asleep, and when she woke up, the car was parked and it was late afternoon; she could tell by the color and position of the sun. All the windows were rolled down, and a gentle breeze wafted through them. She wiped dried drool from her chin and sat up. They were parked behind Charlotte's Bookstore and

Café. She scooped Sozzani from where she was curled up on the driver's seat and entered the store, scrubbing at the corners of her mouth to make sure there was no crusty drool left.

Camille was always self-conscious at Charlotte's, but especially in her summer uniform of gym shorts, a thrift-store T-shirt with some inanity printed across the front like DOUBLE BUBBLE DON'T BURST MY BUBBLE, and Keds. No one here was particularly dressed up, but their casual wear was like Patagonia Bermuda shorts and Chaco hiking sandals.

Camille knew that Charlotte's had once been a one-room storefront in California, but Evelyn had moved it to the Georgetown Waterfront the year before. It had focused only on books by and about the "capital D" Diaspora. She'd never been to Oakland, but she could imagine the store wasn't quite like this. Now, somehow, it was a sprawling general-interest shop with creaky hardwood floors, views of the Potomac, and entire sections that sold things like silk bookmarks, novelty bookplates, and coffee mugs with sayings like TEACHING IS MY SUPERPOWER.

Camille was headed upstairs to the offices to look for Evelyn when someone tapped her on the shoulder. She turned around, ready to explain her trespass, but she snapped her mouth shut when she saw who it was. He was the most attractive man she had ever seen, even including Trayon Evans, a junior in last semester's conversational Japanese class. The first thing she noticed about this man was how much darker his skin was than his hair, which was a lovely gradient of blond. His eyes were both green and blue at the same time.

"Um," he said, clearing his throat. "Sorry, but only service animals are allowed in here."

"Sorry, Camille," piped a familiar voice. It was Ruth, the general manager, who often dropped by Evelyn's with expensive teas and bottles of wine. "Logan is new."

"Oh, it's okay," Camille said, adjusting her grip on Sozzani and staring at Ruth's high-heeled penny loafers in an attempt not to look at the man.

"Camille is Evelyn's great-granddaughter, Logan."

"Where is she?" Camille asked. Her skin was hot and tingly, and she didn't know what to do with herself.

Ruth directed her to the office, and Camille scurried upstairs. She looked over her shoulder once and realized the man was actually a boy, maybe a few years older than her. When he glanced up at her, she turned away and stumbled up the stairs. She was hot with embarrassment but managed to make it to the storeroom, where Evelyn was sitting on a crate, gesturing wildly as she shouted into the phone: "I said fifty units! Don't play with me, Reggie."

Evelyn made a spiral motion with her index finger to indicate that she wanted Camille to leave. Camille obediently turned on her heel and went to the employee bathroom upstairs. She stared at herself in the mirror, turned her head left and right, investigating the prettiness that everyone said she had. She was all right looking, she thought. She sniffed at Sozzani's vagina to ensure she wasn't emitting the gross fishy smell she sometimes did. She wished she had spent more time on her hair that morning. She put Sozzani back down, wet her fingers, and tried to smooth the stray hairs around her edges. She decided she would go look at the travel magazines, which were near the cash register. Nowhere she went in Tennessee carried *Travel + Leisure*.

She practiced a casual look. She wished Su Jin were there, because she was good at talking to boys. But if Su Jin were around, the boy would likely be interested in her. Camille's experience with boys was limited. She'd been engaged in a mild flirtation with Trayon Evans for several months, but it fizzled at the end of the year when he started dating Madison Carlyle, a plain-looking white girl who wore too much makeup. She'd almost kissed Alastair Perkins at Su Jin's party last fall but vomited all over her shoes instead. Things were different now; she was older, wiser.

When she left the bathroom, Evelyn was waiting for her. "Let's go home. You want to pick up dinner on the way?"

There were quite a few options in DC: Ethiopian, Greek, Thai, Salvadoran, Honduran, Chinese. But what Camille really wanted was a Supersonic Double Cheeseburger, limp, salty fries, and a cherry limeade. She shrugged.

"How about Manny & Olga's?" Evelyn suggested.

It was a greasy spot famous for pizza, burgers, sandwiches, fries, and enormous Greek salads. Camille liked Manny & Olga's. It tasted better than Sonic, actually. But it wasn't Sonic.

Camille caught a glimpse of Logan at the register on the way out and tried to gather as many details as she could. He was very tall and a few years older than Camille, but definitely still teenaged, maybe seventeen or eighteen. Though his hair was decidedly blond, his eyebrows and eyelashes were brown, which seemed like the best-case scenario.

In the car, Camille asked Evelyn if they'd be coming back the next day. Evelyn looked away from the road to squint at her. "Did you meet that new kid? Is that why you want to hang out there all of a sudden?"

"What?"

"Don't 'what' me. You think he's cute? Did he say something to you?" It was rare for Evelyn to take this particular tone—not preachy but interrogating.

Camille felt like she was being accused of something uncouth. "No. I just like it there," she lied. She didn't care for Charlotte's, which had shifted away from its diasporic roots and now carried mostly mainstream contemporary texts, the classics, and, to set itself apart, a healthy academic left-leaning offering. She preferred the used-book store closer to home, where each visit was exciting. She wanted to see the boy again. Just looking at him made her feel *something*.

"Well," Evelyn snapped. "I actually had a very special day planned, so no. We will not be going to the store tomorrow."

Camille already knew this meant they would be going downtown to the National Gallery, then out to lunch, as they had done at least once a month since she'd lived with Evelyn.

"Why did you name it after Mama Charlotte?" Camille asked, attempting to gently change the subject, but regretted it immediately.

"Don't try and change the subject! *No* boys, Camille. Haven't we talked about this? You don't need a stupid little boy running after you, you hear me?"

"Yes, ma'am."

Usually unprovoked, Evelyn gave her long, impassioned lectures about how boys were distractions that would get you in trouble every time. Camille was *not* to be one of those "fast-tailed" girls. It was unusual for Evelyn to use language "designed to denigrate women," as Evelyn herself would say, but this was *serious*. Camille was *not* to be a fast-tailed girl.

*   *   *

In the morning, Camille awoke with Sozzani curled up next to her under the sheets. She rolled over to look at the ceiling, which was high and smooth, unlike the one in Tennessee. She would be late for ballet, but she couldn't make herself rush until she was watching the bus pull up to her stop from a block away. Somehow, she was right on time for class. She ran to the barre and stepped into first position like she'd been there the entire time.

She'd been glad to get back to ballet. Here, the dancers were all different colors, and a "community scholarship" brought in girls who would have envied Camille's fifteen-dollar clearance leotard, which she'd worn until it was both too small and the fabric perilously thin. Once, one of those girls complimented Camille on her brand-new Mirella in the dressing room before class, and Camille had peeled it off and handed it to the girl; she had another in her bag. She hadn't especially wanted the girl to have it. She'd just wanted to know what it felt like to show that she had more than she needed.

That day, Camille left the studio feeling exhilarated and walked to Su Jin's house, a boring colonial on a shady street, where her friend was waiting for her on the steps eating sour straws. When she saw Camille, she leaped to her feet and did a few steps of bachata that she'd learned from her public school boyfriend, Alex, in her Samba sneakers. They linked arms and rode the bus back to the Banneker Pool on Camille's side of town, where they dragged their lounge chairs directly into the sun. Su Jin pulled out *Sula*, probably trying to show that she didn't expect Camille to do all her work for her, but Camille couldn't help but feel bad as her friend stared at the same page for too long. *Sula* might have helped Su Jin better understand her, but for some reason, Camille didn't want to share herself, and she didn't want to share *Sula*.

After a while, the girls put on their skates and went downtown for ice cream. Su Jin rambled incessantly about Alex. Every time Camille saw her after an absence of any length, it felt like Su Jin was getting objectively prettier and more attractive to boys. This summer, Su Jin's breasts must have grown at least a cup size.

"What about you?" Su Jin asked when she'd finished her two scoops of rocky road and thrown the empty cup in a nearby trash can. "Did you meet any boys in Tennessee?"

Camille hadn't explained the level of isolation she experienced at her grandmother's house, but she was still annoyed at the question. Where would she have met a boy? The Captain D's drive-thru? The Walmart electronics department? The half acre separating Charlotte's house from her neighbors on all sides? Maybe if she looked like Su Jin. But Su Jin was probably too ethnic for rural Tennessee, too. She shook her head.

"I don't get it. You're so pretty."

Camille shrugged. "I gotta get home for dinner. You should probably take the metro and not the bus," she said, knowing Su Jin knew better than she did how belligerent grown men got on that side of town at that hour.

When she got home, she found a denim dress and a pale pink shoebox marked Loeffler Randall lying on her freshly made bed, and she knew she was meant to wear both to dinner. Camille had gotten the faux-wrap dress several weeks earlier from a vintage shop in Takoma Park, but she'd never seen the strappy sandals before. Dutifully, she got dressed. She wasn't sure where they were going, but when she was with Evelyn, she found it easiest to do what she was told. She looked at herself in the full-length mirror inside the closet and gave herself a quick refresher course on living with Evelyn. Wear a bra. Try not to say "might could" or "fixin ta." Don't call all carbonated beverages "coke." Sit with your legs crossed at the knee or ankle. Greet everyone who makes eye contact with a polite "hello." Smile with teeth. Have something to say when people asked what you want to do when you're grown up. She'd been using these events to workshop a spiel about wanting to be a fashion journalist. Evelyn never said anything to indicate that she didn't like the sound of fashion journalism, but her face said it all. Camille considered adding something about focusing on the ethics and morals of consumerism to see how that went.

"Oh, darling!" Evelyn said as Camille descended the stairs. She was sitting in the living room reading a newspaper, which she dropped when she saw Camille. "I just love that dress on you. And your braid! You are just so lovely." Evelyn pressed her hands together as if in prayer and smiled adoringly. Camille knew Evelyn loved her but, based on the tension between her mothers, she also suspected that her great-grandmother was attempting to compensate for something with her enthusiasm. For what, exactly, Camille didn't know. "And the sandals!"

Half an hour later, she was following Evelyn into an austere modern mansion for a small faculty party, carrying an enormous box from Baked & Wired. Evelyn physically pushed Camille in the direction of Ava, the granddaughter of the dean of Howard's College of Arts & Sciences, who was in the same grade as her but attended a selective public arts school. She liked Ava well enough, but she also found her boring. They spent the entire evening watching *Three's Company* and drinking lemonade. Around nine, Camille suggested they get something to make their drinks more interesting, but Ava looked like Camille had suggested they break both their legs. She was relieved when Evelyn said it was time to go.

What a day, she thought to herself when they got home and she carried Sozzani outside. She looked up at the stars, but there were none to be seen like there were in Tennessee. Her stomach dropped as Sozzani relieved herself.

Camille tried to brighten her mood as she followed the dog inside and began preparing her dinner.

In Tennessee, Sozzani had been eating the second cheapest dog food available. Here, she was back to organic kibble topped with a tablespoon of salmon pâté. This change in diet would likely lead to an upset stomach, Camille thought as she portioned out the food, anticipating coming home to a mess. The dog, like Camille, adjusted easily to eating low-quality food. She wasn't sure it would work the other way around.

"Please don't shit on the bed or the carpet. Go for the hardwood," she told Sozzani as they crawled into bed. Camille opened her white MacBook and picked up where she had left off, scrolling through her own Tumblr page, where, alongside photos of herself and Su Jin in vintage clothes or Su Jin's mother's floor-length designer gowns, she posted pikachu gifs, colorful abstract art, and travel photos.

At some point, traveling to New York would have been enough, but now she'd been there and had found it like DC, just bigger and dirtier. She needed to get somewhere that looked nothing like where she'd been. She wanted palm trees, exotic fruit, crystal-clear water, like Maui. She clicked over from her own page to another window from earlier, where she was fifty pages deep into the Maui hashtag. At the party, she'd overheard someone say they'd just gotten back from Thailand. She typed "Thailand" into the search bar. Like with any tag on Tumblr, there was porn and references to shows she'd never seen but there was also stunning drone footage of floating villages and cliffs rising from water so blue it made her mouth water. She started reblogging and continued dreaming.

*   *   *

On the way to the bookstore the next day, Evelyn told Camille that she needed to keep herself busy. She could work the checkout counter or stock books, and Evelyn would pay her for her time in cash from the register. Camille wasn't sure why she bothered, as she had access to a credit card, but she didn't argue about it. She could use the cash to have someone buy liquor for her and Su Jin with no paper trail.

The boy-man was standing behind the counter when they arrived, so Camille was assigned to the stockroom. She was in there organizing boxes of miniature bonsai tree growing kits when the door swung open and he stood a few feet from her. She gave him a quick once-over. There were holes in the knees of his jeans, and he wore checkered Vans like the ones Trayon wore to school on days they weren't wearing uniforms.

"Hey," he said.

"Hi," she answered with a croak, and they stood looking at each other for a moment too long. She averted her eyes.

"Where's your dog?"

"At home."

"Yeah? What's its name?"

"Her name is Sozzani."

"Sozzani? What kind of name is that?"

Camille shrugged and made fragile eye contact. Today, she was wearing one of the cropped shirts she and Su Jin had made. They'd taught themselves how to use a sewing machine Su Jin found in her basement, and figured out how to crop shirts without losing the original hem. They'd cropped at least fifty shirts this way. They'd had their first and only fight over who would get the shirt she was wearing that day, an exceptionally well-saturated tie-dyed V-neck; she pulled at the hem in a futile attempt to cover her belly button and went back to sorting through the inventory. He probably wasn't there to speak to her, anyway. She sat down on a nearby orange crate and flipped on the radio.

"Sorry," he said. "I didn't mean anything by it."

She looked up at him. His narrow cheeks were rosy. He was there to talk to her, actually, and she'd embarrassed him. Her, of all people. "Huh?"

"It's just that you make me kind of nervous—"

Camille squinted and looked over both shoulders before pointing to herself. "Me?"

"Yes, you," he said, laughing. His teeth were very white but not particularly straight, and his nose looked like it might have been broken at some point, as one nostril sat slightly higher than the other. He was otherwise symmetrical, a beautiful young man with a chiseled jawline and high cheekbones. Camille realized that she was smiling stupidly and made a concerted effort to force her mouth closed. She tried to think of what Su Jin might do or say, or what her grandparents—the best couple she knew—might say to each other.

"You have a pretty smile," he said. "I was just wondering if you had a boyfriend or whatever."

"N-no," she said, still smiling. Su Jin would have definitely put her teeth away by now, but she saw that he looked nervous.

"I was wondering if you might like to hang out sometime," he said.

That night, after Evelyn had gone to bed, Camille left the house through the back gate. Logan was leaning against a tree near the corner of S and 15th, looking out of place in a beat-up denim jacket, worn jeans, and desert boots. They walked a block over to the paved platform in front of the Freemasons temple, where she strapped on her skates, and he walked alongside her as she did some slow laps.

Logan was barely eighteen and had recently graduated from high school, he told her. He was from Oakland, but he'd come to the East Coast to "see what it was all about." He was thinking about going to New York next, but he hated the weather and thought he might just go back to California at the end of the summer. He didn't fit in here, he said. Everyone in DC was working toward some long-term goal: get this degree, that degree, buy a house, and so on. Where he was from, there were people like that, but there were also people who worked just to save enough money to take a two-month surfing trip. It sounded like he was one of the latter.

Like herself, Logan never knew his dad. His mom was an addict and died when he was fifteen. After that, he'd lived with a series of family members and foster families. But now he was finally old enough to live without a guardian. He was renting a room in a house in College Park with a bunch of students.

"School's not for me, though," he said.

"What do you want to do, then?"

He pulled out a Ziploc bag of sunflower seeds and ignored her question. "Got these last week." He gestured for her to hold out her hand, and he gave her a generous handful. It had been a while since she'd eaten one, but she popped one in her mouth, cracked it with her teeth to get to the meat; it was nuttier and chewier than the kind from the gas station. She spit out the shell and popped another in her mouth.

"Good, right? Here," he said before she could answer and handed her the entire bag. "For some reason, that's the first thing I thought when I first saw you: she looks like she'd like a good sunflower seed." He shoved his hands into his jacket pockets. She couldn't believe he was wearing a jacket. It was sweltering. "I gotta learn you don't need a jacket at night here," he said, as if he was reading her mind. "I'm hot as fuck. Anyway, what's your story?"

Usually, Camille would have told only partial truths: Evelyn was her grandmother, and her mother was having financial issues, which was why she lived here.

But she told the whole truth: "I don't know my dad either. I'm from Tennessee. My stepdad was crazy, so my mom sent me to live with my grandmother. But then my grandmother sent me to live with my great-grandmother, Evelyn."

"Your stepdad *was* crazy? Like past tense?"

"Oh," she said. "He's dead. He killed himself."

"Oh, shit."

"Yeah."

They looked at each other. Camille knew that he was significant. His nose, covered with a thin sheen of sweat, was lightly freckled.

"You like living with Evelyn?"

"Yeah, she pretty much lets me do whatever."

"Really? She seems strict."

"Nah, not really. I'm not supposed to talk to boys though. Or eat junk food. But that's about it."

"Am I going to get in trouble for this?"

"She'll never know."

Soon, she was skating fast with Sozzani folded up in her arms like a baby. She almost forgot about Logan entirely until she'd pulled a few laps. When she was feeling more like herself, she slowed down, and when Logan reached for her hand, she let him hold it.

"You roller skate a lot?"

"Yeah. Some of my friends got me into it. It's not really common."

"No," he said. "It's not." He put his arm around her waist. He smelled like the little stores on Florida Avenue that sold incense, essential oils, and shea butter.

Within the hour, she knew she liked him. He was kind, but not in a way that seemed like he was trying too hard. He was unself-conscious in a way that she didn't know was possible. She'd never met anyone like him. He was not like the boys at school, who were nice only when it benefited them and were obsessed with them-selves and their test scores.

She was able to get back into the house undetected that night and snuck out almost every night after that. They had a routine for the rest of the summer. Every night around nine, when Evelyn had fallen asleep with a book on her chest, Logan texted to let her know he was waiting for her outside. She left the house with her skates and Sozzani bundled in her arms.

Sometimes, she showed off her roller-skating at the temple, and sometimes they just sat on the ornate steps and talked. He always acted extremely impressed when she pulled a full arabesque. He had a lot of stories to tell, many of which sounded like hers. He knew what it was like to feel different, but he also didn't mind it, which appealed to her infinitely. She wished she could soak up some of his . . . energy, spirit, something. She'd never liked anyone so quickly, not since Jenny.

Toward the end of the summer, they started walking down to the monuments. Camille hadn't spent much time there, as everyone she knew had already visited on their elementary school field trips. And Evelyn never went anywhere "touristy" because she had a strong distaste for "middle Americans."

The week before school was supposed to start, they visited the Jefferson Memorial. She'd been thinking a lot about how to ask him if he was still thinking about going to New York, until she finally blurted it out as he was reading the inscription on the wall. It came out in mumbles.

He squinted in confusion. "Did I say I was going to New York?"

"You said you were thinking about it?"

"Oh. No, probably not."

She sighed in relief, and he smiled. "Why? Are you tired of me or something?"

She could only smile in response. He kissed her that night.

When Logan dropped her off at home, she skipped to the front door. She was feeling so free that she was not as careful as she should have been on her way inside, not that it would have mattered as Evelyn was waiting behind the kitchen counter with a glass of red wine in her hand. Knowing that she'd fucked up, Camille backed away from Evelyn, who advanced on her with superhuman speed.

"Where were you?" Evelyn said tearfully, as if she were in a soap opera. Before Camille had a chance to respond, Evelyn used her free hand to slap her harder than she'd ever been hit. She dropped Sozzani, and sparks of light appeared in her vision. Evelyn was saying something, but Camille could not hear her because her ears were ringing.

Evelyn

LATE SUMMER 2007

When Camille came to live with her, Evelyn made several promises to herself and, silently, to Camille: she would never give criticism that wasn't constructive. She would believe what Camille said. And she would never, ever hit her.

Evelyn knew Camille had been sneaking out. She was never out particularly late, and there were never any signs that she was coming back high or drunk. She trusted Camille to make good choices—or, if not good, then reasonable. She figured she was probably just puttering around with Sozzani at her ankles. After all, Camille was the cerebral type; she could spend a concerning amount of time just *thinking*. So Evelyn wasn't particularly worried at first.

It was late summer when Evelyn figured it out. She was up later than usual, trying to revise her syllabus for her Women of the Harlem Renaissance course. She was drinking wine at the kitchen island, looking through the formal dining room to the window that looked over the street, hoping her ghost might give her some advice, when Camille and the young man came into sight in front of the house. The kid looked familiar, and she realized he was the new hire at Charlotte's, whom Evelyn explicitly told Camille to stay away from. She hadn't had a hot flash in years, but Camille's presence in her life seemed to come with a similar sensation. She fanned herself with a nearby magazine and paced briefly before she went back to the kitchen for more wine. She hadn't planned on confronting her for sneaking out, but seeing her with this kid changed things in a way that Evelyn hadn't thought enough about.

After she slapped Camille, the regret was immediate, though Camille did not express any shock or dismay. Camille had been hit before; her mother hit her. There were signs everywhere. Camille gave her a practiced look of boredom as she touched her own cheek. Evelyn knew she'd hit the girl quite hard, as her eyes were welling with tears, but her demeanor betrayed nothing else. This was one of the saddest moments of Evelyn's life, watching this fourteen-year-old girl pretending not to be hurt.

Early the next morning, Evelyn sat in the breakfast nook with a magazine, pretending to read, though it was actually open to a perfume ad. She peeled back the sample and found that it smelled strongly of lavender. After her mother died, Evelyn couldn't tolerate the scent of Shalimar, her mother's favorite, and had everything washed and spritzed with lavender, the first flowers James ever gave her. Once James died, she couldn't stand that smell either, but she couldn't get the lavender out of the house. Sometimes, it was comforting, but other times, a whiff sent her into a rage.

When Charlotte was twelve or thirteen, Evelyn had worked herself into an awful mood over it. Evelyn knew that it was around 1968 or '69 because she remembered Nixon's face plastered across everything. Evelyn was on sabbatical and writing her first book, which she somehow managed to do in between drinking too much and going on hours-long shopping sprees. She was taking pills to help her stay awake when she should have been sleeping and pills to put her to sleep when she should have been awake. She spent much of each night and day haunting the house she'd grown up in, with pens stuck through her bun and wearing expensive shoes that would never see the light of day.

The book was going to be an examination of Black gospel songs as literature until Evelyn became very bored with the concept, and convinced her publisher that rich Black people in literature was a more interesting topic. It took Evelyn two additional years to finish the manuscript, but it wasn't very good. She wasn't sure if the book was still in circulation. But in 1968, it was the most important thing in Evelyn's life. The book was supposed to change everything, and Evelyn thought her entire career would be defined by it.

So yes, it was probably in the fall of that year that she hit Charlotte for the first time, and then at least a few times a week for the next five years or so. Evelyn cringed when she realized that her memories of those moments were likely faint compared to Charlotte's.

Evelyn heard Camille clomping on the wood floors in her roller skates, which she'd been told countless times not to do. She opened her mouth but decided against it. The front door opened and closed. It wasn't like Camille to leave without saying anything. Evelyn's stomach dropped like it hadn't since 1974, when she woke up sober the morning after Charlotte left.

The phone was ringing, and the dog was whining. She saw that someone was calling from Florida and decided it must have been a telemarketer; she didn't know anyone in Florida. She poured herself a glass of wine and prepared Sozzani's dinner. She sat in the white Womb Chair she'd bought herself for her seventieth birthday and tried to think about what she was going to say to Camille. Instead, she fell asleep and didn't wake until the phone rang again. She answered it this time. It was Corinna.

"Camille is out. I'll tell her you called," Evelyn mumbled.

"No, I—I called to speak with you."

"Mmm?"

"I hope this isn't presumptuous . . ."

Evelyn took a big gulp of wine and waited for Corinna to finish her sentence. There was a long silence, and Evelyn was impatient.

"Well, what is it, honey?"

"I was hoping I could come stay with you."

Evelyn knew what she was supposed to say. She was supposed to say, "Oh, of course. That'll be just fine." Instead, she said, "Why?"

There was another long pause, and Corinna's voice took on a sharp edge. "Evelyn—" she started. Evelyn hung up before the girl could say something hurtful, then immediately regretted it. It was childish behavior. She dialed *69.

"Sorry, the call dropped," she lied. "Of course, you can come stay, dear."

They had a quick conversation about the terms and conditions of her coming to stay. Evelyn would pay for Corinna's flight, and she would live in Evelyn's carriage house indefinitely. Corinna would get a job, and she would not leave for any extended periods of time without warning.

"She deserves stability," Evelyn said. "Either you're in or you're out this time, Corinna."

After they hung up, Evelyn began her nightly routine and was in bed before Camille got home. Sozzani whined loudly from the floor until Evelyn got up to bring her into the bed.

She tried to sleep but could hardly even close her eyes. After an hour, she got up. It was not Thursday, but she thought she might write to Charlotte early. But when she sat down at her desk, she found that the words wouldn't come.

She headed downstairs but paused in Camille's bedroom door, which Evelyn had personally decorated all in white except for a bright but tasteful abstract painting above the bed. Now, the walls were covered in taped-up posters of cartoons and faraway locations she knew Camille had never seen. The white comforter was still there, but one covered in Keith Haring–style figures lay on top of the unmade bed. Though Evelyn had requested Camille straighten up before she left for Tennessee, the room smelled like a locker room. There were clothes scattered across the floor, the chair in the corner was stacked high with ballet tights and leotards, and Evelyn couldn't even bring herself to look at the bathroom. Charlotte had always kept a remarkably clean room, even as a little girl. Evelyn remembered that very distinctly, though she remembered little else about Charlotte's childhood.

Evelyn went down to the wine cellar, where she grabbed a full-bodied red and unlocked the safe. She stared at the stack of five leather-bound photo albums and various envelopes with important documents inside. She tried to look at her wedding album only once a year, and she'd already done it twice so far, but she pulled it out anyway. She tried not to trip on the way back upstairs. She sat at the head of the dining room table, where she typically graded papers, and swallowed a hearty glass of wine before pouring herself some more. She took a deep breath before she flipped open the slightly warped album.

Evelyn was always seeing and hearing commercials from Walmart and Target offering digitizing services to "preserve precious memories." She did not know what exactly she wanted to leave behind when she died, but it was not wedding photos. Her dress had been fabulous, though; it was always the first thing to catch her eye when she opened the album. The tea-length champagne-colored satin gown was strapless, but a winged detail in the front gave it the illusion of straps if viewed from the right angle. She'd burned it in a fit of grief shortly after James died. Evelyn poured herself some more wine before she allowed herself to look at James's face. For several years after his death, the grief manifested itself in her body. She woke up every morning with aches and pains that she quelled with pills. She could barely eat for years.

It was late but not past midnight curfew when the front door flew open and rattled the house. Camille was always slamming the goddamn door. Evelyn quickly closed the album and listened as Camille's skates thumped and rolled on the floor. Then the girl stood in the doorway of the dining room, chewing gum loudly. Evelyn was not sure what shirt Camille had been wearing when she left, but she was almost positive she was wearing a different one now. Her mascara was running, and her hair was askew.

"What are you doing?"

"Nothing."

"What's that?" Camille asked, and pointed at the table. "Can I see?" She stepped toward Evelyn, who immediately and used both arms to form an X across the top of the album.

"No," she snapped. "You may not. You haven't said two words to me—"

"Fine." Camille shrugged and left the room for the kitchen, where she popped open a can of something, probably the Diet Coke Evelyn kept in the house for her.

Evelyn's response was out of proportion, she knew. But she was convinced Camille sometimes intentionally aggravated her. She'd thought the same thing about Charlotte. Though Evelyn knew better, she didn't always do better.

"Camille?" she called.

"Yes?" It sounded like she was responding from the top of the stairs.

"Come here. I want to show you something."

Camille came stomping back down the stairs. Evelyn noticed Camille was not wearing a bra underneath her T-shirt. Why was she so averse to bras?

"Sit down."

Camille's breasts bounced hard when she took a seat at the table. Evelyn must have been staring because the girl crossed her arms over her chest. "You're going to let me see it now? What is it?"

"It's my wedding album. From my first marriage. To your great-grandfather."

Camille nodded but said nothing.

Evelyn cleared her throat. "Well. His name was James. Your grandmother never told you about him?" She opened the album again.

"No," Camille said and shook her head. "Wow. Look at that dress. Do you still have it?"

"No, I donated it a long time ago," Evelyn lied.

"That's a shame."

"Anyway, that's him," she continued.

Camille cocked her head. "Oh," she said. "What happened to him?"

"He died a long time ago."

"How?"

"He went to bed one night and never woke up."

Camille stared at Evelyn blankly. The girl seemed like she might have been drunk, but Evelyn was too drunk herself to say anything about it.

"He had some kind of heart thing. It's a thing that happens, apparently."

"You mean, you slept by his dead body all night?" Camille said, as if it were part of a spooky campfire tale.

Evelyn narrowed her eyes in an attempt to convey that she was being serious and wanted Camille to be serious, too. "Well, your grandmother and I were both in the bed with him, actually."

Camille looked confused. "How old was she?"

"I think maybe nine or ten."

Another long pause. "Do you have any pictures of Granmama when she was a little girl?" Camille asked, and started to turn the pages of the album.

"Yes. But hold on. Don't you want to know more about your grandfather?"

Camille stopped. "Oh, yeah. Yeah, yeah . . . What did he do?"

"He was a doctor, a surgeon, but wound up being kind of a general practitioner, too. There weren't many Black doctors around at the time."

"A surgeon?!"

"Yes, a surgeon. A very good one, at that."

"Wow. It's just kind of crazy. I've always thought of us as from the wrong side of the tracks. Well, 'us' being, you know, the rest of 'us.'"

She looked down at a posed photo and started to play with the corner of it. Evelyn slapped her hand away.

"That's a very reductive and classist phrase, and I'm disappointed you would use it." Evelyn turned the page to show her another photo of James. "He was a good man," she said wistfully. "He loved Charlotte," she said, and pointed at a picture of James with Charlotte in his lap at a party. "He loved to dance. Loved to dance. You have his eyes. You see?"

"I don't really see it, Mama."

"You'll just have to trust me, darling girl."

They sat in silence for a moment.

"Mama Evy? Can you tell me more about him?"

"Well. Let me think. He liked his collard greens spicy. I used to cook, believe it or not. He liked that show, um, *Beverly Hillbillies*. He didn't have much time off, but he watched that if he could. He put Charlotte in piano lessons because his mother played the piano. She's named after his mother; did you know that?"

When she looked up, Camille was listening attentively. She shook her head.

"He loved to travel. We went to France for our honeymoon. He wanted to stay."

Camille smiled slightly. "Cool."

"You remind me so much of him," she said, because it was true. Camille was of her own mind like James had been. She knew they would have been close had they met. Sadness rinsed over her gently, instead of in the oppressive waves like it once had.

Camille's mouth twitched. "You miss him, Mama Evy?"

"Oh yes, darling girl. It's been forty years; I still miss him." Evelyn felt her eyes growing moist. "He was a good man, Camille. He would be so proud of you." She realized she was having a private moment. "Go on to bed, dear."

Camille seemed to have moved on from the Kitchen Incident. If Camille could move on, maybe Evelyn could, too.

In the morning, Evelyn woke up earlier than usual with a dull headache and immediately went to the cellar to retrieve an album full of photos of Charlotte as a little girl to show Camille. She flipped through it, admiring the pictures in which Charlotte's two front teeth were missing. There were only a few pictures of Evelyn with Charlotte, and almost all of them had been posed in a studio. There were a few family portraits of the three of them in matching outfits, taken by a professional.

In a different album, one with mostly blank pages, she turned to the page with the only photo from her second wedding, though she knew the image by heart. Wayne was not an attractive man. His features were angular, but his eyes were droopy like a basset hound's, in a way that Corinna's were to a lesser degree. He'd had a certain swagger about him, though, a confidence that made him seem more attractive than he actually was. He wore his soft hair slick and combed straight back. He was a self-made businessman—he always emphasized the *self-made*—who owned about a quarter of the commercial real estate in the city and sat on various advisory boards and councils. Evelyn never loved him as much as admired him.

Evelyn's second wedding outfit was not nearly as handsome as her first, but it was quite tasteful—an ivory skirt suit with pearl buttons. They had gone down to the courthouse with Charlotte, and Clementine, the housekeeper, and Wayne's driver, whose name Evelyn could not recall, acted as witnesses. Only Wayne smiled in the group photo. Charlotte, who would have been twelve or thirteen, looked like her dog had just died. In fact, that's what just happened.

That morning, Evelyn and Charlotte had gotten into an argument about what Charlotte was going to wear. Evelyn remembered very distinctly that Charlotte had put on a cotton ruffled dress in a green-and-blue butterfly print. Evelyn wanted her to wear something more formal, preferably in a solid color, but Charlotte refused, sitting on the end of her bed with her hands folded in her lap as Evelyn became increasingly agitated. Evelyn had gone into an absolute rage, throwing dresses out of Charlotte's closet onto the floor and across the room. She couldn't remember what she'd said, but she was sure it was nasty and mean-spirited. At some point, Charlotte's new bichon frise puppy, a Christmas gift from Wayne, entered the room and got itself punted into the wall. Charlotte screamed and crawled across the floor to find that the dog was dead, its neck apparently broken. Evelyn took no responsibility, claiming it wouldn't have happened if Charlotte had just done as she was told. She made Charlotte carry the dead dog down to the garden, and watched her bury it under less than a foot of mulch. Still in the butterfly dress, Charlotte wept the entire time while Evelyn drank wine out of a coffee mug and smoked a cigarette. In the wedding pictures, Charlotte wore a pleated emerald-green dress with a dramatically large satin sash and three-quarter sleeves.

But the photo was not there. She searched inside the safe to see if it had come loose from the page, and found nothing. Frazzled, she headed upstairs as Camille came stomping into the dining room with Sozzani under her arm. She was wearing a T-shirt that barely covered her midriff and bright yellow shorts that barely covered her butt cheeks.

"You really do have a lovely body, sweetheart. I hope you enjoy it while it lasts," Evelyn said, preoccupied.

"Thanks, Mama," Camille said absentmindedly as she poured herself a glass of cranberry juice.

"Can I tell you something, darling girl?"

"Mm-hmm."

"Sit down."

Camille carried the dog and the glass to the table. "Is everything all right?"

"Yes, I just need to admit something to you. I think it's important." Evelyn paused. "I just wanted to tell you that I wasn't a good mother to your grandmother."

"Okay?" Camille said tentatively. She threw her shoulders back and sat up straight, something Charlotte had done as a teenager.

"And I feel like I owe you an apology."

Camille pointed at herself, looking confused. "Me?"

"Yes. Things would have been very different if I hadn't been such a bad mother."

Camille nibbled at her bottom lip. "I wouldn't have been born, though, I don't think. Right?"

"It's such a blessing that someone so beautiful came out of so much ugliness," Evelyn said, and reached for Camille's hands. And Camille let her hold them. "I'm sorry I hit you the other night. That was a horrible mistake, and I swear I'll never do it again."

"Okay. . . ." Camille shifted her weight in her seat. Sozzani stood on her back legs to lick Camille's chin. "You sick or something?"

"No, sweetheart." It occurred to Evelyn that Camille might have never received a true apology. Evelyn wasn't sure she'd ever been properly apologized to either. Nor was she sure all of the apologies she volleyed at Charlotte counted. She hoped she was doing it right this time. "Will you forgive me?"

"Yes, Mama. Of course."

"Good," Evelyn said. She moved her chair closer to Camille's and held the girl's face in her hands.

"What do you think about going to pick up a cell phone for you today?"

Camille smiled wide, exposing all of her gorgeous teeth. "Really?"

Evelyn released Camille's face and turned back toward the photo album. "I was going to wait for your birthday, but it's probably about time. I want to be able to reach you if I need to." She sucked air into her lungs and opened the album again. "But first, let me show you these pictures of your grandmother. She really was a pretty little girl."

Camille

AUGUST 2007

Camille's fifteenth birthday began with a long, slow brunch on the patio at the Old Anglers Inn, where Evelyn ordered two glasses of champagne with a wink. After a heaping plate of Belgian waffles with whipped cream and delightfully ripe strawberries, Evelyn gave the "okay" sign to the waiter, who appeared moments later carrying a tray with three boxes covered in silver wrapping paper and tied with pink ribbon. Other people in the restaurant were looking at them, and Evelyn was smiling the widest Camille had ever seen.

"Go ahead," she said. "Start with the biggest one."

Camille heard herself giggle as she reached for the box. Inside was a miniature version of Evelyn's newest handbag, a Prada Galleria. Evelyn had bought the full-size bag on a whim on a recent trip to Tysons, and Camille had been eyeing it ever since.

"I figured you just needed one big enough for your phone, keys, wallet, and that little Pod thing." Evelyn was referring to the iPod that appeared at the foot of Camille's bed one morning the week before. Camille knew Evelyn was still trying to apologize. This constant pandering would eventually start to feel disingenuous, but Camille wasn't there yet.

Today, she gushed over the bag, the perfect shade of bubblegum pink. Camille was developing an "aesthetic," as she called it. In just a few weeks, she'd graduated almost entirely from gym shorts and T-shirts and had spent hours scrolling through eBay vintage boutiques. She wore her pants and skirts high around her natural waist, favored pink, and loved tight or shiny dresses, accessories covered in marabou feathers, and suits with short skirts. Best of all, she knew she could get attention on the internet merely by posting halfway decent pictures of herself wearing the clothes on her Tumblr page. The attention was deeply satisfying, almost as satisfying as buying the clothes in the first place. Camille tossed the bag over her shoulder and posed for Evelyn's BlackBerry.

She opened the other two boxes. Inside one, she found a delicate gold chain necklace, and the next contained a bracelet with equally delicate golden charms in the shape of a flower she didn't recognize.

Evelyn leaned over. "It's a calla lily, darling."

"Oh, cool," Camille said.

"It symbolizes a new beginning," she said. "I wanted to give it to you years ago, but it's custom made, and they just couldn't seem to get it right. Do you like it?"

The cone-shaped bulbs were just about a centimeter in length, but very detailed, down to the delicate waves that crested toward the pointed apex of the bulb. "I love it," she said and turned so that her grandmother could fasten the necklace around her neck. "It's beautiful."

Camille no longer wanted to know what happened between Evelyn and Charlotte anymore. She had her own relationship with each of them now, and though she understood that she could never completely separate the relationships from each other, she also did not want to bear the burden of everyone's hurt by knowing what they had all done to each other. And she didn't want her love for any of them to change, not even the ephemeral relationship she had with her mother. She'd rearranged herself and her life enough. She wouldn't do it again, not even for her mothers.

*   *   *

Camille had invited her closest friends, Peach and Su Jin, for a sleepover, and was required to include Ava, Emma, and Parvitha as well. They all arrived around five p.m., and Evelyn quietly absconded to the Hay-Adams for the night. Shortly after Evelyn left, Su Jin opened her Louis Vuitton Keepall and pulled out several bottles of champagne and a bottle of Svedka.

"Happy birthday!" she exclaimed.

"How did you get that?" Emma gasped.

Su Jin shrugged. Camille knew Su Jin's parents were largely absent and mildly negligent. Her biological father, almost two decades older than her mother, died when Su Jin was very young, leaving a dozen mid-Atlantic car dealerships to her mother, which she ran with incredible efficiency, despite having cheated her way through business school. Her mother quickly remarried Mike Harris, a doctor from Maryland with political ambitions. By the time Su Jin was in middle school, he was a congressman. Between running the car dealerships and stumping for her husband, Su Jin's mother was often otherwise occupied, and her stepdad never had much interest in Su Jin.

Peach, who'd arrived in their friend group only a month earlier, after they met at a school preregistration event, had replaced Katrina as Camille's second closest friend after a Myspace Top 8 Incident. She'd gotten kicked out of an international boarding school in France, and was tall, thin, and very beautiful. She spoke with a strange accent, and though she didn't talk very much, it was almost always to suggest doing something transgressive when she did. Peach constantly played Tetris on a lime-green Game Boy Color that she carried with her always. Camille was positive her real name wasn't Peach, but she couldn't prove it.

The other girls were from wealthy, healthy homes. Emma's mother owned a bridal boutique in Georgetown, and her father taught at Georgetown Law. Parvitha's father was an ambassador from India. The girls attended Evelyn's dinner parties with their parents, but she'd never quite clicked with either girl. She was unsure why she had to be friends with them, but Evelyn had made it abundantly clear that Emma and Parvitha should *always* be invited—along with Ava, of course. Camille didn't care as they were all boring and didn't get too much in the way.

The girls poured their drinks into water glasses and scurried up to Camille's bedroom, where they gathered around Parvitha's white MacBook to watch YouTube videos of singing Harry Potter finger puppets. Emma, Parvitha, and Ava howled with laughter and occasionally talked about the boys they had crushes on, none of whom knew they existed. Camille, Peach, and Su Jin had far more *mature* things to discuss.

Soon, Peach pulled out her Game Boy, and Su Jin rolled off the bed and began to sloppily braid Peach's rose-gold hair. Camille rubbed Sozzani's belly. Su Jin whispered something in Peach's ear, and her friend smiled a mischievous half smile without looking up from her game. The only thing that Camille did not like about Peach was that she felt like they were in competition for Su Jin's attention, though Su Jin had never actually done anything to make her feel her best-friend status was in jeopardy. Camille inched across the bed toward Peach and Su Jin, but Ava was in the way.

"I'm going to get more wine," Camille said, signaling to Su Jin to follow.

"We should drink out of actual champagne glasses," Su Jin said on the way down the stairs. "Peach, Camille's grandmother has the coolest champagne glasses. You'll see."

Peach said nothing as Camille got three gilded glasses down from the cabinet, and Su Jin expertly poured the wine.

"How're things with that boy, Camille?" Su Jin said after she took a long drink of champagne.

"What boy?" asked Peach.

Camille felt her cheeks get hot. Logan had said he was staying in DC, but she hadn't heard from him in several weeks. She didn't want to seem desperate by initiating contact, though he was well within reach, as he was still working at Charlotte's. But she missed him. She couldn't say all that, though. She shrugged like she didn't think about it all the time, like she was fully in control of the situation.

"Is that what you were talking about on Tumblr?" Peach asked, referring to Camille's recent totally vague yet somehow painfully vulnerable post. Camille wasn't even sure why she'd written it, let alone posted it.

She changed the subject. "Speaking of Tumblr . . . have you seen the notes on my last post? It's crazy."

The girls settled onto the stairwell with their wine, and Camille started braiding Peach's hair while Su Jin pulled up Tumblr. Su Jin was popular on the site, but most of her traffic came from being mentioned in Camille's posts. While Camille believed Su Jin had the upper hand in their real-life friendship because of the wealth and privilege she'd enjoyed since birth, Camille's larger online following gave her something to feel superior about. Su Jin gasped when she saw how much attention the picture of Camille on the steps of the Lincoln Memorial was getting. It wasn't really all that impressive. Camille was wearing a pale pink thrifted sundress with white Keds, and sitting with one foot planted on a higher step than the other. She was smiling and looking away from the camera like something funny had just happened outside of the frame.

"Say—" Peach lifted one finger and tapped Camille's knee. "Can I ask you something personal?"

Camille frowned. She knew Peach was about to ask about her family. "Sure."

"Why do you live with your grandmother? Where are your parents?"

"My mom is sick," she lied. "And I don't know my dad."

"I don't know mine either," Peach said. "My mom was having an affair. They got divorced before I was even born."

"That makes three of us," Su Jin said, which annoyed Camille. Your father dying when you're little and never knowing your father are completely different, she thought. And Su Jin's mother was *definitely not* sick. She frowned at Su Jin, but Su Jin was still scrolling through Tumblr.

"Can I please have a photo credit on this? Pleeaaaaassse."

"Okay, I'll do it later," Camille said, feeling magnanimous. She finished her glass of wine, which had gone straight to her head.

Camille wondered if her mother had ever had a friend like Su Jin. For as long as Camille could remember, Corinna did most of her socializing with David and Charlotte, playing cards and drinking brown liquor. Charlotte didn't really seem to have any friends either. Every week, a couple of women came by to get their hair done, but Camille was pretty sure those weren't her friends. And Evelyn had "friends" that she invited over for catered dinner parties, but she probably didn't have long, confessional conversations like she and Su Jin did. Wait. Were Charlotte and Corinna each other's only friend? That was too sad to think about.

"More wine?" Su Jin offered.

The girls went out back with their wine and sat on the deck. It was late, but it was still very humid. They used cushions from the patio chairs as pillows and lay on their backs as they talked about the approaching school year, but Camille was still thinking about her mother as she fell asleep—more specifically, about who Corinna had been when Camille was little. She had once loved her mother so much.

Camille woke up at the first light of dawn and stirred her friends to go inside. They both protested.

"Y'all going ta bahrn," Camille said, not yet awake enough to keep her drawl from slipping through. She looked around to see if anyone had noticed and was preparing to ridicule her. No one had. They went back to Camille's bedroom, where the other girls were tucked into Camille's bed. One of Ava's green eyes popped open.

"Your house is haunted," she said.

"That's what my grandmother says, but I ain't seen nothing," Camille said and quickly corrected herself. "I mean, I haven't seen anything." She frowned at Ava's hair, which had been brutally twisted into a bun, but chunks of which had escaped and formed stiff peaks around the perimeter of her scalp like a crown.

"Well, I saw a lady. Clear as day. She was standing in the doorway of your bedroom."

"You were probably dreaming," Camille said dismissively. "You sleep with your hair out?"

Ava frowned, both eyes open now. "I forgot to bring something," she explained.

Camille knew she was lying. "Can I wash it and do it?" she asked, forgetting herself.

"What do you mean 'do it'?" Ava touched her head nervously.

"You know what I mean. I mean, *do it*." Camille really wanted to do something about Ava's hair. It would have been so pretty with just a little tenderness. That same summer, Camille washed Charlotte's hair for the first time. Her hair was starting to go coarse with age and felt more like Camille's own hair, more familiar.

"I don't know."

"Please? I'll twist it for you so you can have nice little curls when you take it down."

Later, Camille tilted Ava's head back into the enormous kitchen sink. She was pretty sure this sink had never been used like this, maybe in a past life, when the folks who haunted the house were still alive. Evelyn was always talking about how she'd bought the house because Virginia Johnson Douglass, or whatever her name was, had lived there.

Ava closed her eyes when Camille started to massage her scalp with her acrylic nails but opened them after a moment and looked up at her. "You're pretty," Ava said. "You could be a model."

Camille shrugged. "Thanks."

"That's so lucky," Ava said. " You'll never have to work too hard for anything."

"That don't sound true," Camille said and was mad at herself for letting her vernacular slip through yet again. "My grandmother was really pretty. When she was young."

"Ms. Evelyn? She is still pretty."

"No, Evelyn is my *great*-grandmother."

Ava squinted. "How old is she?!"

"Not that old. Like seventy-five or something."

"How's that possible?!"

Camille frowned, and Ava tried to correct the misstep. "Sorry," she said. "I didn't mean anything by it."

Camille shrugged and continued massaging Ava's scalp. Her hair was turning into thick kinky curls in her hands. Ava was better than pretty. She had light skin and light-colored eyes, like her grandmother and great-grandmother, though they couldn't save Charlotte, it seemed.

"Ms. Evelyn lets you do whatever. My mom and dad are *always* in my business."

The other girls, seated at the big, teak table, laughed loudly about something. Somebody snorted.

"I wish my mama was in my business."

"Well," Ava said, "where is she?"

"Tennessee."

"Why don't you live with her?"

Camille looked down at Ava, who looked back with her pretty eyes. They were not celery green like Evelyn's, but a rich, almost emerald shade. She found that she couldn't speak, couldn't explain, not even as nebulously as she had the night before.

"Oh," Ava said, lowering her eyes. She recovered quickly: "Hey, you should run for homecoming queen."

Camille turned off the water and grabbed a towel from the counter.

"I'm on the homecoming committee, and if you sign up first, no one will run against you." She was looking at Camille with raw admiration that made her uncomfortable. "Then we'll be able to spend more time together this year."

"That's not really my style," said Camille as she combed the conditioner into Ava's hair, which she was surprised to find was nearly waist-length.

"Oh," Ava said with a look of grave disappointment. It occurred to her then that Ava *badly* wanted to be her friend. But Ava was too happy, kind, and well adjusted. They didn't have much in common.

Camille was in the middle of using a woody, botanical leave-in conditioner to twist up Ava's hair when Evelyn came home. The other girls were sitting around the table eating chocolate chip pancakes Emma had made.

"Should I come back later?" Evelyn asked. Camille could tell she was smiling by the sound of her voice. "Oh, all right. You've pulled my arm," Evelyn continued, still smiling, but she was at Camille's side.

"I do need to talk to you at some point today," she whispered in Camille's ear. "It's important."

Corinna

LATE SUMMER 2007

Corinna could have flown to DC, but she needed time to think. So she drove. She arrived at Evelyn's doorstep, carrying a large box, two days after Camille's birthday. She'd hadn't wanted to impinge upon any of Camille's plans for that day. Evelyn answered the door holding a champagne flute and wearing an immaculate white linen pantsuit. Her dainty gold earrings matched her necklace and bracelet.

"Well, helloooo," Evelyn said, stepping aside in a pair of espadrille wedges. "How *are* you?"

The house was a meat locker, Corinna noticed as soon as she stepped in. She'd always associated air-conditioning with wealth. In the front sitting room, all the furniture was bright white. Corinna didn't even know you could buy furniture that color.

"Oh, I'm all right."

"Some wine? Red or white?"

"Oh, that's okay. Water is fine."

"Sparkling or still?"

"I'm sorry?"

Evelyn smiled like Corinna had made a joke, batting a hand at her. "Come this way. You can set that big ole thing down," she said, referring to the box, which had been professionally wrapped in pink foil and tied with at least three bows in varying shades of purple.

She followed Evelyn to the enormous kitchen, where Evelyn poured her a tall glass of ice water.

"I don't know where that girl is. I told her to be home by six. What time is it?"

"Six thirty."

Evelyn clicked her tongue. "Our reservation is at seven."

Just then, the front door slammed open, and girlish laughter spilled in.

"Camille!" Evelyn said, shoving the water glass into Corinna's hand as she rushed back toward the front door. "You better not have those goddamn skates on my *floor*." Corinna peered down the hall at Evelyn, Camille, and a thin, pretty Asian girl whose large breasts were barely covered by a sporty racerback top. Camille was sitting facing the door, untying graying roller skates.

"Goodbye, Su Chin," Evelyn said.

"*Jin*. Su *Jin*," Camille corrected.

Su Jin clomped down the front steps on her roller skates and waved goodbye over her shoulder. Evelyn slammed the door.

"Where have you *been*? I told you to be home by six. Do you know what time it is?"

Camille was still untying one of her skates. "I know, I'm sorry. It took longer to get back than we thought."

"Well, you could have called. I didn't get you a cell phone for nothing. And I don't like you hanging out with that girl, anyway. She's *fast*. You *know* I don't like to use that kind of misogynistic language, but there really is no other way to describe that girl. Why don't you spend more time with Ava or Parvitha? They're such nice girls."

Oh, what Corinna wouldn't have done when she was Camille's age to get a lecture like this one, for someone to show some interest in not only her *life* but her *reputation*. She was happy for Camille. Really, she was. But she also felt a little bit of something else. Was it *envy*? No way, she thought. What kind of person—what kind of *mother*—is jealous of her own daughter?

"Yes, ma'am," Camille answered.

"You're just saying that to placate me."

Camille got up from the floor. She was both skinnier and shapelier than Corinna remembered, though only a month had passed since they'd seen each other.

"Now, come say hello to your mother. This top looks nice on you."

Evelyn wrapped her arm around Camille's waist and ushered her in Corinna's direction. Corinna realized she hadn't drunk any of the water. She didn't want to look strange, like she had been standing there this entire time with a glass of water she'd asked for, so she took one sip and then dumped the rest into the sink.

When she turned around, Camille was there looking bored. "Hi, Mama," she said.

"Hi, baby. How are you? Can I hug you?"

Without waiting for a response, Corinna wrapped her arms around her daughter, who didn't immediately hug her back. But she was patient and waited. The girl was almost too thin to hold, she noticed. Briefly, Camille proffered a tepid tap-tap on Corinna's back and then went stiff as a board. Corinna wanted to hug her tighter. She'd heard on the radio that hugging improves relationships. Instead, she backed away from her daughter.

"Camille, go put on something for dinner. We're already running late," Evelyn said. "I'll call the restaurant."

A few minutes later, Camille came clunking down the stairs in a pair of heavy wedges much like the ones Evelyn wore, but higher. Evelyn, who was reclining with her eyes closed in a pristine white chair shaped like a kidney bean, sprang to life to examine Camille's outfit. Camille wore a knee-length chiffon dress patterned with pictures of book covers. Her hair was gathered on the top of her head in a big, neat bun, and she'd put on mascara and lip gloss. She snatched a tiny bag off a nearby table and slung it over her shoulder. When it landed against Camille's hip, Corinna saw that it read PRADA in gold against a black background. Corinna had, of course, heard of Prada but had never seen a piece in person.

She assumed they would leave from the front of the house. Instead, they went out back, where Evelyn flipped a switch to reveal a sparkling white Range Rover. Evelyn loved the color white, she noted. It struck her as ostentatious to have so many white things and not worry about them getting dirty.

They rode in silence. Corinna wanted to ask where they were and what they were seeing but kept quiet, sometimes stroking the box in her lap. She occasionally glanced over her shoulder at Camille, who slouched in the back seat with her legs splayed, her dress creating a convenient hammock for her cell phone, covered in pink rhinestones. The phone periodically made noise, but Camille stiffly looked out of the window. Corinna imagined a world in which she could reach into the back seat and touch the baby hairs at Camille's temple, but she could already feel the devastation when Camille would, inevitably, pull away. When they reached their destination, Evelyn expertly parallel parked the car. Though people were clearly waiting in the front of the restaurant to be seated, Evelyn walked into the main room, where they were greeted warmly and escorted to a massive, semicircular booth toward the back. Corinna slid in first and was blocked in on either side by Evelyn and Camille. Before they could say a word, three glasses of sparkling wine arrived at the table. Corinna raised a finger to protest the glass in front of Camille, but Evelyn shushed her like she was quieting a baby.

"Camille is allowed a glass here and there," she said.

Corinna's tongue became tangled in her mouth. She thought she might choke before she finally coughed: "Wh-what?"

"We'll talk about it later, dear," Evelyn said as if they were discussing the length of Camille's nails.

Corinna had many questions. For one, why would the restaurant risk losing their liquor license just to please Evelyn? Evelyn must have been more important than she realized. Before Corinna had a chance to speak again, her grandmother raised her glass.

"Cheers?" she said.

Begrudgingly, Corinna lifted her glass to join Camille and Evelyn's. The glasses clinked, and they drank. An unsettling silence followed, then Evelyn took her napkin, shook it out to her side, and placed it in her lap. She folded her hands on the table. Every movement she made seemed perfectly choreographed.

"Well," Evelyn said, and sighed. "I suppose we have a lot to talk about."

Corinna cleared her throat. "I'd like to give Camille her birthday present, if that's all right." She wanted to kick herself for asking permission.

Evelyn nodded and Corinna slid the box across the booth to Camille, who eyed it but made no motion toward it.

"*Camille,*" Evelyn said through a wide, fake smile. "Open your gift."

Camille half sighed, half groaned as she pulled the box into her lap, then realized it was too cumbersome and put it back on the table. She tore messily through the wrapping paper and paused when she saw the brightly colored shoebox. Camille smiled so briefly and meagerly that Corinna would have missed it if she'd blinked. She reached into the box and lifted a bubblegum-pink suede roller skate with glittering magenta wheels.

"Oh, wow," Evelyn said, smiling. "Look at those. They match your new bag! You're having one hell of a birthday week, aren't you?" She finished her wine, turned away from the table, and lifted her finger before pointing at her empty glass. "Camille *loves* pink, doesn't she? That *exact* shade."

Corinna hadn't known that her gift would match Camille's tiny Prada bag. She'd just been drawn to the skates at the boardwalk shop in Gulf Shores.

"Thank you, Mama," Camille said and gently tucked the gift back into the box, seeming slightly more buoyant.

"You were just talking about new skates, weren't you, darling?" Evelyn said. Corinna couldn't help but feel like Evelyn was showing off how well she knew Camille, and there was no greater currency than being closely acquainted with Camille. The waiter arrived with Evelyn's champagne, and she popped on her reading glasses.

"Are we ready to order?" the waiter asked.

Corinna fixed her mouth to say no, but Evelyn talked over her and ordered for everyone.

"We'll start with the calamari, panzanella, and bruschetta. I will have the snapper. My lovely granddaughter will have the crab cakes. And her mother will have . . ." Evelyn paused. "The scallops." She snapped the menu shut with a big smile. "Do you know where your name comes from?" she asked Corinna before the waiter was gone.

"No."

"It's a song." Evelyn took a large gulp of wine. "Corinna, Corinna. Your grandfather loved that damned song." She paused again. She made the same series of gestures to get herself another glass though she hadn't yet finished the one she had. "I suspect that's where your mother got the name."

"How's it go, Mama Evy?" Camille asked.

"Well, I'm not much of a singer. I'll play it for you when we get home. We have other things to discuss. Isn't that right?"

Corinna could not keep her eyes off Evelyn's teeth, which were so white they seemed unused.

"Camille, I've invited your mother to move into the carriage house."

"Okay." She shrugged. "You already told me that."

"Camille," Corinna said, holding her daughter's gaze. "I came here to make you my priority."

Camille broke eye contact, took her napkin off the table, and placed it in her lap with a dramatic flourish, then groaned with the same tone Evelyn and Charlotte used. Corinna didn't like that Camille was turning out so much like them. Camille had always had a little bit of an edge to her, especially once she got to be school-aged, and Corinna didn't really understand why. Yes, Corinna had turned to corporal punishment when she did not know what else to do, but only as a response to the girl's increasingly bad behavior. Corinna looked at her daughter. Camille's new life probably only reinforced her aloofness. Before, she had only been pretty. Now, she was beautiful and well dressed, with nearly limitless resources. Isn't this what Corinna had wanted?

"Camille," Evelyn said.

"What?" she answered sharply before inhaling half of the wine she had no business drinking.

"*Please.*" Evelyn caught the girl's eyes and held her gaze.

At this, Camille softened. "Sorry," she said.

"I think it's for the best. For all of us. Our family has a history of disconnecting"—Evelyn paused as her wine arrived along with the appetizers, then continued when the food runners were gone—"I don't think that needs to continue."

Corinna opened her mouth to explain further, even though Camille hadn't asked, but Evelyn gave her a pleading look, and she closed it. It was the most vulnerable she'd ever seen Evelyn be in person.

Camille reached for a piece of bruschetta, ate it in two bites, and washed it down with the last of her wine.

"Is this about all those letters you send Mama Charlotte?"

Color rushed to Evelyn's pale cheeks, and she leaned forward in her seat. "Did you read them?" she asked Camille.

"No," Camille said. "Well, I did see the ones where you just said 'I'm sorry.'"

Evelyn's shoulders relaxed, and she leaned away from the table a bit.

"I read them," Corinna said.

Evelyn lifted her glass again and tilted it back, but it was empty. She didn't seem to notice. Corinna blinked, and the glass was full again, as if by magic.

"I assumed that you knew about all of that," Evelyn said. Corinna hadn't considered this. Perhaps that's why Evelyn had always been so cool to her. For fear of what, though? "We can talk about it later, Corinna," she said finally. "Camille doesn't need to be involved in this right now."

Corinna saw that Evelyn was gripping her fork with great force, and she shrank back into the booth when it struck her that the only reason she wanted to tell Camille was to exercise some agency. Camille didn't need to know yet. If Corinna was still working on what to do with the information, what would Camille do with it?

"Well, Camille," Evelyn said, her voice shaking and her gaze low. "Won't you tell us about your classes this year? Fairfax-Washington has some of the *most* interesting classes. Isn't that right?"

Camille rolled her eyes, picked up a fork, and stabbed at the panzanella. The bits of crusted bread deflected her jabs, and Corinna could practically smell the frustration emanating from Camille's skin. "Yeah. I'm taking something called 'Study Skills,' ceramics, cryptology . . ." she answered flatly. "And umm, some other, basic sh-stuff." Then she threw the fork down, picked up the salad plate, and skillfully shook some of the soggy mess onto her smaller appetizer plate. Evelyn frowned at this, but Camille wasn't paying attention.

"What's cryptology?" Corinna asked, trying to sound bright.

"It's the study of codes."

"Speaking of 'ology,' I was just listening to something on the radio about agnotology."

"What's that?"

"The study of ignorance."

*   *   *

That night, there was a knock on the carriage house door, and Corinna found Evelyn outside in satin pajamas, holding a bottle of wine and two glasses.

"May I come in?"

Corinna stepped aside, and Evelyn strode into the small but comfortable living space.

"I haven't been here in a long time," she said. "I haven't had any overnight guests since Camille moved in. You like it?"

"Yes, it's very nice."

"Good," Evelyn said, then popped the cork on the wine. "Come sit."

They sat together on the gray sofa and Evelyn began to pour the wine; it was an expensive-looking sauvignon blanc. "You like white, yes?"

"Yes, I prefer it." Though she didn't know what was in the guesthouse, Corinna considered making a cocktail, but she felt paralyzed by Evelyn's presence.

"That's because you have a light palate, I can tell. You like seafood, yes?"

"Well, I grew up eating what was available, and that didn't really include much seafood."

Evelyn winced at this. "Right. Of course." After a moment, she added, "I just wanted to say something."

Corinna nodded.

"I don't make a big deal about alcohol with Camille because I'm hoping it will lose its elusiveness, and she'll have a healthier relationship with it than I do. Or your mother."

"Experimenting?"

"It's working so far," Evelyn snapped. "By the time your mother was fourteen, she was drinking like a fish. She probably thinks I didn't notice, but I did. She came in late, and she vomited every Sunday morning like clockwork. Camille isn't binging like that."

Corinna took another sip to give herself time to consider what Evelyn was saying, but this gave Evelyn permission to move on.

"And," Evelyn began, "I think I wrote that I wanted your mother to get rid of you."

"You did."

"I'm sorry I said that."

"But you meant it."

"Well," she said and took another sip of wine, "wouldn't *you*? If it happened to Camille?"

Corinna almost choked.

"See," Evelyn said. "If the same thing happened to Camille, you'd want the same thing."

"Yes, but—" Corinna took her own large sip of wine. "That's not even the—"

"Worst thing I did."

"Yeah."

Evelyn stood up and started rustling around the kitchen. Eventually, she produced a tin of anchovies and a sleeve of crackers. It surprised Corinna that she and Evelyn shared a taste for the same snack. "You're right," she said. "It's not the worst thing I did. But it's the worst thing I did to *you*."

Corinna felt she couldn't compute what had been said. She sat in silence while Evelyn continued talking, and heard none of it.

"It never would have happened to Camille," she surprised herself by saying, finding that she was angry. "I wouldn't have let it happen, Evelyn. And even if it did happen, I wouldn't have lost my daughter like that."

Evelyn's shoulders slumped. She closed her eyes and deflated further, but she seemed like she was fighting back angry words. And then, suddenly, she straightened. "I made mistakes."

"Listen," Corinna retorted. "What you done to my mama, you done to me. It shouldn't have been like that. She owed me better, and I owe Camille better. I'm giving her more than better. You do your part in 'better,' and that's just about all me and you got to talk about."

Evelyn blinked hard and fast. "Fair enough."

Corinna couldn't sleep that night. She sat on the couch, slowly drinking the remaining wine and watching *I Love Lucy* on mute. Corinna continued to reflect on who was responsible for whose trauma and came to the conclusion that the details didn't matter. She wanted to move, if not *on*, then forward.

In the morning, she apologized to Evelyn, who nodded.

"I accept your apology. But you weren't wrong. I owe you an apology as well. I hope you'll accept it."

Camille

FALL 2007

Riding the 96 bus to school, Camille was thinking about how much her mother annoyed her. She hated how her mother chewed, how her afro was almost always dry and flat on one side, how she wore the same nonslip restaurant clogs every day, how she sounded like a backwoods country bumpkin saying things like "finna" instead of "I am about to" and asking after her friends by saying things like "How's Su Jin an 'em?" Her mother, who had never been on a plane until recently, didn't even know what country Santorini— one of Camille's dream destinations—was in.

She jumped off the bus and ran a long block to the school, slowing when she reached the curving driveway and approaching her friends, who waited for her by the school's heavy oak front doors every morning.

Camille had matured significantly over the summer. She'd grown two inches, her breasts had bloomed to a C cup, and her hips had spread into an hourglass shape. She hadn't been unpopular before, but things had changed. Every morning, whether she took the bus, roller-skated, or was dropped off by her grandmother, Camille burst through the front doors of Fairfax-Washington like it was her own personal playground. And people turned to look at her. And they weren't just looking at the way she accessorized her school uniform, which had always been a cut above. They were looking at *her*.

She was not the most popular girl in school—that would have been Lauren DuMarre, who was pretty, smart, white, and wealthy. But Camille was up there. She controlled a different class than Lauren DuMarre, queen of the white, old-money scions. Camille was lady of the ethnic, the new money, the scholarship students, the offspring of academics. While she was technically of a lower status, it didn't mean the general population did not respect

Camille. Just the week before at a party at Jennifer Wang's house, Anderson Bradford had explained to her:

"It's a matter of preference—my 'cup of tea'—if you will. I must acknowledge that an excellent oolong is an attractive tea, right? But it's just not *my* 'cup of tea.' I'm more of an Earl Grey kind of fellow, an English Breakfast kind of guy. You understand."

Camille had, indeed, understood. She could be as objectively beautiful as science would allow, but she was still a Black girl. And not even a light-skinned Black girl with fine curly hair and light-colored eyes, like Ava. Her skin was gourmet hot chocolate–colored in the summer and milk chocolate–toned in winter. In a couple of years, she would be mistaken for Bangladeshi in a Singapore airport. But for now, she was the Blackest person she knew. Her hair, which had been cared for exclusively by Jeannette for the past three years, was not "kinky," per se. Still, her hair was naturally very, very tightly curled, though she usually had Jeanette do a steaming, smoking-hot "Dominican blowout," or, if she was feeling confident, she had Jeanette use soft twisting rods to create looser curls. The tidiness of her hair depended on the humidity and the right combination of products. Though she'd cut the relaxer out of her hair, she'd never really gotten the hang of her natural hair. This day, Camille's hair was blown-out bone-straight with tiny braids at the front pulled away from her face and bobby-pinned in the back.

As much as parts of her yearned for the level of riches and privilege her classmates had, she knew it was not attainable. She would have to settle for moderate generational wealth and the upper-middle-class status provided by her great-grandmother. In a way, Camille had everything anyone could possibly want. She had money, privilege, loving family members, and beauty. Still, she wanted something else. Or needed it?

One thing bothering her was her lack of a boyfriend. She and Logan had recently started texting again, but there wasn't much forward motion, and she hadn't seen him since school started. She avoided going to the bookstore in case he was there making out with his new girlfriend or something. The boys she would have considered dating were either white boys who couldn't take her home to their crusty families, or Black boys who wanted to date white girls. She would have happily dated Raj Patel, a very beautiful junior with pretty eyes and a head full of dense, black hair, but she felt that wouldn't work out either, as they were from such different cultures. Camille could have had anyone she wanted, but the relationship would have been carried out in near secrecy within the school walls and dark corners at parties. That's not who Camille wanted to be. Her mother was that kind of girl, she had a feeling. Camille hadn't come all the way to DC to be like her mother. Maybe she wished that's what the yawning, gaping hole in her heart was about.

Camille had a regular day at school. She bossed Su Jin and Peach around. She didn't eat anything at lunch. She flirted with Henry Alexander IV (whom everyone called Hank) in biology. In study hall in the library, she was staring off into space in front of her algebra homework when her phone buzzed. She looked around to be sure the librarian wasn't nearby and opened her phone in the lap of her gray wool pleated skirt.

Hey, read a text from Logan. Blood rushed to her face as she tapped out several messages and deleted them before deciding on a simple: hey;) She immediately regretted the winky face. She also wished she hadn't responded so quickly.

Camille had several hours of ballet classes after school, but she was distracted. Her pointe instructor, Mrs. Wallace, followed her around across the floor clapping her hands and hollering her name in time with the music.

"Camille! Where is your head?!" Mrs. Wallace shouted—nearly belligerent—between exercises.

This sort of singling-out rarely happened to her, and she would have found it mortifying under different circumstances. But she was still thinking about the winky face emoticon.

After ballet, she got on the bus. She was unusual among her classmates in that she used public transportation, and she lived almost downtown and not in Upper Northwest, Northern Virginia, or Bethesda. When people arrived at Evelyn's home, they were often surprised by how nice the house was and how many of the houses on the street were equally lovely. People were also amused by how Camille skated around the city when the weather was nice and she wasn't exhausted, including often skating to and from school. It took Camille a while to understand what this shock and awe were actually about, but Camille wasn't concerned with "politics."

Camille pulled out *A Lesson Before Dying*, which she was reading for English class, and almost immediately her phone buzzed in her jacket pocket. She stared at the back of the head of the man sitting in front of her while she debated whether or not to reach into her pocket. She knew it wasn't her grandmother or mother because they only called. It might have been Su Jin or Peach, but she doubted it; they would both be deep into their homework or internet activities at this hour. She opened her thin, bejeweled flip phone and read the message: lost my phone. been thinking abt u. She forced back a smile, flipped her phone closed, and slipped it back into her pocket. She wasn't sure she believed him, but she couldn't help but feel glad.

The house was quiet when she arrived home, only a few lights on toward the back. She expected Evelyn to greet her in the front hall, as she usually did, but it was dark and empty.

"Camille? That you?" she heard her mother call.

Camille rolled her eyes. She wanted to go upstairs to kick off her penny loafers and pull off the leotard, which was giving her a bad wedgie. She was wearing it underneath all of her school clothes because she couldn't be bothered with getting completely undressed and then dressed again after ballet.

"Yeah?" she groaned loudly.

"Come here, please."

Camille shuffled down the hallway, loudly sighing. Her mother was sitting at the end of the dining room table with a glass of red wine and a dog-eared copy of *Who Moved My Cheese?* She was always reading corny self-help books and quoting them in casual conversation. Sometimes, Camille overheard her mother reciting what sounded like motivational speeches out loud to herself. "There is no such thing as a hopeless situation" was one of her favorite lines.

"Yeah?" Camille said when Corinna failed to look up from her book.

Corinna flipped the book over and folded her hands on the table. She smiled. "I just wanted to say hello."

"Hi," Camille said, a mocking tone in her voice. She was actually annoyed with herself for her general attitude, but she really couldn't help it sometimes.

"How was school?"

"Fine."

"I heard you had a test today in geography. How'd that go?"

Camille sighed. "Fine."

It had gone great, actually. She'd known the answer to every question and finished so quickly that her teacher graded it in front of her while the rest of the class was working. Mr. Peele, who was young and handsome, smiled when he handed it back to her: "Congratulations, Miss Jackson." But Camille didn't know how to convey any of this to her mother. Or maybe she just didn't want to.

"Anything exciting or interesting happen today?"

"No, not really."

Camille's phone buzzed in her jacket pocket. She pulled it out, but it was only Su Jin asking about weekend plans.

Corinna sighed. "Did you eat?"

Camille had not eaten anything since breakfast. She usually didn't eat dinner unless Evelyn was around to watch her. "Yeah," she lied. "I had a sandwich after ballet." She looked up to see if her mother appeared to believe her. She didn't.

"There's some soup on the stove."

Camille stared at her mother and shrugged. "Okay."

Camille

DECEMBER 2007

Once Logan came back into the picture, Camille dedicated much of her free time to him. On the weekends, she sneaked out to see him. He always brought her sweet little gifts: a tiny mason jar of fresh honey, shrimp tacos, a handmade friendship bracelet–style collar for Sozzani. He told her all kinds of stories about himself and listened carefully when she told hers. He was not the first person she'd ever talked to about Jenny; she'd told Su Jin, Peach, Evelyn, and her allergist. Each of them had grimaced and said, "That's crazy" or "That's awful." And that's where the conversation had ended.

"That must have messed with your head," Logan said as they sat on the steps of the Portrait Gallery at eleven thirty on a Saturday evening, sharing a gyro. The streets were uncharacteristically quiet, a major disappointment considering how much the pair enjoyed people watching. She handed the gyro back to him, and he took a bite while she was still holding it, which felt insanely intimate.

"Yeah."

"What happened after that?"

She paused. Then she told him about Samantha, her mom, and her general anxiety about the direction of her life, something she didn't realize she had until she said it out loud. He didn't flinch; he even asked questions she'd never asked herself, like "When no one in your house reacted like you thought they should, did you think violence might be normal?"

"I see why you have a hard time trusting people," he said a bit later.

"What? I trust people."

"No, you don't."

"Just because—"

"Okay," he said. "Forget I said anything."

But, of course, she could not forget it. To fill the awkward silence, he talked about his new side hustle, redoing and rebuilding furniture. "I started in high school. You can buy like a two-dollar dresser and repaint it and fix it and just resell it as 'upcycled,' and people go crazy for it. I've been taking shit to flea markets on the weekends and killing it. I can spend like a hundred dollars on materials and come home with a thousand. Around here, people will spend an insane amount of money for an old coffee table dressed up to look new. Sometimes, you don't have to do anything at all."

Camille knew this was not the kind of man she was supposed to be interested in. He didn't have a pedigree. He didn't even have a family. He had no money, and no degree or desire for one. But she liked him. And he was kind, handsome, not crazy, and usually smelled nice. What else did a fifteen-year-old need?

"Obviously, the time I spend on it isn't free, but if I had more time, I could make more stuff. My roommate Dominic rents a moving van on flea market days. He builds guitars and parts for guitars. And we just take it all out there. And we come back with nothing. Well, nothing but cash." He laughed. "Every time."

Camille couldn't stop smiling. Logan and her grandfather would get along famously, she thought.

"I'm saving up for a trip," he continued.

"A trip where?"

"Haven't decided yet. Might stay when I get there, though."

"Oh," she said. "Cool."

"We could go together, maybe." He nudged her with his shoulder.

She barely slept that night. She was too busy smiling and giggling under her down comforter. Early in the morning, Evelyn knocked on Camille's door and opened it before she had a chance to say anything.

"Hello?" Evelyn said and took a loud sip of coffee. "We have an early breakfast reservation in Bethesda. Let's get going, please."

Camille swung her legs out of the bed and listened to Evelyn return downstairs, grumbling about something. Half an hour later, they were seated in a restaurant seemingly constructed entirely of marble and glass. An older woman played soft piano music. Evelyn was humming and reading the menu with her reading glasses resting at the very tip of her nose. Camille was watching the woman play the piano. She tried to imagine Charlotte sitting there instead.

"I know you're seeing a boy," Evelyn said without looking up, rousing Camille from her daydream.

Camille's face grew hot, like when she'd drunk a couple of glasses of sparkling rosé at one of Su Jin's stepdad's fundraisers. Camille looked down into the enormous menu in her arms. The menu was absurdly large for how few things were listed on it.

"That white boy from my store this past summer."

Camille stared at her lap.

"Look at me, Camille."

When Camille hesitated, Evelyn pounded the table just hard enough that the restaurant quieted and turned to look at them. Startled by the show of anger, Camille met Evelyn's eyes. Evelyn folded her hands on the tablecloth, then leaned across the table and whispered, "What do you have to say for yourself?"

Camille had nothing to say for herself. It was true. She was "seeing" the white boy from the store.

"You're not to see him," Evelyn said. She snatched her napkin off the table and snapped it like a whip before placing it delicately in her lap. "We have this rule for a reason."

"What's the reason?" Camille asked, her eyes averted.

"I'm sorry?" Evelyn snapped. "You're not in a position to be asking questions, are you?"

"But—"

"But not a *goddamn* thing, Camille."

"Have you told my mother?"

Evelyn shook her head. "No, she'd *die* if she knew."

Camille didn't care much for her mother's opinion, but she breathed a sigh of relief.

"And I won't tell her if you stop seeing him."

Before they ordered their food, Evelyn watched Camille delete the contact from her phone, an action she seemed to think was less reversible than it was. They ate breakfast in near-total silence, but much to Camille's surprise, Evelyn placed a hand on the middle of her back as they left the restaurant.

"There's plenty of time for dating," Evelyn said, Manolo Blahniks clicking as she crossed the marble floor. "You're so beautiful. You know that? But I'd prefer you date someone *more* . . ." She waved her free hand in the air. "How do I say?" She paused. "*Colored*." The valet pulled up in the glimmering Range Rover. "And inspired, perhaps. Ruth told me he's not in school. He said in his interview he didn't even plan on going!" Her hand on Camille's back was growing colder with each passing moment.

But Camille thought: Not going to college? Imagine that.

Evelyn continued: "You're so lovely, truly a beautiful young woman. I'm not just saying that because I'm your great-grandmother, and I love you. Maybe I didn't tell Charlotte this enough, and that's why things have gone the way they have with her. I taught her that a man was the prize, not that *she* was the prize."

Evelyn was talking to herself, Camille realized. It was like she was workshopping something, repeating herself and rambling. "You can have your pick, can't you? I'd like to see you with some-one with a little status, you know? You're going to graduate from a prestigious school and go on to a wonderful university. You'll go to Howard, obviously . . . They have a wonderful journalism program. That's still what you want to do, right?"

Eventually, it would occur to Camille how absurd it was to ask a fifteen-year-old what she wanted to do with her life. But at the time, being a journalist sounded right. She liked to write, and she loved the idea of traveling the world. And it was a profession Evelyn recognized as legitimate. So Camille nodded, then men-tally composed her next text message to Logan:

We gotta be more careful.

Camille

SPRING 2008

When Camille arrived home late Thursday night of Easter weekend, Corinna was sitting in the front room holding a glass of brown liquor. Camille knew immediately that her grandmother was nearby. Charlotte and David were seated on the white leather couch in the front room. Charlotte was wearing a yellow linen pantsuit, and David was in khakis and a new-looking rugby shirt. Camille had never seen her grandparents so presentable. She rushed to the couch and wrapped her arms around them both. She'd last seen them for a few days in December but hadn't been nearly as exhausted from school and ballet as she was now. Her feet, knees, and thighs constantly ached, and Evelyn had convinced her that she needed to take physics and AP calculus so that her Howard application would look like she was "challenging herself," so she was always on the verge of either a migraine or some kind of anxiety attack. Evelyn praised her often but could also be very pushy. She called it "encouraging," but Camille, on her worst days, thought of it as nagging.

"Oh, sweet, sweet girl," Charlotte and David cooed together, and Camille crawled into Charlotte's lap like a small child. No one else in the entire world would have described her as "sweet." She'd grown cold in her new life, and she knew it. Later, when she'd slid from her grandparents' laps, she opened her cell phone to answer a text from Logan, now saved in her phone as Rashida from Afro-American literature, which wasn't even a class she was taking.

My grandparents are here. Unavailable.

She showered and struggled to find something to wear. Evelyn would want her in something dressy for dinner, but she didn't want to be dressed more formally than her grandparents. She decided on a vintage bell-sleeved floral baby doll dress from a shop on 14th Street, but no one commented on it when she came downstairs.

In the dining room, she sat next to David. "I got something for ya," he said and winked, before producing a box of Milk Duds seemingly out of thin air. "You're looking thinner. Your grandmother feeding ya?"

"Yes, Grandaddy," Camille said, tucking the box under her thigh. "I'm just dancing all the time, you know?"

David took her hand and kissed her fingers. "Sweet girl," he said. "So talented. And smart. I hear you're doing physics. Now, what's that, exactly?"

"Oh, Grandaddy," Camille replied, cupping his thick, veiny hand in her own. "It's so hard. I hate it." She could just barely hear all three of her mothers in the next room having some kind of heated debate in loud whispers.

"Oh, but the hard things are the things worth doing. Somebody famous said that, ain't they?"

Camille felt tears welling and pain swelling in the back of her throat. Her lower lip quivered, and before she knew it, she was crying.

"What's the matter?" David asked.

She slipped her hands away and covered her face. She didn't know why she was crying. "I'm not unhappy," she said through gasping breaths. She knew she was supposed to be happy. But she just *wasn't*.

"Now, don't let your granmama see you crying like this no more," he said and handed her an intricately folded napkin to wipe her tears. "She's ready to take you home as it is. Unless you *want* to come home." His navy-blue eyes stretched open like those of a pleading kitten.

"No, no, Grandaddy. My friends are here. I like it here," she said as she dabbed at her eyes.

"Well, dry them tears then," he said, smiling. "You been keepin' up with the Tornadoes?" he asked, just as Evelyn and Charlotte entered the room.

"No," Camille said, trying not to sound annoyed.

"Well," he said. "Johnny Washington had hisself a great season. I'm tellin' ya. Did you know we used to know his mama?"

Camille had just seen Johnny Washington in a commercial for car insurance. He'd pulled up close to the camera in a shiny red Corvette and pointed right at the camera. *You can save money with America's Best.* He smiled an enormous, almost clownish, white smile. It looked like it had been edited onto his face, but Camille knew that was his real smile because she'd seen him at a meet and greet at Food Lion once when she was grocery shopping with Charlotte. They hadn't even gotten close to him, but it was almost impossible to miss his grin.

"No."

"Yeah, before you was born. Your granmama was best friends wit his mama. Used to come by the house sometimes."

It seemed odd that her grandmother had never mentioned knowing the mother of the most famous football player in the country. "Why she never talk about it?"

He shrugged. "They fell out."

Dinner was uneventful. They ate food Evelyn must've had delivered as she never cooked anything complicated, but she was making unusual efforts to pass it off as her own, transferring it into her own dishes and putting it in the oven just so that she could pull it out and place it on the table. Evelyn said James, Charlotte's father, liked food that took a lot of time and effort, but she hadn't had the same kind of patience since he died. Almost everything Evelyn ate was cold, or required little preparation, or both. She ate yogurt for breakfast, salad for lunch, and a piece of salmon or chicken for dinner with a side of lightly steamed vegetables. Tonight, there was roast chicken, macaroni and cheese, string beans, and sweet potatoes. Camille hadn't eaten anything with butter or much oil for months. Her mood immediately improved upon her first bite of chicken.

"You're eating like we don't feed you," Evelyn said from the end of the table.

"She is *awfully* skinny, isn't she?" Charlotte said with a smirk.

Camille looked at Charlotte, who was very politely holding a knife and fork, and then to Evelyn, who was gripping her utensils with great force.

"You *must* realize she's dancing twenty to thirty hours a week. I'd be concerned if she weren't so thin."

Charlotte scoffed.

"She's healthy," David chimed in. "That's what's important, isn't that right, Corinna?"

"That's right, Daddy," Corinna answered without lifting her eyes.

"And I think she looks *perfect*," Evelyn said.

"I didn't *say* she didn't look good. I'm just—"

"Well, what else matters, Charlotte?" Evelyn was still in the exact pose she had been in at the beginning of the exchange, midway through cutting open a chicken breast, her knuckles turning white from the tight grip on her utensils. "Hmm?" She looked like she did when a server delivered the wrong order to her table.

"Well, I can—"

"Oh, Lotte," David interjected. "Can you pass the sweet potatoes? They sure are good. Only thing coulda made 'em better was some marshmallows on top. Ain't that right?"

Charlotte passed the elaborate crystal dish. "Yes," she muttered, apparently begrudging. "They're good."

After dessert, when the adults were starting to show signs of drunkenness and David was entertaining the women with stories from the bayou, Camille excused herself to the kitchen. She knew there was a second pecan pie sitting on the marble counter. The small piece she'd allowed herself earlier hadn't been sufficient. She couldn't remember the last time she'd had something sweeter than a ripe strawberry. She used to resist Evelyn's "clean eating" habits but had grown accustomed to them. Her skin was clear, and her bowels were regular. And best of all, she was skinny. She might have been relatively naturally thin, but she was not naturally ballet skinny.

She planned on just cutting herself another slice. It couldn't hurt. She went to the utensil drawer and pulled out the biggest spoon she could find. She repositioned the pie so that her body would conceal it from anyone who was to enter the room. She plunged the spoon directly into the center of the pie. She took an enormous bite, and before it was completely chewed, she took another bite. Her phone was buzzing in her dress pocket, and she ignored it.

"Camille, what are you doing?"

She turned to find her mother in the kitchen doorway. "Nothing."

"Don't look like nothing. Look at this pie."

Camille looked down at the pie, which now featured a few large craters.

"You feeling okay?"

Camille wasn't quite sure. "Um," was all she could muster.

"What are we going to do about this pie?" Corinna picked up the dish. "Go back to the table before they wonder where you are," she said. "I'll fix it."

At the table, David was still talking, and Charlotte and Evelyn stared straight ahead at adjacent walls. She excused herself shortly after David started his story about the ghost he'd seen on Frenchmen Street in 1973, which she'd heard at least four dozen times. He swore up and down that he saw a beautiful woman in old-timey clothes who he thought was a street performer turn down a dark alley. She was cute, and he went to talk to her, but she turned again and walked straight through a wall. Well, sometimes it was a wall, and sometimes he followed her through the back door of a bar and she disappeared into the crowd, but that was the long version. She knew he would go for the long version to diffuse the tension in the room. She couldn't help but flee; grabbing Sozzani from the living room, she went to her room and closed the door.

Corinna

EASTER WEEKEND 2008

Evelyn had ordered food from a restaurant in Georgetown that didn't do takeout, only catering. Two men in chef's whites delivered the food in an unmarked van.

Charlotte stood in the corner of the kitchen, sipping a glass of red wine with unusual restraint, as Evelyn attempted to transfer the food from the aluminum serving trays to a set of elaborate crystal serving dishes. Corinna took over when she saw how much Evelyn's hands were shaking, but Evelyn stood close by.

"She wasn't supposed to see this part," she whispered. "Can you make it look like it was cooked in the bowls? Keep the baked part of the macaroni on top? Maybe swirl the potatoes?"

The jig was undeniably up, but Corinna did as she was told, scooping much of the macaroni from underneath the baked crust and delicately transplanting the crust to the top of the bowl.

"No one would believe the macaroni was baked in that dish if that's the look you're going for," Charlotte shot from the other side of the kitchen.

Corinna looked over her shoulder at her mother, who had taken a seat at the island. Her glass was empty.

"I mean, I've never seen either of you cook a damn thing in my life," Charlotte said, her face so blank Corinna thought she was done, but she continued. "I mean, who are you *actually* trying to fool, Evelyn?"

Corinna was afraid to look at Evelyn because she was not sure what she might find. She tried to telepathically tell her mother to shut the fuck up. But Charlotte poured herself more wine and kept going.

"I know what you're trying to do," she said. "You're trying to remind me of what I couldn't."

"Oh, Charlotte," Evelyn said with unusual sweetness in her tone.

"Don't 'oh, Charlotte' me!"

"Mama," Corinna said, trying to stop her mother from doing what she did best: escalating a situation into chaos. She was beginning to understand that David wasn't exactly the sole aggressor, though it had taken her a long time to see it.

Charlotte continued to run off at the mouth, while Evelyn took it. Corinna wasn't listening to what her mother was saying, but

Camille was in the next room, so she tried to drown Charlotte out: "Mama, stop it! Hush!"

Corinna took her mother's arm in one hand and her mother's wineglass in the other and guided her out of the kitchen to the dining room, where Camille and David were talking. Corinna forced her mother into a seat, refilled her glass, and left her there.

When she returned to the kitchen, she asked Evelyn: "Do you have any marshmallows for the yams?"

"Yams?"

"Sweet potatoes, whatever."

Evelyn seemed to snap out of a trance. "Oh no. No. I don't keep sugary things like that in the house."

"Well, I'll give it a good swirl, make it look a little more home-made maybe," she said.

"You don't think Camille heard those things she said?" Evelyn asked as she watched Corinna swirl a wooden spoon on the surface of the sweet potatoes.

Though Corinna was concerned about the same thing, she reassured her grandmother: "Camille too caught up in her own little bullshit. I wouldn't worry about it if I was you."

"She is awful self-centered, isn't she?"

Corinna smiled and saw, out of the corner of her eye, that Evelyn was also smiling.

"But that's what we wanted, right?"

"Well. It kind of is, I suppose."

After dinner, Camille went upstairs almost immediately, and everyone's shoulders dropped several inches as soon as she did. David stopped telling his favorite ghost story and finished his drink. They were silent for a moment.

"I think y'all ought to keep that girl out of y'alls mess," David said. "As best you can, anyway."

"Which mess?" Corinna asked. Charlotte and Evelyn both cut their eyes at her, but she didn't mind. She crossed her legs and took a long sip of her drink, a concoction she'd mixed up in an attempt at making a Long Island iced tea taste like actual iced tea. She'd failed and she could feel the liquor wafting toward her skull.

"She's having a hard time is all I'm sayin'," David answered. "That's even without all the drama."

"Trauma's more like it."

"Hard time?"

"I think this world's just new to her is all. She'll be all right, but I don't want it being no harder on her than it need be. I don't think she needs to know about . . . you know."

Corinna wasn't sure she agreed, but nodded anyway. She headed upstairs, where she knocked on Camille's door and listened for footsteps. Camille opened the door as if she were hiding out from the police. She poked her head out and looked left and right.

"Yes?"

"Can I talk to you?"

Camille shrugged and sat down on the bed, where Corinna joined her.

"Are you okay with school or whatever?"

"Yeah, why?" Camille had crossed her arms over her chest. Her chest was getting big; she must have gotten that from Delia, whose breasts were large enough to smother an adult man. The women on their side were B cups at most. She'd hoped Camille would get a nice balance in between. The dog was panting loudly from her spot by Camille's hip.

"I—You just don't seem like yourself."

"I *definitely* am myself. What would you know, anyway?" her daughter asked. "You haven't even been around." Camille folded her arms tighter, but suddenly, her body language softened; she dropped her arms a little bit, and her shoulders sank away from her ears.

Corinna was stunned by her daughter's vulnerability. Her brain felt like it was rattling in her skull as she tried to figure out what to say next. She decided to try and match Camille's apparent openness. "That's fair," she said and watched to see what Camille would do next. Camille's arms dropped entirely, and her hands rested in her lap, but she didn't look up.

Corinna reached to touch her daughter's knee and was surprised that Camille allowed her to. "But listen, I let other people raise you when I didn't think I could. I just wanted you to have what I didn't. I hope that means something to you." She retreated her hand. "It's okay if it doesn't. Maybe one day, it will."

Camille sighed loudly and rolled her eyes. "I get it." She paused and then added, as if it pained her: "That doesn't mean it didn't fucking hurt."

Corinna bit her tongue so she didn't say what she wanted to: "You don't know what pain is" or "Watch your damn mouth."

"I understand," she said instead, because that was true, too.

*   *   *

In the morning, Corinna went into the second bedroom in the carriage house. David was snoring, and Charlotte was sitting up against the headboard with her head bowed.

"Mama?" Corinna whispered from the doorway. "Mama," she said a little bit louder when Charlotte didn't respond.

"Mmm?" Charlotte answered without lifting her head.

"What you doin'?"

"What does it look like?"

"Prayin'."

Charlotte nodded.

"Why?"

"I'm trying to forgive my mother."

Corinna stared at Charlotte in silence.

"You're still here?" her mother said after a moment.

"How's prayer going to help?"

Charlotte sucked her teeth and lifted her head. "I'm doing the best I can, okay?"

"Can we talk?"

"Now?"

"Yes."

As if greatly inconvenienced, Charlotte huffed, but she got out of bed. "I'll meet you in the kitchen."

The kitchen was half the size of the one in the main house, but at least twice the size of the one in Tennessee. As she prepared to brew a pot of coffee, Corinna thought about the coffee her mother made from packets of blackened dust and hot water. In the past, Corinna had replenished her mother's stash of instant coffee before she noticed. Here, everything magically replenished itself by way of the mousy housekeeper. There was no need to go to the grocery store unless you were looking for something that wasn't on the weekly list. And the coffee came in impractically small bags of whole beans. She ground the beans, placed them into the filter, filled the tank, pressed the appropriate buttons, and waited. She looked out the window and saw the Astroturf leading to the main house. Inside, Evelyn swept past the glass door in her white satin pajamas and robe like a ghost.

"This place is *haun-ted,* you hear me?" Charlotte said as she entered the room. "Last time I was here, I swear I saw a damn ghost. And last night, I couldn't sleep. I went outside to smoke, and I just felt like something was following me, watching me."

"It was probably Evelyn."

"It wasn't." Charlotte took a seat at the table. "Coffee ready?"

"I been here months and ain't seen nothing of the sort." Except she had seen something strange: her bed was always made within an hour after she got out of bed. At first, she'd thought it was the housekeeper, but then it happened on the woman's day off. Corinna knew it was something otherworldly, but she decided not to be afraid and never to speak about it, either. Shit really popped off in the movies as soon as someone said something out loud about the ghost, and Corinna didn't need any more drama. The coffee maker beeped. She carried the carafe to the table.

Charlotte rolled her eyes as Corinna poured her a cup. "You ain't got to believe me. I know what I felt." She lifted the mug and crossed her legs. "What did you want to talk about?"

"I think you know, Mama."

Again, Charlotte huffed. "I'm doing my best, I said."

"Are you really?"

"I'm still your mother. You can't talk to me any kind of way," she said weakly, but she avoided Corinna's gaze. "And I'm not ready to talk about it, okay?"

"Not talking about it only gives it power."

"Where'd you read that?"

"I don't remember."

"Well, it doesn't matter because it's already got a hold on me." Charlotte's eyes were open, but they were blank. She looked old, withered, and small to her daughter. "And I can't shake it." Then she seemed to return from where she'd been. "Can I smoke in here?"

"I'd rather you didn't," Corinna said, but her mother was already lighting a cigarette and sucking on it like it was bringing her back to life.

"Well, I hope you can at least forgive for your own good, Mama," she continued. "You don't have to be angry for the rest of your life." She finally took a sip of coffee, but her jaw and hands trembled.

"I don't think you understand, Corinna."

"What?"

Charlotte squared herself to the table. "You got any liquor in here?"

Corinna stood and fetched the rum, which Charlotte promptly poured into her coffee. "What don't I understand, Mama?"

"It's too late for me, sweetheart. My heart is too hard."

"Your heart isn't too hard, Mama. You love Camille, and Daddy, and . . ." She hesitated. "Me."

"And that's all it can do."

Corinna shook her head. "That's not right. Everyone can forgive. I've forgiven you."

Charlotte became still as a statue. Then, she took a breath. "I'll keep trying, but I don't think it's going to happen for me, sugar," she said, then ashed her cigarette into the potted plant on the table. "Pour me some more? Why does it matter so much to you anyway?"

"Because it would be good for everyone, especially Camille."

"Is this all about getting Camille to forgive you? You think she'll
see me forgive Evelyn, and that will mean she has to forgive you?"

It was Corinna's turn to roll her eyes. Then she took a gulp
straight from the bottle of rum and poured some more in her
coffee.

"Fortunately for you, I don't think it's too late for Camille. You
can still turn things around."

"How?"

Charlotte shrugged. "You keep asking me these deep-ass questions. I don't know. You're familiar with my work." She swigged
the last of her second cup of coffee. "Do what I didn't do."

"Pay attention?"

"That sounds right. Now," she said, and sighed. "Pour me another
damn cup of coffee."

Camille

EASTER WEEKEND 2008

"I have a lecture this evening," Evelyn said. "I would like to have
dinner after with everyone and have a conversation about the way
things are going."

"Okay, where?" Camille asked.

"Well, not you. Everyone else. You're staying here."

Camille fought back a smile. She couldn't have hoped for a better
opportunity to sneak Logan in, finally. They had never really been
alone together indoors.

A few hours later, she was staring at herself in her bathroom
mirror, half-drunk off a half bottle of something white from Evelyn's wine fridge. She'd carefully selected a pair of tight-fitting,
pink velour lounge pants that read *Juicy* across the behind, and
a silky cropped camisole, and twisted her hair up into two thick
buns on the top of her head. At eight, she answered the door to a

smiling Logan. She was already quite drunk by then. She led him to the family room with the gigantic television and brown suede couch where she and Su Jin sometimes watched TV. Other times, Camille did homework in it when Evelyn wasn't around to lecture her about how she couldn't possibly be learning very much in front of the television. Camille turned on a *Degrassi* rerun and opened a new bottle of wine.

"Are you allowed to do this?" Logan asked.

"Allowed to do what?"

"Have me over?"

Camille shrugged and collapsed into his side. He wrapped his thick arm around her. They sat in silence for a moment.

"You could be a model if you wanted. Is that what you want?" he asked.

"What?"

"To be a model or whatever? I thought that's what the Tumblr thing was about."

She shrugged. "Tumblr isn't really about anything."

"You like the attention, don't you?"

Camille frowned. Logan had a Tumblr, too, but he seemed to use it only to reblog pictures of the ocean and quotations about surfing.

"I didn't mean it like that," he said.

"You don't care about attention?"

"I just think I learned to live without it." He took a gulp from Camille's glass.

"That sounds nice."

"Pretty sure it's a symptom of child neglect, so don't get too excited." He adjusted his white V-neck tee.

Camille opened her mouth to tell him she was neglected, too. But that wasn't right. Not *really*. She had always been taken care of. She never went to school dirty or hungry, like some of her elementary school classmates had. "Oh," she said instead.

He smiled. "If you were a model, you could travel and whatever. Like we talked about."

They had been talking about travel a lot lately. She'd been reading about study abroad programs, which eventually led to more general travel blogs. There was no place in particular she wanted to go, though she was particularly drawn to Central and South America. She was taking Spanish in school. She liked the rhythm of the language and the history of the land. But she would have leaped at the chance to go anywhere. For someone so worldly, Evelyn only really traveled if she had to for work.

Camille knew Logan wanted to get away from DC. He didn't say it, but she knew he was staying because of her, which was the most incredible bit of information she had ever known.

In her wildest daydreams, Camille thought about leaving with Logan to go on an adventure someplace exciting. But she wasn't going to graduate for another year and a half. And her mothers wouldn't let her go anywhere with him. And why would she go somewhere with someone who she wasn't even sure was her boyfriend, anyway? It was a total pipe dream.

He put his arm around her and pressed his lips to hers. She felt herself go stiff, though they'd been in this situation a few times, each time always going a little bit further than before. Feeling her breasts over her shirt became unhooking her bra became peeling her top off entirely, and so on. Something about this moment felt more serious. Were they skipping steps? She wasn't sure. But she did know what was about to happen. She'd fantasized about it, though she hadn't really thought it would happen so soon. Both Su Jin and Peach were already having sex. Sometimes, they treated her like a kid because she was still a virgin. They were also the only people she'd ever heard speak candidly about sex. Charlotte had given her many talks about what not to do, but never what to do. And her school's sex ed hadn't been great. She'd read about it in books, though. During her young adult literature phase, she'd learned that it was supposed to hurt, supposed to be between a committed couple, and supposed to be "special." Most importantly, you were supposed to be "ready."

"What's wrong?" he whispered against her neck.

Her skin buzzed. Her cheeks stung, and her mouth was watering like she'd tasted something tart. Her nipples were hardening under her shirt, and there was a throb between her legs. "Nothing," she said, because there was nothing wrong; she liked him, felt comfortable with him.

Things happened very quickly after that. She fell limply onto her back, and he undressed her, seeming to grow new, additional arms to touch her with. He pulled his sherpa coat underneath her "to protect the couch," he said. He knew exactly what he was doing, and that was a comfort to Camille, who'd heard stories about boys who didn't. He didn't need to pull away to fumble with the condom he produced from his back pocket, and she was reassured by the sound of the latex unfurling; it sounded familiar, almost like food packaging being unwrapped.

She was thinking about the sound a package of bacon made when he slid inside her and released a moist, hot, girlish sigh into her ear. It didn't hurt. The discomfort was equivalent to a dentist messing around in her mouth. And it didn't stay uncomfortable. But it didn't feel as good as the moments leading up to it. She didn't know what to do with her hands, so she placed them on his back. She wasn't sure if she was supposed to feel something physical or emotional. She closed her eyes and tried to relax.

It wasn't long before he became very still, and his pelvis collapsed heavily onto hers. Instinctively, she stroked his back. That was when she noticed the two long scars that ran at least six or so vertical inches up and down his back, parallel to his spine. There were two of them. She couldn't even see them, but she was alarmed at the violence that must have created them. These were not surgical scars; they were very straight but uneven, and there were *two* of them. He kissed her cheek and ear before pressing his face against her neck.

Camille excused herself to her en suite bathroom with the condom, which she dropped in the toilet. She thought she was supposed to bleed, but there was nothing on the toilet paper other than clear, viscous fluid she recognized as her discharge. On the second wipe, the fluid was pinkish. But that was it. Wasn't there supposed to be enough blood to ruin the sheets? What had the coat been protecting the couch from?

Still seated on the toilet, she opened her cell phone and texted Su Jin about what she'd done. Then she texted Evelyn that she'd had to order dinner because there was nothing in the house. She had left only an hour earlier with the rest of the family for George Mason, which was more than an hour away. Camille likely still had all night to do whatever she wanted.

In her closet, she changed her moist underwear and put on a new pair of satin pajamas. When she walked back into her bedroom, Logan was standing with his back to her at the bookshelf by her desk. It startled her. She wasn't sure she was ready for him to see her room. He turned to look at her.

"Nice PJs," he said with a wide smile. He flopped onto her bed and tucked his hands behind his head. "You want me to tell you about my scars?" He smiled rakishly, like an illustration of Huckleberry Finn on the cover of a crusty paperback.

Camille sat on the other edge of the bed. She had an ominous feeling that all the girls before her had probably asked about his scars. And maybe there was something wrong with her for not asking.

"Fine. You're going to tell me anyway."

"When I was fourteen—when my mom was still alive—I was jumping a fence with my cousin and got snagged on the barbed wire."

Camille winced. "Are you fucking with me?"

"Yes," he said and smiled. "You got me. I was actually attacked by a bear."

She rolled her eyes. "Well, what happened after that? Were you, like, dangling from the fence or something?"

"No, I didn't dangle from it. But it was really more like razor wire, so it was pretty fucking sharp. I didn't even realize I'd been cut until my cousin Brody saw it and screamed like a little girl."

"Then what?"

"I think I fainted or something. I woke up, and I was at home. My mom was in the middle of a *wild* bender. She didn't want to take me to the hospital. I would have died if her fucking boyfriend hadn't showed up to beat her ass and make her."

"Your mother's abusive boyfriend took you to the hospital?"

"Yeah, he was like 'Colleen, that boy gon' die!'" he said in a bad southern accent. "I think he was from Texas."

"Wow."

"He was a piece of shit, but he saved my life. Crazy how that can go, isn't it?"

"That's a good story," she said. "Did you just make it up?"

He laughed. "I wish."

"Are you mad at your mom?"

"No, she's dead."

"You can be mad at dead people."

"What's the point of that, though?"

"Where do you get all this well-adjusted shit?"

"Court-ordered counseling, mostly," he said.

Camille laughed. She felt warm. She had a strange urge to rub her nose against his, but she refrained.

"You ever considered therapy?"

"What?" She pulled away from him and pushed his arm off of her and onto the bed with a thump.

"That's not nice." She crossed her arms over her chest and pouted.

"It's not an insult. I just think it might benefit you." He laced his callused hands through hers. "I'm glad I got to see you."

Without really thinking about it, she joined him at the top of the bed and threw back the covers. She took his arm and wrapped it around herself. She hadn't been held much lately. It was like she'd reached a certain age and her body became off-limits. Her grandparents still hugged her but not nearly as much as they once had. She pulled the covers up over them, and he smiled at her.

"I like you," he said.

"Why?" she asked, knowing it shouldn't have been her first reaction.

He pulled his shoulders up by his ears and touched her hair. "You dress cool. And you smell nice." He tapped playfully on her forehead. "And you got a lot going on up here. You're a thinker with a lot of thoughts."

Then the front door slammed. She could tell it was her mother because her mother was always so heavy-handed with doors, probably because none of the ones at home in Tennessee closed right. Camille froze. "You can't be here."

He took the cue and rolled across the bed and into the bathroom. She was sitting up in the bed as if she were getting ready to sleep when Corinna stood in the doorway.

"Oh, you're still up."

"I was reading," Camille said, touching the copy of *The Sound and the Fury* conveniently located on her bedside table. "What are you doing home? I thought you all were going to dinner to have a chat or something."

"I was sent home."

"Why?"

"Beats me." Corinna squinted suddenly and sniffed suspiciously. "Camille?"

"What?"

"Have you had a boy here?"

"No!"

Corinna stepped into the room and switched on the overhead light. She stepped back and shook her head. They stared at each other for a moment before Corinna headed toward the door of the en suite bathroom and turned the handle. "Goddammit, Camille."

"Mama, I—"

"Get out of here," Corinna said almost gently to Logan, who sat on the plush rug looking rather boyish. She repeated herself more firmly when he didn't move. He had the nerve to smile and wave as he left, but he left without his coat. She knew because he turned right toward the stairs and not back toward the den. It was cold outside. She made a mental note to retrieve the coat as soon as possible.

"You wanna explain yourself? Who is he? What is this?"

"Well, his name is Logan," Camille said and immediately regretted using his real name, which Corinna would likely report to Evelyn, who would know she hadn't obeyed months earlier. She paused. "Don't tell Mama Evy, *please.*"

"We'll determine that once you tell me what's going on here."

"I met him at the store over a year ago."

"You've been having a relationship since then?"

"Well—" Camille found herself scrambling to find words. Corinna hadn't called her out on anything in many years. "Well," she tried again. "I don't know," she said finally and turned her gaze to her hands.

"You don't *know*?"

"I like him very much, Mama," Camille said. Her voice sounded genuine and childlike in her ear. She also sounded like someone else. She wasn't certain how true what she'd just said was. She liked him, but she probably didn't know him well enough to like him "very much." But it suited the moment, so she rolled with it.

"Sounds like there's a 'but' coming."

"He says he likes me, too."

"But?"

"I don't know if—I don't think he's my boyfriend."

Corinna sighed. "Jesus. You all talk on the phone when you're not together or something?"

"Yes'm."

Corinna sighed and took Camille's hand, something she hadn't done in years. "You've slept with him, then?"

Camille's face felt hot. "Just once."

Corinna smiled sadly. "You used protection?"

"Yes'm."

"How old is he?"

"Eighteen." She lied. He was actually nineteen.

Corinna flinched. "Eighteen?" She inhaled. "That's a little old for you, don't you think?"

"Yes'm," Camille agreed, though she hadn't thought about it much. Her friends dated college-aged boys, sometimes even older. Lots of girls did. "Girls mature faster than boys," everyone seemed to agree.

Corinna shook her head, still holding Camille's hand. "Let me just tell you something, okay? I thought I was in love with your father. He was a tall, handsome young man. But I misunderstood love on a very basic level. Do you understand what I'm trying to say?"

Camille thought about it. "No," she said.

"Before you were born, things were pretty volatile. Your grandparents fought a lot. I didn't know what a couple was supposed to be like. And they weren't exactly . . . Well, I put a lot of time and energy into caring for them. I didn't really even know your grandmother very well until you were born."

Camille nodded. This part made sense to her.

"The important thing is that I didn't know what love was supposed to feel like when I thought I was in love with your father."

"What are you saying?"

Corinna squirmed. "That you . . . might not know what love is supposed to be like either. I want you to be careful. Promise you'll be careful? Not just with your body, but, you know, with your heart?"

Camille did not fully grasp what her mother was saying but nodded because she knew Corinna wanted her to.

"All right then. I guess we'll have to get you on birth control."

"Do we have to tell—"

"No, I think it would only make things more complicated to tell Evelyn and Charlotte," Corinna said, to Camille's relief. "But don't think you're in the clear. That was very risky behavior. Not to mention dishonest. Where's your phone?"

Corinna sounded so much like a TV mom, Camille didn't know what to think. But she did as she was asked, producing the flip phone from under a pillow.

"Tell your friends you're grounded till next Friday."

"What does that mean?"

"It means no phone or computer, and you're not going *anywhere* but to school and dance and home."

Camille had heard of such things on television and in movies but had never experienced punishment that wasn't physical. Still, she knew she'd gotten off easy. She sent a few texts and handed over the phone.

"When you're ungrounded, we'll get you unlimited texting or whatever." Corinna stood up to leave but quickly sat down again. "Can I hug you?"

Camille pressed her face into her mother's neck; it smelled strongly of raw shea butter instead of the funky chemical-smelling oil sheen she used to use.

Charlotte

EASTER WEEKEND 2008

Charlotte was under the impression they would be attending a lecture after dinner. But when Evelyn said that Corinna should head home, Charlotte knew there was no lecture. She was being cornered. They'd driven for over an hour, presumably in the direction of the imaginary event. Evelyn had even pulled onto campus and asked for directions. But they sat in an empty parking lot. David, who had been snoring loudly in the back seat, roused.

"Good," he groaned. "I need me a cigarette." He slowly exited the vehicle and hobbled to a nearby bench. Charlotte watched him roll a cigarette. He looked much older than he was and was skinny like an invalid or a drug addict. Even his brand-new clothes had taken on a secondhand quality because of how they hung off his frame. He was clean-shaven, but his hair was greasy.

"There is no lecture," the women said in unison after a long, uncomfortable pause.

Charlotte sighed, and Evelyn started talking. "I'm not going to ask for your forgiveness," Evelyn said. "I just wanted to talk to you about Camille."

Charlotte snapped her head to look at her mother. "I forgive you," she lied.

Evelyn exhaled sharply, and tears welled in her eyes. "Do you?"

"I do," she said, nodding. Maybe if she said it out loud, it would become true. She could manifest it, like Corinna was always talking about doing. "That don't mean I'm not angry."

"I think forgiveness means—" She stopped herself, which was probably wise because Charlotte was already feeling trapped. Everyone, including Charlotte, knew how Charlotte could be when she was feeling vulnerable. Evelyn wiped at her eyes, inadvertently transferring a bit of mascara to the sleeve of her white silk blouse, then sighed. "So you're still angry?"

"Of course I'm still angry."

Evelyn clicked her tongue. "I'll die with this heavy on my spirit. Is that what you want?"

Charlotte rubbed the space between her eyebrows as if anything could soothe the great ache radiating from her skull. Charlotte had been forgiven. So why not Evelyn?

"Everything I do is penance to you, Charlotte."

She couldn't forget what her mother had done to her. Evelyn's favorite means of punishment was corporal, and it didn't take much to get her going: chewing too loudly, wearing the wrong shoes, talking "improperly," spending too much time in the sun. When she was fourteen, Charlotte's lip was almost always split; as soon as it was near healed, Evelyn found something new that she'd done wrong. When Wayne came around, he intervened, sometimes even catching Evelyn's hand before it could make contact. He could be kind. Eventually, he used that kindness against her.

Evelyn had changed over time; Charlotte could acknowledge that. But Charlotte's pain had not. She wanted to let it go. But she didn't know how. All she knew was that being near her mother put pressure on the wound. And it wasn't the kind of pressure that stopped the bleeding, just the kind that hurt. Or maybe it was more than a wound, more than skin deep. It was like the bones of a limb had been shattered, and she'd done nothing to mend it; she just went through life with her dangling, useless arm.

"I can't forgive you," she said. It lifted a small weight from Charlotte's chest to admit it.

"I've tried and I can't. What you did is unforgivable," she continued, waiting for Evelyn to interrupt her, but she didn't. "You hurt me. You were never there when I needed you, not once. Not when Daddy died, not when that man came in the house. You fucking knew, the whole time. How could you not? You're a fucking mother. I'm a shit mother myself and—"

"You, of all people, know it's not that simple. Giving birth doesn't make you a mother, Charlotte."

"That's your excuse?"

"I didn't say it's an excuse. I'm just saying—"

"What could you possibly say to make it right?"

"You're right. I can't."

Charlotte considered getting out of the car but knew her mother had intentionally driven to this remote location for the express purpose of making it hard for her to get away.

"Corinna forgives you and look what happened after she released that anger. She's free. She's living. I'm not even asking for your forgiveness for my benefit—"

"It's different!"

"Different how?"

"I never put a hand on Corinna, and I never would have let happen to her what happened to me. I wouldn't have brought a damn villain in the house."

"Villains come in all shapes and sizes."

Charlotte ignored that. "And I'm not like Corinna. I'm not good or smart like her. When she gets knocked down, she gets up. Lord knows where she got that from, it sure ain't from me."

The women stared at each other.

"Well, I tried," Evelyn said, surrendering.

But Charlotte wasn't done. "Can you even say out loud what you did?"

"I could but I would never get it right in your eyes, would I?"

Charlotte deflated. "We're leaving first thing in the morning," she said.

"I had plans for Easter brunch."

Charlotte didn't respond. She rolled down the window and waved to David, who hobbled back to the car, wincing with each step. "What's going on?" he said.

"There's no lecture."

"Then what'd we come out here fah?"

"Ask Evelyn."

The urge to leave was viscid. But she needed to say goodbye to her girls.

*   *   *

Early the following day, she went to Corinna's bedside. She didn't wake, so she kissed her daughter gently on the cheek. Then she went to Camille, whose eyes immediately popped open. She sat up quickly, as if an alarm had gone off.

"What's the matter?"

"Nothing, baby. I'm just leaving."

"Leaving? Like to go home?"

"Yes, baby. We're going home."

"But we were supposed to have brunch."

"I know, but I need to go."

"Why?" Camille's brow furrowed.

"The ghosts, baby. They're getting to me."

The girl looked like she might cry. "Everyone says that this place is haunted, but I ain't seen no ghosts."

"That don't mean they don't exist," Charlotte said and lifted the comforter. Camille slid back underneath. Charlotte tucked the blanket around the girl's body like she'd done when she was little.

"Go back to sleep." She leaned over to kiss Camille's forehead. "I love you."

"I love you, too, Mama. Tell Grandaddy I love him, too."

"I don't got to tell him. He knows."

"Will ya tell him anyway?" She looked like a little girl again.

Charlotte wished she could take a snapshot of this moment and use it to replace all of the ugly memories she toted around.

"All right. I'll tell him for you."

On the way down the stairs and back to the carriage house to collect her things, she saw the photograph on the very edge of the dining room table, as if it had been left there for her. Quickly, she crumpled it in her palm and tucked it into her bag.

PART IX

"Or Something"

Corinna

SPRING/SUMMER 2008

THE AUTHOR OF *The Secret*, a self-help book Corinna had been reading, said that you must trust the universe to give you what you ask for. If you ask more than once, you are not trusting the universe to provide. Corinna thought she had been extremely clear with the universe.

The universe provided the other things she asked for. She got a job at the Front Page, where the happy hour crowds were enormous, and the drinks were expensive. Happy hour actually meant something in DC. Back at Copperhead, nobody wanted to work that shift, because no customer came in between four and seven unless they didn't have a job, and then they couldn't pay the tab anyway. In DC, people in suits and business casual dress started coming at three thirty every weekday. And they drank heavily and tipped well, sometimes staying for dinner. Conversation was easy; all she had to do was talk about Tennessee. It was like being from another country: folks loved her accent, loved to ask about the "political climate," and loved trying to warn her about the northern winter. Because people had more varied—and sophisticated—tastes, she was able to show off her skills in "mixology," as her Front Page manager called it. Best of all, she always left her shift with a few hundred dollars in cash.

She'd also manifested herself a nice place to stay; she was living in Evelyn's carriage house, which was larger than the one she'd lived in for the majority of her years. Corinna did not understand the logic of having an entire additional house in your backyard, especially if the main house had as much space as Evelyn's.

She liked the carriage house, though; it was the closest she'd ever been to living alone. She also had an excellent view of Camille's bedroom windows from her own second-floor bedroom. She'd missed so much of Camille's life, she was desperate for whatever she could get.

She watched Camille talk on the phone, read, do homework, take pictures of herself, or stare blankly at her computer screen. Her bedroom was one of the few places where Camille smiled freely. She smiled just like Johnny; she even had the same teeth, except Johnny had gotten veneers once he started making real money.

Camille spent a lot of time looking in the mirror, and at first, Corinna thought she was admiring her own reflection. But she looked too closely, leaning across the bathroom counter to get her face as close to the mirror as possible. Corinna had done the same thing when she was Camille's age but stopped when she'd realized there wasn't much to be done about the way she looked; she accepted that she was nothing special and moved on. Camille, however, scrutinized her face. That was Corinna's contribution to Camille's inheritance. Her father gave money, her grandmother passed along her temper and mannerisms, her great-grandmother handed down sophistication and intelligence. Corinna? Self-loathing and insecurity.

Corinna guessed that Camille had a boyfriend, because every night around nine, she got a call that lasted anywhere from thirty minutes to a couple of hours. At first, she thought it was Su Jin, but she'd also seen the two girls alone in Camille's bedroom, and their energy was different. The girls were like Delia and Charlotte used to be, laughing and sharing inside jokes and Arizona Iced Teas.

The problem was that Camille was not allowed to have a boyfriend. The rule was Evelyn's, though Corinna thought it was a good idea for Camille to get some experience with dating while she was young.

So when the nine p.m. phone call had materialized as a very tall, very tan white kid in Camille's bathroom, Corinna knew she would say nothing to Evelyn. She didn't know if she was doing the right thing. Most likely, she wasn't. But she couldn't afford to push Camille further away. So she told Camille what she wished someone had told her about the female reproductive system. They went to the gynecologist and got a birth control prescription. Corinna programmed an alarm on Camille's cell phone to remind her to take the pill at the exact same time every night. Yes, she lamented to herself that Camille was *so* young. And at times she questioned the young man's intentions.

But, well. If Corinna had the time or energy, she could write a very thick book of all the things she wished were different. What she did know, almost immediately, was that the universe was finally providing what she'd asked it for: an opportunity to get closer to her daughter. And like *The Secret* told her, "*How* it will happen, *how* the Universe will bring it to you, is not your concern or job. Allow the Universe to do it for you."

Corinna saw a lot more of Camille after the Bathroom Boy Incident. She was still moody and mouthy, but she was moody and mouthy *with* Corinna, and not *against* her. Instead of clomping loudly upstairs when she got home, she stopped in the kitchen or dining room to say hello. Sometimes, on the weekends, she came out to the carriage house with Sozzani while Corinna got ready for work.

The day after the school year ended, Corinna asked Camille to lunch. They walked arm in arm to 17th Street. The quiet restaurant they chose was frequented mostly by gay men and tourists, but it also had some of the best casual Italian food in the city. They sat in a quiet corner. Corinna drank an Aperol spritz and Camille ordered Diet Coke with no ice.

"Mama?" Camille asked.

"Cheers me," Corinna said, lifting her glass. "To the end of your sophomore year." They clinked glasses.

"Can I ask you something?"

"Of course."

"Have you thought about dating?"

Corinna paused chewing on a large chunk of chilled bread. This question had never occurred to her. But she didn't have to think very hard. It took her years to recover from what happened to Isaac, if she were even fully recovered.

"No, I don't think I'm ready, baby."

"What do you mean by 'ready'?"

Camille stared at her, and Corinna tried to discern the girl's feelings on the matter. "I don't know, actually. I figure I'll know it when I feel it."

Their food arrived, a helpful interruption. Camille had a small plate of pasta with pesto sauce and shrimp. Corinna had lasagna. She watched Camille put the tiniest sprinkle of parmesan on her meal.

"You might consider telling Evelyn about Logan."

Camille bit her lip, but still managed to make a noise that sounded like "I can't."

"What do you mean? Why not?"

"Because she told me to stop seeing him months ago."

"What?!"

"I don't know how she found out, but she made me delete his number and everything. I said I wouldn't talk to him."

Corinna nearly dropped her drink. Instead, she swigged it. "Jesus."

"I *had* to."

"Did she say explicitly that you couldn't speak to him?"

"Yes, very clearly."

Corinna leaned across the table in an attempt to communicate the gravity of what she was about to say. "Camille, you realize you've made me an accomplice in this, and it's worse because you didn't tell me this *very* important—"

"I know," Camille said, and half shrugged. "I'm sorry!"

"It is very important to Evelyn that she *feels* like you're obeying her," Corinna said.

"Mama, I *know*. I'm sorry," she said, but she sure didn't look sorry. "Maybe *you* could tell her?" Camille offered with her gaze low as she attempted to excise a shrimp from its shell using her butter knife and fork.

Corinna wanted to reach across the table and do it with her hands. Instead, she wiped her mouth to ensure there wasn't any sauce around it, which gave her time to think. *The Secret* would not help her here. This was *7 Habits of Highly Effective People* territory. Think win-win.

"Or we can just keep this between us for a while," she suggested. "After all, you're young. She might never need to know. You just have to promise me you'll be honest with me about *everything*." This way, Evelyn wouldn't have her idea of well-being disrupted, and Corinna would have something private to share with Camille. Win-win.

"I will."

"You tell me when you're with him. You tell me what he says and does. If I get the slightest impression you're not being truthful, I swear I'll tell both Charlotte *and* Evelyn."

Camille smiled. "I *promise*, Mama."

"You're taking the pill like you're supposed to?"

"Yes'm."

"I'd prefer you not," Corinna said, then paused and spiraled her fork around above her plate. "You know."

Camille nodded.

Corinna was pleased to be back in the driver's seat of her daughter's life, even if it had to happen like this. She was in the most intimate depths, when she'd previously been on the absolute margins. She thought she'd lost Camille forever to Evelyn's world of Prada and perfect table manners. But here she was, with influence over her daughter's choices. She could try to guide Camille down a path of fulfillment and happiness, whatever that meant.

Evelyn

EARLY SUMMER 2008

After she submitted her grades, Evelyn did nothing for a week. She didn't write, read, or check on the store. Camille would be in school for another couple of weeks, and Evelyn sat on the back deck to drink Corinna's cocktails, eat chocolate, and reflect on her life choices. Most of the time, she was trying to locate the precise moment she'd failed as a mother. She usually pinpointed it as her choice to marry again.

Wayne had pursued Evelyn with gusto. He insisted they get married quickly. Evelyn couldn't remember why she agreed. Or maybe she could. She'd felt vulnerable as a single woman living alone with a young daughter. Not in terms of her physical safety, but her social safety. She could pay people to keep her body safe, but she could not pay anyone to maintain her position in society. That's probably why she married him. She thought she'd had her chance at true love with James. And that was gone, so she would have to settle for convenience.

Soon after they were married, she and Wayne lost interest in each other. Evelyn had her work, and he had his. They spent time together only in public at social events, which worked for her. She was teaching, researching, and writing; she didn't have time for any more courtship. She was still drinking too much and popping the pills she'd started taking in the aftermath of James's death. But she was remarkably productive. In the five years that Evelyn was married to Wayne, she wrote seven books, published twenty-two papers, and was promoted to full professor. People were writing about her and talking about her like she was a living legend. She was at the absolute pinnacle of her career. It was everything she wanted and was told she could not have.

And yet, her family was rotting from the inside out.

Women can do both, have a powerful career and a strong family, Evelyn now thought. Obviously, they do both all the time. But Evelyn hadn't. She still asked herself all the time how she let it happen. She could never come up with a good answer, other than she was truly, truly, deeply selfish. Or maybe she'd had no business being a mother.

But if she had never been a mother, there would be no Corinna or Camille. She'd been given a second chance at family, love, and happiness. Did she deserve it?

At first, she'd kept her distance from Corinna. Though she looked like Wayne, genetics graciously didn't go much further. She had many of Charlotte's mannerisms—throwing her shoulders back when she was nervous and gnawing on the inside of her cheek when she was in deep thought—but her own way of moving through the world. She was gentle with her words, unlike the other women.

The more Evelyn got to know and understand Corinna, the more she saw herself in her granddaughter. She had an incredible work ethic. Evelyn hadn't known a service job like bartending could require passion, skill, and specialized knowledge, but Corinna was always experimenting with new cocktails, and she checked out books on the subject from the library every week. Evelyn credited her own genes for Corinna's dedication to her craft.

Charlotte had been a phenomenal pianist, but Evelyn knew she didn't *love* playing, not the way Corinna enjoyed messing around with cocktails or the way Evelyn committed to her research. Charlotte started playing because there was a piano in the house, one that had belonged to Charlotte, James's mother. As soon as she showed interest in it, James found her a teacher. Evelyn was fairly certain Charlotte's continued interest was the result of encouragement from her father. Evelyn also encouraged her, but for different reasons. Charlotte had needed something to help her stand out from the other girls. Evelyn had worried about Charlotte's marriage prospects practically from the day she was born. So, when Evelyn was paying attention to Charlotte, it was to criticize her. It was years into Charlotte's absence that she understood this about herself.

She wouldn't make the same mistake again.

*   *   *

"Can you do something with me? It's kind of important," Corinna asked Evelyn. She was seated at the dining room table, staring at a copy of the manuscript for *Gwendolyn Bennett's Burden: An Examination of Women, Sacrifice, and Literature in the Harlem Renaissance.*

"Hmm?" Evelyn asked, though she'd heard Corinna perfectly well.

"Can you go somewhere with me?"

She glanced up at Corinna, who was looking very good lately. She'd finally deep conditioned her hair and was getting facials regularly, so her previously chalky brown skin appeared radiant and healthy. "Depends on where. I have a lot to do before I fly out." She was leaving for a conference in San Francisco in the morning.

"I just need you to go somewhere with me."

Evelyn yanked off her reading glasses. "*Where*? For *what* reason?"

"Evelyn, *please*?" Corinna clasped her hands together like a child. Her shoulders dropped. "Right now?"

"Can you be ready in ten minutes?"

"What do you mean *ready*? I don't even know where we're going. Do I need to change my clothes? How long will this take?"

"What you're wearing is fine. Shouldn't take too long," Corinna called over her shoulder.

Forty-five minutes later, they had taken a cab because Evelyn didn't want to be bothered with parking and Corinna said they were already running late. They were standing in the swanky but generic-looking lobby of the Watergate Complex. Corinna was hurriedly sending text messages. A large man in a suit was walking toward them, but Corinna didn't seem to notice.

"Corinna," Evelyn said and nudged her granddaughter just as the man was upon them.

"Ms. Jackson?" the man said, and both women nodded instinctively. "Follow me."

They followed the man to a sixth-floor apartment. He knocked twice but didn't wait for a response and opened the door. When they entered the apartment, another large man was sitting on a leather couch that Evelyn recognized as a Moore & Giles. The apartment was tastefully decorated in neutrals. It was obviously someone's secondary residence, she guessed, based on the lack of clutter or personal effects. The art wasn't great, just reproductions on stretched canvases, but that could be forgiven, she supposed.

"Oh, wow," the man said. "Mrs. Evelyn Gwendolyn Jackson."

Evelyn was surprised to hear her own name.

"I'm sorry," he said. "*Doctor.*" He stood over them now. He was impressively tall. And seemed familiar somehow. Evelyn was looking to Corinna for explanation when the man reached for her hand and planted a kiss on it. "I am just so honored." Corinna averted her eyes.

This man was easily six and a half feet tall and broad-shouldered. As she looked at him carefully, she realized he was the man from the lidocaine patch commercials and the ads for that kitschy, overpriced chain restaurant.

"Oh, this is terribly rude of me," the man said. "I'm not used to introducing myself. My name's Johnny. Johnny Washington."

The football player, that was right.

"Corinna." Evelyn glanced over at her granddaughter, who was wearing a plastered-on smile. "What is going on?"

"When Corinna told me you were coming," the man said, smiling cartoonishly wide, "I was so excited that I would get to meet *the* Dr. Evelyn Gwendolyn Jackson. You know, I read your last book, *A Reimagining of the Talented Tenth*, in one sitting."

He ushered her toward the sitting area. where a gigantic television was playing two different football games side by side. He grabbed the remote and turned it off, then tossed the remote carelessly aside as he guided Evelyn toward a beautiful armchair made of plush velvet. This was luxury furniture if she had ever seen it. He was new money, but at least he wasn't gauche. She almost forgot where she was.

"I've always wanted to attend one of your lectures, but I can't really do things like that without being recognized, and I didn't want to take the focus off you, so I try to watch on YouTube when I can. I just saw the one you did at Cornell in 2002. Do you remember that one? I'm sure you do so many. And you don't remember everything you say everywhere you go. I would love to hear your thoughts on Obama—"

"Johnny, that's not what we're here for," Corinna interrupted. She had joined them in the sitting area.

He looked surprised that Corinna was there at all. He laughed loudly and heartily, slapping his knee. "That's right. That's right. I hope you'll excuse me, Doctor. I'm just so honored and overwhelmed to have you in my home. Well, my fourth home, really. I just bought it. You like it? Check out the view."

"I'm sure it's lovely," Evelyn said without looking away from him. The couch looked child-size under his gigantic frame. She ran her fingers along the seams of the chair. Everything was as it should be. There was no rug underneath the coffee table, though. That was a mistake.

Corinna was sitting in an armchair identical to Evelyn's, looking like she didn't belong there. Evelyn wanted to pull the woman's shoulders back and lift her chin. Still, she projected more authority than usual. Evelyn watched as Corinna produced a two-inch binder from her bag, flipped it open, and paged through the document protectors. Finally, she stopped, wet her fingers, and pulled a few things from inside of a plastic sheath.

"You wanted her grades," Corinna said, handing over the pages. "And what else?"

He took the papers and smiled again. "That's excellent," he said. "I'm glad she's doing well in that school. It's more expensive than the tuition for Cassidy and Ashton combined," he said, smiling.

"That're my twins," Johnny said, looking at Evelyn. "They just turned ten." He stood up and took three giant strides to the galley kitchen to retrieve a framed photograph of five light-skinned children and handed it to Evelyn, who reluctantly took it. He pointed at each child. "Cassidy, Ashton, Whitney, Junior, and Avery, the baby. Camille's my oldest, obviously," he said.

Evelyn should have known. She'd seen that smile somewhere, and it wasn't on TV. "Wait a minute," Evelyn said. "You're her *father*?" She addressed Johnny but was looking at Corinna, who wouldn't look at her. "Camille's *father*?"

Corinna, who was flipping through the binder again, looking quite composed.

"Oh, I assumed you knew," Johnny said. "I know she's been living with you for a while now. Thank you for that. Fairfax-Washington is an *excellent* school. Much better than that trash high school me and you went to. Isn't that right, Corinna? Do we think the president's kids are going to go to Fairfax-Washington, too? Assuming it's Obama, of course. Anyway, I guess it's best to start talking about college. I'm fine with her going wherever she wants, but I was hoping she might consider . . ." He trailed off. "I'm sorry. I didn't offer y'all anything. Water, tea?"

"She was not allowed to know," Corinna said, more to Evelyn than to Johnny. "That was part of the agreement if you recall."

Johnny sat down again. "Well, I certainly thought you'd tell her before bringing her here."

"You told me the money was from a *settlement*," Evelyn scoffed.

"Can we talk about this later, please?" Corinna said, finally making eye contact with Evelyn. "What else did you want, Johnny? Oh, her school picture." She produced a picture of Camille in which the girl was smirking like she'd just said something slick.

Johnny held it in both hands. "She's *really* beautiful," he said.

"I brought the DVD from her last ballet performance. She had a lovely solo. Isn't that right, Evelyn?"

Evelyn nodded. "That's right. Very talented young woman."

"Oh, good. I'll watch it tonight," he said.

"So," Corinna said, sounding confident. "Let's talk money."

"You're taking me to the cleaners as it is," he laughed. He appeared to be joking, but Evelyn wasn't so sure. It wasn't making sense, the whole thing.

Corinna shrugged. Twenty minutes later, he was writing a check for twenty thousand dollars. Evelyn was in awe.

Corinna smiled as she accepted the check. She folded it in half and placed it in her bra. "Pleasure doing business with you, Johnny."

"Yeah, yeah," he answered, looking defeated.

"See you in a few months? Same time. Same place."

Corinna stood with her bag under her arm like a proper businesswoman, her hand extended. He shook it.

"But don't forget your promise."

"Oh, right," Corinna said and turned to look at Evelyn. "I said you would sign his books."

"I brought all of them," he said. "Even the ones no longer in print."

Evelyn could have slapped Corinna when he wheeled two suitcases into the room.

"I have two copies of each. One to read, one to collect. Some of these will be worth a lot of money someday, you know? Especially this one from 1970 . . ." he said. Evelyn could have vomited at the sight of her first book: *To Be Rich, Gifted, and Black.*

She flipped the book over to see a picture of herself looking rather snide, and frowned. "This isn't still in print, is it?"

"No," he said. "It's selling on Amazon for almost a thousand dollars. I got mine a few years ago—"

Evelyn stopped listening. By the time they left, almost an hour later, she was thoroughly furious, primarily because Johnny had talked nonstop. He had an entire conversation with himself under the guise of talking to Evelyn. It occurred to her that a less-sophisticated person might have been flattered that he was speaking to her at all. And then it made sense: Corinna and Johnny.

"I'm sorry that took so long. He's a talker. He definitely didn't pass that on to Camille," Corinna said once they were on the sidewalk. They quickly hailed a cab.

"So Camille doesn't know?"

"No."

"She's never asked?"

"Well, kind of. But not really."

"And what do you say?"

"Not much. I told her when she was little that he'd moved away."

"And your mother doesn't know? How did this happen?"

"Well, his mother used to be good friends with my mother. And we went to high school together, me and Johnny."

"And Charlotte had no idea?"

"I don't really know if she knows."

"It was a one-time thing?"

"I'd rather not talk about it. It's embarrassing."

"Shame has no place in this family anymore. I would have thought you knew that by now."

Corinna exhaled sharply. "Well, it's just that he always had a girlfriend—she's his wife now. I thought we were in love or whatever. It was dumb. That's really all there is to it. He was about to go off to Vanderbilt, and everyone already knew he was going to be a big star. A kid would have ruined it. It was a different time."

"And this is where all that money comes from?"

"Yeah."

"Well, I'll be damned. And there's *more* money than I've seen?"

"Yes, a lot more. When she turns twenty-one, she'll be a multi-millionaire."

"I'll be god*damned*," Evelyn smiled, seeing her granddaughter through new eyes. "You're a hustler, Corinna. You know that?"

Corinna shrugged. "He bought that condo with the idea that he could have some kind of relationship with her. I said no. He said he would let it go if he could meet you and you would sign some books, so I agreed."

"Corinna, you're lying."

"I'm not lying." She looked at Evelyn, almost smiling.

"That mother*fucker*."

"Yes, exactly."

"Well. You could have warned me."

"Would you have gone?"

"Of course, I would have," Evelyn said, offended. "What makes you think I wouldn't have?"

Corinna shrugged again, reverting back to the girl-woman Evelyn had always known. And Evelyn had another revelation that should have been obvious. "Do you think I resent you?"

Corinna turned to look out of the window, and Evelyn addressed the back of her head. "Well, I don't. What happened was painful for me, but I can't hold that against you. Not even I could do that." Evelyn realized she was telling the truth as she was speaking. "I'm proud of you, Corinna. I'm honored to have gotten to know you."

Corinna slowly turned around to give Evelyn a weak smile.

"For what? Shaking down a hardworking Black man?"

Evelyn chuckled. They were in front of the house now. Evelyn gave the driver too much money, and they parted ways at the front door without a word. Evelyn stood in the wine cellar with her hands on her hips, thinking about what she'd learned. Selfishly, she'd thought Corinna was trying to show her something, but it had nothing to do with her; she was merely a prop.

Still, Evelyn was impressed. Corinna would do anything for Camille. She would expose her vulnerabilities and secrets for Camille's benefit. And she expected nothing in return. It was astonishing, really. Corinna was not the perfect mother, Evelyn knew. But she was trying her damnedest. She would likely die haunted like Evelyn would, still racking her brain for what she could have done differently for her daughter. But she and Corinna were not the same. Evelyn was staring at an exposed cork in a bottle when her vision began to blur with tears.

If she were honest with herself, she might have understood that what she felt was relief that her mistakes hadn't ruined everything that came after her.

She didn't want anything from the cellar. She went upstairs and got a bottle of sauvignon blanc so chilled it was uncomfortable to hold. She carried it to her bathroom and drew herself a bath filled with chamomile, the scent she'd chosen to replace lavender. Lavender reminded her of Charlotte and their home in Atlanta. She'd searched the address recently to find that the home still stood and had been recently put up for sale. She'd clicked through the photos and found that, while it had been renovated, the changes were almost all cosmetic; the structure was ultimately the same.

The Atlanta house was almost certainly haunted. In the decades after her parents' deaths, Evelyn sometimes heard her mother humming like she had when brushing her hair or examining her skin in the mirror. What would Pearl think of what had become of them and her various degrees of daughter? Was her mother's pride something she needed to add to the litany of items that tortured her and that she could do nothing about it? She backed away from the question, and returned to thinking of her mother and her mother's ghost, both beautiful and pale. She did not remember her mother perfectly, but she did remember her scent, her hands, her voice.

She thought of the ghost in her current home. She hadn't seen or heard much from her ghost lately, especially since Corinna moved in. Maybe it was because the book was essentially done. Maybe she was resting. Maybe she was haunting someone else.

Charlotte

SUMMER 2008

Charlotte didn't have much going on, and hadn't had much going on since Corinna left. So she busied herself with other things. She taught herself to knit from a pamphlet in the grocery store checkout aisle. Sometimes the Goodwill had brand-new skeins of yarn. She sat on the porch and knitted hats for babies, which she donated. She spent a lot of time thinking, though she didn't want to. Primarily, she considered the rest of her life. She was fifty-two years old. If things went well, she easily had another twenty years on earth, and she didn't know what to do with them.

Foolishly, she'd never considered her girls would leave and never come back. She'd lost her vision for the future when Corinna left and reappeared in DC. She'd thought Corinna would come back to Tennessee eventually, but that had been a silly thing to think. Obviously, she would choose her daughter and not her mother, as Charlotte had done decades earlier. That may have been her last motherly act for Corinna, though she still wondered if it would have been more motherly to leave Corinna and not be her mother at all. Either way, she'd chosen her baby over her mother, as all mothers should.

She'd chosen Corinna over Evelyn, but she knew she didn't become a true mother until Camille was born. And she'd found more than "atonement," as Evelyn put it; she'd found purpose. She didn't even know who she'd been before she became Camille's protector. It had been all she needed for a long time—until now, really.

She still had David, who needed her the most; he probably wouldn't survive without her. But it wasn't the same. Her feelings for and about him were not unconditional. The love she felt for him was partially dependent upon his love for the rest of the family, she'd come to understand.

She continued doing the hair of her longtime clients. They all wanted the exact same thing they'd always wanted, either a roller set or a silk press, both of which she could do with her eyes closed. Some wanted their grays dyed or their entire head colored a deep, unnatural black, but that was the greatest deviation from the norm.

She went to the library a couple of times looking for books she'd heard Camille mention but found that she still didn't have the patience to read anything unless it was instructional. At the library, she perused the bulletin board, where a notice caught her eye: "Need Help Making Your Next Step? Try Counseling." She tore it down and read it front and back. The language seemed directed at teens, but she figured there had to be something similar around for older women who defined themselves by the people they cared for. Standing there, in the icy library, she understood that she was not her own person. She was most her "own" when she was an addict. She took the flyer with her though she had no plans for it.

The next day, she returned to the library, where she used the card catalog to locate books about mothers. The books were primarily focused on adult daughters, which made sense. She might have benefited from one of those. One of the book covers read: *The Mother Wound: A Path to Healing and Forgiveness.* Healing sounded like a fantastic thing to do. But it wasn't for her. She didn't deserve to heal. And forgiveness? She had been forgiven though she didn't deserve that either. Though she said she was done talking about forgiveness, she wasn't done thinking about it. Maybe her wound was just too deep. Maybe she'd been so hurt for so damn long that she didn't know how else to be. Maybe she was afraid of what was on the other side.

Before she left, she stopped by the bulletin board again. The counseling flyer she'd taken before had been replaced. She took this one down as well, though she knew the other one was still in the passenger seat of her LeBaron. On the back of the flyer, there was a list:

Your counselor can help you:

1. Create and organize goals
2. Brainstorm solutions to problems big and small
3. Boost your self-esteem
4. Improve your interactions with friends and family

She put this flyer back and looked at it a little bit longer. There were a lot of flyers on the bulletin board. Why had this one caught her attention? It didn't even have one of those little illustrations that Camille called "click art" or "clip art." She decided she would float the idea to Corinna. It sounded like something they all might benefit from, but might be most effective for Camille.

Next to it, another flyer got her attention: "SEEKING: piano teacher," next to a little picture of a piano. At the bottom, the page was split into a fringe with a phone number on each piece. She unpinned the flyer, folded it, and stuffed it in her shirt pocket. At home, she pulled it out over dinner at the kitchen table and showed it to David.

"What's this here?" he said, holding the paper at arm's length. His vision was going.

"It's a piano teaching job. What you think?" she asked.

He shrugged. "What's this got to do with us?"

"I played piano, you know."

"Oh that's right."

"I can still play."

"So you think you can teach it?"

This wasn't what she wanted to hear. "Never mind," she said. She snatched the flyer out of his hand and continued eating her TV dinner lasagna. David was like a shell of himself when the girls weren't around. He was quieter, slept later, went to bed earlier, and rarely listened to music.

"Maybe you ought to find yourself something to do," he said. "The girls likely ain't coming back. Camille's damn near grown."

"I gotta take care of you."

"You think I'll be around as long as you?"

"Why would you say that?"

He shrugged his bony shoulders.

Charlotte decided to make the call. There couldn't be many qualified candidates in the area, not that she was entirely qualified herself. Truthfully, she'd never loved playing the piano, but did it because of her father, who'd placed her on the bench beside him when she was four or five.

"Your grandmother Charlotte was a pianist. She could have been famous," he told her.

"Why wasn't she, Daddy?"

"Well," he said, turning the sheet music. "She was Black, and she died."

She knew then that she was supposed to be who her grand-mother couldn't be. And she hadn't done that. It was really too damn late to do much to change that, but maybe she owed it to her grandmother to do *something* with the rest of her life. That's something people liked to say. "We owe it to our ancestors." But perhaps she owed it just as much, if not more, to her descendants.

Corinna

SUMMER 2008

The morning after she'd worked a double, completely alone aside from the barback who moved through space as if it were molasses, she fought her way out of a dark, cavernous sleep when her phone rang. It was her mother.

"What are you doing?" Charlotte asked. "Did I wake you up?"

"Yes."

"Oh," she said. "Well, I was just calling to say hello. It is ten a.m. and all."

"Okay." Corinna's knees ached.

"You worked last night?"

"Yes."

"You're getting too old for that kind of work."

This comment stung, though, all of the evidence pointed in the direction that her body was struggling to keep up with the work. But what else was she going to do? Become a lawyer? A doctor? She wanted to hang up.

After a silence, Charlotte said: "What you think about me teaching piano?"

Corinna squinted at the ceiling above her. A twinge of pain hit her between her shoulder blades. "Huh?"

"I can still play, you know?"

"Start all over, Mama. From the beginning?"

"Well. I found this flyer at the library . . ."

It took a moment, but Corinna realized her mother was confiding in her. She sat up straight in bed so that she could listen better. Charlotte was thinking about becoming a piano teacher.

"Sounds like a great idea, Mama."

"Thank you," Charlotte said. "I thought so, too."

After she said goodbye, she got up to make a pot of coffee and attempted to stretch her back, but she was already feeling energized. She and her mother had gotten over some kind of hump.

From where she stood, she could see Camille sitting on the back patio, having her own phone call. Carrying a large cup of coffee, Corinna crossed the yard to the main house, where Camille sat cross-legged on the patio loveseat with Sozzani snoozing in the nest of her legs. She wore an open-knit cropped polo shirt, and high-waisted shorts. Corinna would never understand Camille's clothing choices. Corinna was about to open the door to the main house when her daughter threw her head back in laughter. It must have been that boy. Corinna noticed a magazine by Camille's folded legs, open to a spread about new museums opening across the world.

Corinna went inside and sat at the heavy teak dining room table. Evelyn had left early that morning for California, so she sat in Evelyn's usual seat and tried to experience what it felt like to be her as she sipped her coffee. It wasn't even eleven yet, but she went down to the cellar to fetch a couple of bottles. She descended the spiral staircase, thinking of little more than how she would choose her wine. She wouldn't pick anything expensive. Though Evelyn said all the time that she should "feel free" to help herself, Corinna could not mindlessly drink a five-hundred-dollar bottle. But Evelyn didn't organize the wine in any discernible manner; it was the only thing she was lackadaisical about, probably because of how swiftly inventory moved.

When she reached the bottom of the staircase, she noticed a flickering yellow-green light on the wall. She knew it was on the door of the safe where Evelyn kept all the important documents, but today there was a red light she'd never seen, and it intrigued her. She flicked on the ceiling light to illuminate the vast cellar. The safe was not fully closed, and though she should have just clicked it shut, instead she opened it all the way to see the file folders and photo albums inside. She pulled out the first album; it was bloated with age, and the pages were crisp and browned. She put it under her arm, then hunted for a moderately priced wine but found that everything cost at least a hundred dollars. She would have to pull something out of the wine fridge.

When Corinna emerged from the cellar, Camille was standing in the kitchen drinking from a large bottle of mineral water and flexing her feet. She was no longer on the phone but staring blankly into space. She was good at that.

"Hey, Mama," she said without looking up.

"Hey there."

Corinna laid the photo album on the counter and hugged Camille. Then she went to the wine fridge.

Sozzani trotted in when she heard the fridge open. "She probably thinks that sound was the refrigerator," Camille said.

That's where they kept the dog's salmon pâté, in a container the size of a mayonnaise jar, which a butcher in Georgetown hand-delivered to the house. Corinna had once signed for it: the jar cost as much as her weekly grocery budget back in Chilly Springs.

"You ready to leave, baby?"

The next day, Camille was heading to Tennessee to see her grandparents, leaving Corinna on her own in DC.

"I haven't even started packing," Camille admitted.

"Girl."

"I know, I know," she said dreamily, clearly still thinking about something else.

"Well, go on and get started. I'll help you. Be up in a minute."

Camille obeyed, taking her bottle of water and her dog and leaving the room.

Corinna poured herself a glass of chilly sauvignon blanc and sat down at the table, where she opened the album. The pages were a heavy stock, and the photographs were attached with some kind of glue, like in a scrapbook. The first few pages featured photos from Evelyn's first wedding, where she looked young and happy. She resembled Camille, especially in the way she held her mouth: like she was getting ready to say something slick.

After several pages of those, there were a few of Charlotte as a baby and little girl. She looked like a happy child, and she and Camille at the same age were practically identical apart from complexion.

Corinna flipped back and forth between the photos of Charlotte and Evelyn, searching for signs that she belonged to these women. She looked closely at James, her grandfather, but she couldn't find herself there either. Camille had his eyes: big and simultaneously dark and bright. She gave up and continued paging through the album, and toward the back she found a ghostly rectangle where the paper was still creamy white. Underneath, someone had written in an exceptionally neat hand: Wayne, Evelyn, Charlotte—1970. Corinna traced the edges of the square with her finger. This is where she would have found herself. She sighed, grateful the image was missing.

She carried the album back downstairs and put it in the safe, closing the door securely. Back on the main floor, she grabbed the sauvignon blanc and carried it upstairs. Camille was sitting at the foot of her bed, hunched over her laptop, which was linked by cable to her iPod.

"This don't look like packing."

"I was updating my playlist," she said.

"Well, where's your suitcase?"

"In the closet."

Corinna went to Camille's closet, which was filled almost to capacity. Hanging clothes were squeezed tight, and the two dressers overflowed. Shelves on one side were packed with layers of handbags, and on the other with shoes, many of which were highly impractical. The sheer abundance was overwhelming. Even in the sea of loud colors and funky textures, Corinna quickly spotted the hard-sided neon-pink suitcase. She looked around for a place to set down her wine and eventually put it on a shelf of clumsily folded scarves. She needed two hands to pull the suitcase out from underneath a pile of coats. Why did the girl have so many god-damn coats? Could she even conceivably wear all of these clothes? She looked through some of the dresses, many of which were old or "vintage," as Camille insisted on calling them.

She decided to try and organize the coats. The first one she grabbed was a fairly sensible plaid tweed peacoat. The second was a hot-pink cape with fur trim. The third was a heavy, vibrantly pat-terned bomber jacket. Corinna had had one coat from the ages of thirteen to eighteen, and it hadn't even been a coat but a used Le Coq Sportif windbreaker that she'd felt extremely lucky to find on half-price day at Goodwill. Camille owned at least a dozen, and they were just stacked on top of each other like at a donation center.

Corinna was just about to give up when Camille appeared in the closet doorway.

"You know, I started to feel you moving when I was only a few months pregnant with you?" She poured herself another glass of wine.

"How would I know that, Mama?"

Corinna ignored Camille's tone. "They said, 'It's too early! It's just gas!' But I knew it was you."

Camille started opening drawers and flinging clothes into a pile on the floor.

"You was a vigorous baby." Corinna started folding the clothes from the floor and placing them in the suitcase. "It was a tough pregnancy. Have I ever told you that? I was sick from beginning to end. And you moved *constantly*, like a cat trying to get out of a bag."

Camille sighed. Corinna took a large gulp of wine and poured herself some more, despite a nearly full glass.

"And it was such a hot summer, you hear me?" Corinna went on, continuing her folding. "It's hard work growing a person."

Camille knelt down to help her mother.

"Emotionally and physically. I cried so much. And you came out looking nothing like me."

Seeing Camille's frown, Corinna realized she was drunk.

"You look like everybody but me. You look like your granmama, your daddy. Everybody but me."

"Mama—"

"I really hoped you would look like me." Corinna closed her eyes, trying to pull herself together. When she opened them, Camille was staring at her, her mouth slightly agape.

"Mama, are you okay?"

Corinna wiped at the corners of her eyes and cleared her throat. "I'm sorry. I was just looking at your grandmother's photo albums."

"And they made you sad?"

"Well, yeah. Have you seen them? It's very sad."

"I've seen one of 'em." Camille's brow furrowed as much as her taut, youthful skin would allow. "What's sad about them?"

Corinna stared at her daughter. How had they looked at the same photos and had such different reactions? "Your dead grandad, for one."

"*Your* dead grandad."

"What's that supposed to mean?"

"*My* grandad's not dead."

"Well, actually—"

"My grandad's not dead," she repeated and started folding T-shirts.

"It was also seeing Charlotte as a completely different person."

"Why's that sad?"

Corinna thought about this for a moment. Camille's experience was not the same as her own. Of course, she'd known this, but it had never seemed quite so plain. She'd grown this child in her body, and yet this child was not an extension of herself. How was she meant to understand this girl and give her what she needed? She knocked back the trace of wine at the bottom of her glass.

"When you see that boy, don't let him talk you out of using a condom. That's how you got here."

Camille looked around as if disoriented by the breakneck speed of the change in subject. "I'm on the pill, Mama."

"There are plenty of other reasons to wear a condom. Don't get your feelings hurt. And you get up and you leave if he starts in with some 'it doesn't feel the same' or whatever nonsense these boys are talkin' 'bout these days," Corinna said, feeling like she needed to lie down. "Any red-blooded boy would rather do it with a condom than not do it at all."

"Okay, Mama." Camille was no longer folding T-shirts, instead sitting on one hip and fiddling with the zipper on her shorts, a zipper that her little boyfriend might pull on. Was she even listening? Corinna tried to imagine what she was thinking, but the girl's thoughts were increasingly impenetrable, which frustrated her. All she could do was talk and hope her daughter listened.

"You hear me, Camille?"

"Yes, ma'am."

Camille

SUMMER 2008

Camille was in her usual place between her grandmother's knees having her scalp greased in preparation for cornrows. They were about halfway done when Charlotte realized she was out of salon clips.

"There's some more in my bedside table," Charlotte told her.

Camille obediently went inside and into her grandparents' bedroom, where her grandfather was sleeping. She opened the drawer of the side table gently to avoid waking him. It was full of junk, which she tried to rummage through quietly. She found six lighters, two small packages of Kleenex, four lottery tickets, some dice, several dollars' worth of change, a couple of hairbrushes, some costume jewelry, a pack of Swisher Sweets, and several keys, but no salon clips. At the bottom of the drawer, she found a photograph. She picked it up and squinted at it. It was a posed photo of three people: a young Evelyn in a light-colored structured suit, a man in a dark suit, and a teenage girl wearing a formal dress. It took her a moment to recognize the girl as Charlotte. Who was this man? Must have been Evelyn's second husband, whom nobody liked to talk about. He sure was ugly, especially compared to her first husband.

"I didn't find any clips," she told Charlotte, who turned to look at her. "But I did find this." She showed her grandmother the photograph, and she went white as a ghost.

"What's that doing here?"

"I found it in your drawer."

"In my room?" Charlotte snatched the photo and stared at it closely. "You swear to me you found this in my drawer?"

"Yes, Mama."

Charlotte rose out of her seat.

"Mama," Camille said, pointing at her half-done hair.

"Oh, that's right," Charlotte said. She sat down again, and Camille resumed her seat on the ground, deducing that she shouldn't ask any questions about the picture, not that she knew what those questions would be. They sat in silence as Charlotte continued braiding.

"I forgot I took the damn thing with me," she said.

"You did? Why?"

"Yeah, so your mother wouldn't see it." She sighed loudly. "It's hard to say why."

"You don't have to tell me," Camille said. She knew what she needed to know. The man looked just like her mother, in a way that he definitely shouldn't have. And it made her want to vomit. But she just sat there as Charlotte continued braiding. Her butt bones and spinal column ached even though she was sitting on a couple of couch cushions. Camille felt like she'd been punched in the throat. This was exactly the kind of thinking she'd wanted to avoid. She squeezed her eyes shut, not wanting to cry in front of

Charlotte. She didn't want to show Charlotte that this information had any impact on her because she didn't want this ugly old man to have any more power over them than he'd already had.

When Charlotte was done braiding, she raked her long, slender hands and her spiky nails through Camille's scalp and hair a couple of times.

They didn't speak about the picture after that. And they never did locate the salon clips.

That night, Camille sat on the floor between her grandparents' knees as they watched *Three's Company* reruns. She wasn't paying much attention; she was thinking about her mother's "father" and her own "father." They were both nameless, faceless, bodiless, inconsequential. Her grandad, of no blood relation, was real, present, and loving. He'd fulfilled his role so well that there was no cavity where those men should have been. It almost felt like a betrayal to consider those men as anything other than what they were: absent.

She laughed when her grandparents laughed, though the show really wasn't that funny. But the clothes were cool, she thought. She wondered, had her father been in the room she was sitting in, laughing at farcical sitcoms with her mother? She didn't know. She didn't know if she wanted to know. She wondered if she looked like him and if it had been hard for her mother to look at her, like it must have been hard for Charlotte to look at Corinna. Maybe that was why things had gone so wrong, with the beatings and such? If that were the explanation, Camille knew she would feel obligated to "forgive and forget" because it wasn't her mother's fault, right? But if it wasn't her mother's fault, then whose fault was it?

She went to bed that night with her body tired and her mind hurtling around the same questions again and again. She tucked her face into the pancake-flat pillow and tried to smell her mother, but she smelled only laundry detergent. Too much time had passed since her mother had been there.

When she was still awake after several hours, she got up and headed to the kitchen to root around for something to put her to sleep. The moon was bright that night, and she easily made it to the kitchen, where she found her grandmother, her pale face illuminated, at one of her favorite posts: the kitchen sink. She was smoking a cigarette, but after each puff, she tapped the ash off the end, and pressed the butt to the photo in her hand, putting small, blackened holes into it. Camille could tell she was burning away faces, and had already obliterated her own.

Charlotte turned and looked at Camille, who was still standing in the dark hallway, with a strange look that churned Camille's stomach. "What are you doing up?"

"I couldn't sleep."

Charlotte picked up the lighter nearby and lit what was left of the photograph on fire, then dropped it into the sink. "You want some tea or something?" Charlotte started opening cabinets. "We probably got some allergy medicine somewhere. You want that?"

"Will you lay down with me?"

Charlotte looked over her shoulder into the sink, where the photo must have stopped burning in the sink and turned into ash. "Yeah, baby. Of course."

They went back to Camille's bed and nestled closely together, so her grandmother's breath grazed her shoulder.

"You thinking about that picture?" Charlotte whispered.

Camille nodded.

"Don't."

"Can I ask you something? Does it bother you that Mama looks like him?"

"It used to."

"Why not anymore?"

"I think I just moved on."

Camille flipped over to face her grandmother. "Moved on?"

"Maybe that's not the best way to put it. Let me think."

Camille waited. "Well, it's more like," Charlotte started. "What's happening now has become more important than what happened in the past. . . ." She trailed off.

Camille didn't say anything.

"I haven't forgotten what happened. I just think my own hurt became less important right now than doing right. Does that make sense?"

Camille nodded.

"I don't think I've forgiven or forgotten or whatever, though, and that's a real problem for me. I don't want you and your mama to be like that. You especially."

"Why me especially?"

"Because your mama really wants to do right by you. She's trying. Evelyn, too. Don't let this change how you see her. They both love you."

"You didn't want to do right by Mama?"

"I didn't know how at first, and it took me a long time to start trying to figure it out. Does that make sense?"

It made a lot of sense. Her mind's eye, previously staticky like a television with its antennae crossed, was now clear, in technicolor. She nodded and rolled over again. Charlotte stroked her arm as she fell asleep.

Charlotte

JUNE 2010

At Camille's high school graduation, the girls wore white dresses, a tradition Evelyn said was sexist. Still, she unearthed an old dress of Charlotte's—a Mexican wedding gown of delicately embroidered white cotton—and had it hemmed to midcalf so that Camille could show off a very expensive pair of strappy Manolo Blahniks. Charlotte braided Camille's hair into a crown; she plucked some baby's breath from a bouquet in the kitchen and tucked it into the folds.

At the ceremony, Corinna and Evelyn were extremely friendly. Each time Charlotte looked over at them, they were smiling and whispering to each other. It physically pained her; she felt it in her gut, her heart, her lungs, her back, her knees, behind her eyes, everywhere.

Charlotte stewed in the moist heat. She thought of her own high school graduation, which she'd missed because she'd run away from home. She wondered what folks said after she didn't show up. What lies had her mother told to cover up her disappearance? Sweat dripped from her forehead into her eyes and melted her mascara. She cursed herself for not wearing the fancy waterproof version Corinna had offered her.

"You're prideful," David was saying a lot these days. "Prideful about your mama. Prideful about some damn—whatchu call it?—mak-scurrah. Stubborn as can be."

Charlotte dabbed underneath her eyes and her fingers came away with a bit of inky black. They were only on the *F* part of the alphabet. She fanned herself with the thick program. She'd only looked through it to find Camille's name. Underneath it said she planned to attend Howard to study journalism and English. Charlotte knew about Howard, and journalism and English made sense. Thinking about her granddaughter's plans, she felt some of her bitterness release. She continued to fan herself.

"Damn," she said out loud.

"What?" David asked from his wheelchair, where he'd been confined for the past three months.

"It's hot." She looked at him, really the first time that afternoon, and saw that he was pale. "You okay?"

"Yeah, why you say that?"

"You're 'bout as pale as—"

"I'm fine. Worry about yourself."

Finally, Camille walked across the stage. Everyone beamed. The white woman in front of them whispered loudly to the older woman sitting next to her: "She could be a model."

Charlotte's mood improved a bit more, but she knew she needed to leave DC as soon as possible. Camille was headed to Mexico with her friends. Without Camille there, there was no point in staying. The whole arrangement gave Charlotte heartburn, and there was no place to smoke. So, she and David started back to Tennessee in the wee hours of the morning, and arrived home in the early evening, just in time to sit on the porch, drink, smoke, and listen to Robin Trower.

The next morning, she woke up to find that David was gone. He was still a little warm to the touch, but it was clear that he was dead from the grayish color of his skin and the stillness of his body. She'd been through this before, but this time, she'd had a feeling it would happen. His pain had been getting worse, and he was barely able to stand anymore. He'd said on the drive back to Tennessee several times: "I just wanted to see my baby graduate," and "I don't want to bother you no more, Charlotte," and "I'm tired of this body."

She kissed him and pulled back one of his eyelids. She tried to commit the particular shade of blue of his eyes to memory, but knew she would fail.

She took a seat on the front porch steps when they took his body away, and she was still there when Corinna arrived that night from the airport.

"Oh, Mama," Corinna said, and her tone was eerily familiar. "Let's get you inside. You smell horrible."

Corinna, however, smelled very good, Charlotte noticed. She smelled like laundry and baby powder. She'd cut her hair almost to the scalp, which suited her, and wore two thin, gold hoop earrings in each ear. She did not look like the girl Charlotte thought she'd always known.

Corinna helped her up and put her in the bathtub filled with painfully hot water, just like Charlotte liked it.

"I loved him, you know?"

Corinna offered a scant smile.

"We fought a lot, but I always loved him. You know that, right?"

"Of course I know that, Mama."

"I loved him because he loved you."

Corinna inhaled and exhaled.

"It was his heart, I bet. It just gave out," Charlotte croaked. "That's how my father died. Did you know that? Your grandfather died like that. And your father, too," she said, letting it slip for the first time. "Heart failure."

She looked expectantly at Corinna, who was sitting on the edge of the tub, but the girl just filled an empty shampoo bottle with water.

"Why'd you stay, Mama?"

"Well, it wasn't as simple as staying or going."

Corinna seemed to chew on this for a moment.

"You know how complicated relationships can be."

Corinna frowned, and Charlotte waited for her to say something, though she already felt like she was being accused. "I didn't know what I was supposed to do. I didn't have any idea, watching y'all."

Charlotte felt a chill run down her spine. "Well, I loved him. And I guess I was also afraid to be alone." She added after a beat. "With you." She wasn't sure why she admitted it.

Charlotte looked up in time to see her daughter nod. "I get that," Corinna said. "It's scary. Raising a child on your own."

"You just don't get why I chose him?"

"I didn't say that. I understand why you chose him and why you stayed. I ain't like the answers, but I know 'em. . . . Now close your eyes," she said.

Charlotte obeyed. The warm water felt like an ointment.

"I told Camille about it, about you and Daddy fighting and all that."

Charlotte felt her head snap from left to right as if possessed. "Why would you go and do that?"

"It's best she know what she come from."

Charlotte didn't have the energy to argue with that.

*   *   *

Later, they sat on the porch steps so Corinna could braid Charlotte's hair.

"Now what am I supposed to do?" Charlotte asked as Corinna started to oil her scalp. "I've got *nothing*."

Corinna sighed. "You have them little piano lessons."

Charlotte nodded. She was enjoying the children she taught.

"And you got me, and you've got Camille." She placed a glob of something on Charlotte's scalp, and immediately she knew it wasn't Blue Magic. "And," Corinna continued, "Evelyn, if you want."

Charlotte sniffed the air and realized it was coconut oil that Corinna was using. Because the girl was so quiet, Charlotte tilted her head back to check on her. Corinna was just sitting there grinning, teeth showing, eyes crinkled, grinning. David was dead, and she was sitting there smiling.

"You got a job waiting on you," Corinna added. "It's all set up, whenever you're ready. Now, put your head back down."

Charlotte sucked her teeth and bowed her head again so that Corinna could continue the oiling. Again, she tilted her head back to look at Corinna, who took her head and gently moved it back into position; this annoyed Charlotte, but she'd done the same thing to Corinna many times, but with much more force. "What on earth are you talking about?"

"You're going to play the piano up at Johnny Washington's restaurant in Nashville."

"What?"

"Just what I said. You going to play piano for Johnny Washington's restaurant—"

"I heard you! But how'd you work that out? I didn't know you still talked to him," Charlotte said.

Corinna shrugged. "I just called in a favor."

Charlotte's mood lifted. When her hair was done, they sat on the front porch like they used to and put on David's favorite Robin Trower album, *Caravan to Midnight*.

"Did you know he's British?" Corinna asked as she poured more bourbon into her lemonade.

"Who?"

"Robin Trower."

"Shut up," Charlotte said, and laughed. "Your daddy had me thinking this man was born and raised in the bayou."

"Let's get you to bed."

Corinna tucked Charlotte into the bed in the second bedroom because the funeral home people had offered to go ahead and dispose of the mattress. She smoothed a few stray hairs from her mother's face. Charlotte closed her eyes when Corinna lingered for a moment.

"Will you forgive me, Corinna?"

"For what, Mama?"

"Everything."

"I do. I forgive you every day," she said, and though Charlotte already knew it was true, it was good to hear.

Camille

SPRING 2010

Toward the end of Camille's junior year, as she was taking her first standardized tests, she realized she had a problem: she didn't want to go to college. Though she'd done well in school, she didn't take any particular pleasure in it. Learning was okay, but she didn't need school to do that, did she? Maybe it was Logan's influence. He'd taken a couple of business classes at the community college, which he said were useful because he'd figured out what he wanted to do before he spent money on school. Su Jin wasn't too keen on going to college either. But Su Jin had finally just been diagnosed with dyslexia and ADHD, and Camille understood why she wouldn't want to go to college and continue struggling. But Su Jin's mother allegedly had a plan to get her into an Ivy League school. She'd started a fashion blog on WordPress, and Camille proofread her posts. She was doing well, better than Camille had done on Tumblr, which she'd more or less abandoned for the material world.

She already knew she could and would get into Howard, but there she would likely need to work just as hard to absorb information she saw no real need for. She didn't really want to "go away" to college either, unless she could be close to Logan. But she was partial to the way things were between them.

Still, Camille did what she was supposed to: applied to Howard and got in. Graduated from Fairfax-Washington in the top ten of her class. Danced a solo at her year-end recital. And for herself, she planned a postgraduation trip with Su Jin, Peach, and Peach's girlfriend Jyoti. Camille wanted to go to Phuket, but nobody wanted to do the long plane ride, so they settled on Mexico. She and Su Jin both surreptitiously invited their love interests, though she and Logan still weren't official, and Logan and Alex both agreed to come.

One afternoon a few weeks before graduation, Logan texted her to say they were going to do something: wear something nicer than usual. On this particular night, Evelyn wasn't home. She'd taken Amtrak to Philadelphia earlier for a conference and wouldn't be home until Monday, and her mother would be working until the bar closed.

That evening, she spent two hours trying to look nice but not too nice, like she'd tried but not too hard. She decided on tight black skinny jeans, a cropped bell-sleeve top, white high-top sneakers, and large gold hoops. She told her mother that she thought Logan was finally going to take her on a "real date" like Corinna had been in her ear about.

"What y'all doing is cute, but try not to fall in love with him till he takes you on a date," her mother said. "That was my mistake."

At some point, Camille started developing real feelings for Logan, beyond infatuation, and wanted to figure out what it meant to be a couple.

When she looked down from the upstairs front window at eight o'clock, Logan was standing across the street whittling a piece of wood. She could see the beautiful veins in his hands from where she stood, and she felt pretty sure she was in love with him. It was uncomfortable, but also effervescent. She hated it.

She was relieved to find that they were dressed at a similar level of formality. He was wearing jeans and shoes without holes and a stiff flannel shirt, probably the nicest outfit she'd ever seen him in. He surprised her with a kiss on the lips while she was still fumbling with her keys and her impractically small cross-body bag.

"You look really pretty," he said, still really close to her face.

Camille dropped the keys. "Thanks."

He kissed her again. She was feeling jittery, as if they didn't talk on the phone every day and weren't having sex as often as they could.

"Where are we going?"

"Dinner and a party at my house." He touched her neck and kissed her again but with tongue. "Or we can just go to my house. No dinner. No party."

She must have frowned.

"I'm just kidding. Let's go."

They got on a train to the end of the Green Line, and from there took a bus to a strip mall with a dog groomer, a 7-Eleven, and a taco place at the end with picnic tables in the parking lot.

"I know it's not what you're used to, but you'll love it," he promised, eyes gleaming.

She never went that far on the Green Line, or anywhere that required multiple modes of transportation. Logan had tried to get her to come out to his house a few times, but she wouldn't even look at the bus schedule. Her mother said not to go out of her way for a boy who wouldn't go out of his. He always managed to make it to her, anyhow.

The guy behind the counter at the taco restaurant seemed to know Logan. Then he ordered for both of them in really good Spanish.

He turned to look at her. "You want horchata or agua fresca?"

She noticed the way he said horchata sounded almost exactly the way her Spanish teacher (who was from Mexico) said it. She didn't know. "Um," she said, "whatever you're having."

They sat down, as far away as they could from a family with far too many small children.

"This is different," she said.

"Good different?"

"Yeah, good different. For sure."

"You don't sound sure." He extended his hands across the table, and she slipped hers into them.

"I'm sure," she said, and nodded vigorously.

They looked at each other. His eyes were impossibly bluish-greenish, and his face was improbably easy to look at, even the crooked nose.

She took a sip of her agua fresca. "Do you like living here?" she asked.

"Yeah," he said, quickly and sharply. "Why? You looking for some place to be?"

"Well," she said, just as the food arrived.

"I got us both two tongue and two carnitas."

"Tongue?"

"Yeah, like cow tongue. You'll like it. Try it," he implored her. "Squeeze some lime on it."

She did really like it. When they were done with their tacos, he ordered a couple of Coronas and squeezed lime into them, too. He always seemed to know what he was doing; she found this very attractive. She would have done anything he told her to do at that moment. Her mother would not approve of this kind of thinking, but her mother wasn't there. She dipped her finger in the remaining salsa, sucked it off, and followed it up with a sip of beer.

"Good, right?"

Camille reached across the table and took his hand. She rubbed the back of his hand with her thumb which had become code for sex.

He looked at his hand and then looked at her, smirking. "Now?"

Her mother wouldn't like this behavior either. Corinna said it was important for it to "feel special." Camille had once asked for clarification. "You shouldn't just be doing it *wherever*, you know?" Corinna had said, but Camille didn't understand why not. She liked having sex "wherever." However, her outfit wasn't well suited to such behavior; she didn't want to risk something happening to the very delicate chiffon sleeves on her expensive vintage top. This was a problem she knew her mother had never had.

"Later. This is vintage Versace." She gestured to her shirt.

He snorted. "I don't know if Versace has a place at this party."

"Versace has a place everywhere."

"If you insist."

They walked about fifteen minutes to Logan's house, mostly along a busy main road. She hadn't expected much from a house full of college-aged kids. It was in disrepair, with rusted metal awnings and foot-tall weeds where shrubs might have been, but it was actually a refreshing shade of sunset pink, like the pink of her Prada bag and roller skates. And the paint job looked new.

"It's pink," she said, gesturing at the monstrosity.

He shrugged. "That's your favorite color, right? I painted it for you."

She smiled. "No, you didn't."

"You're right. The landlord dropped the paint off, said it's all he had, and he'd take a few hundred off the rent if we did it ourselves."

It was a nice coincidence, though.

"It's . . . not nice," he said.

"I like it," she lied. Her grandparents' little house in Tennessee was in better condition than this house. And that was saying a lot.

"The party probably hasn't started yet. We can just go to my room for a bit."

It was ten, and there were a lot of people in the house when they entered, more than just his roommates. How was this *not* the party? The scent of marijuana was strong, and the tile floors were so sticky she thought she might lose a shoe. The music was a bit too loud.

Logan put his arm around her and held her close, introducing her to everyone: the dozen or so people in the living room smoking and laughing at nothing that Camille could see or understand, the guy sitting at the kitchen table with a toddler on each side, the six people hanging out in the backyard. They were all kind; no one was belligerent or impolite. They were all certainly nicer than any group she'd seen gathered at a Fairfax-Washington house party, or a dinner party at Evelyn's house, for that matter.

Logan grabbed a couple of beers from a dirty refrigerator that looked like it had been hit with several shotgun blasts. After, he guided her toward the back of the house to his room. She instinctively reached for the light switch but found only the wall.

"There is no overhead," he said and pulled the chain on a large floor lamp that looked like the kind on a movie set, but wasn't particularly bright. In the warm lighting, she found that the room was neat and clean, especially compared to the rest of the house. The bed was stacked on top of wooden industrial pallets but was tidily made. There was a dresser and a desk, both orderly. The walls were covered in layered tapestries, but they were the only clutter. Instead of a closet, his clothes hung on what looked like a luggage cart without wheels. His four pairs of shoes were neatly arranged on the velvet platform below. A surfboard leaned against the entire structure. She sat on the bed as he drew the curtains.

"I forgot the bottle opener."

While he was gone, she looked around for signs of other girls. She wasn't sure what they would be—maybe a pair of earrings? She flipped the pillows, looking for smudges of makeup. The light wasn't very good, and she didn't want him to catch her doing this, so she stopped and folded her hands in her lap and tried to appear natural. She heard his footsteps and sat up very straight. He was smiling when he walked through the door, holding different bottles than the ones he left with.

"It's the champagne of beers," he said as he handed her one. She didn't know what time it was. She didn't want to violate her generous midnight curfew, even though there was no one home to enforce it. Her mother most likely wouldn't check to see if she was in bed when she got home. Appearing to read her mind, he continued: "Why don't you just stay the night?"

It sounded like a bad idea. But he kissed her, and his mouth was cool from beer.

"We've never had a whole night together."

Evelyn would have had a heart attack if she knew where she was. The last time they'd had a conversation about Logan, Camille left feeling ashamed. But . . . His lips were full, and she liked the way he was looking at her.

"I'll think about it."

She liked the idea of waking up next to him. She took a large swig of beer while Logan felt around for the zipper on her top. She unzipped it herself and let the blouse slide down her shoulders, but then had to pull it up over her head to remove it entirely. She placed it on the back of his desk chair.

"You look pretty in this light," he said as she returned to sit next to him on the bed. "You look pretty in any light . . . but *really* pretty in this light." He mimed taking a photo with his hands.

She smiled. Suddenly, her mother came to mind. She was probably her exact age when she thought she was in love with Camille's father. She didn't know most of the details, but she knew her father had a girlfriend at the time, and he never introduced her to his friends. Logan might have also had a girlfriend, but he had introduced her to his roommates and a few of his friends. That was something.

While she was thinking about this, Logan undid her bra. The room smelled like patchouli and neroli, like incense. Her bra slid down around her elbows. Her breasts were naked, but she never felt exposed in front of him, never felt the urge to hide her body.

"You want some pot?" he asked.

She shrugged, feeling like an idiot, as he produced a large blunt from a small box she hadn't noticed on the floor.

He lit it and handed it to her, then said, "I'm gonna get some more beer. Hold on."

The party must have officially started because the music was getting louder and louder. Led Zeppelin blasted from the backyard, and Kanye West boomed from inside the house, so loud that the windows rattled. She took a hit, rolled onto her back, and fell into his pillows.

When he returned, he set down four more bottles of beer by the bed, took the joint with one hand, and reached for her with the other. Her mother told her a few key things: if you want to stop, say stop; you can say no and you can say yes; always use a condom. She wondered what her mother had been told, if anything. She wanted to stop thinking about her mother. The room was hot. His mouth was cool. She remembered something else her mother said: "I wish I knew that sex was something you do with someone and not something that is done to you." Camille understood more and more what her mother meant by this. There were times when he pulled her clothes off so quickly that she barely registered the removal, feeling like an object.

"Slow down!" she shouted over the noise as he yanked down her jeans.

He paused and looked at her like she'd been speaking another language. Then, like it suddenly made sense to him, he mumbled: "Sorry, okay."

He pulled off his own shirt, and she felt more like an actor and less like a prop when he made eye contact with her. She put her arms around his neck. They held eye contact until Logan cracked a smile.

"What?"

"We're gazing into each other's eyes," he said, smirking.

Camille rolled her eyes. "Can we open a window?"

He shook his head. "They're painted shut."

"What?"

He shrugged. They finished their beers and lay down.

He sighed his familiar little sigh when he slipped inside of her.

He pressed his forehead to hers. She'd been led to believe—by books and television—that sex was painful, especially the first time. Even her mother said it hurt. But she'd never bled or felt pain. Her ob/gyn had warned her that bleeding after sex was often due to inadequate lubrication.

"Meaning," Dr. Jones had leaned in to say. "Not enough fore-play. Women not getting . . . worked up. You know?"

Camille nodded, though she'd never had that problem.

When it was over, he rolled over onto his back and grabbed his perspiring beer from the floor. She wished he'd stayed for just a moment longer.

She put on his T-shirt to go to the bathroom down a dark hall-way, apparently the only place in the house not overrun by people, aside from the couple breathing hard against the wall. She stepped around them to get to the bathroom, where she hovered over a chipped toilet seat to clean herself up with rough tissue from an enormous industrial-size roll of toilet paper. She went back to Lo-gan's bedroom, feeling less enamored with his lifestyle, and wasn't surprised to find that he wasn't there. She fell onto the bed to fin-ish her beer. She opened her phone. There were no missed calls or texts, and it was barely eleven. She plucked the blunt out of the ashtray and relit it. She opened another beer. She still hadn't decided about staying the night. She wasn't feeling particularly in-clined to do so, though she did want to stay with Logan, just not in that house on the mattress on wooden pallets.

Logan returned. He was smiling and carrying more beer. He sat down next to her on the bed. She put her phone down, and he kissed her.

Still close enough to kiss her, he asked: "Can I give you some-thing?"

"Sure," she said. He opened the same box from which he retrieved the weed.

"Here," he muttered. "Give me your hand. Your right hand."

She gave him her hand and he slipped a ring onto the ring finger. She thought the ring was beautiful, a dainty gold thing with two interlocking, amber-colored stones, but obviously not particularly precious or fine.

"What's this?"

He shrugged. "Do you like it?"

"Yeah," she said. "It's pretty."

"Then, it's yours."

"What's it mean?"

He shrugged. She squinted at him. He squinted back. "What do you want it to mean?"

Camille rolled her eyes. "Are you asking me to be your girlfriend?"

"Is that what you want?"

"Logan, are you fucking serious? We've been—"

He cut her off. "It can also just be a ring," he said and pressed his lips to hers. "We don't have to call it anything."

She wanted to throw something, though she wasn't sure why. He sensed her anger.

"Okay, I'm sorry. I'm sorry. Okay? I'm asking you to be my girlfriend."

"Why wouldn't you just fucking say that?" She started getting her things together to leave.

"Camille," he said.

"I'm going to college in the fall. I don't need a boyfriend right now, anyway."

"You know we're together. And you don't even want to go to college."

"What's that got to do with anything?"

"We could do something else instead."

"What are you talking about, Logan?!" she shouted, already pulling on her jeans. "Say what you mean!"

He took both of her hands in his. "We could travel, like we talked about. I've got money saved up."

Camille snorted, only half-dressed. She felt suspicious of him in a way she never had. "You must think I'm stupid."

He shook his head. "I definitely don't think you're stupid. You're the smartest girl I know."

Camille felt tears coming on. She really, really did not want to cry, afraid of showing her hand. Jenny Rhodes came to mind. Who knows who Jenny could have been? She could have traveled the world, or she could have stayed in Chilly Springs until she died in a car accident or of old age. But she hadn't had the choice. Camille had all kinds of choices. It felt foolish not to choose the one that would make her happiest. But she had her mothers to think of.

"We can't do that."

"Why not?"

"Because," she said, gesturing, as if it were obvious. "Everyone's counting on me."

"I don't get how that's your problem." He stood up. "I think I know you pretty well. You've been my *girlfriend*," he paused, "for like a year. And I think you're better than doing what's expected of you. You're capable of much more."

"That's corny, Logan," she said as she softened.

"Will you stay? Tonight? We don't have to talk about any of this. We can just have a good time."

It was obvious that he didn't get it. He didn't have anyone counting on him. He didn't understand the immense pressure of being the beacon of hope for three generations of women. But she had hope—where she hadn't previously—that maybe she could make them proud and make herself proud at the same time.

Corinna

SPRING 2010

When Camille returned from her spring break senior year, Corinna decided to sit her down and tell her about Valencia. It wasn't a "secret" after all. She was just being cautious about who she introduced to her family.

She found it difficult to pin down Camille at home, though. She was always headed somewhere or doing something. It wasn't until almost the end of the school year, when they were in the car headed to pick up Camille's prom dress from the Neiman Marcus at Tysons Galleria, that the two of them were alone together.

"I didn't go to prom, you know?" Corinna said.

"Because you were pregnant. I know."

"Well, that and there was no way I could spend money on something like that."

"I know, Mama."

"I just hope you're grateful for all the ways you've been blessed."

Camille massaged her temple. "I am." She sighed loudly. "Actually, I wanted to talk to you about something."

Corinna braced herself. "Yeah? Is it about your date? The Wilson boy?"

Camille's prom date had been hand-selected by Evelyn. He was not a very good-looking young man, but his father was a major donor to the university.

"No," she said. "After graduation—" she started.

"You want to go somewhere other than Howard? I told Evelyn. We can talk about it. Where are you thinking? It's a little late, but maybe you could do a postgrad year somewhere. I've heard of that."

"Mama. Can I speak, please?"

"Well, I don't like your tone, but go on."

"I was thinking about not going to school *yet*."

Corinna felt her jaw clench and saw the blood leaving her knuckles as she squeezed the wheel. They weren't far from the mall. "So what would you do instead?"

Camille wrung her hands.

"Camille?"

"Um."

"This isn't about that boy, is it?"

"Well—"

"You wanted to speak, so speak!"

"It's not just that!"

"So it is about the boy?"

"It's about a lot of things. Lots of people take gap years."

"To build schools in Africa, not gallivant with their low-life boyfriends."

"Low-life?"

Corinna was yelling before she knew it. "I *let* you see that boy, so that you wouldn't sneak around and get pregnant or get some goddamn STD. And this is how you act? You have everything you could possibly want, and you've managed to find something *else* to want? We're driving damn near to the middle of Virginia to get your goddamn custom prom dress, for fuck's sake! You want, want, want, want, Camille!"

Corinna pulled sloppily into a space on the outskirts of the mall parking lot. Camille sat with her arms crossed, staring blankly ahead.

"The answer's no!"

Camille reached for the door handle, but Corinna held down the button for the power lock.

"I'm not done speaking to you."

Camille rolled her eyes. "You were fine with a gap year—"

"I said *postgrad*. You're going to Howard in the fall, goddammit! Do you hear me?"

After a long pause, Camille responded: "Yes, ma'am."

"Let's go get this dress," Corinna said, feeling ashamed of her behavior. She'd just read *ScreamFree Parenting*, and she was definitely not adhering to its principles.

Inside Neiman Marcus, the tailor had Camille try on the champagne-colored satin gown with the cowl neckline. She looked beautiful and also miserable.

"It's perfect," the small woman said. "Are we happy with it?"

Camille nodded unenthusiastically.

"It's stunning," Corinna added as the tailor handed her the receipt. Evelyn had already paid for the dress and the alterations—a total of twelve hundred dollars, more than most people's wedding gowns cost. She felt herself getting angry again. *Ungrateful little brat*, she thought.

They left the mall with the garment bag slung over Camille's shoulder. Corinna put her arm around her daughter's slight waist and squeezed.

"I'm sorry," she said. "For yelling."

Camille didn't say anything.

"I didn't need to raise my voice like that."

Camille just looked at her shoes as they approached the car.

"Camille. Hello?"

"Yeah, okay. It's fine."

"I'm just trying to look out for you. You know that, don't you?"

"Yeah," Camille said as she hung the dress up in the back seat of the car.

"You want ice cream?" Corinna asked as soon as they were on the road back to the city.

"I have plans with Su Jin," Camille said flatly.

"Okay, well. I need to talk to you about something."

"Okay." She gestured as if to say, Go on.

"I'm seeing someone."

Again, Camille gestured for Corinna to continue, but Corinna promptly lost her nerve. She didn't want to complicate the tensions she'd just created.

"That's all. I just wanted to let you know that I'm seeing someone."

"Well, that's *something*, Mama. Hope he's not a low-life."

Corinna's face flushed with anger. Their relationship was so much closer to normal than it had ever been. And Camille was so much more normal than Corinna could have imagined; she was self-absorbed and occasionally petulant, like a television seventeen-year-old. This was what Corinna had wanted, she reminded herself. Still, she wanted to strangle her sometimes.

Corinna forced a smile. "What are you and Su Jin gonna get up to?"

"Nothing."

Corinna sometimes felt that Charlotte had chosen David over her, but she had come to understand the compulsion to choose a partner over a child. After all, she married Isaac and stayed with him rather than be with Camille. She didn't want Camille to feel like Corinna would ever choose someone over her again.

That night, Corinna tied down her hair, drank half a bottle of wine, and stared at the *Andy Griffith Show*, thinking about her daughter the whole time. What mattered to Camille? In order of apparent importance: clothes, her boyfriend, her friends, the internet, ballet, her grades, then everything else, including her family. But what would she become? It wasn't that Camille was vapid; Camille was smart and interesting. She said she wanted to be a journalist, but Corinna got the distinct sense that Camille wasn't convinced about this career choice. If Camille's future was what mattered, would it be okay if she became a trophy wife? One of those internet personalities? A model? An MTV VJ? A fitness instructor? A bartender, like her mother? Perhaps she couldn't think that far ahead. Camille was only seventeen. If she didn't get pregnant, she had a lot of time to make those kinds of decisions. And she had real options. Whatever she chose would be her choice, at least more so than most of the "choices" Corinna had made.

Camille

SUMMER 2010

A few days after her graduation ceremony, Camille was eating roasted sunflower seeds given to her by Logan while roller-skating toward the Mall to meet up with Su Jin to attend an art exhibit at the National Gallery. The weather was pleasant. She'd had a shrimp and avocado burrito for an early lunch. Her recent conflict with her mother was far from her mind. She was thinking about what to pack for her upcoming trip to Tulum. She, Su Jin, and Peach were going to spend five days at a rustic mountain resort, and five days at a beachside resort. Camille's mother knew that they had also invited along their boyfriends and girlfriend (in Peach's case), but no one else's parents knew. Her phone rang with the tone she'd assigned to her mother. She ignored the call, planning to call her back after she'd arrived at her destination and changed into her shoes. But then she called again and again. Camille had a bad feeling, so she braked near the Verizon Center. She held on to the tall black gate that surrounded the American Art Museum building while her mother delivered the news about her grandfather.

She'd always known her grandfather wouldn't live a particularly long life, as his body was so broken and his health so bad, but he was only in his late fifties, and she'd expected a little more time with him. Charlotte had been in an unusual hurry to get back to Tennessee and must have driven nonstop to get there. As she skated back toward home, Camille wondered if her grandmother had known somehow that her husband was dying and wanted him to die at home in his own bed. The idea of looking at a loved one and seeing death raised goose skin on Camille's arms.

When Camille arrived home, she found Corinna tossing things into a suitcase.

"We're leaving right now?" Camille asked.

"Not 'we.' I'm going on ahead. You and Evelyn can come in a day or two."

Camille sucked her teeth, tears welling in her eyes. "But why?"

"Who knows what kind of state your granmama is in."

Camille left the carriage house and slammed the door behind her.

Evelyn was of little help for Camille in her time of grief. Her forte had never been condolences, and it was clear she didn't know what to say. So she left her alone. Camille sat in the den with the lights off and watched the Independent Film Channel. In the late afternoon, Su Jin appeared in the den door. "I texted you," she said.

Camille had texted her to let her know what happened but hadn't checked her phone much after that.

"Your grandma let me in," she said. She sat down next to her and unzipped her backpack and pulled out a box of Snickers ice cream bars and two splits of champagne.

Despite feeling like someone had ladled a hole in her chest, Camille felt lucky. Her friend snuggled up next to her and they quietly watched *Amelie*, which happened to be playing back-to-back.

Su Jin spent the night with her on the couch. In the morning, she woke up with her cheek resting on the crown of Su Jin's head.

She thought of her grandfather.

He'd gotten off easy. He told her this himself, little by little, over the years. She could tell it eased his spirit a little to know that she knew, and that she forgave him. She found it easy to forgive him, because he spoke honestly (as far as she knew) about what he'd done. This was more than she could say about her mothers, with their "I did the best I could" or "I did what I thought was best." Corinna never even acknowledged the savage beatings she'd given Camille, hardly said anything about the way she passed Camille around to her grandmother and great-grandmother. Though Camille had begun to forgive her mother, she still struggled from time to time, and thought she might have had an easier time if her mother could have said out loud what she did. But she wasn't sure of all the things her mother had done wrong; she wasn't even sure what her mother had done right. Maybe it wasn't right, but it was more straightforward for her grandad, she thought.

She found her phone and opened it to find a couple texts from Logan. First, the typical good night. Then, in the middle of the night: Su Jin told me about your grandfather. I'm around if you want to talk.

She wasn't sure she wanted to talk, but she did want to see him.

Two hours later, she and Su Jin were showered and skating to the National Sculpture Garden to meet Alex and Logan. The boys were sitting by the massive fountain appearing to be deep in conversation, even though they'd met only a few times. Logan had a way of doing that with anyone he met.

The couples split up. Alex and Su Jin went to the café. Camille and Logan remained seated by the fountain.

"Sorry about your grandad," Logan said. "I know you were close."

"Thanks."

He reached for her hands, and they sat silently as if they were praying. Camille's mind was blissfully blank for the first time since she'd learned her grandfather had died. Logan tended to have that effect on her. He calmed her.

After a while, he spoke. "I apologize if this is the wrong time to ask, but I was thinking about something."

Camille nodded.

He continued: "When we go to Mexico, what if we just stayed?"

Camille's instinct was to say yes, but she had been conditioned to do otherwise. She shook her head. "I don't think so. Not so soon after my grandad." The trip was in two weeks.

"You're still going on the trip, though."

"Well, yes. That's been my plan. But he *just* died."

"Okay, okay. I'm sorry. I shouldn't have brought it up."

Hours later, after they'd eaten ice cream, pupusas, and skated up and down the waterfront, Logan walked her home. Usually, that meant they stopped a block away from Evelyn's house on the corner, but they weren't careful this time. They walked nearly to the house before Camille noticed Evelyn standing on the stoop watering the plants. Camille had never once seen Evelyn do that. It shocked her so much that she froze. Logan's arm was draped across her shoulder and their fingers were laced. Something made Evelyn look up and Logan retreated his arm, but it was too late. She told him to go.

Camille thought of turning away, but that felt like admitting a misdeed. She approached her grandmother as proudly as she could.

"Are you crazy?" Evelyn asked her, appearing intimidating from the highest step on her stoop.

"I—"

"If you say you love that boy, I will spray you with this hose."

Feeling possessed, she said, "I love him." She'd known it for quite some time, but had never said it out loud, not even to Logan. Evelyn did not spray her with the hose. Instead, she tossed it into the yard.

"Turn the water off, will you?" Evelyn said before turning to go inside.

Camille turned off the spigot, then followed. She expected the altercation to continue, but Evelyn was gone. The door to the master bedroom slammed. She wasn't sure what to do so she headed toward her own bedroom. By the time she got there, she was in tears. She cried herself to sleep.

Camille and Evelyn ignored each other for the next two days. Then Corinna said she was "ready for Camille." It had never been discussed if Evelyn would attend the funeral, but she bought two tickets to Nashville when the time came.

The short flight was uncomfortable. Neither of them spoke. But when they landed and were waiting for Corinna to pick them up, Camille realized she had something to say: "I didn't do it to spite you."

"I know that," Evelyn said without looking at her.

"Then why are you so angry with me?"

"I just wanted more for you." Evelyn finally looked at her, and Camille saw there were tears welling in her eyes.

"I'm only seventeen, Mama. I haven't ruined my life. Not yet, anyway." She cautiously added: "I'm on the pill."

Evelyn looked like she had swallowed her own tongue.

Just then, Corinna waved at them. Charlotte was also in the car, but she got into the back seat with Camille. They held hands but didn't speak.

The car ride to Chilly Springs was uncomfortably quiet. Camille used the time to think about what Evelyn meant by "more." What could Camille want more than love? Money, perhaps? A good education? A career? She thought of what Logan said at the sculpture garden. Camille had wanted to go to Mexico—or somewhere like it—since she was twelve years old and started using her journal as a scrapbook for places she hadn't been. She'd never stopped pasting pictures of water into her journal, eventually getting particularly interested in hot springs. But she'd started adding other images, too: food, hotel rooms, mountains. She frequently visited the *Condé Nast Traveler* website to watch white people enjoy exotic locales. She'd taped an enormous aerial-view poster of a beach in the Seychelles on the ceiling of her bedroom so it was the first thing she saw when she woke up. Perhaps, she and Evelyn had very different definitions of "more."

They were about fifteen minutes away from Charlotte's house when Evelyn asked if Corinna knew about Logan.

Corinna did not hesitate. "Yes," she said, without taking her eyes off the road.

"He's at least three years older than her, Corinna."

"I know that."

"And you let it happen?"

"*Let?*" Corinna said. "What was I supposed to do? Kick her out? Run her off?"

Camille could see Corinna's face but not Evelyn's. Corinna's face was full of rage. Evelyn went silent. Then the entire car went silent. The car was so quiet, Sozzani's breathing was deafening and the sound of Corinna itching her dry elbows unsettled her.

Corinna

JUNE 2010

They were almost home when Charlotte decided she had something to say. Corinna's stomach dropped before her mother completed her sentence.

"I think you're overcorrecting," Charlotte said.

Corinna wished she could climb into the back seat and muzzle her.

Corinna saw where her mother was going. "Mama, come on now—"

"For what you *let* happen to me," Charlotte finished.

"Now you wait a minute!" Evelyn turned around toward Charlotte like she was prepared to fight her, then spoke through gritted teeth. "I'm tired of having this conversation. Forgive me or don't! Move on or don't! You're only hurting yourself, Charlotte."

Corinna pulled onto the gravel driveway, unsure of what to do next.

Camille was on her way out of the car before the car was even off.

Charlotte got out next.

Corinna and Evelyn were left alone in the car.

"Leave me be for a minute, please," Evelyn said.

Corinna hesitated.

"I don't deserve your pity," Evelyn said, her lettuce-colored eyes reddened and watering.

"But Mama," Corinna said. "You do. If you don't deserve pity or forgiveness, then I don't either. None of us do."

Evelyn frowned. "That's ridiculous, Corinna." She furrowed her brow and shook her head. "What you've done and what I've done are not the same. You're ill-advised at worst, Corinna. Don't talk like that."

"Before your mother had to remind everyone how wicked I am, I was going to say that you did what you thought you had to do. I know that you feel like you can't say no to Camille. That's you trying to be a good mother. I get that. I'm not completely dead inside." Evelyn sank into her seat. "But I don't think it's the right choice."

"Well, I weighed my options, and I decided not to push her away." They sat in silence for a moment. When Corinna finally looked at Evelyn, she was dabbing at her eyes.

"Let's go inside, have a drink," Evelyn said. "I'll try to understand."

*   *   *

On the day of David's funeral, Corinna requested to ride alone with Camille to the funeral home.

"Well?" Camille said when they were more than halfway there. "I assume you want to talk to me about something."

Corinna hadn't figured out exactly what she was going to say. She sighed. Valencia said she was reading the signs wrong. Camille wasn't going to "rebel." She was respectful and grateful. But Valencia didn't know Camille, how adversarial Camille could be, had always been. And Corinna had felt something brewing.

"Don't do anything stupid," she said.

"Huh?"

"You heard me."

Camille rolled her eyes. "Can we go inside, please?"

Corinna pressed the child lock so Camille couldn't get out.

"Whatever you're thinking, don't do it. You're up to something, I know it."

"I'm not up to anything, Mama. Can you let me out, please?"

Corinna released the child lock, and Camille huffily exited the vehicle.

Corinna found her mother and they walked hip to hip into the chapel area, where David's body lay inside the cheapest-looking casket Corinna had ever seen. The two women stopped to stand in the middle of the aisle as other attendees, mostly neighbors, former coworkers, and Charlotte's clients, moved awkwardly around them, carrying little plastic cups of orange juice and programs printed on paper so thin Corinna could have comfortably blown her nose with it. Charlotte hadn't allowed Corinna to help with the funeral planning, and it showed.

It was a bare-bones ceremony, lasting fifteen minutes at most. There was a slideshow playing pictures of only David and Camille as the pastor gave a generic speech about death and heaven. There was no one to carry the casket to the gravesite. Corinna had to clarify with the funeral home if it would be taken or if they had to figure it out themselves. Corinna wished Charlotte had asked for help.

They went home and sat around the house for the rest of the day.

Corinna woke up in the middle of the night in the bed she was sharing with Evelyn, Charlotte, and Camille. The full-size bed was nowhere near big enough for the four of them, but Charlotte hadn't replaced her mattress.

Without looking around, Corinna sensed her mother was missing; she knew she would find her on the porch smoking and drinking something brown. When Corinna stepped outside, Charlotte did not turn to look at her. They sat in silence for a while, smoking.

"Can I just ask you one thing, Mama?" Corinna asked as the sun began to come up.

"What?" Charlotte said without looking at her, tapping the ashes from her cigarette.

"Why did you keep me?"

Corinna watched Charlotte run her tongue along with her teeth for what felt like an ungodly amount of time. "I don't know," she said finally.

"That's not good enough," Corinna said. "I deserve a real answer."

Charlotte inhaled sharply. "Why did you keep Camille?"

"That's not what we're talking about."

"Well, I'm pretty damn sure it's the exact same answer."

Corinna recoiled. "And how do you know that? You were *raped*, Mama."

"You wanted someone to love you, right?" Charlotte put out her cigarette and gripped the rocking chair's armrests while Corinna stared at the side of her face. She looked *old*, with her dark undereye circles, and her crepey skin. "Hmm?" she asked accusingly. "That's what it was, wasn't it? You'd gotten to be eighteen years old, and you felt just about as *empty* as could be, didn't you?" She finally looked at Corinna. "Am I wrong?"

"No."

"Well, there's your answer," Charlotte said, and picked up the cigarettes again.

"But Mama. Did you love me? When I was a baby?" Corinna said, and immediately regretted how silly it sounded.

"Of course I loved you!" Charlotte insisted, but it didn't ring true to Corinna.

"Can you just admit that—" Corinna started before she knew what she wanted her mother to admit. Perhaps that there was something Corinna needed from Charlotte that she never got? It would never happen.

"Leave me be, Corinna," she muttered, a cigarette between her lips. "Please."

Corinna inhaled deeply and stood to go inside, but just as she put her hand on the door, Charlotte said, "Hey."

Corinna looked over her shoulder at her mother, who looked small and childlike in her chair. "Yeah?"

"I have regrets, and I'm sorry," Charlotte said before taking a hearty sip of her drink. "I loved you best I knew how."

"Thank you for saying that, Mama."

Corinna returned to the bedroom. Somehow, Evelyn and Camille had both turned and were sleeping facing the wall, their heads on black satin pillowcases, because "satin is anti-microbial, better for your skin." Corinna preferred standard cotton.

She fought the inclination to climb back into bed, and instead, watched them until Camille stirred. Not wanting to get caught staring, she went to her parents' bedroom and saw that David's "good" cane, a solid wood one she'd ordered online that he used only when he left the house, was leaning against the bed's headboard. Corinna felt her first pangs of grief as she took the wooden cane and put it with her things.

Camille

JUNE 2010

Two days after her grandfather's funeral, Camille was delivered back to the airport by her mother. She hadn't been consulted about whether she would still go to Cancun. She'd told her friends that she wasn't sure, and they seemed to assume that she wouldn't. Her ticket was back to DC.

"Go back to Evelyn's and get your things," Corinna said. "And go. You'll regret it if you don't."

Camille would be at home alone for forty-eight hours before her flight to Mexico. When she realized this, as she waited in the security queue, she texted Logan that she wanted to see him.

Later, in her bed, her back to his front, she told him that she would stay with him in Mexico.

"Wait, really?"

"Yes."

"Whoa. Okay. Wow."

Camille hoped for more enthusiasm. Her disappointment must have been obvious.

"That's amazing. I didn't think you would. What changed your mind?"

Camille wasn't sure, exactly. Something about the way her mothers used the word *let* had disturbed her. They were angry with each for what each of them had or hadn't allowed. She didn't want to be angry with her mother for not letting her do this. She paused to consider the consequences and the danger, but not for very long.

"Everyone's made all my decisions for me, where I go, who I live with, what I do—"

She cut herself off before she could start crying.

"I get it," Logan said.

By the time they flew to Cancun, they had a loose plan.

With their friends, they were scheduled to stay at a rustic jungle lodge in Quintana Roo and then a more posh beach resort in Tulum. After that, they would stay and work in downtown Tulum for a few weeks, until they had enough money to move on.

Camille had fun despite near constant low-grade anxiety. They hiked, drank strong tequila, danced, bathed in hot springs, lay by the pool, swam in the ocean. She and Logan bathed and slept together. They had their first argument outside of the spat about the ring. This time it was over a four-hundred-dollar restaurant bill she and Su Jin had rung up. Logan wasn't responsible for it but couldn't understand it: "You won't be able to do that when it's just me and you—you know that, right?"

"Of course I know that, I'm not an idiot."

"I didn't call you an idiot."

"You might as well, if you think I think I'm going to run all over South America with my grandmother's credit card."

"You don't understand money, do you?"

"Have you heard nothing I've said this whole time? I grew up poor. What's the real problem?" She wrapped her arms around his neck and pressed her forehead to his, a move she'd learned from him.

"I think I'm feeling insecure," he admitted with astonishing ease.

She wished she understood her own feelings so well.

The night before the group's last resort stop, Camille went to Su Jin's room, where her friend was sitting in the hot tub on the balcony, Alex nowhere to be found. She was drinking straight from a magnum of champagne, which she extended to Camille.

"You wanna get in?"

Camille was still wearing her bathing suit, so she climbed in. Su Jin put her arm around her. They hadn't spent much time alone together, and she wished for a moment that it was just them on the trip. When would they get a chance to do something like this again? There were the summers, but Evelyn would insist Camille have internships or jobs or take classes, she felt certain. Camille felt more resolved in her decision not to return home, though she was realizing there were details she hadn't thought through. For one, she was still seventeen. Several times, she went to Google and started to research what might happen. Every time, she stopped herself, frightened of what she might find. She worried about Sozzani, who was staying in a dog hotel. Would she feel abandoned? Get sick with depression? Still, she was determined to go through with it, to find out what would happen.

"I have to tell you something."

Su Jin smirked and leaned forward, looking drunk. "Is it juicy? Sexual?"

"No, it's serious."

Her friend frowned and stuck out her tongue, like she'd tasted something sour. She looked very pretty in the low light, with her hair floating around her chest as if her head was emerging from a coal-colored lily pad. Camille took a large sip from the champagne bottle. It tasted crisp and lemony.

"Are you pregnant?" Su Jin asked.

"No, I'm not fucking pregnant." If Camille were pregnant, she knew she would have an abortion. No question. No hesitation. She wouldn't even tell anybody.

"Okay? So what's so serious?"

"I'm not going home."

Su Jin stared at her blankly. "What do you mean?"

"I mean, Logan and I are going backpacking for a while."

"For a while? How long is that?"

Camille shrugged. "I don't know, but I don't plan to go to Howard in the fall."

"You don't plan to go to Howard in the fall?" Su Jin repeated softly and incredulously.

"Right," Camille said. "Because I don't want to."

"Because you don't *want* to?" Su Jin closed her eyes and shook her head slowly from left to right. "Wow. I never really thought we had a choice in the matter."

"And that's exactly the problem, right? They tell us to do this, do that, or we're not doing 'right.'"

"Yeah, I mean. I don't know, Camille. What's your plan, exactly?"

"I'm just not going home with you guys."

"Is Logan putting you up to this?"

Camille thought for a moment. He wasn't not putting her up to it. He had planted the seed and watered it, but she didn't think anyone could say he was forcing her. "No," she said, trying to sound confident.

"Well." Su Jin tucked a piece of Camille's hair, which was slowly curling up tightly from the steam, behind her ear. "I think it's brave. You'll write me?"

"Of course, I'll write you," Camille said, and took another large gulp of champagne. "Wouldn't it be easier to drink this out of a glass?"

Su Jin shrugged. "A glass might break."

Camille got up to retrieve a glass, both relieved that Su Jin hadn't tried to talk her out of it and frustrated that she hadn't.

Corinna

SUMMER 2010

After the funeral, Corinna took an indefinite leave of absence and stayed with her mother in Tennessee. Camille had gone to Mexico, and Evelyn back to DC. For a while, Charlotte seemed to go about her normal routine, except for the gaping hole of no one to care for. She got up in the morning, smoked while she cooked eggs, watched several hours of daytime television and smoked, made sandwiches for lunch and smoked, started drinking around four p.m. on the porch and smoked, made dinner and smoked, sat up late, listening to music, and smoked. For a few days, Corinna went along with it. Charlotte seemed fine; she hadn't shown much emotion in the days after David's funeral.

"How are you feeling, Mama?" Corinna asked her mother late one night over one of their nightly games of spades. She indiscriminately put a card down, knowing her mother would win anyway.

"Feeling about what?" Her mother was closely focused on her hand.

Corinna was exasperated. "Your dead husband."

"Oh, I'm okay. He was in a lot of pain." Charlotte continued to stare at her hand before finally playing the trump card and winning the game. Again.

"Don't be a sore loser," Charlotte said to Corinna's frown, and pushed her glass across the table. "Make me another one of those whatchamacallits."

Corinna had been making French 75s, which Charlotte really enjoyed. Charlotte leaned back in her seat and watched Corinna prepare it in a regular wineglass because Charlotte didn't have champagne flutes.

"I've been meaning to say that I'm proud of you."

Corinna couldn't help but smile, but she turned away so her mother wouldn't see, then carried the cocktails back to the table.

Charlotte unfolded her arms to wrap her delicate hand around the glass and took a sip. "That's a good cocktail," she said. "You think Camille and that boy going to last?"

Corinna shrugged. She really didn't know. "I think he loves her. Whatever that means for kids that age." Her mother smiled a little. "I think they got something better than me or you ever had with men, you know?"

Charlotte lifted her drink and extended her pointer finger. "Now, you damn right about that."

An image came to Corinna of her mother's blackened eyes, cracked ribs, and bloody lips. "I told her about you and Daddy. And me and her daddy."

"What you tell her about Johnny?"

"Not much. Just tried to make it a teaching tool, told her not to settle for scraps."

"That's a good lesson." Charlotte rubbed her chin. She finished her cocktail in one sip, and changed the subject again. "Have I ever told you what happened with Evelyn?"

"No."

"Okay, well. Make me another cocktail, and I'll tell you."

Charlotte

SPRING 1974

Charlotte was just six weeks short of graduating from high school when she realized she was pregnant. It was the absolute worst-case scenario. She'd gone years without this happening, and was weeks away from never having to sleep in that house another night. She even thought she could figure out how to get out sooner, and was working on her mother for an extended trip to Europe.

She knew a bit about abortion. She'd seen *Alfie*. She hadn't seen that episode of *All My Children*. She'd never had many friends. If she did, she would have known she had options. She didn't trust the few friends she did have enough to tell them what had happened to her. So she kept it to herself. She let it *fester*. That's the word that came to her mind about her situation. A disease or cancer.

Wayne was in the UK doing something for work. He often left town but had never been away for so long, and Charlotte could relax for the first time in years. She almost felt happy, especially since Evelyn was practically nonexistent at home. She did occasionally appear in the late evening to antagonize Charlotte about her future or to demand that Charlotte play something for her on the piano, but other than that, Charlotte could exist unbothered.

One afternoon Charlotte came home to find Evelyn standing at the top of the grand staircase wearing a satin robe and with curlers in her hair. She was smoking a cigarette out of a dramatically long holder and looking down at Charlotte like she'd never seen her before. Charlotte thought about turning around and leaving, but Evelyn began to descend the staircase, her high-heeled slippers clicking on the impeccably polished wood. Time moved like cold molasses as Evelyn made her way down.

"I got a call from the school," Evelyn said at the bottom of the steps. Charlotte was not sure what the call might have been about, but she knew she was in for a bad night. "They said you're failing every single subject. Is that right?"

Charlotte lowered her eyes, held her books close to her tender chest, and nodded.

"Look at me!" Evelyn shouted, and Charlotte smelled the alcohol on her mother's breath, a terrible sign of what was to come. She looked up and was not surprised when Evelyn hit her in the face with an open palm. "You're in danger of not graduating. Do you know that?"

Charlotte knew she should say something, anything, if she didn't want to get hit again, but no words came to her.

"Do you know how *embarrassing* that would be for me, Charlotte?" Evelyn started to pace the foyer, another terrible sign.

"I'm sorry, Mama," Charlotte said, though she hadn't called her mother "Mama" since she was very young, and had no idea where it came from. Evelyn slapped her harder than she ever had, and Charlotte fell to the wooden floor, making her school oxford come untucked from her skirt and revealing just a sliver of her moonlike stomach. Charlotte didn't notice in time to stop her mother from seeing. When her ears stopped ringing, and some of her vision returned, Evelyn was standing over her, her eyes wild.

"And you know what else they said? They said there's rumors you're pregnant," Evelyn said, her voice a little too calm, standing over Charlotte. "Is that true?" She reached for Charlotte's arm, but Charlotte crawled away on her hands and knees until she was able to get the balance to stand and run for the stairs. Evelyn kicked off her slippers and gave chase. Charlotte looked over her shoulder only once and saw a woman who was practically rabid. "I'll beat it out of you," she screamed, just before Charlotte reached her bedroom door. She slammed it in Evelyn's face and locked it, but Evelyn threw her small body against the door with such force that the wood cracked.

Charlotte went to her nightstand and dug through the deep bottom drawer until she felt the cool metal of the gun she'd stolen out of Wayne's study shortly after he left so that he wouldn't be able to use it against her. He hadn't yet, but she wasn't sure what he was capable of. She pointed it at the door, and when the door flew open, sending splinters flying, she cocked it. Her hands were shaking badly. Evelyn came lunging through the door with her fists up and her teeth bared, but when she saw the gun, her demeanor changed instantly. She straightened her back and spoke calmly: "You have ten minutes to get yourself and that goddamn abomination out of my *fucking* house, Charlotte. And don't you come back until that baby is dealt with."

Tears streamed down Charlotte's face. "You let this happen!" she shouted, her finger twitching on the trigger.

Her mother smiled wanly. "It's his, isn't it?"

Charlotte nodded, and Evelyn put her hand over her eyes and sighed deeply. "Like I said, you have ten minutes to get the hell out of my house," she said without looking at Charlotte, then turned and left without another word, the scent of liquor and lavender bath salts trailing behind her.

Less than a month later, while soaking her swollen feet in the motel bathtub, Charlotte saw in the newspaper that Wayne was dead: "Black Atlanta Business Magnate Dead at 51." The headline was buried deep in the business section of the *Tennessean*. She did not read the article, but she did write her mother months later.

Mother,
I hope you are happy now that you are alone. It seemed that's all you ever wanted. I have decided to let you know where I am always so that you may never truly be alone as long as you know that I am somewhere thinking of you and how incredibly you failed to love me. And you have a granddaughter. I named her Corinna. Like the song.

Charlotte

Her mother's letters came once a week after that, always on the pink stationery the color of a sunset.

Corinna

SUMMER 2010

"You took the gun with you?"

"Yeah, I sold it for liquor money, I think."

"How can you be so nonchalant about it?"

Charlotte shrugged. "I wouldn't say I'm nonchalant."

"You seem it to me."

"And that's *key*, isn't it? Appearing nonchalant?"

"What do you mean?"

"I mean, look at *you*."

"I don't know what you mean. I'm fine."

"You think all them books you read are going to fix what ain't right inside of you?" Charlotte laughed dryly as she sat with one arm draped over the back of her chair and a cigarette in hand.

Corinna said nothing, knowing her mother was right. Or something resembling right.

*   *   *

She'd been back in Tennessee for a few weeks when Evelyn called. She was standing by the window in her former bedroom eating barbecue-flavored sunflower seeds and watching a deer graze. She hadn't heard from Evelyn in a while and assumed she was still angry.

"Where's Camille?"

"What do you mean?" Corinna checked the date and time on her phone. Camille should have been back in DC the night before. "She's with you."

"She's not with me, and she's not answering her phone."

"Well, she's not with *me*."

"Call her. Maybe she'll answer *you*," Evelyn said, a hint of spite in her voice.

Corinna went to the kitchen to use her mother's landline, know-ing she would answer if Charlotte called. Camille answered almost immediately. "Hi, Mama."

"Where are you?"

"Oh," Camille said, obviously surprised. "I didn't realize it was you."

Corinna's neck and cheeks warmed with rage. "You're still in Mexico with that boy, aren't you?" She heard Camille take a deep breath. "Did you miss your flight?"

"You could say that."

"Camille, you better get your ass on the next flight to DC."

"No."

"No?" Corinna's fist was balled up tight by her side. "You're going to—" The line went dead. She was lightheaded and short of breath. She'd seen this coming, and it still made her want to crawl out of her skin. "Mama?!" she called, though Charlotte was stand-ing less than a yard away at the sink.

"What? Why are you shouting?" Charlotte dramatically plugged one ear with a finger.

"Camille is still in Mexico."

"She miss her flight or something?" Charlotte was smiling.

"You knew?"

"I didn't."

"You did! Why are you smiling?! She told you, didn't she?!" Corinna was standing over her mother, whose smile was gone, but there was still a sparkle in her eye.

"She didn't tell me, I swear." Charlotte tapped her cigarette on the ashtray.

Corinna waited for Charlotte to continue. There was more to be said. "Well?"

"I just *knew* she was going to do that. I could feel it."

"*Feel* it?"

"Soon as you told me she wanted to do a gap year, I knew she was going to figure out how to do something like this. You know how that girl is. Stubborn. Hardheaded."

"I saw something coming, but I didn't see this."

"Maybe you weren't paying as much attention as you thought."

Corinna pulled out a chair and collapsed into it.

"You want her to be like you," Charlotte said. "She's of her own mind. She'll figure it out. Or she'll figure something out. What you don't want to do is make it so that she don't want to talk to you. She'll be all right."

Corinna wanted to slap her mother. "She's *seventeen*." And she thought about her mother's words. "And what the hell do you mean 'like me'?"

"You know: grateful, forgiving, accommodating, dutiful, blah, blah, blah."

"I've given her *everything* she could possibly want! Look at her life!"

"Corinna, you did what you should have done. What I should have done, what my mother should have done. There is no reward for it, believe it or not. Well, other than a daughter who does what she wants. That's the reward. And you sure as hell got that," Charlotte said, fighting back laughter. She popped a couple of Corinna's sunflower seeds into her mouth.

Corinna stared at her mother, who was using both hands to hold her chipped mug of coffee, one that read WORLD'S GREATEST GRANDPA. Camille had picked it out almost ten years earlier at Goodwill, insisting her grandaddy needed it. "It's the boy that's the problem," she said.

"Why? You assume it's like what happened to you and me? Trust your work, Corinna. She's grown."

"No, she isn't!"

"She thinks she is! That's the same damn thing!"

That was enough for Corinna. "Will you call her? I want to hear her explain it to you."

"Does she know you're still here?"

"Tell her I'm not. She trusts you. Use your cell phone."

Again, Camille answered almost immediately. The conversation began quite differently, and they used much softer tones with each other, speaking slowly and gently.

"Your mother is really worried. What's going on?"

"Well, I just don't want to come home right now."

"Why not, baby?"

"Well, Mama. You know I've had to move around a lot, right?"

"Sure, baby, sure."

"And I get why, I think."

"Mm-hmm." Charlotte finished her coffee and shoved the mug at Corinna for a refill.

"I wanted to make a choice for myself."

"It's more complicated than that, ain't it, baby?"

Corinna did not want to walk away at this moment, but Charlotte pushed her, and Corinna resisted the urge to push her back. Charlotte cut her eyes in her direction as she refilled the mug. When she returned to Charlotte's side, Camille was midsentence:

"Not angry," she said.

"I understand, Camille. But don't you think you may have gone about this differently?"

"Well, maybe. But I tried to talk to her about it, and she wouldn't listen. It was just college, college, college. Or some kind of postgrad program. And that's not what I wanted."

"I hear you."

"I just wanted to do something on my own."

"I hear you, but your mother doesn't see it that way, baby."

"What should I do?" Camille had never asked Corinna this question, in any context. She *should* come home and do as she was told.

"*Personally*," Charlotte said, and Corinna prepared to be angry, "I think you ought to do what you think will make you happiest, if you feel safe. We'll handle the rest later, dear."

Corinna grabbed the phone from her mother and slammed it into the wall. As Charlotte watched her, she stomped on it with her bare foot. Somehow, the phone managed to ring, but Corinna stomped on it again.

"You should have told her to come back! She would have listened to you!" Corinna said, realizing she was in tears. "You owe me!"

"You got to let go of that idea, Corinna. Your books don't tell you that?"

PART X

"Not On, but Forward"

Camille

CAMILLE DID NOT return that summer. She and Logan stayed in Tulum for a bit. She sold most of the things she brought with her at a consignment shop, including her suitcase, keeping a few T-shirts and her underwear and adding a few pairs of hiking shorts, a pair of stiff jeans, and boots. She also had a couple of "nice" outfits for work in restaurants. She carried it all in a strategically packed backpack and duffel bag. Her already workable Spanish became nearly fluent quickly. Eventually, they were able to buy a decent motorbike and continued along the Yucatán, headed south toward Belize. They slept mostly in hostels and stayed close to the coastal tourist spots where it was easy to find work.

She thought her mother might put out an alert via INTERPOL, or send a bounty hunter, or something, but she didn't. She thought her mothers would have shut off her phone, but they didn't; it seemed her mother had actually changed her phone plan so that she still got service wherever she went. She cut up her credit cards in Caye Caulker after not using them for several weeks, and intended to sprinkle the pieces in the ocean, but Logan said that was bad for the fish, so she kept them as souvenirs. She'd prepared herself to rely on Logan but quickly understood that though she was smart to travel with a large white man, she could have survived on her own if she was wise about it.

As they traveled farther and farther south, Camille felt less and less like she belonged to the women who raised her. Yes, she belonged to them in that they were in her bones, body, and soul. But she was not *theirs*, and *they* were not *hers*.

In the mountains of El Salvador, she and Logan hiked something called a "stratovolcano" to a mirador recommended by some other travelers. As they approached the summit, several thousand feet above sea level, the air became increasingly thinner and chillier. This was something she couldn't have done several months earlier. She'd been fit from ballet but didn't have the stamina for something like this. But they'd been hiking a lot, at least every third day. Her thighs and calves were growing thick and ropey with muscle, and she could keep up with Logan for miles-long runs along the beach.

When they arrived at the lookout, Camille felt her literal heart float up in her chest as she looked out over the endless Pacific. She'd seen the Pacific before, but from this incredible height, it was spiritual. She was so *small* in the grand scheme of things. She was a meaningless speck of dust. She hadn't wound up here by any cosmic accident. She'd been placed here. She was meant to be here, seeing this. She was there because of choices other people made. Even her audacity in refusing to return to DC was not her own; she'd inherited it. This was a dazzling revelation that she didn't know what to do with.

"You okay?" Logan asked and put his arm tightly around her.

She realized she was crying. "Yeah," she said and wiped at her tears with her filthy hands.

He kissed her forehead. "Makes you feel small, right?"

"It's overwhelming," she agreed.

They held hands as they descended the mountain. That night, when they were slow-dancing in a dark bar, Camille thought briefly about the immediate future. It was August, and her eighteenth birthday was days away. The school year would begin only a few weeks after that. She talked to each of her mothers when she was in major cities and had service, but she usually kept in touch by writing emails from internet cafés. Charlotte, who got an email address expressly for this purpose, told her the night before that she wished she'd done what Camille was doing. Corinna had stopped asking her to come home weeks earlier. Instead, when they planned to stop for longer than a week, she sent boxes with socks, cash, and birth control pills. Evelyn continued to beg her to come back and start the school year as planned. But Camille still had things to think about.

Several days later, they were in Tegucigalpa, staying in a single room in a decent hostel with a "business center," where she waited in line for an hour for a computer. Her mother had written a long email with no paragraph breaks. It was so long that she printed it out on the beige dot-matrix printer, then took it to her room to read it on the small balcony. Her mother was not a talented writer. Mostly, she rambled about how she was beginning to understand that Camille was her own person, but one segment stood out to her:

> I think I have tried in some ways to move on, but I think the goal is to move forward. We take what we have, and we learn from it. What I think I mean is that if we move 'on,' we are leaving what we have and starting something completely new. We don't need to do that. We need to make progress.

We move not on but forward. Camille liked the sound of that.

Corinna

LATE SUMMER 2010

One night, Corinna went to Adams Morgan with Valencia and drank too much too quickly. When she got home, it was still early.

She went through the front door of the main house to feed Sozzani and get some food for herself. Evelyn was sitting at the dining room table, staring at a page in a photo album. As Corinna approached, she saw that the album was open to the page with the missing photograph.

"I've thought about tearing this damn page out," she said. "You've seen this, haven't you?" She pointed at the place the picture should have been with a sharp nail.

"Yes," Corinna said and took a seat at the table.

Evelyn was drinking champagne out of a deep wineglass. "But I don't know. Can't erase it entirely. What do you think?"

"I agree. It's history."

Evelyn turned the page a couple of times, but all the ones after that were blank. "I just wish I knew where the hell the damn picture went." She turned back to it. "It's probably for the best. You don't want to see it, do you?"

"I don't," Corinna said, though she wasn't sure it was true. "Maybe the ghost took it," she added, feeling drunk.

"You've seen her, too?"

"Well," she said. "I haven't *seen* anything. But something makes the bed and folds the laundry. Sometimes makes the coffee."

"She's a helpful spirit, is my belief."

"Mama says she seen her."

"What'd she say?"

"Just said she was kind of old-fashioned."

"They used to call this area the Strivers' Section. It's where the Black strivers lived. I think she's a writer. She helped me write my last book." Corinna laughed. "I'm serious. I swear she did. She left notes on my papers."

Corinna smiled and took a sip from her grandmother's glass.

"You think a ghost would do your laundry, but you don't believe a damn ghost would be my editor?"

"You've seen her, then?"

"A little bit. Never the entire face or body or anything like that. It's like a metaphor," Evelyn said thoughtfully. She was always saying something was a metaphor for something else. Corinna had read a few of Evelyn's books, and they were rife with metaphors she didn't understand. She figured this would be one of them.

"A metaphor for what?"

Evelyn smirked. "For trauma, Corinna. Only your mother can see her clearly because she experienced the trauma firsthand."

"That's not a very good metaphor, Evelyn. Trauma doesn't fold the laundry."

Evelyn tapped the side of her head. "Think *harder*, Corinna," she said, condescension in her tone. "We can *learn* from trauma. We can become better, more efficient, if we do the *work*."

"Whatever." Corinna was not in the mood for a lecture. "Have you heard from Camille today?"

"She must be off the grid somewhere because I couldn't get through on the phone, but I sent her an email."

This was the most Evelyn had acknowledged Camille's world travels to Corinna. "Did you tell her you'd get her a ticket home?"

"Of course, I told her I would get her a ticket. Her birthday is coming up, and I figure she might want to be here for that."

"She's not coming back, Evelyn, not until she wants to."

"You could still make her come back."

"I can't make her do anything," Corinna said. "I always wanted her to be independent. She's doing it, isn't she?"

"Is that really how you see it?"

"Not always." She still badly wanted Camille to do only what she wanted her to do, how she wanted it to be done. But why? Because she'd grown her in her body? That wasn't what it really means to be a mother, anyway. Growing a child in your body does not make you that child's *mother*, Corinna knew that. She'd given Camille everything she could figure out how to give, but she couldn't tell the girl what to do with it, as it could only lead to anger and resentment for them both.

At some point, she would need to tell her that there were millions of dollars in the bank with her name on it, and she hadn't figured out how to do that yet. Honestly, she was frightened of what all that money might do to Camille, though it had once seemed like the only way to save her from a life of misery like her own. But that was before she knew Evelyn, or who Charlotte had once been.

"I wanted her to have what I didn't and be who I wasn't. I just kind of expected that meant college and a career at a typical pace. Turns out"—Corinna drank again from her grandmother's glass—"I was wrong."

Evelyn's brow ruffled in the way it did when she was surprised by someone else's insight. "That's an interesting way of thinking about it. Where did you read that?"

"I didn't read it anywhere." She'd come to this conclusion from various conversations with her own mother. Evelyn nodded. "Besides, telling that hardheaded girl to do anything is like paying her to do the opposite."

Evelyn laughed at this. She closed the album and squeezed Corinna's hand. "I trust you to do what's right for her, I do. I'm sorry if it doesn't always seem that way. I'm hardheaded myself, you know."

Corinna took her grandmother's hand. "Thank you for saying that. But shouldn't the daughter of a good mother be more obedient?"

Laughing again, Evelyn shook her head. "Well, I sure as hell wouldn't know." Evelyn's profile was lovely, especially when she was laughing. Her eyes sparkled, and her delicate laugh lines crinkled around her eyes and mouth. She squeezed Corinna's hand more tightly. "I got some peaches at the farmers market. Make us some bellinis? We can watch a movie upstairs."

Evelyn

FALL 2010

Evelyn had been furious when she learned what Camille had done. It was insolent, childish, a silly adolescent rebellion. She also equated it to what Charlotte had done. All of this work, all of this energy, only to wind up with the same result, both girls running away from her. What had she done wrong this time? She thought she'd done so much better, maybe even gotten it *right*. She wrote to Camille often, as she had with Charlotte. She called every day, left long voicemails. She *begged* her to come back. She even prayed for it to happen.

She was also spending more time with Corinna and actually listening to her. Corinna spent a lot of time thinking out loud about whom she wanted to be as a mother. Evelyn admired that about her. Sometimes, it even made her wish that she had done motherhood differently. But also, she couldn't change the fact that she had never wanted to be a mother. She wasn't at peace with her choices, but she had been working on being at peace with her life as it was, until Camille went and ran off. It hurt her until it finally dawned on her that it wasn't about her. The revelation came over her suddenly while she sat at her desk not working. She opened her email and instead of writing another lengthy, pleading message, actually read what Camille had written.

> Mama Evy, I read your last email, and I know you think I'm being childish and angry, but I feel like I owe it to you, Mama, and Granmama, to figure out who I want to be. Y'all didn't really get a chance to do that. I just want to take my chance.

Sure, she could say that Camille could "find herself" at school or after college, that she was welcome to take all the little summer trips she wanted. But she was getting tired of wishing things were different. She was nearly eighty years old. She decided to let it go. Camille was smart. She would be okay. If she wasn't, at least she was doing what no one before her had: whatever she wanted to. That, in and of itself, was rewarding.

Evelyn wrote back: You owe it only to yourself.

Still, Evelyn wanted Camille to come home because she missed her and loved her. More than that, she *liked* Camille. She was brave and smart and had her own ideas. She wore clothes that Evelyn wouldn't have had the nerve to wear. She had a smart mouth, played loud music, didn't listen very well, and couldn't keep her damn room clean. But honestly, Evelyn admired her. And envied her. That *was* the point, wasn't it?

That fall, Evelyn taught as usual, which was a pleasant distraction from thinking about Camille getting robbed, raped, or murdered in the mountains of Bogota or wherever the hell she was that week.

Corinna came home in November with a very handsome woman. "Evelyn, I wanted to introduce you to someone," she said. Valencia's hair was steel gray, and she wore it in a tightly cropped bob.

Evelyn had known for a while that Corinna was seeing someone but had decided not to involve herself until Corinna was ready. Evelyn hadn't expected a woman. A different version of herself might have had something to say.

Valencia seemed kind, and she looked at Corinna like James had once looked at Evelyn.

A few months later, Corinna moved out of the carriage house and into Valencia's bungalow in Arlington. Evelyn was devastated again. What had she done? Why was everyone leaving her? When she thought about it, though, she saw it was good, especially for Corinna, who badly needed something of her own, besides her daughter and her cocktails. Also, she was able to realize that, like Camille's choice to go to South America, it wasn't about her.

With both of them gone, Evelyn was back where she'd begun: alone. It was a different sort of loneliness than she'd had before, less harsh and dark. It was peaceful.

She still thought about Charlotte, though she'd given up on being forgiven by her. She knew her daughter was doing well, playing piano at some restaurant in Nashville. But she'd done what she could. Like Corinna had said about Camille, she'd given what she could give, and she couldn't tell Charlotte what to do with it.

Camille

SPRING 2011

Camille learned of Valencia via email. Her mother wrote a thousand-word essay on how she'd met Valencia at work, how Valencia was a forty-five-year-old nonprofit CEO from upstate New York, how long they'd been seeing each other, and why she hadn't said anything sooner. Camille had vague recollections of her mother telling her she was seeing someone, but being so self-absorbed, she had never followed up. At the end of the email, Corinna wrote: Same-sex marriage became legal in DC this week, and Valencia and I have decided to get married. I would love it if you would come.

"Part of me is outraged," she told Logan. They were living in a tent in a remote part of Peru as part of something calling itself an edu-commune. Neither of them knew what that meant, but they'd had trouble finding somewhere else to set up camp. He was sprawled across the pile of sleeping bags they called a bed. He was peeling an orange by lantern light and struggling to keep his eyes open. In the commune, Logan put his carpentry skills to work, building and fixing furniture for up to twelve hours a day. When she did see him, he wanted to have sex, not talk. But he was obliging her. Camille was holding the printed pages of her mother's email. "I think because, like, how dare she have a life that doesn't involve me. And how dare she ask me to come back after all the drama. It would take two days just to get to the airport."

"Yeah, especially after she didn't take care of you for so many years."

"But then I'm mostly, like, good for her. She deserves it. She's had really shitty luck."

"Come lie down."

She nestled against him. "I guess it doesn't matter what I feel."

"It matters how you feel, babe."

"What does it mean if I don't go?"

He yawned loudly. "I don't think moms are allowed to be offended by that kind of thing."

His breathing deepened. He was asleep. She envied how easily he fell asleep. Even after a full day of work, she couldn't fall asleep that easily.

The wedding was in two months. She had some time to think about it. She'd spent the last few weeks working with the smallest children on the commune. They were mostly toddlers and a giant infant with bright blond hair whose mother worked in the kitchen. She did her best to teach them numbers, the English alphabet, and more. The kids were from all over, some of them indigenous, some of them children of foreign hippies, and some she had no idea where they'd come from or whom they belonged to. Most days, the kids followed her around the commune, the baby on her hip as they explored together: she showed them how to plant rice and corn; they milked the skinny cows and collected eggs. All of this was new to Camille, too, and, sometimes the kids taught her. They called her Tía Maestra. For the first time, she felt she had purpose. She didn't care to disrupt her work, but she missed her family.

The kids she taught had never received a proper education, it probably wouldn't ruin them to have a substitute for a week or two.

To her surprise, Logan disagreed with her decision to go back to the States. They were already doing a delicate dance with visas, and this would only complicate matters. What if she wasn't able to come back? They would be separated and Logan wouldn't have the money to come back. No one was begging to pay for him to come back to the US. But Camille had already made up her mind. Even without the impending wedding date, she felt that she couldn't wait.

Though Corinna offered to pay for him as well, Logan stayed behind. They'd finally moved from the tent into a small one-room cabin with a functional bed. He said he didn't want to lose it, which was a remarkably convenient excuse not to come back with

her. She hadn't argued with him about it. Perhaps they could benefit from some time apart.

When she arrived in DC after two days of traveling, she headed
to Evelyn's. When she saw Sozzani, she cried. The poor dog was
only seven pounds when she left, but was now so overweight that
she was nearly immobile.

"Mama, why is my dog so fat?"

Evelyn put her fists in her hips and narrowed her eyes. "You tell me."

Camille wished she could take back what she'd said. "Sorry, thank
you for taking care of her."

"You taking her back with you?"

"I wish I could," she said, but as she told Evelyn, the South
American mountains were no place for an overbred dog with
chronic breathing problems.

She went to her room, which looked like a magazine-spread
version of itself. The posters had been unstuck from the wall, the
bed had been made with hospital corners, new pieces of storage
furniture containing organized makeup and skincare products
were located inside the bathroom and closet. The closet had been
reorganized to contain the clothing and shoes it held, and the
entire suite had been painstakingly cleaned. She sat on the bed
and stroked the sheets like she'd never seen or touched anything
like them. She took a hot shower and washed her hair, which had
grown nearly waist-length. When she was done, there was a fine
film of grayish, reddish dirt on the tile floor. She looked at herself
in a full-length mirror for the first time in ten months and smiled.

She dried off, braided her hair, and twisted it into a tight bun.
She put on a pair of crisp linen pajamas and got into bed, though
the sun was still out. When she woke up, she hadn't realized she
had fallen asleep. It took a moment to orient herself in her old
bedroom. She looked around and was startled when she saw her
mother standing in the doorway, smiling with all her teeth.

"Hi, Mama. Did you get your teeth whitened?"

"Yes! For the wedding," Corinna said, still smiling as she sat on
the edge of the bed. "I'm so happy to see you!" She squeezed

Camille so tightly she thought her ribs might crack. "I missed you so much!"

Up close, she saw that her mother's skin was clear, her short 'fro neatly trimmed and moisturized, and her eyes bright. She was wearing a green dress and gold jewelry, including a pair of hoops that Camille recognized as her own.

"What time is it?"

"It's eleven a.m.! Get up, get dressed. Let's get lunch. And then I want to introduce you to Valencia."

They went to brunch at Le Diplomate. Camille had missed out on a lot while she was gone. Corinna had launched a cocktail blog not long after Camille left and had been approached about writing a book of drink recipes. A bar opening up on U Street had hired her to "design" their cocktail menu.

Corinna was effusive as she described it all, in a way Camille had never seen or heard before. She took this opportunity to stuff her face with buttered croissants and oysters before her entrée arrived. When the lobster Benedict and breakfast potatoes arrived, Corinna took a breath. "Well?" she said.

"What's next for you?"

"Um," Camille said through a mouthful of breakfast potato. "We don't have much of a plan at the moment." Logan wasn't much for plans, which had seemed fun a year earlier and now seemed reckless and juvenile.

"Well. You look well. You feel well?"

Camille mulled this over. Yes. She felt well. She was wearing some of her old clothes and felt strange in them. It wasn't about fit as much as about comfort; she didn't feel prepared to climb a tree or harvest sugarcane, nor could she teach a child to build a rain shelter.

"Yes, I feel really well," she said, her mouth full of another bite of lobster, eggs, and English muffin.

Corinna smiled warmly. "And Logan?"

"He's fine, too." She wasn't entirely sure if he was fine. He was working very hard and wasn't talking as much as he once had. They weren't spending nearly as much time together as they had at the beginning of their journey, mostly getting private time in the outdoor showers, late at night by the fire, or in the moments before falling asleep.

"I meant more like you and him."

They were still a couple. They still had sex. She still loved him, he still loved her, but things were shifting. It was no longer enough to just be in love, though it had never been just that. She trusted him. He saw her when it felt like no one else did. If it was just love, she wouldn't have followed him. He was smart. He was safe. He insisted they eat peanut butter for breakfast while they were saving money to leave Panama City. They'd had only a few fights, and it was always over the same thing: the quality of the accommodations. He didn't care about anything besides convenience, but she wanted clean sheets, a place to shower. She wasn't sure how to tell her mother all of this. "Yeah, we're good."

"You're still getting the pills—"

"Yes, but I was thinking of getting an IUD while I'm here."

Corinna smiled. "That's a good idea."

"Can I ask you something?"

"Anything."

"How did you and Valencia happen?"

"Are you asking if I've been gay this whole time?"

Camille hesitated. She wasn't as concerned with her mother's sexuality as she was curious how Corinna had once lain down with a man and had her. "I think I'm really asking about my dad."

"What about him?"

"Did you love him love him? Like you love Valencia?"

Camille knew her mother was in love because of the way she spoke and moved like an improved version of herself. Camille recognized that she and Logan had been like that at some point.

"No." Corinna shook her head. "I didn't. But I'm glad you're half him. Couldn't have chosen better genes."

Unexpectedly, this was the answer Camille hadn't known she was looking for.

Still, Camille managed to stew about it. Why hadn't her mother sought out love when Camille was younger, so that she would know what it was supposed to look like? She suddenly had a headache.

They rode the train and walked to Valencia's house. Valencia was a beautiful, statuesque, intelligent, and kind woman who really loved Corinna. It was clear. In real time, Camille struggled with feelings of profound bitterness. Why had she been made to watch her mother suffer when it could have been this way the whole time?

Corinna showed Camille her office, a strange, triangle-shaped studio in the backyard. "It's called an accessory dwelling unit. You can order it online. It's insulated. I bought it myself—can you believe that? I'm self-sufficient." She handed a cocktail recipe printed on cardstock to Camille. "I named it for you. It's a Jungle Bird with a sophisticated twist. Get it? I'm going to put it on the menu at Fraise, a new place opening on 18th Street."

Camille did not read what she'd been handed. "Cool," she said.

As they walked back toward the house, Corinna slipped her arm around Camille's waist, and Camille put her arm around her mother's shoulders.

"When does Granmama get here?"

"Friday night."

"Isn't the wedding Saturday morning?"

"You know how she can be."

Camille nodded.

Corinna rubbed her cheek against Camille's bare shoulder. "You inspire me. To make good out of bad. To make the most of what I have."

"How?"

"I'm not sure. I suppose if I didn't have you, I might not have pulled myself together. I wouldn't have had reason to."

Camille saw her mother differently. Corinna was more than her mistakes and her capacity as a mother. She'd done a lot with a little, and she was a kind, generous person doing her best. If she'd hurt Camille, it hadn't been on purpose.

Camille felt lucky to have a mother whose lead she could follow. She knew the women before her hadn't had that luxury.

Evelyn

SPRING 2012

Evelyn had known fall 2011 would be her last semester at the university. She managed to finish teaching her classes, but her health declined very suddenly as soon as finals were done and her grades were in.

She didn't have to ask Camille to come home; she came on her own. She became Evelyn's caretaker: she prepared her meals and her medication, made sure she walked around a bit every day, and didn't get too much sun.

Every few weeks, Camille's man showed up for a couple of days. Evelyn took the time to get to know him. He was actually an okay guy. She could tell he was impulsive, though, and he didn't have any proper family.

"He doesn't have any roots," she told Camille as she prepared lunch. "He's all his own person." Logan was outside directing the landscaper, though no one had asked him to.

"He can't help that, Mama," Camille said, her eyes still on the vegetables she was chopping for the soup. Evelyn was primarily interested in soup.

"I know. I'm just saying be careful."

Camille sighed.

"You're smart. You're independent. You don't have to settle. You know that," she said. "You're in love with him, aren't you?"

"Of course I'm in love with him, Mama. What else do you think I'm doing? Dating him for my health?"

Evelyn smiled. "I'm glad that's how you see it."

Camille rolled her eyes. She'd only recently learned about her massive trust fund. And she hadn't had the kind of response Evelyn thought she might. She hadn't done anything. She was still teaching in South America and completing her degree in short spurts when she returned to the States. Eventually, she would need to settle down and gather up her credits. But she wasn't showing any signs of doing so any time soon. She was too in love. Not just with Logan. Evelyn didn't fully understand it, but she saw that Camille was happy and that had to be enough.

"You need to invest some of that money, Camille. You do."

Camille continued chopping. "Can't do anything with it yet, Mama. Not twenty-one."

"And I can have someone write up the prenup—"

"Logan and I aren't getting married."

"Ever?"

"I didn't say that."

"Well, I won't be around forever. Let me talk to Carl, that lawyer."

"All right. If that will make you happy."

Camille dumped the vegetables into the hot oil, then pulled the chicken out of the oven and started pulling it apart. She'd learned to cook somewhere in Central America, and she was actually quite good.

"Are you happy?" Evelyn asked after a few moments.

"I'm happy, Mama. You know that."

After lunch, Camille brushed Evelyn's thinning hair and secured a large sunhat on her head so they could sit outside on the deck. Evelyn had thought she would die alone or in a nursing home. Instead, she was drinking expensive wine every day with her great-granddaughter, who cared for her beautifully.

"I don't deserve this," she told Camille every night.

"You took care of me; I take care of you."

"Don't worry. I won't hold on too long. You've got things to do."

"Don't talk like that."

They kissed each other's cheeks. Left, right, right, left.

"Good night, darling girl. I love you so, so much."
"I love you, too."

Corinna

JULY 2012

When Charlotte flew in for the funeral, Corinna picked her up from the airport and took her to Evelyn's house. Corinna had hated seeing Camille fritter away her youth taking care of her great-grandmother there. "When it's over, I'll continue being young," Camille insisted, "but I really want to do this, Mama. At least for a little while."

"Until June. Then I'm hiring someone," Corinna told her.

"Why June?"

"It's five months from now. I think that's a suitable amount of time."

"You can't make me leave."

"I know I can't make you do anything, but I can hire someone." Camille rolled her eyes.

Then Evelyn died in June, and Corinna hadn't had to hire anyone.

Charlotte and Corinna arrived back at the house at ten thirty in the morning to find Camille sitting on the front steps looking lost. Corinna decided to make mimosa margaritas, pulling out the lime juice, orange juice, tequila, and champagne.

Charlotte and Camille melted into each other on the low-slung couch. They sat hip to hip, and Charlotte wrapped her arm tight around Camille as they talked to each other in low voices. Obviously, whatever was happening was not for her, Corinna knew, but she delivered them the drinks in champagne flutes.

"Where's Logan?" Charlotte asked.

"I don't know. He's coming."

"You two have such an interesting relationship."

"Why? Because I don't track his every move?"

"That's not what I said. Anyway, anyway," Charlotte said and lowered her voice again.

Corinna returned to the kitchen and poured herself a straight tequila. She took a shot and looked over at the dining room table. She could picture her grandmother sitting there grading papers and muttering to herself. A pang of sadness hit her in the gut.

Johnny invited himself to the memorial service, which was standing-room only. She introduced him to Camille.

"You're the guy from the insurance commercial," Camille said with a look of absolute disinterest, and didn't wait for a response before she walked away.

Johnny's wide smile froze on his face. He held it for just a beat too long.

"She can be icy," Corinna explained. "I think it's a defense mechanism."

"Did you tell her who I am?"

"No."

"That's just how she is?"

Corinna could only smile. Johnny had become one of the most famous football players of all time, and Camille had treated him like one of those pesky Greenpeace canvassers asking for money on the street.

"Well," he sighed. "She is very beautiful. That gets you far in life, don't it?"

"Well," Corinna responded. "It helps. But she's also very intelligent."

"Thank you for raising her. I sometimes wish things could have been different."

"Different how?"

"Maybe I could have been in her life more."

"Well, it is what it is," Corinna sighed and finished the wine in her plastic cup.

"I guess she's nearly grown now."

"I wouldn't say that, no."

"What?"

"That she's nearly grown. I don't think you're ever really grown."

Charlotte

JUNE 2012

Charlotte had found some peace in the role of being needed, but everyone who needed her was gone. David was dead. Corinna and Camille were both doing well enough without her. Charlotte knew she'd been banished. She could not forgive, and that made her incompatible with the rest of the family. Evelyn, Camille, and Corinna were living harmoniously—not together in the same house, but they were getting along. Corinna was married again and working as a "mixology influencer," according to some local magazine spread. Camille was back and forth between the United States and South America doing God knows what. She said she was patching together an international education degree. It seemed like she and her little boyfriend were still serious, but Charlotte couldn't be sure. Evelyn was doing exactly what she'd always done.

Charlotte stayed away, though she spoke to Camille and Corinna a couple of times a week, and they came to see her for most holidays. But she was no longer the nucleus. Maybe that wasn't the right term, but Charlotte hadn't been to school in over thirty years and didn't like to read, so she wasn't good at analogies. But she knew the nucleus was the powerhouse, the command center; she knew this because she'd heard Camille say it at some point. And it stuck with her—that idea.

When Charlotte thought about it, she hadn't been the nucleus since Camille had come out of diapers. Camille was the center of things. And, over time, Charlotte learned to love her from a distance. David had said something about it before he died: "Sometimes the best thing you can do for someone you love is stay the hell away from them," he said, apropos of nothing. "I bet you wish I'd done that." And she'd known what he meant.

And yes. She tried. She tried to forgive, forget, move on, move *forward*, like Corinna was always saying. She tried them one at a time, all at once, and in various configurations. It didn't work. She couldn't let it go.

What, exactly, was "it"? Well, everything was "it." What wasn't "it"?

So she waited. She waited for her mother to die. She considered that she might feel worse after it happened. She would probably feel guilt of some kind, but it was better than the sick feeling she got when she was near her mother: the shakiness of her hands, the pummeling and punishing memories that she couldn't shake. No, she'd made the right choice, she thought.

Then, her mother died.

It had been her plan all along that Evelyn die without her forgiveness. She didn't know what she expected, but she felt very little. A large part of her was relieved that she no longer had anyone to hold this nasty grudge against. She was free. But she was also forced to acknowledge how much space her mother had been taking up in her life. And she wasn't sure that had been the way to live. There was no reason she had to welcome her mother back into her life, but she could have released some portion of the pain a long time ago.

"Forgive your mother," Charlotte said to Camille.

They were sitting together on the low-slung couch in the rear of Evelyn's house, drinking morning cocktails. Charlotte's eyes were moist.

"What?" Camille said. She had visibly been thinking about something else.

"I said forgive your goddamn mother."

"I already did," Camille said. Charlotte heard her say this, but she wasn't really talking to Camille; she was talking to herself.

"Don't do it for her. It's not about her. Do it for *you*. Forgive your mother."

Acknowledgments

FIRST AND FOREMOST, I thank my husband, Dennis, who believed in me and this book before I did. Thank you, so much, for listening to me read draft after draft after draft (year after year). Your support and encouragement never wavered. I don't know how I got so lucky. I couldn't have done this without you.

I thank my daughter, Margaux, who—before she was even born—pushed me to write this book and to learn something from it. I hope this book makes you proud someday. Similarly, I owe a great deal to my female ancestors and the women who mothered me.

An enormous, heartfelt thank you to all my siblings (including the ones I came to by marriage) for celebrating with me and for loving my daughter (this helped me write this book and helps me continue to write in so, so many ways). Your support is so dear to me and I couldn't and wouldn't trade it for anything.

I thank the folks who provided amazing childcare so that I could work: my sister-in-law Amanda Casey, and friend Rachel Wynn.

I am eternally grateful to every student I've ever had for teaching me something about reading, writing, and dedication.

I have so much gratitude for the people who worked with me to make this book what it is today. The earliest readers of this book were Yael Kiken, Barrett Smith, Lauren Francis-Sharma, and Molly Tilghman. Thanks to my grad school friends: Molly (again), Amanda Miller, Zeynep Cakmak, and Ken Fleming for strategizing and celebrating with me every step of the way as this book went from a glorified outline to what it is today. I thank my agents, Susan Ginsburg and Catherine Bradshaw, for seeing something in that glorified outline, pulling it out of the slush pile, and reading the submission over and over and over again. Your encouragement and feedback helped me turn *Grown Women* into something I am fiercely proud of.

Of course, many, many, many, many thank yous to my first editor, Micaela Carr, for loving the book, and to Emily Griffin for picking up the baton, championing this book, and bringing us to the finish line.

Also, I thank myself for not giving up, even though I really wanted to sometimes.

About the Author

SARAI JOHNSON grew up in the South, primarily in Nash-ville, Tennessee. She studied journalism and English at How-ard University and later earned a master's degree in literature from American University. She has taught writing at both her alma maters and with several nonprofit writing programs in the DC area. She lives in Alexandria, Virginia, with her husband, daughter, and dog.